Surviving Amber Springs

USA TODAY BESTSELLING AUTHOR

SIOBHAN DAVIS

WWW.SIOBHANDAVIS.COM

Printed by Amazon
Paperback edition © December 2018

ISBN-13: 9781790930159

Editor: Kelly Hartigan (XterraWeb) editing.xterraweb.com
Cover design by Robin Harper https://wickedbydesigncovers.wixsite.com
Photo by Sara Eirew.
Cover Model: Chen Haskin
Formatting by The Deliberate Page www.deliberatepage.com

Note from the Author

This book is only suitable for readers aged eighteen and older due to profanity, sexual descriptions, and sensitive subject matter. This book includes topics related to gun violence, rape, and suicide. If any of those subjects are triggers for you, then I recommend not reading this book.

Thank you, and I hope you enjoy *Surviving Amber Springs*.

Part One

Prologue

"Claire! Get your butt down here already!" Ethan hollers up the stairs as I stifle another yawn, running the comb through my long almost-white-blonde hair one last time before leaving my bedroom. My twin and I are alike in so many ways, but his early morning sunny disposition is definitely *not* a trait we share. If it wasn't for Ethan dragging my ass out of bed each morning, I know I'd be late for school every damn day.

"Where's the fire?" I inquire as I step into the homey kitchen a couple minutes later. My nostrils twitch at the delicious aromas wafting through the air, and my tummy rumbles appreciatively.

"I cooked bacon and eggs, and I didn't want it to go cold." My only sibling places a warm plate in front of me before striding to the refrigerator, his long legs eating up the distance in no time.

I pull up a stool at the island unit and sit down. "Wow. You're really spoiling me today," I remark, glancing at the stacked plateful of pancakes on the counter. Pancakes *and* bacon and eggs? Something's up. "What's the occasion?" Ethan is always up first, so he fixes breakfast, but he doesn't usually go to this much trouble.

"Do I need a reason to spoil my sister?" he asks, pouring me a glass of orange juice.

He smiles as he hands it to me, but something about him is off. I scrutinize his face as I sip my juice, observing the extra layer of scruff on his chin and the noticeable bags under his eyes. "Hey." I put my glass down and touch his arm. "Is everything okay? You look like you didn't get much sleep."

"I'm fine. Stop worrying and eat." He presses a kiss to the top of my head before claiming the stool across from me.

Mom and Dad have already left for their respective places of work, so it's just the two of us. As usual. We eat in silence, and there's a tension in the air that rarely exists between us. Ethan and I have always been super close, even more so since everything went down the summer before tenth grade, which is why I know something is bothering him.

When I've finished eating, I get up to take my empty plate to the sink. "Here, you can take this." Ethan hands me his barely touched breakfast. "I guess I'm not hungry after all."

I put both our plates down on the counter beside the sink and wrap my arms around my brother from behind. "Please tell me what's wrong. Let me help."

God knows I owe him that. That summer, when it felt like I was destructing from the inside out, Ethan was there for me. Helping me get through it, one day at a time.

He swivels around on the stool, pulling me into his chest. I lean my head on his shoulder and sigh. "Nothing's wrong, B. I'm just a bit stressed. First day nerves and all that."

Ethan's endlessly protective of me and always the first one to jump to my defense whenever it's needed. But it works both ways, and I want him to know I'm here for him. It hurts that he's clearly dealing with something and deliberately shutting me out.

I lift my head and eyeball him, staring into his bright blue eyes, so similar to my own. "You're like the antithesis of nervous. What gives? Seriously. What's going on?"

His Adam's apple bobs in his throat, and he claws a hand through his short blond hair. While my shade of blonde is more akin to Mom's pure, white-gold hair, Ethan has the same hair color as Dad. A kind of dirty-blond color that all the girls love.

My brother has no shortage of admirers, but he hasn't had a girlfriend in a long time. He's still crushing on Lucinda Jamison. Still harboring hope she'll leave that douche she's going out with for him. She doesn't deserve Ethan, and she isn't good enough for him, but try telling him that. I wonder if his current odd mood is in some way connected to her. It wouldn't be the first time, that's for sure.

"You know I love you, right?" He cups my face. "You know I love you more than I love anyone else in this entire world."

I stretch my hands out on top of his. "I know, and I love you too, in the exact same way, but you can't keep protecting me forever. And I can handle it. Whatever is weighing on your mind." I squeeze his hands. "I'm good, E. I'm happy and I want the same for you."

He presses a kiss to my forehead. "This is something I need to deal with by myself, but I don't want you to worry. Once you're fine, I will be too."

Cryptic as ever, but I know there's no point pursuing it. Ethan can be stubborn as fuck when he wants to be, and I don't want to end up arguing on the first day of senior year. This is a milestone for both of us, and I'm determined this year is going to be epic.

"Okay, you win. I'll drop it." I circle my arms around his neck. "I love you, big bro. So, so much." Ethan was born six minutes before me, and he never lets me forget it, but I always know his teasing is in good humor.

"Love you too, little sis." He pulls me in close, squeezing me so hard it's a wonder I can breathe. "I'd do anything for you. You are all that matters." His voice sounds clogged with emotion, and when he finally releases me, I'm startled to find tears pooling in his eyes.

"E, I—"

He puts his finger on my lips, silencing me. "Nope. Not another word. Scoot. You better get dressed before Cam arrives."

"I was thinking I'd ride with you today. I can message him."

Ethan shakes his head. "I want to get to school early, and I know he wants to drive you. He'll never let me live it down if I take that from him."

I roll my eyes. "You've been best friends with my boyfriend since you were three, E. You, of all people, know he isn't one for dramatics. If I want to ride with you, he'll be cool."

Gently, he removes his arms from around me, sliding out of our embrace. "Ride with Cam, B, and I'll see you at school." A pained look washes over his face, but it's gone so fast I'm not sure I didn't imagine it.

I'm still pondering his weird behavior as I traipse up the stairs to my room and into my en suite bathroom. I take a little extra care getting ready today, slicking some gloss across my full lips and applying blush and mascara. The girl staring back at me in the mirror looks happy and glowing with vitality, and I smile at myself, glad I've finally turned a corner and put the past behind me.

I'm perched on the edge of my bed, toeing my shoes on when a subtle clicking sound pricks my ears. Wooden floorboards creak outside my room, and I pause what I'm doing, frowning. "E?" I call out. "Is that you?" Eerie silence greets me, and all the tiny hairs on the back of my neck lift as a blanket of unease creeps over me. My heart pounds behind my chest, and I can't shake this ominous sense of dread that has materialized out of nowhere. I'm rooted to the spot, willing my body to calm down. The last thing I need is an anxiety attack before school.

The roar of an engine distracts me a couple minutes later, and I race to the window in time to see Ethan's SUV pulling out of the drive. Air whooshes out of my mouth, and I shake my head as I walk back to my bed. I'll give myself a coronary overthinking things.

Brushing aside the strange sensation, I finish getting ready and then check the time on my cell. Cam's late which is most unlike him. My boyfriend is almost as anal about good timekeeping as my twin. I call Cam, but he doesn't answer straightaway, so I ping him a message. He calls back about five minutes later. "Did you forget about me?" I tease.

"Never, babe. That's a virtual impossibility. You know you occupy my every waking minute."

I grin like a loon. "Then get your sexy ass over here."

A frustrated sigh leaks through the phone. "That's what I was calling to tell you. Something's up with my truck. It won't start. The engine just keeps turning over. You'll have to grab a ride with E."

"He's already left, but it's cool. I'll just take Mom's car today. She's going out with the girls after work, so she got my dad to drop her at the doctor's office on his way to the hospital."

"E's gone to school already?"

I pick up on the instant strain in his voice. "Yeah. I know, he's a freak, but you know E. He hates being late for anything."

"If you two didn't look so alike, sometimes I'd forget you were twins."

"We're more alike than unalike," I reply, jumping to defend my twinsome as I always do.

"I know that too." He pauses for a beat. "Was he, ah, okay this morning?"

Clearly, Cam knows what's going on with my brother. Even though it doesn't surprise me that Ethan confided in his best friend, alarm bells start ringing in my ears. That worrisome feeling returns. "You know what's up with him?"

A pregnant pause trickles down the line. "Yeah." He sighs, and it does little to reassure me. "I need to go, B, but I'll talk to you later. Love you."

"Love you too," I mumble absently, staring off into space as the line goes dead. That horrible, ominous feeling is back, and I'm scarcely holding my anxiety at bay. It's been a while since I had a panic attack, and I'm sure as shit not going there today. Placing my head between my knees, I draw deep breaths, in and out, cautioning myself to calm down. Just because Ethan doesn't want to tell me what's bugging him, it doesn't mean I need to overreact. It's probably just girl trouble, like I initially suspected.

After a couple minutes, my breathing has evened out and I'm back in control. Grabbing my bag, I head to the door, but it won't open. I frown, scowling at the door, before trying again. I twist the handle firmly, shaking and rattling it, but it doesn't budge.

What the hell?

Dropping my bag on the floor, I wrangle both hands around the handle and tug on it, repeatedly, aggressively, to no avail.

I stare at the door, and my mouth turns dry. Those antsy feelings I worked so hard to repress overwhelm me, and I'm shaking all over.

I'm locked in.

And I don't have a good feeling about this.

Even though I know it's futile, I grab the door handle again, shaking it violently, over and over, as frustration gets the better of me. But it's no good. I'm definitely locked in, trapped in my bedroom with no way out. If there wasn't a thirty-foot drop from my window to ground level, I might risk scaling the side of the house, but there's no way I'm taking that chance.

I drop to the floor, leaning my back against the door, sighing loudly.

There's only one person who could've done this.

Ethan deliberately locked me in my bedroom.

But the million-dollar question is why?

7

Chapter One

Four Months Later

I tiptoe out of my new bedroom, quietly easing the door shut with military precision, although there's probably no need to invoke stealth mode now that Mom's sobbing has stopped. The usual arguing has replaced her tears. My parents' shouts still echo in my ears as I creep out the front door and take off running in the direction of the town.

As I run through the dilapidated suburb we now call home, I can empathize with Mom, a little. It's hard moving across the country, moving away from the only place you've ever known as home, even more so because this new reality is so altered from our previous existence. But it's not like we had any choice.

Remaining in Amber Springs was *not* an option.

Not after what Ethan did.

And if my aunt and her husband hadn't offered us a lifeline, we'd still be stuck there, living our own personal hell. Aunt Jill and Uncle Tom don't live here in Kentsville. They live in a neighboring suburb—they have for the last twenty years—and Tom owns a thriving real estate business. His connections came in handy when we needed to flee Arizona. A friend of his had been trying to rent out his house for a while so he was happy to offer it to us at a knockdown price, and the decision was made.

As I sprint past run-down houses, graffiti-strewn walls, abandoned warehouses and storefronts, and streets in need of a little TLC, I offer up silent thanks to Kentsville for offering us much-needed shelter, and I fervently hope Maryland remains the safe haven it promises to be.

I slow down in front of the communal park, resting my hands on my knees as I attempt to bring my breathing back under control. Sweat clings to my brow, plastering my newly dyed hair to my face. I straighten up and glance at my surroundings. I'm on the outskirts of the main town with a large park on my right and a row of stores and businesses on my left. This part of town is a lot more affluent with modern buildings, and the streets are clean and tidy. Laughter trickles out from the bar situated on the corner, and it's the only sign of life at this late hour.

Tying my hoodie around my waist, I shiver in spite of my hot, sweat-slickened skin. The frigid air swirls around me, rapidly cooling me down as I step inside the park.

It's pristine and well-maintained with neat flowerbeds and freshly mown grass. Lighting is a little sporadic, but I'm not frightened. After what I've lived through, it takes a lot to freak me out now. I'm a hell of a lot stronger and tougher than I used to be even if my vulnerabilities still linger under the surface. Some might say I've lost the softer parts of myself, but it's simpler than that—without Ethan, I'm only half the person I used to be.

Some days, I'm so mad at him for leaving me. Other days, I miss him so much I wish he'd taken me with him. Everything always felt right when we were together, and now, I feel lost, aimless, and I struggle to find the will to go on. It's only for my parents that I do. They don't deserve to lose another child, and right now, I'm the glue holding this family together.

Which is laughable because I'm the least together person I know.

I follow the path to the central area of the park and drop down onto the nearest bench, cursing my stupidity. I slipped out of the house without any supplies, and I would happily trade a limb in exchange for a bottle of water right now.

I only took up running in the aftermath of the shitstorm in Amber Springs. It was either that or resort to self-harming again. I needed some form of outlet, and running became my saving grace. If Ethan were here, he'd laugh himself silly at the notion of me running. I've never been the sporty type, unless you count cheerleading, but I'd given that up by the time I was fifteen. Ethan was the one who inherited the athletic genes. Not me. I was the academic one, and he was the sporty one. They were the roles we played, and now, it feels like I'm trying to be everything, but there's no way I could ever take Ethan's place. He was too Goddamned special. I don't care what everyone is saying about him. They didn't know who he was, and he isn't defined by his last act on this Earth.

A heavy weight presses down on my chest, and tears prick my eyes, just like every time I let my mind wander. Like every time I think of my twin. Or that morning. And all the different ways it could've gone down. I should have pushed him. Insisted he tell me what was on his mind. Maybe I could have prevented it.

But I'll never know now.

Because Ethan is gone and we're the ones left to pick up the pieces.

"Watch out!" a deep, clearly masculine voice shouts, and I snap out of my depressive inner monologue, pivoting on the bench in time to see a football winging its way toward me. It's not enough of a warning to avoid impact, and the ball smacks into me with brutal force, knocking me to the ground as if I've just been leveled by a truck.

Stars explode behind my eyes, and pain radiates across my skull and shoots up my spine. I curl onto my side, and a little whimper escapes my lips.

"Fuck. Shit. Crap." A shadow looms over me as the sound of additional footfall reaches my ears. I'm having trouble focusing, so when a guy crouches down in front of me, I'm seeing three of him. All I can distinguish is that this guy is big. Massive shoulders, powerful thighs, and rippling biceps. "Are you okay?" he asks, sounding concerned.

"Don't ask stupid questions," another male voice says. "She's clearly not okay. She's probably got a concussion or something." He bends over me too, and the first signs of self-preservation set in.

"Get away from me," I rasp, forcing myself to sit up and scooting back a little. My head spins, and I don't feel too hot, but I've got to get a handle on the situation. Despite my knowledge of self-defense, if any of these guys make a move, I doubt I'll be able to engage any protective technique. "Leave me alone, or I'll scream."

"Back the fuck up," another guy says, his voice carrying authority. "You're crowding her."

The two guys straighten up, and the skinnier one of the two extends his hand toward me, offering to help me up. "We don't mean you any harm. You're safe with us. I promise."

My vision is becoming clearer, and I look up at him, examining his face to see what it tells me. It's hard to make out his exact features in this dim light, but he looks genuine. Still, I don't trust people for a reason. Especially teenage boys who are random strangers. Ignoring him, I grab my cell from my back pocket, almost crying when I see the cracked, black screen. Dad will go apeshit when he realizes I've broken my cell. I'll be lucky if there's money for a new one. I attempt to stand, and the ground sways around me, or at least that's the way it seems.

"Careful." The skinny guy tentatively takes my arm, helping to steady me as I straighten up.

"Don't touch me!" But even as I say it, I clutch onto his arm to stop myself from falling.

"Let us help. You're hurt, and you might need to see a doctor."

A laugh bursts free of my mouth before I can stop it, and the three guys look at one another and then at me like I'm cray-cray. "My dad's a doctor. I just need to get home," I explain.

"No offense, sweetheart, but we're not letting you leave by yourself, so either we escort you home or you let us take you across the road to get checked out." His tone brokers no argument.

"What's across the road?" I ask, looking over his shoulder at the other two guys, hanging back in the shadows. "And why should I trust you? I don't know any of you."

He shoots me a blinding smile, and now that my vision has properly corrected itself, I can see him more clearly. He's cute with messy dark hair that falls into mischievous eyes, a strong, smooth jawline, and a gorgeous mouth. As I cling to his arm, I realize he's not all that skinny either. He's not as bulked up as the first guy, but he's no skinny dude—he's lean but strong.

"You're new to town, right?"

I narrow my eyes. "How can you tell?" *Do I have newbie written on my forehead or something?* I mean, I know Kentsville only has a population of fifteen thousand, less than half the size of Amber Springs, but still.

"We know everyone who goes to Kentsville High, and, trust me, there's no way we would've missed you." He waggles his brows, grinning flirtatiously, and my mouth hangs open.

"Are you seriously hitting on me right now?" I remove my hand from his arm, putting a little distance between us.

"Skeet. Quit this shit and let's go," the taller of the trio says, taking a step forward. This guy is well over six foot and seriously hot with dark hair, styled long on top and shorn at the sides, and a chiseled jawline you could cut glass with. Unlike his two friends, he has a thin layer of stubble on his chin and cheeks. He pins me with a look that seems to penetrate skin deep. My mouth turns dry, and I almost cower under his intense stare.

"Axel, I'm trying to put the girl at ease," Skeet says. "Just give me a minute."

The other guy, the one who hit me with the ball, rolls his eyes, sending me an amused grin. My eyes almost bug out of my head at the sheer size of him. He's practically got boulders for shoulders and biceps so big they're straining the sleeves of his thin jacket. His dark blond hair reminds me of Ethan's, and the usual pang slices across my chest.

I wrap my arms around my waist, my gaze bouncing between the three of them. I should be terrified, in the pitch-dark, in an unknown town, with three hulking strangers surrounding me, but I'm not, and I can't wrap my head around that. Perhaps my instincts are better now, and I'm sensing these guys are sincere when they say they mean me no harm.

"I'm Skeet Taylor," the cute one says, pointing at himself before turning to his buddies. "That sullen bastard is Axel Thorp," he adds, jerking his finger at the hot one, "and the idiot who threw a ball without checking is Heath Gilchrist. We've lived in Kentsville our whole lives, and most everyone knows who we are. Feel free to text a friend our names. That way, if anything happens to you, they know where to come looking." He shoots me a lazy smile before winking.

"Awesome," Heath says, strolling to his buddy's side. "I'm sure she's really at ease now."

"I'm standing right here. You don't need to speak about me in third person."

"You're right, and I'm sorry." Heath drags a hand through his hair, messing up his careful styling. "About the ball in the face. I wasn't expecting anyone to be here this time of night."

"Apology accepted." A shiver works its way through my body, and I untie my hoodie and put it on, zipping it up to my chin.

"Here," Heath says, removing his jacket. "Put this on. That hoodie won't keep you warm. Judging from your accent and the way you're dressed, I'm guessing you're not used to the cold winters in Maryland."

"No, I'm not, and I didn't stop to think before I went running." But that doesn't mean I'm taking some stranger's jacket, so I shove it back at him, pretending I don't see the confusion crossing his face.

"You like to run?" Skeet asks me, but his eyes automatically lock on Axel's.

I nod. "It helps keep me sane."

What the fuck, Blaire? Why the hell did I admit that?

Skeet looks contemplative as he eyeballs Axel. "I think we might have just discovered your female alter ego," he quips, and I arch a brow.

"Don't." Axel growls the word. "Come on. I'm freezing my ass off out here." He turns and walks away, shoving his hands in the pocket of his skinny jeans and pulling the collar up on his weather-beaten black leather jacket.

"Don't let his broody exterior chase you away," Skeet says, offering me his arm. "Axel's got his demons, but he's a good guy."

"One of the best," Heath agrees.

"Where are we going?" I ask, brushing Skeet's arm away.

"Axel's brother Griffin manages the bar on the corner," Heath starts explaining as we walk. "And he lets us hang out in the back room to play pool. We can stay there until you feel well enough to go home."

"Honestly, I'm feeling much better now," I lie.

"Yeah, I'm so not buying that." Skeet walks protectively by my side as he sends me a disbelieving look.

"Are you always this … persuasive?"

He chuckles. "You really don't want to know." His eyes twinkle with mirth as he smiles at me. "I can be extremely persuasive when I see some-thing or some*one* I like."

My cheeks heat at his obvious meaning, and I'm glad it's dark and they can't see. It's been a long time since anyone flirted with me, and it feels nice. Normal.

"I bet you say that to all the girls," I retort, letting him steer me out the main entrance of the park.

"Only the ones I deem worthy."

"Wow. Healthy ego right there."

"You've seriously no clue. Don't encourage that shit," Heath says, smirking.

We cross the road together, and Skeet stops at the door to the bar, his hand resting on the wall. "Before we go in, I think we should at least know your name."

My name.

It should be simple. As easy as breathing. Just let the words flow off my tongue.

But it's not simple. It's as complicated as it can be. Besides, my name doesn't define who I am anymore. I lost my identity the day my brother died. In more ways than one.

I'm conscious of both guys watching me with abject curiosity written all over their faces. I've got to get better at this or my true identity won't stay hidden for long. I plaster a fake smile on my face. "It's Blaire. Blaire Adams."

Blaire Simpson died in Amber Springs Academy the same day Ethan Simpson did.

Chapter Two

"Follow me," Axel says the instant we step inside the cozy bar. It's surprisingly modern on the inside with leather-backed chairs and stools clustered around shiny walnut tables. Lighting is low, and music thumps from speakers dotted around the room. There is only standing room left, and it's clear the bar is a popular spot. Axel doesn't wait for a reply, spinning on his heel and walking through a side door.

"Friendly, isn't he?" Heath says, failing to hide his smirk.

"He's cool. I understand guarded better than most." And there I go again. Spewing the truth when my survival rests on me living a lie.

"Shit, Blaire," Skeet exclaims when we step into the brightly lit back room. The space is small with a large pool table occupying most of the real estate in the room. A battered brown leather couch rests against the wall in front of a small wall-mounted TV screen. "That's gonna bruise bad." I flinch when he touches my cheek without invitation, and he instantly retracts his hand. "Sorry. Boundary issues sometimes."

"Try *all* the time," Heath supplies, tossing his jacket on the corner of the table. "Have a seat, Blaire."

I maneuver around them, dropping down onto the couch in grateful relief.

"Take these," Axel says, not making eye contact with me as he drops a couple pills in my palm. "For the pain." He raises his eyes as he hands me a bottle of water, and I have to work hard to stifle my gasp. He has the most piercing silvery-blue eyes I've ever seen. And my impression of him back at the park did not do him justice. Didn't do any of them justice, I realize as I quickly glance at Heath and Skeet too.

Holy hotness. These three are gorgeous. Each uniquely so. Skeet's messy, long hair curls around his ears and the nape of his neck, only begging to be touched. And cute is too simple of a word to describe how adorably good-looking he is with his striking green eyes and flirtatious smile.

Heath looks even bigger under the glare of this light, and his biceps are well-defined under the tight long-sleeved Henley he's wearing. He has a preppy all-American boy look about him, and I'm betting the girls at Kentsville High are all up in his space.

There's no denying Axel has the bad boy rebel look down pat. Now that he's lost the leather jacket, I can see he's ripped in all the right places too. He's not as bulky as Heath but bigger than Skeet. With his eyebrow piercing and the tats creeping up the side of his neck, he emits a dangerous vibe that is intoxicating.

All three are clearly hazardous to my health. But it's good to know my hormones are still working. And that I'm capable of attraction to the male race.

After Cam dumped me— unceremoniously and without any hesitation—I doubted I'd ever feel anything for any guy again. Cam failed me when I needed him most, breaking my heart apart all over again. Ethan would be so disappointed in him if he were still here.

"Liking what you see, Blaire?" Axel asks, dragging me out of my head. He narrows his eyes at me, and his gaze holds a challenge.

I could try to talk my way out of it, but I don't want to tell any more lies if I can help it. Where I *can* be truthful, I *want* to be honest. "As a matter of fact, yes. You guys are seriously hot."

Heath throws back his head, howling with laughter. Axel's gaze sharpens on me, and a muscle clenches in his jaw, but apart from that, he's a blank canvas, giving nothing away. Skeet props his butt against the pool table, grinning at me like it's his birthday and Christmas combined. "I knew there was a reason I liked you. And I think fate put you in our path today."

Heath groans. "Dude, you sound like a total pussy when you start spouting all that fate crap."

Skeet shrugs, not flummoxed in the slightest. "Do I look like I care?"

"Take the pills," Axel commands in a voice that says he means business.

"How can I be sure it's not rohypnol you're giving me?"

Axel plants his large hands on the couch on either side of me before leaning into my face. I'm not sure if he means to be deliberately aggressive, but it's intimidating as fuck all the same. His warm breath coasts over my face as he stares impassively at me. "Because if I wanted to fuck you, it'd be consensual. I don't have to drug any girl for sex."

I swallow the bile flooding my mouth and work hard to keep a cool composure. After my heart rate has calmed down, I'm able to assess this more logically. I don't need to know Axel to believe him. I just do, and I bet girls are crawling all over his moody, sexy ass.

I spot the packet of pills on the armrest of the couch, and it's a familiar brand, which erases any last doubt. Making a production out of taking the pills, I slowly open my mouth and drop them in before carefully bringing the bottle of water to my mouth, suctioning my lips around the top and gently tipping the contents into my mouth. I maintain close eye contact with Axel the entire time.

Skeet chuckles. "Where the hell have you been all my life?"

Axel straightens up, reinstating distance between us, while I send Skeet a flirty smile, relaxing for the first time in hours. "Hiding?" I tease.

Oh, the irony.

"Please tell me you're sticking around town?" Skeet asks, sinking into the couch beside me.

"I've just moved here with my parents, and yes, we're not planning on moving anytime soon." Although that will totally depend on whether our secret remains a secret.

"Cool." His smile is genuine, and I find myself smiling back at him. For the first time in months, I'm smiling.

It's almost miraculous.

"If you're done hitting on her, I need to attend to that bruise." Axel glares at his friend, but Skeet shrugs good-naturedly.

"Work your magic, bruh."

Axel crouches in front of me, and his face softens a smidgeon. "May I?" He gestures at the small medical kit resting on his knee.

I'm surprised he's asking permission. He looks like the type of guy who just takes what he wants, but I'm not ungrateful. I nod. "Thank you."

19

He probes my injured cheek with gentle fingers, sending fiery tingles all over my skin. My heart careens around my chest like an out-of-control race car when his fingers move up, and he carefully examines my forehead, pressing soft fingers into my skull at the hairline. "Does any of that hurt?"

I have to smother my snort of hilarity and clamp my lips shut to avoid telling him the only place I hurt is between the apex of my thighs. I shake my head instead, working hard to maintain a nonchalant expression on my face.

"I don't think there's any permanent damage. You'll probably just have one hell of a headache until the pills kick in."

"How can you tell?"

My question is greeted with silence until Skeet breaks it. "Let's just say Axel likes to fight, and he's had more than his fair share of knocks to the head." Axel shoots Skeet a deadly look that instantly mutes him.

"Well, okay, and thanks." I stand.

"Where the hell do you think you're going?" Axel's eyes narrow to slits.

"Home. It's late, and my parents have probably discovered I've snuck out by now."

"Text them," Axel snaps. "You're not leaving until the medication has kicked in, and then Heath'll drive you home."

I fold my arms across my average-sized chest, glaring at him. "I'm perfectly capable of walking home."

"Not happening, sweetheart." Skeet pulls me back down beside him. "It's not safe to go roaming these streets at night, and none of us would sleep tonight if we didn't make sure you got home safely. There's no point arguing with us. Trust me."

"Okay." I roll my eyes as I relent, but I'm secretly pleased. It's been a while since I've had anyone I could count on, and it can't hurt to make some friends before school starts on Monday. We've arrived just in time for the start of winter semester which is better than starting midway through where my appearance would be more noticeable.

"Want to shoot some pool?" Heath asks, quirking a brow.

My grin is sly as I nod. "Sure. I haven't kicked anyone's ass at pool in a long time."

Skeet slaps a hand on his thigh, grinning as he tilts my face toward him. "Hot, feisty, and you know how to play pool. Can I get on one knee now?"

I shake my head, but I can't contain my grin. "Is he always this full on?" I shoot the question in Heath's direction.

"It depends on the company, but in your case, I'd say yeah."

I jump up, wincing a little as a dart of pain shoots through my skull. "Who's up first?" My gaze bounces between them as my smile spreads.

I whip their asses, one a time, and by the time I've wiped the floor with Axel, I can't keep the smug grin off my face.

"Where the fuck did you learn to play like that?" If I didn't know better, I'd say there's a hint of awe in Axel's tone as he admits defeat, laying his pool cue down on the table.

"My twin brother taught me." My smile falters a little as a multitude of memories surge to the forefront of my mind, threatening to drown me. My life is so intertwined with Ethan's that no memory is safe. It hurts so much to think about the past, but I'm also terrified of the time when the past fades, because it's all I have left of him now. My chest heaves painfully, and that's my cue to leave. I want to be in the sanctity of my bedroom before I have my usual breakdown.

"Is that so? I'd like to play him sometime," Axel continues, unaware of my imminent meltdown. "See if the teacher is as good as the student."

My lower lip wobbles, and tears automatically prick my eyes. I don't know if it'll ever get any easier, but I might as well put it out there now, get this part over and done with. With any luck, they'll share the news around school, saving me from having to repeat it again. "He's … he's … dead. He died." A lone tear slips out of the corner of my eye, trekking down my face. I grab my hoodie. "I need to go."

"Wait." Axel takes my elbow, peering into my eyes. "I'm sorry."

I nod, fighting tears the whole time. I thought it might be easier here, but I have a feeling it could be harder. At least here I can say my brother died and people will react the right way. I won't have to face the snide comments and disgusted looks. Here, Ethan is humanized. He's not the monster everyone in Amber Springs believes him to be.

And that's why it's going to be harder than I imagined.

Here, I might actually find a way to properly grieve.

And facing all those emotions terrifies me.

It was easier, in some ways, to just lock it all away in Amber Springs, to hide my feelings and pretend like I was an emotionless droid.

"It's okay," I whisper. "It just hasn't been that long, and I'm still processing."

Skeet appears in front of me, pulling me into his arms without hesitation. I surprise myself by letting him hug me. And God, does it feel good. After a couple silent minutes, he releases me but takes my hand instead. "Come on. Let's get you home."

Heath's SUV looks brand-spanking-new if the clean interiors and new leather smell are any indication. Axel sits shotgun in front while Skeet sits beside me in the back, keeping a firm hold on my hand. His fingers entwine in mine, and it feels like the most natural thing in the world.

"Where to?" Heath asks, twisting around to look at me.

"Melville Place."

His eyes instantly dart to Axel's, but he says nothing, nodding as he starts the engine.

"Give me your cell," Skeet says, holding out his other hand.

"Why?" I narrow my eyes suspiciously.

He chuckles. "So I can add our numbers and get yours."

"My cell's toast," I admit, pulling the ruined phone out. "It was in my back pocket when I took a tumble in the park."

Skeet frowns. "My dad's good with repairs and shit. I can have him take a look. See if it's fixable."

I very much doubt it's fixable, but there's no harm in letting him look, and if, by some miracle, he can repair it, then it will, at least, save an awkward conversation with Dad. Money is really tight these days, and I don't want to ask for funds for a replacement phone if I can help it. "Have at it." I put the phone in his open palm and he slips it in the inside pocket of his jacket.

"Which house is yours?" Heath inquires as we turn onto my road a few minutes later.

"The last one on the end."

Heath pulls the car up in front of the run-down two-story house, and I try to mask my embarrassment. The front yard is like a jungle with grass that looks like it hasn't been cut in years, weeds galore, and over-grown, misshapen shrubbery along the edges. The realtor's sign hasn't been removed yet, and it's faded, crooked, and about to fall down, adding to the general derelict vibe the house emits. Peeling paint and worrisome cracks decorate the front façade of the property like a neon sign that screams *rental*. At some point, someone gave a crap about this house, but it's been poorly neglected since.

"Thanks for the ride." I wind my hand around the door handle.

"No problem," Heath replies with a small smile. "And I'm sorry again. I hope you're feeling okay."

"I'm fine. Honestly," I say, before climbing out of the car. Skeet hops out his side, and I stall on the sidewalk. "What are you doing?" I whisper.

"Walking you to your door," he whispers back.

"Not necessary, and if my parents see you or the others, they'll prob-ably freak."

Skeet looks up at the pitch-dark house. "I don't see any lights on. I think everyone's in bed."

I glance up, acknowledging his observation. There was a time when my parents would stay up until both their children were home safe and sound. That's just another thing that's changed around here. Some days, it feels like I'm invisible. Like I died with Ethan that day, for all my parents notice of me. My heart hurts all over again, but I force it aside, adept at disguising my true feelings. Skeet wraps his hand around mine, tugging me forward. "You don't need to do this, you know," I protest.

"I know, but I want to."

"Why?" I ask when we're on the porch, standing in front of the door.

"Because I like you, and you intrigue me, and I'd like to get to know you better." I'm not sure what face I make, but it's enough to have him backtrack a little. He extracts his hand from mine, holding up both palms. "As friends, Blaire. I swear you don't have anything to worry about with me. Or Axel or Heath either."

"I know."

"And you're new to town. It can't hurt to have friends who can show you around and help you navigate the halls of Kentsville High. You're a senior too, I'm guessing?" His smile is disarming, and I find myself relaxing.

"Yeah, and you're right, it can't hurt." I slant him a grateful smile. "Thanks for tonight. I had a good time."

"We did too." He pulls my hand to his lips, planting a soft kiss on the back of my knuckles. "For the record, I'm glad you moved here, Blaire."

I want to tell him me too.

But I'm reserving judgment.

Waiting to see if this move turns out to be the right decision.

Or another disaster waiting to happen.

Chapter Three

"Where's Dad?" I ask the following morning as I pour myself a cup of coffee.

"He has an interview at Johns Hopkins so he left early," Mom confirms, sitting down at the kitchen table.

"Oh. That's good."

"It's only a temporary part-time position. But it's a start."

I nod, shooting her a tentative smile. "When do you start your new job?" Uncle Tom has given Mom an administrative position in his real estate firm. It's quite a step down from her previous role managing the doctor's office, and it's more than an hour's commute each way, but beggars can't be choosers.

"Monday." She sips her coffee, looking absently out the window.

"So soon? What about the unpacking?"

"The unpacking can wait. We need the money." She levels me with an earnest look. Her hazel eyes lack their usual warmth, and the fine lines around her mouth seem more pronounced. We've all changed in the aftermath of Ethan's death. My parents have literally aged overnight, and whatever remnants of my youth I was clinging to are long gone.

"I understand, and I wasn't criticizing." I hope she knows that.

She reaches across the small, chipped kitchen table, clasping my hand. "I know, sweetheart." Her eyes probe mine. "How are you feeling about everything? Do you think you could like living here?"

My heart surges with joy at her questions. It's been so long since she's shown any real interest in me, and I didn't realize how badly I needed to know she still cares. I hear how that sounds—like I'm a selfish bitch, but my parents are all I have left in this world, and they've shut me out, a lot, these past four months, and it hurts. They aren't alone in their pain and their grief, but it's almost like they believe they are. Like I couldn't possibly be going through the same things. Feeling the same emotions.

Ethan was my *twin*. We were as close as two siblings can be, but more than that, he was my best friend and my biggest advocate, and I miss his larger-than-life presence so Goddamned much.

"I'm doing okay," I admit. "As well as can be expected." I pause, wetting my dry lips, wondering if I should say this. "I miss him," I whisper with tears swimming in my eyes. "I miss him so much."

Tears trickle out of her eyes, and she tightens her grasp on my hand. "I know, sweetie. I miss him too, but I'm still so … angry with him. And confused. How could he do that? *Why* did he do that? I still can't make sense of it."

A wave of guilt jumps up and slaps me in the face, and I avert my eyes, staring at the tile floor as if it's the most fascinating thing.

She releases my hand, slouching in her chair and audibly exhaling. "At least here we don't have to deal with the public backlash, but it doesn't stop the inner turmoil," she murmurs, more to herself than me.

"Do you think they'll find out?"

She eyeballs me. "Not if we stick to the plan." I nod, and she reaches across the table to me, taking my hand again. "I know we haven't been there for you, and I hate myself for that. We both love you so much, honey, and I'm sorry if we haven't shown you lately. Everything has just been so hard, but things will be better here. I promise."

A couple hours later, I'm wading through some of the boxes stacked against the wall in the small living room when the doorbell chimes. Mom looks over at me, panic evident in her gaze. "Who could that be?"

Wiping my dirty hands down the front of my jeans, I scramble to my feet. "It's probably just a neighbor welcoming us to the area. You stay here. I'll get it."

The look of relief on her face is instantaneous, and my heart hurts. Mom has always prided herself on being an upstanding member of the community. Appearances matter to her—not in the obnoxious sense of the word, but holding the respect of her neighbors, coworkers, and the community at large was always important to Mom. Which is why she took it so hard when that respect was wiped out overnight.

I couldn't have given two shits about that, but I did hate how Ethan's character was decimated even if I understand exactly why people started spewing the shit they did.

I pull the door open, and my eyes pop wide.

"Hey." Heath smiles, flashing me a perfect set of blinding white teeth, and I'm momentarily dazed. "Sorry to turn up without warning, but I wanted to give you this." He thrusts a brand-new iPhone at me.

My brow furrows. "What's this?"

"Chris couldn't fix your cell, so I got you a new one."

"Chris?" I arch a brow.

"He's one of … he's, ah, Skeet's dad."

"I can't accept that." I push his hand away. "It's way too expensive."

"I'm the reason your cell is broken, so that makes it my responsibility to replace it." Taking my hand, he wraps my fingers around the phone. Delicious little tremors shoot up my arms at the contact, and I lean against the doorframe to steady myself.

"And I'll happily accept a replacement once it's a like-for-like replacement." This is the latest version iPhone and a step up from my old iPhone. This time, I take *his* hand, placing the cell in it. "This is too much."

A massive grin spreads across his mouth, and my forehead scrunches up in confusion. I've no idea what I said that so's amusing. "Did I say something unintentionally funny?"

He shakes his head, running a hand through his blond hair. "It's just refreshing to meet a genuine girl. One who isn't out for what she can get."

"Does that happen to you a lot?" I inquire as I sense the presence at my back.

"More than I'd care to admit," he adds, glancing over my shoulder.

"Are you going to introduce me, honey?" Mom inquires, stepping alongside me with a fake smile plastered on her face.

Crap. I'll be in for it now. "Mom, this is Heath. I met him and his friends last night. They go to the local high school, and they're seniors too."

"It's a pleasure to meet you Mrs. Adams." Heath extends his hand, engulfing Mom's much smaller one as they shake hands.

"Likewise. I'm glad my daughter is making some new friends." Mom beams at him, a genuine smile this time, and I stare at her as if she's grown ten heads. I thought the whole plan was to stick to ourselves and go about our business as quietly and invisibly as possible, which is why I assumed she'd rip me a new one for already breaking the rules. She shivers, pulling the sides of her cardigan more firmly around her body. "We'd invite you in, Heath, but we're still unpacking, and the place is a mess."

"Oh, that's fine, Mrs. Adams. I just stopped by to give this to Blaire before heading to the gym." He grins as he thrusts the cell at me again. This time, I take it, slipping it quickly into the front pocket of my jeans before Mom pays too much attention to it.

"Thanks," I mutter as he steps back.

"No problem. Guess I'll see you Monday at school."

I nod. "Guess so. Um, bye."

He walks to his car and gets in, waving as he drives off.

"Come in, Blaire. It's freezing, and we're letting all the heat escape." Mom places a hand on my back, ushering me inside as she closes the door. I return to the living room, removing items from the box I was working on while silently praying she lets it drop.

"So, do you want to explain what that was all about?" she asks from the open doorway, planting her hands on her hips while piercing me with a stern look.

I silently curse in my head as I admit everything.

🖤🖤🖤

I arrive early to Kentsville High on Monday morning, and it's probably the first time I've ever been early to school of my own devices. Ethan would be so proud of me. The usual pang hits me square in the chest, and it takes considerable effort to put one foot in front of the other and step inside the building. I slam to a halt when confronted with the security checkpoint just inside the main entrance door, a cold sweat instantly breaking out on my forehead as I walk through the metal detector.

Gulping over the wedge of emotion clogging my throat, I tug my black hoodie up higher on my head as I make my way to the school office.

Once I've gotten my schedule, locker combination, and signed some paperwork, I step back out into the much busier hallway, hoping I'm going in the right direction.

My cell pings in my pocket and I smile as I open my new message. All three guys had messaged me yesterday, helping make today a little bit less daunting.

SKEET: *Where u at?*

ME: *Walking to locker.*

SKEET*: #*

ME: *212*

By the time I arrive at my locker, all three guys are already waiting. They are in a huddle, chatting quietly, oblivious to the interested looks they are picking up from all quarters. Or maybe they're used to it and they don't really notice anymore. The hallway is busy, and the loud hum of conversation tickles my eardrums. I bite down on my lower lip as I approach them wondering how I'm going to maintain a low profile if I start hanging with these guys. But if it's a choice between this and being a complete loner, then I know which option I'm going for. "Hey." I grip the straps of my backpack as I force out a shaky smile.

All three guys jerk their heads up, peering at me. Skeet and Heath are smiling, but Axel is wearing a neutral expression I'm guessing is his usual face. "Good morning, beautiful," Skeet says, yanking the hood off my head and smoothing my hair back off my face. "Depriving the world of this gorgeous view is a sin," he explains with a cheeky wink.

Axel tosses his gaze toward the ceiling, and Heath just laughs before whipping my schedule out of my hand. "Let me look." He skims his eyes over it. "You're taking a lot of advanced classes." He nods appreciatively. "And most of the same ones as me."

"Cool." I shift from one foot to the other, unaccustomed to such concentrated attention. Sure, Cam was attentive and didn't shy away from PDAs but having three guys focused on me at one time is a little overwhelming. While Heath is appraising my schedule, Skeet is toying with strands of my hair with a weird look on his face.

"Your hair is fascinating," he muses, threading his fingers through my newly dyed now wavy hair. "Is this your natural color?"

"No," I semi-lie. In my hasty attempt to change up my appearance before we left Amber Springs, I made a complete mess of dying my pure blonde hair dark, and now it's a weird combination of brown and blonde that actually looks artfully stylish, as if I'd planned on it turning out like this. Because my hair is so long and thick, it obviously needed two packs of dye, but I didn't know that before I set out to do it. I've never had cause to do anything other than cut my hair in the past.

My long, straight blonde hair was my defining feature in Amber Springs, so even though I've only just dyed my hair and I'm wearing it loosely curled now, it still alters my appearance considerably which I'm hoping will deflect anyone from guessing who I really am on the off-chance anyone saw one of the papers from that time or happened upon an online article and makes the connection.

"Well, I really like it." Skeet's smile is flirtatious in the extreme, but it's strangely comforting.

"Could you be any more obvious?" Axel deadpans, leveling an intense look at his friend.

"Could you be any grumpier?" Skeet retorts, slinging his arm over my shoulder. "Blaire and I are friends, and I'm just being *friendly*. You should try it sometime."

Heath chuckles. "I think senior year just got a whole lot more interesting."

"I should get going," I say, ignoring all their comments. "I don't want to be late for my first class."

"You're in AP World History with me," Heath confirms with a slight grimace.

"Why the scowl?" I inquire.

"I'm really behind with studying in that class, and my grades are dropping. My parents are *not* happy."

"It's one of my favorite subjects. I don't mind studying with you if you think that'd help?"

"Uh, yeah! As if anyone could turn down such a tempting offer," he says, waggling his brows before slanting a cocky look in Skeet's direction.

"Let me look at that." Skeet grabs my schedule from Heath's hand, quickly taking a photo and texting it to the others. "Now we all have Blaire's schedule, and we can ensure one of us is with her at all times."

"Stop, you guys. Seriously. I'm a big girl, and I can handle myself."

"You'll be grateful you have us looking out for you," Skeet continues. "As soon as the male population gets a look at you, they'll be crawling all over your sexy ass, and, that'll bring every mean girl out with swinging fists. Trust me, hang with us and we'll make sure you navigate Kentsville High like a pro."

"This isn't my first rodeo," I admit, opening my locker and shoving some books inside. "And I happen to be pretty handy with my fists too."

"That kind of statement will not deter him," Axel supplies, lounging against the side of the wall watching me with that penetrating lens of his.

"I'm not trying to deter anyone," I reply, banging my locker shut. "I'm just explaining I can defend myself."

God knows I've had to do enough of it the past few months.

"Good to know," Skeet says, darting in and lightly kissing my slightly bruised cheek. I've disguised it with makeup, but it's still a little sore to the touch. "But we've got your back, baby, and we're going nowhere, so you'd better get used to it."

Chapter Four

I walk with Heath to class, and he insists I take the seat in front of him. The morning period goes quite fast. Some teachers quietly acknowledge my presence while others force me to introduce myself, which I hate, but I get it done. By the time lunch comes around, I'm used to the inquisitive stares. It makes me hugely uncomfortable, but at least it isn't openly hostile. It's more akin to healthy curiosity which I can deal with, and hopefully, the attention will die down soon. The student body is large, so one new student shouldn't pique interest for too long.

When I leave math class, I'm surprised to find Axel waiting outside. This is the only class I've had all morning without one of them in it. He's leaning with his back against the wall and one leg raised at the knee. A pretty brunette is talking to him, her hand resting possessively on his chest, but he isn't paying her any attention, staring intently at me as I step out into the hallway.

He pushes off the wall, ignoring the girl, and stalks toward me. "C'mon. The others are holding a table in the cafeteria." He jerks his head forward, and I step into line beside him, shooting the girl an apologetic look. She glares at me with thinly restrained annoyance.

"I don't want to piss your girlfriend off. Why isn't she coming with us?"

He doesn't look at me as he replies. "She's no one, and I don't do girlfriends."

"Like, not ever?" I inquire.

He brusquely shakes his head, and that's as much intel as I'm getting. We walk in silence the rest of the way, and I try to memorize my surroundings and ignore the envious looks and heated stares leveled in my direction.

A shrill whistle rings out the second we step foot in the cafeteria, and several heads swivel in our direction. The urge to yank my hoodie up over my head rides me hard. I keep my head down as I follow Axel to a table at the back of the room. Skeet stands, holding out a chair for me, and I chew anxiously on the corner of my mouth, feeling eyeballs glued to my back.

"Dude, quit that shit," Heath says, coming up behind us. "Can't you see you're freaking Blaire out?" He places a tray loaded with food on top of the table and sits down.

Skeet's face falls a little. "Shit. Sorry, Blaire. I'm doing it again."

"S'okay," I lie, dropping my bag on the ground. "I just prefer to keep a low profile."

"You want me to get you something?" Axel asks with a raised brow.

I shake my head as I slide into the seat alongside Heath. "I brought lunch with me." To admit such a thing back at Amber Springs Academy would be akin to social suicide. While Kentsville High isn't a private school crammed full of pretentious assholes, I'm guessing it's not the done thing here either, but I really couldn't care less.

Money had never been an issue for my family until that fateful day. Sure, we weren't filthy rich like most of the kids at the Academy, but my parents had good jobs that paid well, and I didn't want for anything. Once news spread, both my parents were let go from their jobs, and money's been super tight ever since.

Six months previously, my parents had used up most of their savings buying a three-acre plot of land on the outskirts of Amber Springs. The old ramshackle house that came with the land was uninhabitable, so they'd pulled it down and were in the process of building a new house. Every spare penny was pumped into the build, so when everything happened, they were stuck without savings, without jobs, and saddled with land and a half-built mansion no one in town would dare venture onto let alone make an offer on. We literally fled here with the clothes on our backs and a few boxes of possessions. Mom sold her car and her jewelry, and that's what we've been surviving on ever since.

Buying lunch in school is a necessity I can't afford anymore. At least, not until I find a job. I'm hoping I'll be able to find work around here so I can at least ease that burden from my parents.

"I've got extra," Heath says affably, pushing his tray at me as Axel strides to the food counter. "Take what you want."

I grind my teeth down to the molars and knot my hands into fists in my lap. "I'm not a charity case," I hiss as red-hot anger replaces the blood flowing through my veins. "Is this some kind of 'help the poor girl' intervention? Is that why you're paying me attention?" I glare at them.

"No!" Skeet is quick to deny my hastily drawn assumptions. "Of course not!"

"Whether you have money or not doesn't factor into it," Heath calmly says, and that only irritates me more for some reason.

"Screw this." I bend down to grab my bag when a meaty hand wraps around my wrist.

"It's not charity, and we like you for *you* not what you have or haven't got. I was just being a friend. Friends share stuff without any motive, right?" Heath's tone is pleading.

"Don't leave," Skeet adds. "Please."

I rub the back of my neck, only staying put when I realize my little outburst has drawn more unwelcome attention. Ignoring everyone, I remove my lunchbox and unwrap the sandwich I prepared before I left the house this morning. I chew slowly as I try to calm down. The sandwich tastes like sandpaper, and I'm afraid I might choke over the lump in my throat, so I only manage a few mouthfuls before I discard it, appetite vanished.

Skeet and Heath are conducting some type of silent conversation when I finally lift my head up a couple minutes later. Now that the heat of my anger has faded, I'm a little embarrassed at my behavior. They stop, both turning to me with uncertain expressions, and I feel like a Class-A bitch. The guys have been nothing but nice to me, and I know Heath didn't mean anything by it. It's my issue. Not theirs. "Um, sorry. Touchy subject."

"It's cool," Heath says, his clear blue eyes examining mine. "But I really didn't mean anything by it."

"You should count yourself privileged," Skeet teases. "Heath doesn't share his food with anyone. Like ever."

"Shut it, assface. You make me sound like some greedy, selfish motherfucker."

Skeet leans into my side. "Heath is the school's star quarterback, and he's fucking anal about what he puts into his body. We've known him since he was three, and all he's ever wanted was to play NFL." He shoulder-checks me, making sure Heath is listening when he delivers his parting sentence in a faux solemn tone. "He's very responsible, and he takes it all really seriously."

"As seriously as a heart attack," Axel agrees, joining us.

"It's why he rarely shares his food, because his diet is carefully planned and controlled. You'd want to see what this guy can put away." Skeet thumps Heath in the upper arm, smirking at him.

"There's nothing wrong with being dedicated," Heath protests, giving his friends the middle finger.

"You're not just dedicated," Skeet retorts. "You're *obsessed*."

Heath ignores his friends, pinning the full extent of his attention on me. "Just because I take my training seriously, eat carefully, and rarely drink, these dicks think I'm obsessed."

"There's nothing wrong with having dreams or being passionate about something you care about," I say. "My brother played football too, and he was very committed. Controlled his calorie intake, drank protein shakes like he owned shares in the company, and worked out in the gym like a fiend." I clamp my mouth shut the instant the verbal diarrhea comes to a halt. I don't know what it is about these guys that has me opening up about Ethan. I've gone months without talking about him and now it's like I can't stop.

Perhaps that's why.

But I'm conflicted.

I want to remember my brother the way he was. Not as the sum of his last act on this planet. But guilt is wreaking havoc with my insides, because we weren't the only traumatized family left behind, and it all churns in my gut, twisting me into knots.

Is it wrong to feel guilty for thinking about my brother? For missing him? Or is it natural, irrespective of how horrified I am at what he did?

I don't know how to resolve all the messy emotions churning inside me.

"He sounds like my kind of guy," Heath says in a softer tone than usual. "I'm sorry I never got to meet him." Sincerity underlines his tone.

"Me too," I whisper. "He would have liked you. I can already visualize the bromance in my mind's eye."

"What happened to him?" Axel asks, and all good humor dies.

I don't want to lie to the guys, but I can't admit the truth either. However, if I'm vague, that'll just make them curious, and curious isn't a good thing when it comes to this. So, I say the only thing I can think of. I let my hair fall around my face, curtaining me. I don't feel quite so bad if I'm not eyeballing them while I'm lying. "He was sick. Cancer."

"Fuck."

"Yeah." I rub a hand over my aching chest. "Can we talk about something else? Anything? Please."

We lapse into a momentary period of silence until Skeet jumps in to fill it. "We heading to Lance's party on Saturday?" he asks, his gaze dancing between his two buddies.

Axel pauses in between eating. "I'm in."

"Sure. The season's over, so I can let loose a little." Heath shrugs.

"What about you?" Skeet pins me with puppy dog eyes. "Please say you'll come. We can pick you up around nine."

"I'll think about it," I say, knowing there's no way I'll attend. Parties and me have a checkered history, and that's not something I want to get into, now or ever.

"Hey, sexy." A glamorous blonde leans over Heath from behind, kissing his cheek as she drapes her arms all over him.

"Cassie." Her name is a virtual growl rolling off his tongue. He removes her wandering hands with an audible sigh. "Was there something you wanted?"

She giggles, and it's a horrid, high-pitched effort that has all of us wincing. Not that she notices. "That's a loaded question if ever I heard one." She laughs at her own joke, but she's the only one. Axel looks bored, and Skeet looks pissed on Heath's behalf. Heath looks … frustrated. His eyes flick to mine briefly, but Cassie notices, her smile instantly disappearing. "Who the hell are you?" she demands, her tone slicing through me in a way that's familiar.

"Leave Blaire alone." Axel's tone contains considerable challenge.

Cassie eyes me from head to toe, her expression transforming to one of amazed disgust. "*You're* Blaire?"

I pierce her with a cool stare. "If you have something to say, just say it."

She laughs, but it sounds all wrong. "You're all everyone's talking about today, but I wasn't expecting you to be so … *ordinary.*"

"Don't be such a fucking bitch, Cassie." Heath's venomous tone surprises me and Cassie too if her flushed cheeks are any indication.

"Shoo," Axel says, flapping his hand in her direction like she's an annoying insect. I've got to say, the more I'm around Axel, the more I like him. I don't mind that he's aloof and emits this whole intense "don't give a shit" vibe. He's clearly not afraid of speaking his mind, and I get a sense he's a diehard loyal friend. The type that is hard to come by.

"Screw you, asshole." Cassie glares at Axel.

"Wouldn't you love to." Axel smirks, leaning forward across the table. "But. It'll. Never. Happen."

Cassie storms off, tripping a little in her stiletto heels, and my lips kick up. Axel notices, offering me a subtle half-smile in return.

"Fuck me." Heath claws a hand through his hair, and I can't help noticing how his biceps flex and roll under the Henley with the motion. "Do you have to antagonize her like that? You just make that shit harder for me."

I sit up straighter in my chair. *Wait? Is Heath actually dating the clinger?* I thought he had more class than that. Yes, she's stunning, and I'll bet she fucks like a porn star, but I've known her type before. The malicious bitch who tramples over anyone and everyone to get what she wants—namely the most popular guy in school. Then she finds a way to trap him, get a ring on her finger, and her perfect future's locked down. Cassie reeks of it from a mile away, and Heath is the perfect target. He's good-looking and a star football player with a promising future. Plus, he's a really nice guy, but I'm sure she doesn't care about that.

I have a feeling Cassie is going to be a problem. I've had enough experience with malicious bitches to read the signs. Being prepared will help, and I open my mouth to ask about her, but the bell chimes before I can quiz Heath, and we make our way back to class without any further comments on the lovely Cassie.

Chapter Five

The afternoon session is much like the morning one, and I share one class with Skeet and another with Axel. Both experiences couldn't be more different. Skeet spends the whole class sending me cheeky notes and flirting outrageously any chance he gets while Axel basically ignores me.

My last class is with Heath, and he's already seated when I walk into the room behind Cassie. She slides into the seat in front of him, twisting around and smiling. I move past them to take a seat in the back when Heath's hand shoots out, and he holds my elbow, stalling me in my tracks.

"I saved that seat for Blaire," Heath tells Cassie. "So, if you don't mind." He gestures with his eyes for her to move.

Steam is practically billowing from her ears as she sends daggers at Heath. "What if I do mind?" she spits.

He shrugs casually. "Then I'll move someplace where Blaire and I can sit together."

Cassie shakes with anger as she stands, slamming her shoulder into me as she storms to the back of the room like a thundercloud waiting to wreak havoc.

Reluctantly, I sit down, angling my body sideways so I can talk to him. "I wish you hadn't done that. I really don't want her as my enemy."

Heath leans forward, pressing his mouth close to my ear. "I was doing you a favor. Whether you want her as an enemy or not doesn't come into it. Cassie's the head cheerleader, and she thinks she's queen bee around here. Unfortunately, there are plenty of idiots who buy into it. She's been mouthing off to anyone who'll listen all afternoon about you."

"Well, that's just fucking peachy. So much for wanting to blend into the background."

"At the risk of sounding like Skeet, I very much doubt that'd be achievable around here. You're far too beautiful and far too interesting to hide in the shadows."

I blush a little at his compliment, and he smiles. Tentatively, he reaches out, trailing the tip of his finger along my bruised cheek. "Does it still hurt?" he whispers.

"Barely."

"I'm really sorry about that."

"It's forgotten about. Honestly. We're cool." I hastily remove his finger when I hear hushed conversation going on around us. The pointed looks in our direction are a dead giveaway too. "And I'm still not happy about the cell, but I'm only accepting it because I need a phone, but I'm paying you back. As soon as I get a job."

"I don't want your money. It was the least I could do after I broke yours."

I open my mouth to argue when the teacher enters the room, bringing all discussion to an end.

The rest of the week follows a similar pattern. While the whispered gossiping and sneaky looks haven't dissipated, most people leave me alone. Sitting with the guys at lunch every day is both a help and a hindrance. It's clear they are popular and respected and having their friendship means I'm protected but it's also made me a target. The girls in class either glare at me or give me a wide berth, but once they leave me alone, I couldn't give two shits about it.

I'm in the bathroom on Friday afternoon, after the last class of the day, when I'm accosted. I've been expecting this so I'm not overly surprised.

"Clear the room," Cassie snaps at a girl with long coppery-brown hair, and she duly ushers everyone out of the restroom. I continue washing my hands as if nothing's happening. It's only when the door lock clicks into place that I turn around and face her. She's flanked by two girls on either side, and all five of them sneer at me as if I'm beneath them.

"Let's hear it," I say, deliberately keeping my voice level.

Cassie plants her hands on her slim hips, fixing me with a derogatory glare. "Let's hear it? Who the fuck do you think you are? You think you can swan in here and tell me what to do?"

I push off the sink, straightening up, putting my face right up into hers. "I don't really give a fuck what you think. I'm not here to cause trouble, but I won't back down from it either. This doesn't have to be a war, but it will be if you don't walk away."

They all laugh, and I work hard to remain calm, something which is difficult when there's so much pent-up frustration and anger swirling inside me.

She flicks her fingers in my chest, and I see red, grabbing her wrist and squeezing it tight. "Don't touch me or you'll be sorry."

"Shannon." The instant Cassie speaks, a tall girl with jet-black hair cut into a sharp bob steps forward, grabbing me around the neck from behind. I could get out of it easily, but I let them believe they have the upper hand. Another girl steps up, extracting Cassie's hand from my grip as if she's incapable of doing it herself. "Let's get one thing straight," Cassie continues. "I'm in charge around here, and if anyone's calling the shots, it's me. You will do as you're told or face the consequences."

She's comical, and I have to work hard to quell the urge to laugh in her face. No point being stupid. Even though I'm certain my fighting skills are superior to these girls, I'm still outnumbered, and I've been in enough catfights to know girls can be vicious and creative when they need to be.

"So, tell me. What are these rules I have to abide by?" I'm giving nothing away in my tone or my expression, and I can tell that's throwing her. She's probably used to girls quivering and falling at her feet, but I've faced off against much worse. If she knew me, she'd think twice about this.

"Stay the fuck away from Heath. He's mine," she snarls.

Man, she's so predictable. This is almost too easy. "You sure he got the memo?" I can't help pushing her buttons.

"What the fuck does that mean?"

"He doesn't seem very interested is all."

Fire spits from her eyes as she seethes right in front of me. "And you think he's interested in *you*?" She barks out a laugh, and her minions join in. "Heath's not into slumming it, and even if he was, he'd never go for someone like you." She skims her eyes over me, her disgust mounting as she takes in my scuffed biker boots, skinny black jeans, and black hoodie combo.

I never thought I'd miss my uniform at the Academy, but once I started at Amber Springs High, the public high school back home, I realized how underrated uniforms are. There's a lot to be said for being a number, one of many attired exactly the same.

I found it more difficult to hide when wearing my own clothes to school.

Although, it's unlikely I'd find any way to hide in my hometown. Ethan ensured the Simpsons were notorious, and there was no such thing as fading into the background anymore, but I tried hiding my figure behind slouchy sweaters and hoodies, wearing jeans and boots, and trying to look as inconspicuous as possible. It was an epic fail in Amber Springs, but I had hoped it would serve me well here.

Now, it seems, it's only made me a bigger target.

Cassie yanks the hoodie off me, scrunching her nose in disgust at the faded, holey Reckless Scary Bastards shirt I have on underneath. "Do you even look in the mirror? You're a walking disaster. It's laughable you think any of those guys are interested in you. They just feel sorry for you. You're like their pet project for senior year." She rakes her gaze over me again. "Hell, are you even into boys? Or are you a big, hairy dyke?" She flicks her finger at the shirt. "And what piece of shit band is this? You think it's cool? You look like some skanky slut. Is that who you are, Blaire? Is *that* why the guys are letting you hang with them?"

Reckless Scary Bastards is a local band Ethan supported for years even before they hit the bigtime last year. He bought this shirt at their first outdoor arena back home, and he loved it. I've taken to wearing some of my brother's shirts under my hoodies. It helps me feel close to him. To remember all he sacrificed for me. Cassie's personal insults don't bother me. I've heard way worse, but no one disses the shirt. I'm pissed at her dismissal of something that means so much to me, and I've reached my breaking point.

The girl with her arm around my neck isn't paying attention because it's way too easy to disarm her. I shove my heavy boot into her foot, and she yelps in pain, automatically loosening her hold on me. Then I shove my elbow into her gut, and she crumples into a heap on the floor. Another girl comes at me, and I level her with a direct hit to the nose, smashing my palm full force into her face. Blood gushes from her nostrils, and she cries out, stumbling on her heel and crashing to the ground.

"Who's next?" I challenge, and the girl with the coppery hair lunges at me. My boot slams into her stomach before she even reaches me, sending her flying back. Out of the corner of my eye, I spot a clenched fist coming at me. I jerk my head back to avoid the full impact, and her fist only glances off my jawline. I come back, swinging, knocking the girl with the sharp black bob back onto her butt. The others are climbing to their feet now, pissed as all hell. They circle me, and I crouch into a fighting stance. If this is going down, I'm putting up the mother of all fights.

"You know what to do," Cassie commands her crew, examining her nails like this is commonplace for her. Perhaps it is. She maintains position, not entering the fray, happy to watch from the sidelines like all cowards who get others to do their dirty work for them.

They surge together, ganging up on me, throwing punches left and right, but they're disorganized and lacking muscle, and I have moves thanks to the self-defense classes Ethan insisted I take a couple years ago. I give as good as I get. We trade punches and jabs while Cassie and one other girl sit it out.

"Open this door!" An authoritative voice yells from outside, and we all falter, swiping bloody fingers and sweaty brows.

Cassie levels a cunning look in my direction before viciously slamming her forehead into the wall. My mouth drops open. She sways on her feet, her eyes blinking profusely as a small bump swells in the center of her forehead. "You can open it now," she tells the other girl, the only one uninjured in the entire place.

She doesn't need to be told twice, rushing to unlock the door. The principal and vice principal push into the room, instantly surveying the scene. "What on Earth is going on here?"

"It's all her fault," Cassie says, her eyes flooding with fake tears. "The new girl attacked all of us when we were just minding our own business."

The principal levels a stern look in my direction before her gaze sweeps over the other girls. "All of you," she barks. "My office, right now."

Chapter Six

All six of us are propped on chairs outside the principal's office waiting for our parents to arrive. Every time the secretary leaves the room, Cassie hurls insults in my direction, but I tune her out and stare at the ceiling, knowing it's driving her mad and enjoying that fact.

One by one, the girls are hauled into the office with their parents, each one walking out looking suitably chastised. Without fail, they all snarl or glare in my direction—some of the parents included—and I'm guessing I'm being painted as the villain, but I've endured worse, so I ignore them, continuing to stare at the ceiling as if they're invisible.

"Ms. Adams." Principal Ivers calls me in last and I prepare myself for the inevitable lecture. She ushers me inside her office, closing the door after her. "I'm sorry for keeping you waiting, but I was hoping to have this discussion with your parents present; however, I can't locate either one of them and it's getting late, so we'll have to talk alone. If they've any questions, you can tell them to contact me on Monday morning."

She hands me a plain white envelope as she nudges me toward one of the empty seats in front of her desk. "You need to return this letter with their signatures."

I drop into the chair, embarrassed that neither of my parents are concerned enough about my welfare to ensure they're contactable. The principal sits down behind her desk and leans forward, clasping her hands in front of her. "I'd like to hear your version of events, please."

I proceed to fill her in, answering all her questions honestly.

"I understand how difficult things have been for you the last few months," she says when I've finished speaking. "But we don't condone or tolerate violent behavior at Kentsville High, and if it continues, it'll become a very serious matter which could end with your expulsion."

"I didn't start it, and I'd no choice but to defend myself. They ganged up on me. What was I supposed to do? Stand there and let them beat me?"

She sighs, rubbing a tense spot between her brows. "That is not what the other girls have told me. They all claim you were the instigator."

"I wasn't. Why would I start a fight with girls I don't even know? Especially when I'm trying to settle in with the least amount of attention."

Principal Ivers is well aware of my, *our*, situation. We had no choice but to fully inform her, partly because I wanted to use my mother's maiden name to enroll here, yet I had no formal ID, and partly because we knew all would be revealed once my old school sent over my records. The principal was sympathetic once Mom explained, readily agreeing to accept me after she received the transcripts from Amber Springs and saw my solid academic record. Even when things were shit, I always buried myself in my books, welcoming the focus and much-needed distraction so my grades are consistently high and I've a 4.0 GPA.

Although this discussion was conducted over the phone, I felt like the principal understood and was on my side. I told her the abuse I suffered at the hands of other students and my desire to settle as unobtrusively into my new school as possible.

Has she forgotten that? Or she thinks I lied?

She sighs again. "I'm in an impossible situation, Blaire. I have five students all claiming one thing, and you're telling me the opposite."

"I'm the only one telling the truth."

She stares at me in silence for a beat, obviously weighing something up. She wets her lips and fixes me with a solemn expression. "Cassandra McFarland is at the center of enough issues around here for me to believe that, but unfortunately, there isn't much I can do without sufficient evidence. And fighting on school property is not acceptable no matter who starts it. I have no choice but to suspend you for a week. The other three girls who have admitted fighting back have received the same punishment."

"And Cassie gets off scot-free?" I harrumph, not that I'm in anyway surprised. Girls like her always come out smelling like roses.

"You confirmed she didn't physically touch you, and the other girls agree she wasn't involved."

"But she manipulated the whole situation."

"I don't doubt that, but my hands are tied." She stands. "I'm sorry your first week has ended so acrimoniously. My advice to you is to steer clear of Cassandra and her friends. It's only five months until graduation, and then you won't have to ever see them again. Keep your head down. Focus on your studies and stay out of trouble." She walks around the desk and opens the door. "I really don't want to see you in here again, Blaire."

I'm still fuming as I step outside the main building into the fading daylight and stomp down the steps. My parents are going to throw a hissy fit when they hear I've been suspended.

The bus is long gone, so I've no choice but to make the trek home on foot now. Tightening the straps of my backpack, I zip my jacket up under my chin and start walking, following the path through the parking lot which will lead me out onto the main road.

A car pulls up alongside me a couple minutes later, and I jerk my chin up. "We heard what happened. Get in," Skeet says from the passenger side of Heath's SUV.

"I'd rather walk." I need to expel all this pent-up rage before I explode.

"It's getting dark, and we're not taking no for an answer."

God, he's so damned pushy. I give up fighting the inevitable, jumping in the empty back seat and pulling the door closed. "Where's Axel?"

"He's working," Heath confirms as he steers the car out of the parking lot.

"I didn't know he worked. Where?" Maybe they might need some additional help.

"He works at the local auto center," Skeet supplies while climbing into the back seat alongside me. He tilts my chin up with his thumb and forefinger, examining the fresh injuries on my face. "They're fucking jealous bitches," he seethes. "And they'll pay for this."

"Don't get involved. It'll only make things worse."

"I know how to put Cassie in her place without it backfiring on you," Heath cuts in. "They won't bother you again."

"How can you guarantee that?"

"My family is close with hers. Let's just say I have leverage and leave it at that." My eyes meet his briefly in the mirror, and I see the determination on his face.

"I appreciate what you're trying to do, but I'll only look weak if I let you fight my battles."

"Trust me, you look anything but weak. Shit's blowing up online already, and everyone knows you took them on even though you were outnumbered." Skeet slants me a lopsided grin. My heart plummets to my toes at the thought of my name being bandied around social media, causing all the tiny hairs on the back of my neck to lift in alarm.

"And I got a look at the other girls when they were leaving," Heath adds. "There's no denying you can hold your own."

"This isn't some big joke, guys. I got suspended for a week, and that bitch Cassie walked away without punishment."

"You still gave her a nice big goose egg to remember you by," Skeet teases.

"I gave her no such thing. The psycho bitch did that to herself."

"What?" Heath glances at me through the mirror, his incredulity obvious in his expression and his tone.

"She slammed her head into the wall when the principal showed up and then claimed I did it."

"Fuck. She's even crazier than we thought." Skeet's no longer laughing about it.

"All the more reason for you to stay away from her and let me handle this," Heath says, pulling onto my street. "This is because of me anyway. She's jealous I've been spending time with you, and I should've figured she'd pull some kind of stunt."

"It doesn't matter anyway." I peer out the window. "Can't change what's done."

"Will you get any shit for this?" Skeet peers up at my house as Heath pulls into the empty drive. No lights are on, and it doesn't look like anyone's home. It's usually after seven before Mom arrives home from work, and Dad's been on a downer all week because he hasn't heard back about that job yet. I've no clue where he disappears to each day, but he's never in the house when I return from school.

I shrug. "Probably."

"What about the party tomorrow night?" Heath asks, turning around to face me.

"I don't do parties anyway, so it makes no difference."

"You have to come." Skeet links his fingers in mine. "Pretty please?" He pins doe eyes on me, his messy hair almost obscuring them where it falls over his forehead, and it's hard to hang onto my frustration when he's so adorably cute.

"If you don't show up, others will speculate it's 'cause you're scared to confront Cassie and her hos," Heath adds. "We know that's not true, but they don't."

I exhale noisily. "Ugh. All right. I'll come, but I'll probably have to sneak out, so park around the block, and I'll meet you there."

The house is in pitch-darkness when I step inside and it's freezing cold, like icy-tentacles-swirling-through-the-air cold. I crank the thermometer to the highest setting, layering a second hoodie around my torso as I start preparing dinner. I've been cooking dinner all week so Mom doesn't have to do it when she comes in. Therefore, it won't look like I'm trying to butter them up before I drop the suspension bomb.

I make Grandma Adams's infamous lasagna, homemade garlic bread, and a leafy green salad. I've just set the table when the front door opens.

"That smells gorgeous, honey," Mom says, giving me a quick hug and a grateful smile when she steps into the kitchen. "Thank you." She presses a kiss to the top of my head and I wish I didn't have to ruin her good mood with my news. "Where's your father?" She glances around, her brow furrowing.

"I don't know. He wasn't home when I got in."

Her frown grows, and she pulls out her cell, checking her messages.

"Should we wait?" I ask, turning off the oven and removing the piping hot lasagna.

She shakes her head, tapping away on her cell. "No. Let's eat. I'm famished. Your father can heat his up later."

We're halfway through our meal, and I'm trying to pluck up the courage to tell her what happened when the front door slams and the heavy thud of approaching footsteps rings out.

"You!" Dad slurs, swaying on his feet as he points his finger at me. "Want to tell me why I have some message on my cell about a fight at school?"

Mom's gaze bounces between us, and she looks torn, not knowing who to question first. Dad takes the indecision away. "Spit it out, Blaire. What trouble have you gotten into this time?"

His hurtful comment stings, as if I was a regular troublemaker or something, but I swallow back the bile flooding my mouth and explain what went down. As I talk, Dad scoffs and snorts, half-slouched against the counter, looking like he's struggling to stay on his feet.

"Fucking hell, Blaire. We're not even here a week!" I jump as he roars at me. "What the hell is wrong with you children? First Ethan, and now you!"

"Archie!" Mom hops up, glowering at Dad. "It's hardly comparable, and you're drunk."

"So fucking what!" He throws his hands in the air. "That changes nothing. We're still fucked, Mir. We moved all this way, and Ethan's crimes are still following us."

"What do you mean?" I look between both my parents. "Has something happened I don't know about?"

"Let me see." Dad drops down into the chair beside me with a heavy thud, reeking like a brewery. "Your mom's already had to change her cell number, *again*, because some asshole got hold of her new one and was harassing her. I didn't get the job at Johns Hopkins because that asshole who made a false complaint against me has ensured I won't practice medicine ever again, and my once sweet girl is already fighting at her new school." He slumps headfirst onto the table. "I think that about sums it up." A beat later, he lifts his head. "Oh, and my dead son is still a monster. Let's not forget about that."

"Stop it, Archie." Mom is sobbing now. "Don't call him that."

"Why the hell not?!" The words rip from Dad's chest, but they could've been birthed from his splintered soul. "Why the hell not, Miranda!" His voice lowers, and he leans over the table, pain etched across his face as he pleads with Mom. "Have you forgotten what he did?"

"Of course not, but that wasn't him. That wasn't our Ethan." Tears are spilling down her cheeks as she tries to defend my twin.

SURVIVING AMBER SPRINGS 🖤

"He did it, Miranda. We've all seen the footage. It was him." Dad slumps back down in the chair, and an ache spreads across my chest as tears leak out of his eyes.

It's not the first time Dad's broken down in recent months, but it always floors me when it happens. I hate seeing Mom cry too, but there's something so heart-wrenchingly agonizing about watching a strong, proud man like my father dissolve before my eyes. I've been watching it for months now, helpless to do anything to stop it, knowing that time has come and gone.

A sob tears from his chest. "We can't keep deluding ourselves, Miranda. Our son did it. He's guilty as sin. Ethan shot all those kids dead. Deprived all those families of their children. Turned us into villains along with him. And if that doesn't make our son a monster, then I don't know what else to call him."

Chapter Seven

*D*ad is passed out on the couch, snoring his head off, in a haze of stale alcoholic fumes, when I get up the following morning, and a new layer of guilt adds to the existing pile. It's my fault my parents ended up in another humdinger of an argument last night, but I fail to see how I could've prevented it. If it wasn't the fight at school, it would've been some other trigger. It seems like my parents can't go longer than twenty-four hours before coming to blows over Ethan and the shit he's left behind.

Mom has her head in her hands, quietly sobbing, when I enter the kitchen. The sight of her shoulders shaking as she cries kills me. "I'm sorry, Mom," I whisper, tentatively hugging her.

She lifts her head, pinning me with bloodshot eyes. "Why did those girls pick on you, Blaire? Have they figured out who you really are? Is this the story of our lives from now on? We keep running from town to town as soon as people find out?" She grabs hold of my waist, sobbing into my chest. "I can't handle it anymore. Your father is no help. He's depressed, and I don't have the energy to pull him out of it. It's not going to get any better."

She pulls back, sniffling as she swipes under her eyes with the back of her sleeve. "How could Ethan do this? How could he walk into that school and shoot those boys and girls dead in cold blood? Didn't he think about what he was doing? Or give any consideration to how this would affect those left behind? Did he expect to die too, and, what, he was okay with that? I don't understand. It makes no sense. Why, Blaire?"

She stands, placing her hands on my shoulders as she rains questions down on me: questions she's already asked a hundred times or more. "Why did he do it? You must know! You were his twin. You two shared

53

everything. Why, Blaire? Why did my sweet boy turn into a killer?" She shakes me, tears streaming down her face, and my heart ruptures straight down the middle.

"Mom, please," I croak as the familiar weight starts pressing down on my chest. "Please don't do this. I'm struggling with this as much as you are."

She wraps her arms around herself, shaking her head. "I don't think I have the strength to do this anymore." A strangled sob rips from her mouth as she shuffles toward the door. "I just can't. I'm going back to bed."

I stare at the empty doorway for ages after Mom retreats to her bedroom in a sort of numbed aware state. I don't think it's going to get any better. I don't think this is something anyone gets over. Ever. Eventually I move, ghosting around the kitchen as I pour coffee and fix myself some breakfast. I try to force some toast down my throat, but it's futile. My head churns with the usual thoughts, and I know I need to get out of here before I have a meltdown.

Changing into running pants and a top, I pull on my sneakers, clip my iPhone to the waistband of my pants, and strap my water bottle on my arm. I pop the buds in my ear before leaving the house and press play on the music app. It's practically arctic outside as I set off running, and I wonder if I'll ever get used to the colder weather here. While temps cool down in the winter in Arizona, and it can turn icy at night, it's not even close to this level. I never thought I'd miss the humid heat back home, but I do. I'd happily trade the icy cold for cloying humidity any day.

I head in the opposite direction of town, moving farther into the less than desirable parts of Kentsville, sprinting past neglected homes and overgrown parks, vacant, vandalized stores, and an overcrowded trailer park that looks like it hasn't seen any upgrade since the sixties.

But I don't pay much attention to my surroundings, trapped in my corroded mind despite the music thumping in my ears and my repetitive inner mantra pleading for some respite from my destructive thoughts. Running is usually a great distraction, and it's the only thing that helped keep me sane in the aftermath of the shooting and the public vitriol hurled at my family.

It's not that I don't understand. I do. And my heart breaks for their families. They should not have had to endure that. If we're saddled with a life sentence, then they are too. What Ethan did was beyond reprehensible. It doesn't matter who they were, what history existed; those four boys and three girls did not deserve to be killed in cold blood, gunned down in front of their classmates. I don't blame people for the things they've said about my twin. In their shoes, with the facts as they apparently seem, I would probably say the same.

But they don't know the full picture. And it doesn't make any difference now. It won't change how they feel about my brother or my family.

To others, Ethan Simpson will always be a monster.

And my heart aches at the injustice of it all.

I understand the need to lash out, to require some place to vent all the grief and frustration, but the abuse my parents and I have had to deal with crosses a line. We weren't the ones who did the shooting, and we had no clue Ethan was planning that, yet we're the ones paying the price. Both my parents were forced out of their jobs. Thanks to a completely unfounded malicious allegation, my dad is unlikely to ever work as a doctor again, even though it was proven he was innocent. It doesn't matter; his reputation is tarnished. And we're virtually penniless, unable to sell our house or the land my parents were building our new home on. No one wants to live in the house where a mass murderer lived.

I didn't return to Amber Springs Academy after the shooting—there was no way I could— but I still needed to graduate, so I enrolled in the local public school thinking I wouldn't face so much hostility there, but I was sorely mistaken. Even now, I shudder as I recall the months of torture I endured before we left town. Whispered taunts, unhelpfully, resurrect in my mind, and a piercing pain shoots across my chest.

My feet pound the sidewalk as I ramp up the pace, pushing my limbs to extremes, with sweat beading on my brow, determined to outrun my demons.

I feel for the families of the victims. I honestly do. There isn't a day goes by when I don't think about their suffering, but at least they are allowed to grieve. We were denied that, and it still hurts.

Some days I hate Ethan. Hate him for the decisions he made. And for leaving me alone.

But most of all, I just miss him.

He was the best brother a girl could ever hope for. What he did doesn't take away from that. It's not a sentiment I share with anyone, for obvious reasons, but in my heart, in my *soul*, I still love my brother, and I always will. This whole situation is so messed up that there are times when I even feel guilty for admitting that to myself.

How fucked up is that?

Deep down, I know I'll never be able to truly move on in life until I've come to terms with my brother's loss and all the associated implications of his actions. At least here, with hundreds of miles separating us from the past, I know I have a chance at achieving that. I'm not strong enough yet to face it, but one day, hopefully, I will be.

"You really shouldn't be running out here alone," a gruff voice says from behind, and I scream, my heart rate accelerating to coronary-inducing territory. "Relax, it's only me," Axel says, appearing on my right-hand side as he jogs with me.

"You almost gave me a heart attack," I pant, struggling to recalibrate my breathing.

"And you've just proved my point. I could've been anyone sneaking up on you. You can't run these streets unaware, Blaire. It's not safe. Even in daylight."

"I know self-defense," I protest even if I agree he's right.

"I've heard, but that will only get you so far. Not allowing someone to grab you in the first place is your best defensive move."

"I know. It's just I have a lot on my mind, and I got distracted."

He doesn't reply, shooting me a penetrating stare, one of his specialties. My eyes roam over his crumpled running shorts and top. The tats on his arms are clearly visible under the short-sleeved top, trailing the length of both arms and halfway down one hand. The designs are intricate, and I wonder if they have any special meaning.

If he notices my ogling, he doesn't call me out on it, and we both run in silence, matching strides with relative ease. After a couple beats, he clears his throat. "I know a place that's safe to run. I'll show you if you want."

"Now?" I ask, unstrapping my water bottle and bringing it to my lips.

He nods, veering right and ducking down a narrow alley. I trail a little way behind him as I guzzle my water. When I'm done, I quicken my pace and catch up to him. We sprint down a few more side streets, crossing into more respectable residential areas, and after navigating a few roads, he leads me into a small park at the far side of the residential sector.

Tall trees tower over us as we run along the main path, rimmed with neat shrubbery, and down onto the edge of a small lake. Several houses lap the lake on the other side with lawns and docking bays facing out onto the water. A bunch of kids are playing by the water's edge, and a couple of older men are sitting in foldable deck chairs with fishing rods clutched between their thighs.

"This is a good place to run as there are plenty of people around during the day, and at night, it's well-lit and monitored by a private security firm employed by those residents to protect their property," Axel says, pointing at the lavish houses the other side of the lake.

"That's good to know," I huff out.

"You should still get a ride here though or ..." He trails off, and I stare curiously at him.

"Or what?" I prod as we run.

He shrugs, refusing to look at me, and I'm forced to quell my inquisitive mind.

We run for a couple miles, along the path that borders the lake, keeping a steady consistent pace, and even though we're not talking, it's companionable. I've never run with anyone before, and I didn't think I'd like it. But I like running with Axel.

Or maybe I just like him. Period. He has that whole moody, brooding, mysterious vibe thing going on that is seriously attractive.

"Let's stop here." Axel doesn't ask. He tells me. Usually, it drives me bananas when someone tells me what to do, but I kinda like it when he does.

I'm seriously starting to worry about myself where Axel is concerned.

With his tats and piercings, scruff on his chin, his deep voice, intense mannerisms, and the whole bad boy aura, he's as far removed from the type of guy I usually go for as you can get. Cam was my only serious boyfriend, and while he was dark-haired too, he was the classically handsome, clean-cut, all-American boy you take home to meet the parents. Axel is the type you want to hide in a closet and do dirty shit with.

My cheeks flare up as I drop down onto the ground alongside him. Thank God, he doesn't have a hotline to my mind, or things would get awkward real quick. I pull my knees up to my chest and wrap my arms around my legs, staring out at the calm, crystal-clear water. Distant voices tickle my eardrums, and the faint chirruping of birds is the only other sound around. "I like it here. It's very peaceful," I admit, rolling up the sleeves of my shirt, wishing I'd worn a tank and brought my hoodie instead. The top adheres to the sweat on my back, clinging to me like a second skin.

"Yeah. It is."

I tilt my head to the side, looking at him. "How long have you been running?"

"A couple years." He picks up a stone and lets it loose. We both watch as it soars through the air and then lowers to the water, bouncing over the surface four times before disappearing. Angling his head, Axel locks eyes with me, and I momentarily forget how to breathe. His eyes are the most startling shade of gray-blue and I'd challenge anyone to look away when Axel ensnares you in his gaze. I imagine it's akin to being hypnotized. "And you?" he asks.

It takes me a few seconds to de-fog my brain and remember what we were discussing.

"I've only been running four months."

His brow lifts ever so slightly. "You're a natural. Not many girls could keep pace with me."

I shrug, as if I'm immune to his compliment. "I've long legs." *And an abundance of inner demons pushing me to my limits.*

"I noticed." His voice is deep and gravelly, and it sends shivers cascading up and down my spine. How he manages to load so much into such a small statement speaks of real skill. I'm betting Axel Thorp could get any girl he wanted with one of those looks or a few simple words from his mouth, spoken in that panty-melting tone of his. I'm practically liquefying into a puddle at his side and he's barely even spoken to me today. But Axel doesn't need words to make an impression. He has this indescribable presence. An intoxicating magnetism that's almost impossible to resist. An allure that reels you in whether you realize it or not.

58

Electricity crackles in the space between us as we stare at one another. My chest heaves, and his eyes lower to my breasts, lingering for a fraction too long. My nipples instantly harden, and I'm praying he can't see through my flimsy top. He raises his eyes slowly, in tandem with the lifting of his arm as he reaches out, tucking some loose strands of hair behind my ears. My skin ignites in the place where his fingers brush against my cheek, and I can't recall ever having such a visceral reaction to any guy. His hand lingers on one cheek, and my breath falters in my chest again.

"I see you, you know," he adds quietly. "I see what you try so hard to hide."

Panic swells inside me, and I'm not fast enough to disguise it.

He grips my chin, forcing my gaze to remain locked on his. "Don't do that. Don't feel embarrassed. There's no reason to."

If he really saw inside me, if he really knew the kind of person I am, he wouldn't say that. So, I guess my secret's safe after all. But I'd like to know what he thinks he sees. "What do you see?" I whisper.

He leans into me, and we're so close we're almost touching. There's only a tiny gap separating our bodies, and his warm breath steals over me when he speaks, hypnotizing me all over again. "I see a beautiful girl in so much pain she can hardly breathe," he rasps quietly.

I stare into his eyes, recognizing a kindred spirit. "And I think Skeet was right," I supply. "You only see those things because they exist inside you too."

Slowly, reluctantly, he nods while winding his hand around the back of my neck. "I think you might be dangerous for my health, Blaire," he says, staring at my mouth.

"I already know you're dangerous for mine," I whisper back.

Chapter Eight

I really thought Axel was going to kiss me, but he retracted into his shell after our intense talk, and we ran all the way home without speaking. But it wasn't uncomfortable. Being around a guy like Axel *should* make me uncomfortable, but I'm weirdly reassured in his presence. If there's one thing I've learned in this life, it's that there's no point trying to figure out the whys, so I don't expend any energy trying to work him out. I'm just going to go with the flow, and at least, he distracted me from all thoughts of Ethan and the shooting.

"You going somewhere?" Mom asks, pushing my door open, without invitation, later that night. I'm currently standing in my underwear in front of my bed with the entire contents of my closet spread out on the comforter.

"Heath invited me to a party." I tell the truth, expecting her to ground me, and then I'll have a perfect excuse not to go, but she surprises the hell out of me.

"Good. I'm glad you're making new friends."

My jaw slackens as I stare at her. "But I'm suspended from school. Shouldn't you ground me?"

She purses her lips as she eyeballs me. "Maybe, but I want you to be happy here, sweetheart." She crosses the room, tilting my chin up with one finger. "That's more important. Go out and have some fun. God knows you deserve it." She presses a kiss to my forehead, and I'm wondering if aliens have secretly abducted my mom and some extraterrestrial imposter is pretending to be her. I blink profusely as I watch her saunter to the doorway. "And you should wear the purple dress. I always loved it on you. It really brings out the color in your eyes." She quietly closes the door, leaving me in shock.

I don't wear the purple dress. Or any dress. It's not in keeping with the whole inconspicuous look I'm going for. Instead, I'm wearing black skinny jeans, a beaded, lace-trimmed black tank top, and Ethan's faded gray leather jacket. It's too big on me, but I like wearing it, and I'd challenge anyone to make me part with it. My boots have a little bit of a lift, thanks to the wedge heel, making me taller than my five feet nine inches. A light layer of makeup is my only armor as I wave at Mom before snatching my woolen scarf and bailing out the front door. I practically sprint toward Heath's SUV, scrambling in the back before Mom can make an appearance and embarrass me.

"Hey, babe." Skeet leans over and kisses my cheek, immediately threading his fingers through mine. He definitely gives new meaning to touchy-feely, but I genuinely don't mind. "You look gorgeous."

"Thanks." I smile sweetly at him before glancing at Heath and Axel in the front.

"So, your parents didn't ground you after all?" Heath inquires as he drives off.

"No. Mom basically shoved me out the door with the biggest grin on her face."

"I like her already," Skeet jokes, tugging me into his side. He nuzzles his nose in my neck, audibly inhaling. "You smell divine," he murmurs, and my heart flutters behind my ribcage.

"Boundaries." Axel's one-word warning has Skeet flipping him the bird. "And I saw that." Axel returns the gesture from the front without even glancing back, and I can't stop the giggle from escaping my lips.

Skeet grins, repositioning us a little so we're half-facing one another. "Doucheface has a point, I suppose. My family is pretty free with the love and affection"—Heath almost chokes on his laughter and Axel snorts—"and I'm demonstrative with those I care about, but I know it's not exactly normal. I don't want to make you uncomfortable, so if I overstep, just point it out and I'll back off."

"Okay." I drag my lower lip between my teeth as I briefly consider it. "But I'm fine with it."

His answering smile is so wide it threatens to split his face in two. "Cool." He waggles his brows, slinging his arm around my shoulder while smacking a loud kiss off my cheek. "And just so we're clear," he adds, pressing his mouth to my ear and whispering seductively. "I care about you."

His emerald green eyes twinkle with mischief, and there's something so refreshingly different about Skeet that I'm drawn to. He's blunt but never in a malicious way. He's honest and not afraid of expressing himself, and that's a big turn-on. "I care about you too," I whisper, and he tweaks my nose, settling us back into the seat as Heath drives us to the party.

"Wow, this place is something else," I admit, gawking at the magnificent mansion up ahead as Heath navigates the long driveway behind a line of other cars. "Who is this Lance guy? Does he go to our school?"

"We met Lance at Little League when we were three," Skeet starts explaining. "That's how we all became friends. We used to be the awesome foursome, but now we're the awesome threesome because Lance's parents put him into boarding school overseas and we don't get to see much of him anymore."

"But his parents are on a cruise for the next few weeks, and he got suspended for a month, so he's making the most of the opportunity," Heath confirms, before I can even pose the question, parking the car and killing the engine.

"What'd he do to get suspended for a month?" I inquire, watching a bunch of boys and girls exit neighboring cars, making their way around the back of the house.

Axel turns around to face me for the first time with a half-smirk on his face. "You sure you want to know?"

"Now I definitely want to know," I say, unbuckling my belt and sitting up straighter.

"He smuggled some girls into his room and was caught in a compromising position," Heath says, hijacking the conversation before Axel has time to reply.

Skeet roars with laugher, slapping a hand on his thigh. "Dude! Who shoved a stick up your prissy ass?!" He slaps his thigh again. "Compromising position," he murmurs in between chuckling and shaking his head.

Axel's eyes smolder as he fixes me with a heated stare. "Lance was caught fucking one girl while fingering another. The other two girls were fucking each other when the night supervisor walked in on them." He continues staring at me, and I know he's baiting me, waiting to see how I'll react. He thinks he knows me, but he doesn't know everything.

My lips kick up at the corners. "Yep, that'd do it all right." I deliberately wet my lips, still locked in a battle of wills with Axel. "And now I'm really looking forward to meeting Lance."

"Oh, hell to the no," Skeet says, instantly sobering up. "I don't like the idea of you anywhere near that dirtbag."

Axel quirks a brow, breaking eye contact with me to send an amused grin at his friend. "Double standards much, dude?"

"Screw off, Thorp. I love sex, but I'm not fucking around with different girls every day of the week like Gibbons."

"You know it's a fuck you to the rents," Heath says, opening my door and offering me his hand.

Axel thumps him in the arm when we round the front of the car. "Yeah, I'm sure that's all Lance's getting out of it."

Heath scowls at Axel before looping my arm in his. "Stay close to one of us at all times. Lance is a crazy motherfucker, and this party will definitely be wild."

"Sure." My voice sounds calm even if I'm quaking on the inside. I don't want to admit that my anxiety level is off the charts and I've no intention of going anywhere inside that house without one of them by my side.

"What's your poison?" Skeet asks when we make our way into the pool house which has been transformed into party central for the night. Although, calling it a pool house seems ridiculous based on the sheer size of the place. It must have at least four or five bedrooms if the vast living room and opulent kitchen are any indication. There's even a game room with a large pool table and several gaming consoles. Heath made a beeline for it the second we stepped foot in the space.

"I'll have a Coke."

"You don't drink?" he asks, grabbing a chilled can from the refrigerator for me and a couple beers for himself and Axel. The kitchen is teeming with people, most I don't recognize but that's not unusual. I'm still trying to memorize faces and names at school.

"Alcohol doesn't agree with me." I pop the lid on the can and take a few sips, hoping he doesn't pry anymore. He doesn't, but Axel turns that penetrative lens on me, and I can tell he understands there's more to it than my simple statement.

"Rat bastards!" A tall guy with reddish-blond hair shouts over the noise, stalking in our direction. He performs some elaborate man-shake with Skeet before thumping Axel in the shoulder. "S'up asshats?" He grins at them before draining the remnants from his beer and tossing the empty bottle at the sink. His aim is off, and the bottle drops to the floor, smashing into smithereens. People dart out of the way, girls shrieking as little splatters of beer land on them.

"Still can't shoot for shit," Skeet teases, pulling me in close to his side. The stranger notices, and it's almost comical how fast his whole demeanor changes. "Well, hello there, beautiful. Who are you, and where have you been my entire life?"

"Does that line usually work for you, Lance?" I ask with a teasing grin. I'm guessing he's our host although it'll be embarrassing if he's not.

"Like a charm," he acknowledges with a wink.

I laugh, extending my hand. "I'm Blaire. Nice to meet you."

He lifts my hand to his mouth, pressing a wet kiss on my skin. "The pleasure is all mine." He makes no effort to conceal his blatant perusal of my body. "Definitely, all mine," he adds, licking his lips in a suggestive manner as his gaze sticks to my chest. I'm wearing a push-up bra tonight, and the swell of my breasts is visible behind the lace trim of my top. Lance isn't the best-looking guy I've ever seen, but he has a certain charisma and a whole lot of personality which more than makes up for it. With anyone else, I'd call him out for the suggestive comments and sleazy looks, but I just find it funny. I figure he's exaggerating to wind the guys up, and it's not as sinister as it seems on the surface.

So, I'm hugely surprised when Axel gets all offended on my behalf.

Chapter Nine

"*B*ack the fuck down." Axel steps in front of me, pushing his chest into Lance's. Axel has a couple inches in height on Lance, but Lance is carrying at least an extra twenty pounds in weight, and I'm sure he could take Axel if he wanted to. "And apologize."

Lance holds up his palms, grinning like a lunatic. "My girl Blaire knows I'm just messing around."

"I'm warning you now, Gibbons," Axel growls. "Keep your fucking hands, and other parts of your anatomy, away from Blaire." Skeet shoots a loaded look at Lance for added effect.

Lance chuckles. "It's too fucking easy to do this. Chill the fuck out. I'm only fucking with ya. And I'll be the perfect gentleman." Shoving Axel aside, he takes my hand again. "I apologize if I caused any offense."

"I'm cool."

"I'm getting that, but these two." He shakes his head, his gaze bouncing between the boys. "Never thought I'd see the day, but, yeah, I think the Taylor influence is definitely at play here."

The Taylor influence? I frown a little, confused and unsure what he's inferring. Axel locks up tight, glaring at Lance. "You're talking out your ass, and now I'm pissed." Grabbing another beer, he stomps off to the front room without another word.

"Oh, was it something I said?" Lance feigns innocence.

"Something tells me you can't help stirring shit," I say, sipping my soda.

"I've got to do something to ease the boredom at school," he admits.

"It didn't sound like school was all that boring for you," I retort, unable to smother my grin.

Lance slaps Skeet around the head. "Thanks for ruining my chances before I even met her."

"Don't blame me. I never said a word." Skeet tightens his arm around my waist, and I lean into him. "And Blaire is capable of making her own choices. If she wants a ride on your disease-ridden dick, who am I to stop her?"

I burst out laughing.

"I'm not infectious, I swear," Lance rushes to reassure me. "I get tested every quarter. I can show you." He reaches into the back pocket of his jeans, extracting a crumpled piece of paper and thrusting it at me. Skeet and I crack up laughing, and then someone hollers for Lance from outside, and he dashes off, shouting back at me as he blows kisses my direction. "We're not finished this conversation, gorgeous. Later." He winks, and I have to clutch my stomach I'm laughing so hard.

"Oh my God," I say when I finally compose myself. "Did that just happen?"

"Dude's crazy, but he's actually a good guy underneath the persona he wears."

"Let's be serious," a new voice says, and I spin around the same time Skeet does, coming face to face with a very pretty girl with strawberry-blonde hair hanging in wavy lines to her waist. "Dude's got issues, but he knows how to throw a rocking party."

"Shaznay." Skeet grabs the girl into his arms, lifting her clear off the floor. A pang of jealousy hits me as I watch them hug it out. She's squealing, pleading with him to let her down, and by the way she's looking at him, she clearly thinks he hung the moon. I look around for any sign of Heath or Axel, but Axel has disappeared completely, and Heath is in what looks like a tense stand-off with Cassie over in the corner. As if I've called her out, she picks her head up and glares at me.

"Blaire," Skeet says, tugging on my elbow and reclaiming my attention. "I'd like you to meet my little sister. Shaznay, Blaire. Blaire, Shaznay."

"Your sister?" I stupidly blurt, relief flowing over me like a waterfall.

"My *sister*." He enunciates the word, grinning and letting me know he understands exactly where my head went.

"You weren't kidding. She's stunning," Shaznay says, giving her brother a thumbs-up before lunging at me, and folding me into the tightest hug imaginable.

"I told you it runs in the family." Skeet smiles at the startled expression on my face.

"Oh, sorry!" Shaznay releases me, standing back to examine my face. "I've just been super excited to meet you. It's been so long since Skeet has gushed about any girl."

"Wow, thanks for that, sis." His eyes pop wide as he levels a chastising look at his sister.

"Just keeping it real, bro." She grabs him into another quick hug. "And I really did miss your annoying, ugly face."

"And the compliments keep on coming," Skeet deadpans, reaching out for me. He tucks me into his side again, wrapping his arm around my waist. "Shaz has been galivanting around Europe with her godmother the last few weeks," he explains, putting on a fake posh upper-crust English accent that is halfway decent. "They were trapped by Storm Frank and had to wait almost a week to catch a flight out of the UK."

"It was dreadfully tragic," Shaznay says, also adopting a mock-English accent, one that is vastly superior to Skeet's attempt. She pretends to fan her face. "And I *hated* missing the first week back at school."

"Sounds horrid," I agree with a grin.

She pats her chest dramatically. "I'm not sure I'll ever recover."

"Why does shit like that never happen to me?" Skeet bemoans. "And how come you got the awesome godmother and I'm stuck with Liam's conservative sister who would rather walk over hot coals than spend any time with me?"

"Jealousy isn't very becoming, brother dearest," Shaznay reprimands him before nudging him in the ribs with her elbow. "Get over yourself!"

"I need a fucking beer or ten," Heath spews, barging his way into the conversation like a speeding train.

"Have at it." Skeet thrusts a bottle into Heath's hand.

"Let me guess," Shaznay says. "The queen bee is laying down the law again."

"I can't even …" He shakes his head, exhaling loudly as he squeezes his eyes shut. Skeet and Shaznay trade knowing looks. Heath's eyes reopen, and he gives Shaznay a big hug. "Good to have you back, baby Taylor." He messes up the hair on top of her head, and she shoves him off.

"I see you haven't gotten any less irritating while I've been away. And quit with the baby Taylor nickname. That shit was cute when I was, like, five." She narrows her eyes at him.

"Get out. I know you secretly love it," Heath quips. "Makes you feel all special and shit."

"Boys." She rolls her eyes dramatically before pinning me with a conspiratorial grin. "They are completely clueless."

"Heath!" A high-pitched voice shouts across the room, and I don't need to look to know it's Cassie. Her nasally tone is forever imprinted on my brain.

"I can't take any more of her shit tonight." Heath sets his beer down and takes my hand, pulling me away from Skeet. Shaznay looks between her brother and Heath, a look of avid curiosity crossing her face. "Come with me."

I don't appear to have much of a choice as he hauls me across the kitchen and outside. I shiver as a blast of cold air slaps me in the face, and he stops on the patio, removing his jacket and sweater. "Here, put this on." He thrusts his sweater at me. I remove my jacket, bristling as large goose bumps sprout along my skin before the warmth of Heath's sweater glides over my arms, protecting me. It's way too big, but I'm not complaining. His scent swirls around me, and I drink it in as he helps me back into Ethan's old jacket. Taking my hand in his much larger one, he guides me to the edge of the property, and we walk to the end of the small boating deck.

Heath drops down first, a few feet from the edge, crossing his legs and motioning for me to sit on his lap. I comply, without question, resting my head on his shoulder as if it's the most natural thing in the world.

"What's the deal with you and Cassie?" I ask as his arms encircle me.

"My mom and her mom have been best friends since high school, and I've practically grown up with her. Hell, I think our moms had our wedding all planned when we were still in diapers." A shiver works its way through him, sending vibrating tremors rolling through me.

"You deserve so much better than that bitch."

"Don't I know it." He slips one hand under my jacket and starts running it up and down the length of my spine, over his sweater.

I lift my head. "So, she wants to date you, and she thinks I'm standing in the way of that?" I surmise.

His nose scrunches up. "It's a little more complicated than that."

"Care to elaborate?"

He tucks my hair behind my ears when a fresh gust of wind blows strands all over my face. "My dad runs a very successful engineering company, and her dad is at the helm of a massive multi-million-dollar advertising empire. They're working on some new project together, and our families are getting even closer. Last year, my parents really started putting pressure on me to date Cassie. It's not anything new. They've been hinting for years, but now that our dads are partnering professionally, all parties like the idea of cementing the bond between our families." A muscle ticks in his jaw as a thunderous look washes over his face. "Except for me."

"Meaning Cassie's on board with the idea too?"

He nods, and the strain is evident on his face. "My parents are good to me, and they've always supported my NFL dreams. They don't ask much of me, so I eventually agreed but only to get them off my case. I thought we'd date for a while, it wouldn't work out, and then we'd go our separate ways, and neither of our parents could say we didn't try."

"You actually dated her?" I'm shocked. I thought Heath had better judgment and more sense.

"Yeah, and it was a fucking nightmare because it was immediately obvious she was totally into it, and then I didn't know how the hell to get myself out of it."

I sit up straighter, facing him head-on. "I've got to admit, I'm shocked. You're a nice person, and she's really not. I've met her type before, and I can instantly tell she's manipulative and self-centered. I can't believe you thought it would ever work in your favor."

"She hasn't always been a bitch, and we were good friends in middle school, but I never thought of her as anything other than that. I know lots of the guys are into her, and she's pretty, but she was almost like my sister growing up. I was stupid crazy to think I could even pull it off on

71

a fake level. When we were together, there was no chemistry between us, like *zero* chemistry, but I honestly don't think she cared whether I was into her or not."

"Let me guess," I cut in. "She likes the idea of having a hot NFL player for a husband."

Heath nods. "Got it in one."

"How long were you dating her for?"

"Forty-nine days, eight hours, and thirty-two minutes; although, it felt like years."

I burst out laughing. "Oh my God. I can't believe you just said that."

"Honestly, Blaire, it was like a life sentence. I'm surprised I didn't chalk the days on my wall like a prison inmate."

We both howl with laughter at that, and his whole face lights up when he smiles. At this proximity, his blue eyes ensnare me, and the strong line of his jaw begs to be caressed, so much that my fingers start twitching with the craving to touch him. Suddenly, I'm acutely aware of how intimate our embrace is and how easy it would be to kiss him. "If you're no longer with her, how come you have leverage?" I blurt. Anything to deflect the growing electricity in the air.

"Ugh." Air whooshes out of his mouth. "This is the complicated part." He absently starts running his thumb back and forth across my cheek. "She went ballistic when I broke it off with her, screaming and shouting abuse at me before she drove off. She went to some college party later that night and called me at two a.m. sobbing. She was completely shit-faced, and she'd driven her car into a ditch. She wasn't injured, but the car was badly damaged. Her dad would've freaked and grounded her for eternity, so I took care of it. Axel knew a guy, and we made it disappear, pretended she'd spent the night with me at his house and that someone had stolen her car from outside."

"See, you are a nice guy. Most guys would've just washed their hands of her."

He shrugs. "I felt partly responsible for the state she got herself into, and she agreed that we'd continue to pretend we were a couple in front of our parents, which means my parents are off my back, so it was kind of a win-win."

"Ah, now I get it."

"I thought it gave me the upper hand with her, but I underestimated how conniving she really is."

Alarm bells start blaring in my head. "Why? What's she done now?"

"I cornered her tonight to tell her to lay off you, and she only agreed if I promised I'd take her to senior prom." His cheeks pucker as if he's just swallowed something sour.

I plant my hands on his shoulders. "Please tell me you didn't agree to that."

He has the decency to look sheepish. "I didn't have much of a choice."

"Yes, you did! You can always tell her dad what really happened that night."

"That's what I've always thought, but she's completely turned it around on me. She says if I tell her parents she'll tell them I was the one driving and I was behind the idea to ditch the car and claim it was stolen."

"She has no proof to substantiate her claims."

"And I've none to substantiate mine."

"Yes, you do. You said Axel and his friend helped? They're your witnesses."

He clears his throat, looking awkward. "My father won't believe a word out of Axel's mouth, and his friend is not the type I could introduce him to either."

"Why on earth not?"

"It's complicated, and it's not my story to tell," he cryptically replies.

"Heath!" Cassie roars his name from somewhere behind us, and Heath groans.

"Fuck. She's not going to leave me alone now." He lifts me off his lap and stands, helping me to my feet.

"Tell her to go to hell. Let her do her worst. I can handle it."

He clasps both sides of my face. "I've made the deal now, and it's the best way of protecting you. She thinks she has the upper hand because I'm going to senior prom with her instead of you."

"Wait, what?" *Why would she think I'd be going with Heath?*

He moves one hand to the back of my neck. "She can't control anything else I do, and her victory is short-lived, because once we graduate, I'm joining the Gators in UF, and there'll be hundreds of miles between us."

He pulls me in flush to his body, and my heart starts thumping wildly in my chest. "And she sure as shit can't stop me from doing this." His eyes probe mine as he angles his head, lowering his mouth to mine. "If you don't want me to kiss you, now's the time to tell me," he whispers, his lips gently brushing mine.

All logical thought vanishes from my mind as my body takes charge. I cling to his waist, wetting my lips as I stare hungrily at his mouth. Cassie's shouts are drowned out by the thrumming of blood in my ears and the surge of butterflies swarming my chest. "Don't stop," I whisper, staring into his eyes as I close the small gap between us, pressing my lips to his.

Chapter Ten

*H*eath's mouth eagerly meets mine, and he takes charge of the kiss, angling my head even farther so he can deepen our lip-lock. When his tongue sneaks out, teasing my closed lips, I open for him, moaning into his mouth as his tongue tangles with mine. The hand on my lower back pushes me into him even farther while he winds his other hand through my hair, keeping a firm hold on my head and directing our kiss.

His lips are equally soft and insistent as he kisses me like I'm the air he needs to breathe. It's been a long time since I've been so thoroughly kissed, and I'm loving it. This feels different from any other kiss I've experienced. Maybe because Heath is all man and I'm cocooned around his large, strong body, feeling the contours of his muscled torso pressing against me, and it's a heady sensation. I snake my hands up his chest, wrapping them around his neck and running my fingers through the shorn velvety-soft hair at his nape. He groans into my mouth, rocking his hips against me so I'm in no doubt of his obvious arousal.

There's no denying the scorching-hot chemistry we share.

I'm so caught up in Heath that I don't hear her approaching until she's on top of us.

"We still have shit to discuss," Cassie snaps in a pissed-off tone.

Her unwanted intrusion halts our impromptu make-out session, and we both break apart at the same time, going rigidly still in each other's arms. Heath keeps his arms locked around me, holding me close to his body as he turns us to face her. "We have nothing else to discuss."

"You can't go to prom with me if you've been messing around with her."

"Why the hell not?"

"Because it won't look real." She pouts, thrusting her chest out and planting her hands on her hips.

"It *isn't* real. You're blackmailing me into it." Heath sends her a deadly glare.

She cocks her head to the side. "And you're blackmailing me. See how alike we are? You should just stop fighting this. You know we're meant to be together."

She takes a step forward, reaching out with her hand, but Heath catches her wrist, stalling her before she can touch him. "Do *not* touch me."

She extracts her hand, shooting me an evil grin. "Let's not rewrite history, Heath. You *loved* me touching you."

Ew. Is she kidding? I thought he said he despised every second with her, so why the hell would he do stuff with her?

"You pounced on me when I was smashed and not thinking clearly. And you know it was only one time."

"One seriously hot time." She pretends to fan herself, narrowing her eyes seductively at him.

"I wouldn't know. I completely blocked the whole traumatic experience out. Have no recollection of it. At all."

A snort breaks free of my mouth before I can stop it. If looks could kill, I'd be stone-cold dead right now with the venomous look she sends my way.

"Shut your stupid, ugly mouth, skank. And I don't know why you're laughing. It'll be your turn next, or do you actually think he cares about you?" Her eyes flash maliciously as she flings her next insult. "You're just an experiment. They've been looking for someone like you for years. Isn't that right, Skeet?" She yells that last part over her shoulder, and I glance up, spotting Skeet and Axel hanging back in the shadows.

Shit. *How long have they been there? Long enough to see me kissing Heath?* Skeet's made little secret of the fact he's into me, and Axel was on the verge of kissing me this morning, so this looks bad.

"Shut your mouth, Cassandra, or the deal's off," Heath snarls, letting me go so he can step right up into her face. "And if you even think of spouting that shit around school, I won't stop until I end you. Trust me, you don't want to make an enemy of me, and you know the lengths I go to to protect my own."

"Why her!?" The look of disgust as she rakes her gaze over me is obvious.

"Because she doesn't want anything from me except my company."

"Oh, puh-lease." She harrumphs. "Open your fucking eyes, you imbecile. Of course, she wants something from you. Everyone does. Stop being so naïve."

"Maybe in that twisted little world in your head," I interject. "Where I come from, it's a lot simpler. I like hanging with Heath, and there's no ulterior motive. Perhaps if you'd entered into your relationship with the same perspective, things might've worked out differently."

"Don't act like you know me! You think you're superior to me?" She casts a derogatory glance over me again, and I'm really starting to get sick of this shit. Her lips twist into an ugly snarl that is *not* attractive. "I know your type. He may be thinking with his dick right now, but the time will come when he'll see I'm right, when he'll accept the truth that the only one for him is *me*."

She is seriously delusional, but if she wants to deceive herself, who am I to stop her.

Heath shrugs casually as if her words are floating over his head. "Believe what you like. I couldn't care less. Blaire is everything you will never be, and that's why she's worth a million of you."

"You don't mean that," she huffs.

"Eh, yeah, I do."

"That's so … harsh." She actually looks upset, but it's hard to tell if it's genuine or not.

"And I give two fucks, why?" Heath is taking none of her shit, and it's good to see him standing up to her.

A layer of determination creeps over her face, and her features hardens. "Fine, keep your slut. See if I care. But the warning works both ways. If you think you can agree to this now and then turn around and show up at prom with her, you are sorely mistaken. I won't hesitate to end you either. And that includes the bitch."

Wow, she really hates me. Not that the sentiment is anything new for me, but usually, people don't hate me without good cause. It's like Cassie took one look at me and decided instantly I was her enemy.

"Then we have an agreement," Heath says, reaching back for my hand. "And there's nothing else to discuss, so we're getting the fuck out of here." He slings his arm around my shoulders, maneuvering us around a fuming Cassie.

She reaches out, grabbing hold of my arm. "I'll stick to my side of the bargain, but don't cross me, or you'll be sorry."

"Remove your hand, or *you'll* be sorry."

She barks out a laugh, and I yank my arm free from her grip. "It's pathetic that you think I'm threatened by you. You're *nothing*. And it won't take long for everyone to realize that."

"Your claws are showing," Axel says, joining the conversation as he steps down onto the deck. "And jealousy isn't an attractive trait. Neither is chasing after someone who clearly wants *nothing to do with you*." He crosses his arms, slanting her a dark look that'd make Voldemort proud. "Do us all a favor and fuck the hell off."

Her nostrils flare, and she shoves at Axel before stomping off, emitting a choice string of expletives as she goes.

"Well, that was fun." Skeet waggles his brows, grinning at me, not at all pissed like I expected he might be. Maybe he didn't see the kiss after all. "But as much as I'm enjoying it, I think it's time we bail."

"Agreed," Heath starts walking, taking me with him, his meaty hand wrapped protectively around mine. "Grab Shaz, and let's go."

Shaznay pulls me back when we leave the house a few minutes later, and we trail behind the guys as we head toward the car. She talks a mile a minute, chattering away as if we've known each other five years not five minutes. But her bubbly enthusiasm is infectious, and I can't help warming to her. I drift off a little as I watch the guys locked in some sort of intense discussion up ahead. They are talking in low tones, so I can't make out what they're saying, but their tense body language gives them away.

"So, you'll come?"

I snap out of it as she poses the question. "Where?"

"To our place. Tomorrow. To hang with me." Her eyes shimmer with excitement.

"Sure. Once Skeet doesn't mind."

She giggles. "Mind? Are you kidding? My brother will be so hyped he'll be up all night."

"If you say so."

She stops me. "Do you really not see it?"

"See what?"

"How he looks at you?" She glances briefly ahead before lowering her voice. "How they *all* look at you?"

"Are you suggesting—"

"Yep!" She cuts me off, tugging me forward as Skeet calls out for us to hurry up.

"But that's—"

She shoots me a funny look. "My brother hasn't told you yet, has he?"

"Told me what? I'm not sure I'm following." I scratch the back of my head as we approach the car.

"Don't sweat it. It'll all make sense tomorrow."

❤❤❤

Shaznay's comments are still playing on my mind the following afternoon as I drive over to the Taylor house. Mom and Dad had no plans for today, so they let me borrow the car, but I'm on strict instructions to be home by seven at the latest.

As I drive through the salubrious gated community, I can't stop myself from gawking. Every house I pass is a large family home, all with their own unique styles. Following Skeet's directions, I turn into the wide driveway fronting his home and park, staring at the impressive house before me. While it's no mansion, like Lance's house, it's a decent-sized modern family home that looks well-cared for. From the outside, it reminds me a little of the house my parents were building by the lake. A house that had always been their dream. One they won't get to achieve now.

A rap on the window startles me, and I jump in my seat. Adrenaline floods my body, and I have to coax myself to calm down as I smile at Skeet, his face smushed into the window. He says something, but the words are muffled. Opening my door with a big smile, he leans in. "Hey, beautiful."

His green eyes radiate warmth, and I immediately relax. "You coming in, or were you planning on spending the afternoon in your car?"

"Sorry, I was just daydreaming." I take his hand, allowing him to help me out of the car. As expected, he threads his fingers through mine and leads me into his house. "Nice place," I remark, surveying the light wood floors and cream-colored walls. Family photos adorn every wall as he leads me through the hallway and into the kitchen. Shaznay is sitting on a stool at the island unit, bent over and scribbling furiously into a pad, books littering the surface around her.

"Look who I found outside," Skeet says, letting go of my hand and making a beeline toward the refrigerator.

"Blaire!" Shaznay jumps up, enfolding me into a bear hug. "I'm so glad you came." Her smile is sincere. "But would you mind hanging with Skeet for a bit until I finish my assignment? My mom insisted I catch up on all my homework, and I only just discovered this essay is due tomorrow."

"No problem, provided Skeet is down with that."

"Oh, I'm down with it." His flirtatious smile almost knocks me off my feet. "Trust me, this is not a chore."

My cheeks heat a little, and he chuckles. "Want something to eat or drink?"

"Some water would be good."

"Gotcha." He grabs two bottles and shuts the refrigerator door. "Let's go." Grabbing my hand with his free one, he pulls me toward a door on the other side of the room. "Take all the time you need, Shaz. There's no hurry," he hollers over his shoulder. Shaznay shoots me an "I told ya so" look, giving me a thumbs-up.

I follow Skeet down to the basement area which has been converted into livable space. The large room is split in two by a folding wall. On this side is a sizable space with a double bed, walk-in closet, desk, couch, TV, and square table. The small door situated by the closet suggests he has his own en suite bathroom too. "This is yours?" I surmise, spinning around as I take it all in. "It's so cool."

Skeet places the bottles down on the table and pulls me loosely into his arms. "I'm glad you like it. I'm lucky I'm the only son and that real estate is in hot demand upstairs. One of us had to relocate down here after my sister Sage came along, and I volunteered."

"Do you have any other sisters I don't know about?"

"Nope. It's just the three of us."

"Well, you definitely lucked out with this place."

"Best decision ever." He points at a door at the rear. "I even have my own entrance, and the space is large enough that Axel and Heath can crash here if they want to. Plus, there's an added benefit." He steers me over to the middle of the room, sliding the folding doors back to reveal the setup on the other side.

"Holy shit," I exclaim, my eyes popping wide as I look at all the equipment and instruments. "You're in a band?"

"Yep." His eyes twinkle as he leads me to a small leather couch pushed against the far wall. "Have a seat." I plonk my butt down as he walks over to the makeshift stage, grabbing one of the guitars propped against a stool. "My dad, Liam, has been in a band for years. When he's not managing the local hardware store, he's moonlighting as a musician."

Huh. I could've sworn Heath said Skeet's dad was named Chris, but I'm obviously mistaken.

He grins affectionately. "One of the guys dropped out a couple years ago, and he asked me to step in. I've been playing guitar since I was little, and I've watched enough of their gigs to know what's involved, so I said what the heck and went for it. We only play a few times a year, and it's fun more than anything."

"Play something for me?"

"That's the plan." He grins, waggling his brows as he slides the guitar strap over his body. He perches on the edge of the stool. "Any requests?"

"Do you have any original compositions, or it's all cover stuff?"

His foot taps idly off the ground. "We mostly do covers, but we have some of our own stuff too."

"Okay, well play me something of yours."

He thinks about it for a few minutes, absently strumming the strings of his guitar while I settle into the couch.

"This one's called 'Reckless.' This is one of mine," he says before launching into the song. His fingers pluck the strings skillfully as he closes his eyes and belts out the words. I'm mesmerized as I watch and listen. He's holding nothing back, pouring his heart and soul into the performance, and passion oozes out of every pore. Emotion bleeds from the words, and I can tell they have personal meaning for him. The words, and his hauntingly beautiful voice, reach a hand into my chest, squeezing my heart to the point of pain.

He sings about giving up and losing your way, about pain and suffering, and he could have written that song for me. For Ethan. Halfway through, he opens his eyes, watching me intently as he finishes the final chorus. The tears pooling in my eyes fall free, gliding silently down my face.

Quietly, he puts the guitar down and crosses to me. Sitting beside me, he gently cups my cheeks, probing my face with troubled eyes. "What's wrong?"

I can scarcely speak over the lump in my throat. "Nothing, it's just … I really felt the emotion." I press a hand to my chest. "I felt how heartfelt every word was, and it spoke to me. In ways you couldn't imagine."

His eyes roam my face before he leans in, pressing a kiss to my forehead. "That song's extremely personal, and I'm glad you felt an emotional connection, but I hate the thought I made you sad. Made you cry."

"It's not a bad thing." I smile through my fading tears. "You are *so* talented. I can't believe you wrote that, and your guitar playing was flawless. And, your voice is, just, wow. Incredible."

His features soften, and a proud smile plays over his lips before his eyes lower to my mouth. "Fuck, Blaire." His voice trembles. "I don't know how you came to be in Kentsville, but I'm so glad you moved here. I …" He pauses, drawing an exaggerated breath. "I didn't believe it was possible to fall this fast but you … you make me feel alive. Every second I'm in your presence, I feel an intense connection with you, and when I'm not around you, I'm thinking about you." He tilts my chin up a little, still maintaining a hold of my face. "Please tell me you feel it too."

I do. I feel a connection with him. With *all* of them. I finally allow myself to acknowledge that. But, in this moment, I can only confirm what I always feel when I'm with him. Although it's only a partial truth, it's not a lie. "I feel it, Skeet. I feel a connection with you too."

Chapter Eleven

*H*is lips fuse to mine in a nanosecond, and it takes my heart several beats to catch up to the fact he's kissing me. A dreamy, fluttering sensation invades my chest, and I melt into him. His arms cradle me to his chest while he deepens the kiss, moving his mouth against mine with skillful caresses.

Skeet kisses like he sings—with passion and one hundred percent of himself in it. I'm drowning in him, and I don't ever want to come up for air. He continues to hold my face in his hands while he kisses me, as if I'm some precious commodity. My fingers wind through his messy hair, and he whimpers into my mouth, slanting his lips more firmly against mine.

"Ahem." A throat clearing breaks us apart. My heart is careening around my chest like a bull charging around a ring.

"Sorry to spoil your fun," Shaznay says, grinning and looking in no way apologetic, "but Mom's home, and she wants to meet the girl who has finally claimed your heart."

My eyes almost bug out of my head, and I splutter.

"Shaz, quit that shit. You'll scare Blaire away." He hauls me protectively into his side.

"If anyone's scaring her away, it's you and your lack of kissing finesse. Seriously, dude, that was gross."

"I'm not complaining," I blurt, feeling the need to defend Skeet's mad kissing skills.

He puffs out his chest before pressing a chaste kiss on my lips. "Thanks, baby." Then he flips his sister the bird. "You clearly know nothing."

"Oh, I know plenty. I can give you a graphic rundown if you like?" She smiles demurely while deliberately pressing her brother's buttons.

Skeet pulls me to my feet, wrapping his hand around mine like it's second nature. "Sure, if you want me to kill half the guys in school."

Everything locks up inside me, and I freeze on the spot, terror causing my heart to spike to coronary-inducing proportions. I know he's only joking, but it's too close to the bone. "You okay?" he asks, his face suddenly creased in concern. "Did I say something wrong?"

Swallowing back bile, I force a smile on my face and shake my head. "No, don't mind me. I just kinda zone out of it sometimes."

He cups my face again, staring deep into my eyes. "You sure?"

"Yeah. If you must know, I'm just a little anxious meeting your parents, and maybe we should talk first." While I'm deflecting from the real source of my anxiety, I'm not lying either. I don't want Skeet parading me in front of his parents as his girlfriend—if that's what he's planning—without him knowing I've kissed one of his best friends and dreamed about kissing the other one.

"Give us a minute, Shaz. Tell Mom we'll be there in a sec."

"No problem." She barely makes a sound as she leaves.

"Shit, I'm doing it again, aren't I?" he says before I've had time to open my mouth.

"No, it's just, I'm not really sure what's happening here." I look him straight in the eye, and he stares intently back at me.

"What do you want to happen?"

"I'm not sure," I truthfully admit, hating myself the instant the words are out when his face falls. He drops his hands to his side, and I grasp hold of his wrist. "I didn't mean that the way it sounds. It's just, I, ah, I kissed Heath last night." I worry my lip between my teeth while I await his reaction.

Relief is visibly evident on his face, and I'm even more confused. "I know, and it's cool."

I blink several times, rooted to the spot as his statement swirls around my mind. "It is?" Incredulity drips from my tone.

"Okay, look, we need to have a serious conversation." He takes both my hands in his. "Actually, a couple serious conversations, but I know my mom, and if we don't get our butts up there, she'll send reinforcements to retrieve us. Can you trust me to tell you everything later?"

I nod straightaway. If there's one thing I've learned about Skeet, it's that he's always up front. "Good. Just answer me one thing. Forget about anyone else, for now, and just tell me if you want to be with me."

"I do, but—"

He places his fingers to my lips, silencing me. "No buts, baby. And no one else is involved. For now, this is about you and me. I'm crazy about you, Blaire, and I want to be more than your friend. We can take it slow, or go fast, or however you want it, but do you want that with me? If not now, at some point in the future?"

That's easier to respond to. "Yes."

He pecks my lips quickly. "Perfect." My arms encircle his waist as he bundles me up in his embrace. "That's all that matters right now." He presses a kiss to the top of my head. "And don't worry about my folks. I'll look after you. Just prepare for it to be crazy, and make a mental note of the questions you want to ask me. I promise I'll tell you everything after we eat."

♥♥♥♥♥

"Blaire, it's so lovely to meet you." A beautiful woman with shoulder-length dark hair advances toward me, the second we step foot in the kitchen, with a wide, welcoming smile. She's a couple inches shorter than me, but that doesn't stop her from enveloping me in a warm hug that I feel all the way through to my bones. "I'm Chandra Taylor."

"A.k.a. Mom," Skeet adds, taking my hand again. I seriously think Skeet has OCD when it comes to hand-holding.

Mrs. Taylor smiles fondly at her son. "I had to pinch myself to ensure it was real when Skeet told me he'd met a girl and he was actually bringing her home."

Skeet's cheeks redden, and it's so adorably cute. "Can we not do this? You're making me sound like a total pussy."

"That's two dollars." A pretty girl with light-brown hair and the same eyes as Skeet's demands, shoving a clear glass jar stuffed full of dollar bills under his nose.

"Oh look, it's the language police." Skeet tousles her hair before extricating two dollar bills from his pocket and shoving them in the jar. "You'll bankrupt me one of these days, kid."

"I'm not a kid. I'm *thirteen*." She draws the word out before poking her tongue out at Skeet. "Practically a grown up."

"This is Sage," Shaz says, coming up beside us. "She's thirteen going on thirty."

"Nice to meet you," Sage says, ignoring her siblings and thrusting her hand out to me.

I shake it 'cause it's the polite thing to do. "Lovely to meet you too."

"I can't believe you like him. Are you sure you don't need your eyes tested? Or maybe your ears?"

"Funny, ha, ha." Skeet messes up the hair on top of her head again, and she shrieks, jerking back out of his reach. "I can't wait until you start dating. I'm going to give them hell."

"Well, if it's all-out war you want, I guess I'll just have to share some of my stories with Blaire." She smiles sweetly at me, like butter wouldn't melt.

"Between you, Mom, and Shaz, you'll scare Blaire away before you get the chance."

"I don't scare easily," I admit, earning a big grin from Skeet's mom.

"Then you'll fit right in here, honey." She squeezes my shoulder as an older man enters the room. He's wearing a suit and tie and carrying a briefcase which he promptly sets down on top of the island unit.

"Sorry I'm late, sweetheart," he says, kissing Chandra on the lips.

"You're not," she tells him. "I lost track of time when I was going over the Landry file, so dinner won't be ready for a while yet. And Liam and Chris aren't back from town anyway."

"And who is this lovely girl?" he asks, turning his attention to me.

"She's Skeet's girlfriend," Sage replies before Skeet can get a word in.

"Ah, so, you're Blaire." His eyes wrinkle at the corners when he smiles. "I'm Skeet's dad Michael. It's nice to meet you. We all thought you were a figment of Skeet's overactive imagination."

Wow, Skeet must never bring girls home. Though I'm not naïve enough to assume there's been no girls. Not with his looks and personality. I'm sure he has plenty of offers.

"You're all a bunch of fucking comedians today," Skeet deadpans.

"That's another dollar," Sage gleefully confirms, shoving the jar back under Skeet's nose.

"Skeet, can you please make more of an effort with the cussing," his Mom pleads while walking back to the stove. "Especially when we have a guest for dinner."

"It's okay," I offer up. "My brother used to cuss up a storm. My parents gave up trying to get him to quit." The words have vacated my mouth before I've had time to question the wisdom of them. I instantly regret them when I see the sorrowful expressions traded around the room. "You told them," I whisper, gulping as I look sideways at Skeet.

"Yes. I hope that's okay? I just didn't want anyone to say anything and upset you without realizing."

"That was thoughtful, thanks," I croak.

"We're so sorry about your brother," Mrs. Taylor says, walking back over to us. "Skeet said he was your twin?" I nod, smiling sadly. "You must miss him a lot."

"I do. It hasn't been that long, and we, ah, don't really talk about him that much." It's like I just can't stop blurting stuff out. Perhaps it's my brain's way of telling me I need to let out everything I'm keeping locked up inside. But that's a dangerous path to follow. *Once I open the floodgates, who knows what secrets will ooze out?*

"I can't even begin to imagine how horrific it must've been. To watch someone you love go through something like that." She visibly shivers. "Was he sick for long?"

And this is the part where my lies come back to bite me. *Isn't that always the way?* One lie leads to another and then another, and before you know it, you're suffocating under the weight of all the lies and struggling to remember exactly which lies you've told and to whom. It's a slippery slope and one I don't want to fall into.

Thankfully, Skeet jumps to the rescue, saving me from going there. At least, for now. "I'm sure Blaire didn't come here for the Spanish Inquisition. Let's change the subject."

"I hope you like pot roast," his mom says, switching topics without blinking.

A layer of stress lifts from my shoulders. "I love pot roast. Can I do anything to help?"

"It's sweet of you to offer, but I won't let any guest lift a finger while they're here." Her eyes sparkle mischievously. "Besides, I have two slaves right here!" she quips, gesturing toward her daughters. "And the men are always on cleanup duty."

"Christ, it's freezing out there." A tall, thin, older man rubs his hands vigorously as he walks into the kitchen, dropping a worn leather jacket on the back of his chair. He looks a bit younger than Michael, or maybe it's just his ripped jeans, biker boots, and rocker T-shirt make him seem younger than his years. "That smells divine," he says, walking to the stove and kissing Mrs. Taylor on the lips. "What is it, love?"

"Your favorite, Liam." She runs her hand over his cropped hair as he leans in and nuzzles her neck.

My eyes dart to Michael's, and he smiles at me as if it's totally normal for another man to be so openly affectionate with his wife.

"Yo, Skeet, dude, is this her?" I jerk my head around at the sound of another male voice. A guy with long sandy-colored hair eyes Skeet before switching his gaze to me.

"Blaire, this is Chris."

"Hi," I squeak, feeling way out of my comfort zone. *Who are all these men?*

"You're way too gorgeous to be involved with this idiot," Chris jokes, winking at me.

"Geez, thanks, Dad." Skeet glares at him. "I'll be lucky if Blaire's even speaking to me after today."

My gaze is fastened on Skeet, urging him to look at me. *What the hell is going on?* Skeet just called Chris dad, but Michael had introduced himself as his dad, and Liam is way too affectionate with Skeet's mom to just be a friend, so I don't get it.

"You didn't fucking tell her, did you? Asshole!" Shaz shouts from across the room.

"There wasn't time," Skeet mumbles.

"You had time to stick your tongue down her throat!" she shouts back, and I wish the floor would open and swallow me.

"Children. Stop." Mrs. Taylor speaks in a commanding tone that has them clamming up. "Skeet, you need to explain to Blaire. Dinner won't be ready for at least a half hour, so go back downstairs and fill her in."

He nods, looking a little sheepish. "C'mon." He tugs on my hand, spinning us around.

"And no more tonsil tennis until after you've talked," Liam tosses out, much to the amusement of everyone but us.

Please, ground. Gobble me up now.

My face is flaming as Skeet steers me out of the room.

"Oh my God," I shriek the second we step out of earshot. "That was so embarrassing!"

"I told you my family was crazy." He closes the basement door after us and guides me toward the couch in his room.

"What's going on, Skeet? I thought Chris was your dad?"

He pulls me down onto his lap on the couch. "He is. But so are Michael and Liam."

I stare at him, frowning. "What do you mean? You can't have three dads?!"

"Not biologically, obviously," he starts explaining. "Or even legally." His brow scrunches up.

"You're not doing a great job of explaining," I complain.

"Have you ever heard of polyamorous relationships?" he asks, and I shake my head. "Okay, so, you're not really alone in that. Lots of people haven't heard about it or have misconceptions about what it is. Essentially, it's being in a loving, committed relationship with more than one person."

I toss the statement around in my head for a couple minutes. "So, your mom is in a relationship with Michael, Liam, *and* Chris? Is that what you're saying?"

He nods. "Yep. It's exactly that."

Shock splashes across my face. "Wow. I don't know what to say. I mean, how does that even work?"

"Mom's legally married to Michael, but that was only a formality. The four of them held a commitment ceremony, before we were born, and it's those vows and promises they live by."

"Oh." I'm not sure what else to say.

"Are you disgusted?" he inquires, scrutinizing my face.

I take a moment to think about it and then I shake my head. "No. I'm curious more than anything."

He sighs, looking relieved. "I was hoping you'd say that." He kisses the end of my nose. "And I know you have questions, so hit me with them."

Chapter Twelve

"Is it rude to ask who your actual bio dad is?" I hesitantly inquire, chewing on the corner of my mouth.

"Funny how that's often the first thing people ask." He pins me with a lopsided grin. "But I've no clue, and it's never really mattered. I doubt we'll ever know unless we need to for medical reasons or something. As far as we're concerned, all three are our dads. Always have been. Always will be."

"And people know? Like at school and in town?"

He runs his hand up and down my arm as he speaks. "Yeah. My parents have never hidden their relationship, and why should they? It's no one's business who they choose to share their lives with, and once it's consensual and all parties are in agreement, it doesn't concern anyone else."

Except I've grown up in a town, one a bit larger than this one, yet it's still small enough to imagine how people reacted. "I'm guessing not everyone approves."

He grimaces a little. "Try most everyone doesn't approve."

"That must've been hard growing up."

He sighs audibly. "I grew up surrounded by love and affection, and it was only when I started school that I realized my family setup wasn't the norm. We've all come in for some flack over the years. I won't lie; there were times it was tough, but my parents never wavered, and they never let anyone's opinions drag us down. It helps that Mom and Michael run a well-respected law firm in town. While people may gossip behind their backs, their profession has meant we're accepted, at least on the surface, anyway."

"Why didn't they move?"

"Why should they be driven out of their home? My dads grew up in Kentsville, and they all agreed to settle here after they graduated college to be close to their families. Mom was an only child, and both her parents were already dead at the time they met, so it made sense." He leans in and kisses my cheek. "Besides, if they'd moved someplace other than an impersonal city, they would've had to face the same prejudice."

I nod in agreement. "So, your mom's been with all of them a long time?"

He bobs his head. "Yep. Michael, Chris, and Liam were best friends growing up, and Mom met them in college. They've all been together pretty much since then."

"Sounds a lot like you, Axel, and Heath," I venture.

An amused grin tugs up the corners of his mouth. "I'm an open book, Blaire. Ask what you want to ask."

I shift a little on his lap, and he groans, his eyes turning a darker shade of green. "So, have you guys you know … shared girls before?" I cringe as the words come out all wrong. "I mean—"

"It's okay," he interrupts. "I know what you mean, and no. We used to joke about it when we were younger and hornier, but we haven't ever discussed it more seriously … until recently." He sends me a blatant suggestive look.

"You mean until me?" I squeak, half-stunned, half-excited, and half-terrified.

"Yes." He turns me around on his lap until I'm forced to straddle him. "We really should be having this discussion with the guys, but you should know we're all attracted to you and it's already come up in conversation."

My cheeks flush red, but he doesn't laugh like I expect him to. His eyes penetrate mine carefully. "If it's not something you think you can get behind, that's totally fine, but I think we all need to discuss it before things get complicated."

Things are already complicated. Feelings are already involved.

He brushes his fingers across my cheek. "Tell me what you're thinking."

"I'm thinking this is surreal and I'm not sure what to say. It's not something I've ever given thought to before."

"I get that." He rests his hands loosely on my lower back. "Just answer me one thing. You already told me you have feelings for me, but what about Axel and Heath? Do you have feelings for them too?"

Gulping, I nod, and the biggest smile spreads across his mouth. "Well, that's a start." He moves his hand up my spine, along my neck, and into my hair before pulling my mouth down to his. "And I really need to kiss you right now." His breath is warm against my skin as I plant my hands on his shoulders and lean in to kiss him.

It quickly turns heated, and from the way we're seated, I feel the evidence of his attraction hardening against the most sensitive part of me. My body reacts as if on autopilot, grinding against him as a needy moan escapes my lips.

In a lightning-fast move, he has me on my back, his body pressed gently on top of mine as he kisses the shit out of me. I hitch my leg up, coiling it around his hip, and he runs his hand up and down my outer thigh, heating me through the denim of my jeans. He rocks his pelvis into mine, and I see stars, kissing him more frantically as I lose myself to blissful sensations.

"Oh my fucking God!" Shaznay shrieks in a high-pitched tone. I push Skeet off me so fast it's almost a superpower. He tumbles to the floor, chuckling as he wipes my lip gloss off his mouth. "My eyes will never recover!" Shaznay looks like she just swallowed something nasty. "Seriously, I don't know how I'll scrub the image of you two dry humping from my retinas or my brain. You need a cold shower or a muzzle or something." She jabs a finger pointedly in her brother's direction.

"Perhaps you should learn to knock first," Skeet suggests, climbing to his feet and helping me to mine. "And you're overreacting, like always. It's not like we were naked and screwing our brains out."

"Ugh, you are a disgusting pig." She turns to me. "I don't know how you can make out with him."

"Because he's hot and an awesome kisser," I retort with a cheeky wink, earning me a firm peck on the lips.

"God, could you be any more perfect," Skeet muses, snaking his arms around me.

"God, could you be any more puke inducing," Shaznay snarks back.

I laugh, feeling lighter than I have in ages.

"Dinner's ready," she adds. "And we better go before Mom sends Sage down here. I need to protect her innocent eyes from the live porno I just watched."

"Overreaction," Skeet whispers, kissing the top of her head as he tows me with him toward the stairs. "If it was a porno, I'd have Blaire—"

Shaznay clamps her hand over Skeet's mouth muffling him. "Do not even think about finishing that sentence," she warns, narrowing her eyes at him.

"Please don't tell your parents about this," I plead as we exit the bedroom. "It was embarrassing enough before."

"You'll owe me, but your secret is safe with me."

Dinner is a raucous affair, but everyone goes out of their way to make me feel included, and I'm enjoying the banter and the normalcy of it all. After dinner, Skeet goes with his dads to clear the kitchen, kissing me on the mouth in front of everyone before leaving me with a red face and a hysterically giggly Shaznay.

"Shut it." I shoulder-check her as I traipse after her up the stairs.

"Your face is too funny. Sorry, not sorry," she calls out over her shoulder.

I flop down on her large bed, and we both stare up at the ceiling with our hands locked behind our heads. "Skeet told me you were suspended and why," she says, looking sideways at me. "Cassie is a complete bitch with a really nasty streak. Watch your back with her."

"Yeah, I figured that out, but thanks for the heads-up. Anyway, Heath's made this stupid deal with her which he thinks keeps me protected."

"But you understand she's manipulating him, and she'll find some way of getting to you," she finishes my train of thought.

"Yeppers." I prop up on my side using my elbow for balance. "I know we don't know each other well, but can I ask you something personal?"

"Shoot. I'm an open book." I grin, and she quirks a brow. "What?"

"You're so like your brother. He said the very same thing to me."

"Ugh. Don't remind me. Although Skeet's pretty cool as big brothers go," she admits with a wink. "Just don't tell him I said that."

"These lips are sealed." I waggle my brows. "How much of a gap is there between you guys anyway?"

"Only a year."

"So, you're a junior?" She nods. "Ah, that's too bad. I was hoping you were a senior too. That we might have some classes together. The girls all seem really clicky, and it would've been nice to hang out."

94

"We can still hang at lunch if the Three Musketeers give me permission to sit at their table." She rolls her eyes, but I can tell she's just messing.

"That'd be good. Might deflect some of the gossip doing the rounds about me. While I'm grateful for the guys' support, I don't like the additional attention. It's like I can almost feel the daggers embedding in my back the whole way through lunch."

"The guys have always kept to themselves. Heath even forgoes sitting at the table with all the other football jocks, which is so not done, but it only adds to the mystery." She turns on her side, mirroring my position. "You wouldn't believe the number of times girls have befriended me purely to try to get to one of them. Axel and Skeet never date, preferring casual hookups and Heath was exclusively dating Melandra Johnson for a few years before she moved away. He doesn't do the hookup thing, and since he broke up with Cassie, girls have been tripping over themselves to get him to notice."

"You're a mine of information. What else should I know?"

"What else do you want to know?"

"So, they've really never done the whole 'date the same girl at the same time' thing?" It's not that I doubt Skeet, but I'd like to hear it from Shaz, and it'll help steer the conversation where I need it to go.

"Wow, my brother really went there, huh?"

"I thought you knew?"

"I guessed. Like I said, I see how they look at you, and I'm sure everyone at school is wondering. Some asshats used to enjoy provoking us because of our parents, claiming we were dating multiple people at the same time. Not that I have any issue with it, but I'm not sure it's for me."

"Neither do I. That's what I wanted to ask." I bite my lower lip as I think carefully about how to phrase this. I don't want to offend her or have her think I disapprove of her family situation. It might be unconventional, but there's no shortage of love in this house, and they all seem happy, so who am I to cast judgment. It's as I told Skeet; I'm intrigued more than anything.

"Well, how do you feel about them? Are you hot for all of them?"

"Pretty much."

"What have you got to lose?" She straightens up, sitting cross-legged. "I'm sure the guys will go at whatever pace you want and go out of their way to make you comfortable. My parents have an agreement so they each have their alone time, and they all have their own bedrooms and stuff. From what Mom's told me, once everyone is up front about their needs and openly communicates, then you should settle into a routine that works."

"Skeet's going to set up a meeting with the others, which should be interesting."

"Oh, I'd love to be a fly on the wall for that," she agrees, smirking.

"I'll fill you in after."

"You'd better."

A rap on the door interrupts us, and I look around as Skeet pokes his head through the gap. "I don't mean to break up your girly bonding, but it's almost seven, Blaire, and I know you said your parents wanted you home by then."

"Shoot." I glance at my watch and jump up, toeing on my sneakers. "Thanks for the reminder. I lost track of time." I brush hair back off my face. "My dad's a stickler for good timekeeping," I explain.

Shaznay gives me a hug. "I hate that I won't see you at school this week, but I can drop by a couple evenings if you like?"

"That would be awesome. I'll probably go stir-crazy although the principal said she was sending a study schedule and course assignment via email, so that'll probably keep me busy."

"C'mon, I'll walk you out." Skeet, predictably, takes my hand, and I wave to Shaznay as we leave her bedroom. I thank Mrs. Taylor for a lovely dinner, and she makes me promise not to be a stranger, ensuring I know I'm welcome any time. All three of Skeet's dads wave goodbye, and Sage gives me a hug.

"Your family is awesome," I tell him as we walk side by side to my car.

"I think so." He beams at me, pressing me up against the side of my car as he wraps his arms around me. "But not as awesome as you." He lowers his head, but I shove at him.

"Stop! Someone might see."

He chuckles. "They won't care. They like you. A lot. Just like me."

"You're really quite the charmer, aren't you?"

"Just telling it like it is. Now are you going to stop talking and let me kiss you goodbye?"

"Well, when you put it like that, how can I resist?" I circle my arms around his neck, and we move toward one another. His lips are soft and sweet against mine this time, devoid of the heat of our earlier lip sync.

"I think I could get addicted to you, Blaire Adams," he whispers, nudging his nose against mine. Mention of my name brings reality crashing down upon me. Skeet doesn't know who I really am. None of them do. While I understand the need to keep the secret, it's another complication.

How can I contemplate starting a relationship with any of them when I'm keeping something so huge from them? It doesn't feel right, but I promised my parents when we moved here that I wouldn't breathe a word to another soul, and Mom has already reminded me on several occasions. This isn't just about me. My parents' reputations, and their futures, are at stake too.

"Hey, where'd you go?" Skeet asks, concern lacing his tone.

"Sorry. I'm here." I stretch up and peck his lips one final time. "But I really have to go. I'll talk to you tomorrow."

He opens my car door, and I slide inside. "I spoke to the guys, and we can meet up tomorrow night at Axel's place if that's cool with you?" Butterflies scatter in my chest, but I nod. "Wicked." His eyes blaze. "And Axel said he's going running in the morning. He'll wait by the corner for a while if you want to join him."

"Okay, thanks." I move to close the door but not before he steals another kiss.

"Goodnight, beautiful Blaire." He shuts the door, blowing me a kiss through the glass.

I'm still grinning to myself when I enter my house ten minutes later, taking the stairs two at a time. I stick my earbuds in as I switch on my laptop and log in to my school-issued email to download my study schedule for the week.

After I've printed it out and pinned it to my wall, I open the only other email in my inbox. All the blood drains from my face as I read the short, curt message.

This is all your fault and you know it. You should be in that grave, not Ethan. Burn in hell, bitch.

Chapter Thirteen

*S*retch into the toilet bowl until there's nothing left in my stomach to expel. Shivering all over, I wrap my arms around my waist while I lean against the side of the tub. My heart thuds wildly behind my ribcage, and the pain in my chest is so intense it genuinely feels like I'm having a coronary. Tears trickle down my face silently as I mentally replay the message over and over.

I've been so careful since we left Amber Springs, refusing to set up any online profiles for fear of this very thing. I was forced to shut down every social media profile, delete my email account, and change my cell number in the days after the shooting because all the vile comments and messages were physically making me ill.

To have complete strangers commenting on how I deserved to die and random freaks threatening to fuck me up before putting a bullet in my skull had me completely terrified and afraid of my own shadow. As the days turned to weeks and there was no letup in the vitriol or the personal abuse I suffered, I became somewhat anesthetized to it. Letting it all go over my head was the only way I could haul my ass out of bed each morning and at least pretend like I was a functioning human being.

Since moving to Kentsville, I haven't shared my cell number with anyone but the guys and my parents, and I haven't set up any new online accounts or email addresses. The only email address I have is my school-required one, and I've no idea how the hell someone from my past managed to get a hold of it.

We told no one we were moving. Just packed up and left. And I know my parents haven't divulged our new location to anyone.

There wasn't anyone to tell anyway.

Everyone we considered friends shunned us. Either they were too judgmental or too afraid of being targeted by association. Leaving the past in Amber Springs is as much a priority for my folks as it is for me, and I know they won't have said anything to jeopardize our fresh start here.

I push up off the ground on shaky legs, walking in a daze back to my bedroom where I force myself to sit down at my desk. With trembling fingers, I retrieve the email and stare at it, feeling ill all over again. After a couple minutes, I deliberately force my emotions aside, inspecting the message more carefully for clues. I read the words in my head over and over, and something is off. This doesn't feel like the usual asshole trying to freak me out. This is way more personal.

But who knows?

Who could have done this?

And how do they know where I am?

The email is from a well-known email service and the username is truthseeker101 so that reveals nothing about the sender other than he or she fancies themselves as some kind of crusader. I attempt to reply to the message, but it bounces back immediately. Sighing heavily, I print the email, placing the page in a paper folder inside my desk drawer.

I know, from previous experience, not to delete any threatening messages, so I make a folder in my inbox and move the email there before shutting my laptop down again.

All night, I toss and turn, alternating between mental replays of the email and horrific nightmares any time I manage to fall asleep for more than a few minutes. When daylight creeps through the tiny gap in my curtains, I groan, pressing my face into the pillow and silently praying for sleep to come and claim me.

Mom pokes her head through the door a few minutes later. "Rise and shine, sweetheart. Just because you're suspended doesn't mean you have a free pass to lounge in bed all day." She yanks back the covers, and a wave of cool air washes over me, raising tiny goose bumps on my skin in every place where it's exposed.

"I'm getting up," I grumble, swinging my legs out the side of the bed. I yawn as I rub sleep from my eyes, peering up at Mom through a blurry lens. "Go to work. I'll study. I promise."

"Okay." She presses a kiss to the top of my head. "And when your school work is done, finish the unpacking in the living room, and then you can start on dinner."

"Yes, ma'am." I salute her while struggling to my feet.

"Blaire."

She uses that no-nonsense tone with me, and I plaster a fake happy smile on my face. "Go, Mom. Don't be late." I push her out the door and trudge to the bathroom to grab a quick shower.

The nasty email plays on my mind all day, distracting me and forcing me to lose concentration multiple times. I text the guys canceling our get together, feigning contagious illness so they don't show up on my doorstep. I push the food around my plate at dinnertime, unable to stomach anything. I know some people overeat when they're stressed, but I'm the opposite—I lose my appetite and can't force any food down.

The next couple days pass by in a similar manner. Shaznay, Heath, and Skeet text me daily, but I haven't heard a peep from Axel.

It's Wednesday night, and Mom and Dad are at it again, screaming obscenities at one another over the dinner table while I stare blankly at the window wishing I was anywhere but here. Dad's been hitting the bottle again, and he's an ugly drunk. It's not something I knew about him until recently, because neither of my parents were big drinkers before all the shit went down.

The chiming of the doorbell is a welcome relief, and I hop up to answer it. My parents are so busy shouting they haven't even realized someone is at the door. I open it slowly and carefully, sticking my head out as I keep my body wedged behind the doorframe.

Axel's sharp blue eyes cut a line straight through me as he stares in that intense way of his. Fleetingly, his gaze darts over my head as my parents' arguing trickles out into the hallway. Heat creeps up my chest and over my neck, and I have to force myself to maintain eye contact with him. As usual, he's giving nothing away. He jerks his chin up. "Feeling better?"

"Yes."

His eyes bore a hole in the side of my skull, and I know he knows I wasn't ill.

Well, not in the conventional sense.

"Grab your coat. You're coming with me."

At any other time, I'd tell him and his demanding tone to take a hike. But I'm so desperate to escape I don't argue the point. "Give me a couple minutes," I say, and he nods, shoving his hands in the pockets of his jeans as he moves back, leaning against the railing. I race up the stairs, changing into sneakers and a warm sweater. Then I grab Ethan's leather coat and a fluffy scarf and skip back downstairs. I don't bother returning to the kitchen, scribbling a hasty note and leaving it in the hall for my parents instead.

Axel pushes off the railing when I step outside, pulling the door shut behind me. My mouth hangs open when I spot the black and red Harley parked at the curb. "That's yours?" I stupidly ask as we walk toward it.

The faintest of smiles kicks up the corners of his mouth. "Yeah. My grandpa left it to me." He places a helmet over my head, gently tucking my hair in place. "Have you ever ridden on a bike?"

"No, but I've always wanted to." My voice is a little muffled through the helmet, but he seems to understand, nodding with a pleased smile gracing his mouth.

He straddles the bike and pats the space behind him. "Climb on and wrap your arms around me."

I comply, feeling an immense thrill when my body slides forward a little, pressing flush against him. He's warm and strong, and he smells absolutely divine. His cologne is a mix of fresh and spicy notes that perfectly match his personality.

I could literally drown in Axel Thorp right now.

He's like my own hot, personal savior.

Circling my hands around his firm waist, I try my best to ignore the pulsing between my thighs. The engine growls as he kick-starts it while grabbing my hands and holding them more tightly around his body. Now, I'm virtually straddling him from behind, and my libido is going haywire. I always imagined riding a bike with a sexy guy would be hot, but I'd no idea quite how hot until this moment.

I cling to Axel, keeping my cheek pressed against his back as we take off. He maneuvers the streets like a pro, and I'm enjoying the experience enormously. He drives through the main town, veering left, and I hold onto him more tightly as he ascends an incline, bringing us over to the more affluent side of town. My eyes drink everything in as we pass lush, manicured lawns and impressive homes that scream wealth.

Axel pulls into a small retail outlet, killing the engine in front of a row of stores. When the bike is secure, he grips my hips, lifting me off onto the ground in one effortless, smooth move. My entire body tingles from his touch, and I sway on my feet a little, clutching onto his muscular arms to steady myself. He removes my helmet with a gentle touch, helping to brush stray strands of hair away from my face. My skin is inflamed, and I'm on fire from the ride, his electric touch, and the dark, fiendish glint in his eye. I'm seconds away from jumping him when he clears his throat and arches a brow, pinning me with an amused grin. "You liked that a lot, huh?"

"It was awesome," I squeak, hating how easy I am to read.

Bending down, he presses his mouth close to my ear. "I liked having you pressed up against me."

Shivers cascade up and down my spine at his sultry words and seductive tone, and it's a wonder I can stand up straight. I plant my hand on his broad chest, waging an inner battle with my horny libido. I have never wanted to touch anyone as much as I want to touch him in this moment. "Axel, I—"

He presses two fingers to my lips instantly silencing me. I peer into his eyes, wondering what he sees reflected in my gaze. "I know what you need, sweetheart, and I promise I'll take care of you, but we need to do this first." He brushes his thumb against my cheek, and a shudder works its way through me.

"Where are we?" I inwardly cringe at how breathy my voice sounds.

"Heath and Skeet mentioned you are looking for work." He gestures with his head at a store behind him. "My brother's ex owns that clothing store, and she's looking for a part-time assistant. I told her about you, and she wanted to meet up."

My mouth hangs open again as I stare at the funky women's store showcasing the latest trends, excitement bubbling in my veins. "Oh my God, thank you so much!"

"Don't thank me yet," he says, taking hold of my hand and steering me toward the door. "Jacinta can be a bit of a bitch at times. She has a foul mouth, and I'm guessing she won't be easy to work for, but she appreciates those who work hard, and she is offering flexible hours, so it could suit."

"I've only ever worked at a diner, but I'm a fast learner, and I'm not afraid of hard work."

"That's good to know," a female voice says from out of nowhere, and I jump a little as I turn around to greet the newcomer.

A fiery redhead with wide blue eyes swats Axel on the back of the head. "I heard that intro, and I'm less than pleased. It's just as well I like you." Jacinta—I presume— faux glares at him, shoving her tall, thin frame between us as she moves to unlock the door.

"Or what?" Axel retorts, smirking.

"Or I'd slice your cock off and feed it to my pet guinea pig."

"You don't have a pet guinea pig." He shoots her a superior look.

"I'd buy one especially for the occasion," she says, sticking her tongue out at him as she unlocks the door to the store. She steps aside, ushering us in. "Come in before you freeze your balls off."

She flicks a few switches on the wall, and the room floods with light. The store isn't huge, but she's made the best use of the space, and it's decorated in a modern style. "My clientele is mainly young women with an eye for the latest fashions and a healthy budget," she explains as she walks across the room, waving her arms around. "My stock isn't cheap, but it's high quality, and I have a strong repeat business." She hurries behind the counter, retrieving a key, and unlocks a side door. "You're up," she tells Axel, grabbing him by the shoulders and shoving him toward the door. "I'll talk to your girl while you make the coffee. I'll have mine black with no sugar."

"Just like your soul," he quips, ducking down in time to avoid another slap to the head. A devilish glint appears in his eye as he turns to me. "How do you like it?" His tone is deliberately suggestive.

"I'll have mine the same, without the snarky comment, thank you very much."

"Coming right up." He winks before disappearing out of sight.

"So, it's Blaire, right?" Jacinta asks, extending her hand.

I nod, shaking her hand. "Yes. Thanks for meeting with me."

"As you've probably guessed, I'm Jacinta, and this store is my baby." Her smile is proud. "My assistant moved away to college last fall, and I haven't had time to replace her yet, but it's coming into our busy season, and I need another pair of hands. Axel mentioned you were new to town and looking for work."

"Yeah, I just moved here with my parents. I've had a part-time job the last couple years, and I like to keep busy."

Understatement of the year.

Distracting myself is the only way I can avoid the torment in my head.

"How long did you work at the diner for?" Jacinta asks, propping her elbows on the counter as she gives me her full attention. "And what exactly were your duties?"

I give her a quick rundown of my time at the Amber Springs Family Diner, and she asks me a few more questions, suggesting scenarios with imaginary customers and asking how I'd deal with them. Then she runs through the job, outlining the duties. "Any questions?"

"What are the hours?" I inquire as Axel reappears, holding two steaming mugs in his hands.

"We open late nights Thursday and Friday, and it tends to be busy, so it'd be five to nine both days, and eight to six on Saturdays."

"That works for me." My smile is eager as I take a sip of my coffee.

"Okay, well how about we agree on a month's trial period? Can you start tomorrow night?" she asks, drinking from her cup and grimacing a little.

My heart turns cartwheels behind my ribcage at the first bit of good news in ages. I doubt she'd be so willing to offer me the job on the spot if it wasn't for Axel's recommendation, and I'm so grateful to him. "Perfect, and I'll be here. Thanks so much."

Chapter Fourteen

"How long did Jacinta date your brother for?" I ask Axel a half hour later when we're tucked into a booth in a diner a couple blocks from the park where we first met.

"On and off for about three years." His fingers drum off the Formica tabletop as he eyeballs me.

"She seems cool, and she's clearly fond of you. I guess there's no accounting for taste," I tag on the end, joking.

He shoots me a lopsided grin. "Jacinta *is* cool, and I was pretty pissed when her and Griff called it quits for good last year. I miss her around the house."

"She lived with you?" I arch a brow as I sip my soda through a straw.

He nods, leaning back against the booth. "She was kind of a surrogate mom to me growing up."

"What about your real mom?" I tentatively ask, just as the waitress brings our burgers and fries to the table. She isn't subtle about the eye-fuck she sends in Axel's direction, but I'm secretly pleased when he pretends he doesn't notice.

"I haven't seen her since I was fourteen" is all he says before taking a large bite of his burger.

I force a few fries down, and eat, maybe, a quarter of my burger before pushing it away. I want to eat it, but my system is still twisted into knots over that horrid email. I stare out the window, watching a few kids on skateboards, getting lost in my head.

"Hey." Axel taps the top of my hand. "You want to get out of here?"

I nod, glancing at his empty plate, marveling at how fast he devoured his food. He throws a couple bills down on the table before placing his hand on my lower back and steering me out of the diner.

I don't ask where we're going again, trusting Axel in a way I can't explain. He rides through familiar streets, pulling up in front of a neat two-story house a couple blocks from my house. Once again, he grips my hips and helps me down off the bike, and once again, I feel it in every part of me. An overwhelming urge to feel his hands all over me accosts me from out of left field, and I wet my dry mouth and squeeze my core, begging my body to calm down.

Kissing Heath and Skeet was amazing, but I've a feeling that kissing Axel will floor me completely.

As if he can sense where my thoughts have wandered, he takes off my helmet, leans in, and dusts his lips against my neck. A tiny whimper flies out of my mouth, and I clutch onto him for dear life.

"This is my house," he whispers, wrapping his arm around my waist and hauling me into his warm chest. "Griff's at work, so we have the place to ourselves." His eyes penetrate mine, flashing darkly. "You're tense, baby." He threads one hand through my hair, using his other arm to keep me close to him. "I know what you need. Do you trust me to look after you?"

Gulping over the lump of terrified excitement clogging my throat, I nod slowly. He brushes his mouth against mine, sending delicious tremors zipping up and down my body. "I want to make you feel good," he whispers over my lips before slanting his mouth down on mine. I pull him closer to me as we kiss, ravishing his mouth as I let pure, unadulterated need take hold of me. He devours me, kissing me with an insatiable hunger I've never experienced before. I'm writhing against him, twisted into a messy ball of desire, all from a few kisses.

"Come inside before we give the neighbors a show," he teases, taking my hand and leading me into the small house.

The layout is very similar to ours. A narrow hallway with separate living room off to the left, downstairs toilet and under-stairs storage on the right, and a compact kitchen-cum-dining-room at the rear. The house is immaculately clean and tidy with brightly painted walls and newish-looking furniture. "Who else lives here?" I inquire as he starts climbing the stairs, urging me to follow.

"It's just me and my brother. My dad's dead, and Mom's not coming back any time soon."

"I'm sorry," I say, not really knowing how to respond.

"S'kay." He shrugs, reaching a hand out for me when my feet hit the top of the stairs. "It's been almost four years. I've learned to live with it." He pushes a door open, guiding me into his bedroom. A large bed, fitted with wrinkled black sheets, takes up most of the space in the room. A small wooden desk is wedged into the corner, a pile of books stacked in a neat row against the wall. Posters of rock bands and bikers adorn the walls surrounding a mounted TV screen. A game console rests on a shelf underneath, a bunch of games in a neat stack beside it.

I glance around, a little uncomfortable, and Axel notices. He's incredibly perceptive, and it's unnerving at times. Landing his hands on my shoulders, he starts kneading the tense muscles there. "Relax, Blaire. We're not going to do anything you don't want to do." Sweeping my hair to one side, he trails a line of hot kisses up and down my neck. "I just want to help you unwind." I nod, letting him lead me to the bed. "Take off your sweater and shirt, and lie on your stomach on the bed," he commands, kicking off his boots and playing some music from his cell.

I hang my leather jacket on the back of the chair and then strip my sweater and T-shirt off, tossing them on top. I toe off my sneakers and approach the bed with my pulse jumping wildly in my throat. I lie down, fluffing a pillow and resting my head to one side. The pillows and sheets smell like him, and I close my eyes, inhaling the intoxicating masculine scent. The bed dips as he crawls over my body. Heat radiates from him where he hovers over my ass. I tense up a little, jumping when his warm, slicked-up hands land on my back. "Relax, Blaire," he says as he starts to massage my sore muscles.

"Is this okay?" he asks gruffly after a few minutes, and I mumble an affirmative reply. His hands are like magic as they roam my back, working the kinks out. I'm hot from his touch, squirming and whimpering, especially when his fingers *accidentally* brush against the sides of my breasts.

"You want more, baby?" he whispers against my ear, leaning over me as he starts dropping tantalizing kisses across the nape of my neck and lower.

"Yes," I rasp in a breathless voice, not protesting when he unsnaps my bra and the straps fall along my sides. His hands spread out, exploring more fervently, and the ache between my legs is growing in intensity.

"Can I touch you?" he whispers, his fingers tugging at the band of my jeans.

"Please."

"Turn around."

My body tenses ever so slightly at his brusque command, but I do as he asks, too aroused to consider rejecting him. Besides, I feel safe with him. He might look like the quintessential bad boy, but I've seen enough to know he's way more than that, and I don't feel threatened. I trust him to have my best interests at heart. Maybe it's crazy, because I don't know any of them that well, but I'm a better judge of character nowadays, and my instinct doesn't usually let me down. He tosses my bra to the ground while I brush matted hair out of my face, watching while his heated gaze rakes over my bare breasts.

"You're perfect, Blaire." His tone is awed as he brushes his hands over one breast and then the other, gently cupping me. My back arches off the bed as I push my tits into his hands, needing his touch as much as I need oxygen to breathe. "If I do anything you don't like, tell me to stop, and I will."

I blink through the sudden stab of tears pricking my eyes. He's going to so much trouble to reassure me, to let me know I'm in control, without even realizing exactly how much that means to me. I knew my instincts were right about him.

"Touch me, Axel. Please." I reach out, sneaking my hands under his shirt, exploring the dips and planes of his toned abs and muscular chest. "Off. I need this off," I pant, yanking on the hem of his shirt. Without breaking eye contact, he rips it off his body and throws it across the room. My fingers trace over the intricate tattoos that run from his left hand all the way up his arm, down across his chest, and up over one side of his neck.

He shivers under my touch, and I smile at him as he presses his body down against mine until we're skin to skin, face to face. "I want to take your pain away," he murmurs before claiming my lips in a searing-hot kiss.

His hips rock into mine, and I thrust up against him, needing the friction to ease the almost painful throbbing in my panties. His lips trail a path from my mouth to my neck and back again. And then his mouth goes lower, trekking kisses along my collarbone and lower still. He sucks one nipple into his mouth, and I cry out, my body already close to the edge.

All thoughts flee my mind, and I'm adrift in a sea of blissful sensations. This is exactly what I need to let go of the problems troubling my mind. Axel's skillful hands and tongue make me forget everything but how good it feels to have him touch me.

While he worships one breast with his mouth, his hand teases my other nipple, flicking the tautened peak with deft fingers. We grind against one another, and the feel of his hard length pushing into my core sends me over the ledge. I scream his name as my climax rips through me, clasping his hair tight and keeping his mouth suctioned against my breast as I come undone. I ride wave after wave of pleasure until I'm sated, and I sink into the bed, my bones feeling like Jell-O.

"Oh my God," I mumble, feeling my cheeks heating. I've never come without being touched down there before and I'm partly amazed, partly embarrassed. I slide my hand down the gap between us, palming his rock-hard erection, but he wraps his fingers around my wrist, pulling my hand away. "I want to return the favor," I say when he lifts his head, piercing me with an unfathomable look.

In a tender, sweet move, he takes my hand, planting a feather-soft kiss to the underside of my wrist. "I appreciate the offer, but this was about you. All you." He props up on his elbows, scrutinizing my face. "Feel better?"

I can't keep the grin from spreading across my mouth. "What do you think?" I quip, raising one brow.

Dropping onto his side, he pulls me into him, kissing me deeply, and I melt all over again. Cupping my head on both sides, he stares into my eyes. "You terrify me, Blaire, in the best possible way."

"I do?"

"Yeah," he says, moving in to kiss me again as the doorbell rings. He glances at his cell, cursing under his breath. "Shit. I lost track of time. That's the guys."

"What?!" I shriek, sitting bolt upright and grabbing the sheet to cover myself. I reach over the side of the bed, snatching my bra up. "You didn't tell me they were dropping by."

"We need to talk," he replies, scooting out of the bed. "All of us. Before things get messy."

"Hey, Blaire." Heath greets me at the bottom of the stairs with a tentative smile. "You feeling better?"

I blush from the top of my head all the way to the tips of my toes, and Skeet busts out laughing. Taking my hand, Skeet gently pulls me into his chest, kissing the top of my head. "I think it's safe to say Ax took care of our girl."

"Skeet." Axel's firm tone puts him in his place, reminding me of that other side of his personality.

"Living room or kitchen?" Heath asks Axel, deliberately not commenting either way.

"In there." Axel tips his chin in the direction of the living room, and we all traipse inside. Skeet pulls me down on the couch alongside him, instantly snaking his arm around my shoulders. I snuggle into his side, feeling safe and protected.

Heath sits down on my other side, clearing his throat. "So, how are we doing this?" His gaze bounces around the room as he threads his fingers in mine.

"Skeet." Axel leans back in the chair across from us, throwing one leg over his knee. "This is your area of expertise, so you kick off."

With my heart in my mouth, I fix my attention on Skeet, wondering what exactly I've got myself into.

Chapter Fifteen

I look up at Skeet, watching as he shakes his head. "Let's get one thing straight. This is a *team* effort. A *team* decision. A *team* discussion. No one person is calling the shots."

"Don't split hairs," Axel snaps. "We're in agreement on that, but you've lived this your entire life. Heath, Blaire, and I haven't."

"Don't get your panties in a bunch, dude. I'm just making sure we're all on the same page."

A layer of tension settles in the room, and I drag my lip between my teeth before deciding to pull my big girl panties on and kick-start the conversation. "I'll go first." I sit up a little straighter, still keeping hold of both guys. "I like all of you, as friends, and more, and I'd find it really difficult if I had to choose one of you to spend my time with."

My gaze flits between them, slowly, purposely, one at a time. "I've never done anything like this before, but I've kissed all of you, and there's definitely chemistry, so I'm open to exploring this if we keep it low-key and casual."

Skeet angles his body so he's looking me directly in the face. "You're the one in the driver's seat. None of us want to make this uncomfortable for you. You set the pace, and we'll go along with that."

"What if the pace is different with all of us?" Heath asks, dragging his free hand through his hair. "How do we deal with that?"

Skeet looks reflective. "The pace should be natural, and the dynamic will probably be different with each pairing; however, I don't see any issue with that."

"I have no issue with that either, but we're not the possessive type." As one, both Heath and Skeet shift their gaze to Axel.

"What?" he barks. "I've already told you I'm in."

"You can't get jealous," Skeet says.

"And you can't monopolize Blaire," Heath adds, "we need to spend time with her too."

"I fucking get that, and, like I said, I already agreed."

"How does your mom manage it?" I question Skeet, wanting to defuse the mounting tension in the room. I'm also genuinely curious to see how she's made it work all these years. It's so new to me, and while I'm willing to give it a shot, that doesn't mean it's going to be smooth sailing. "Does she have set times or days she spends with each of your dads, or they just go with the flow?"

"There are certain things she does with each of them, but it's not regimented. She makes sure she spends equal time with each of my fathers, and it seems to work."

"I like that idea too. I don't want it to feel like I'm on a set schedule. If I agree that I'll do my best to divide my spare time equally among you, does that work for everyone?" They all nod. "And I'd like it if we kept stuff private. Not that I'm saying we keep secrets from one another, per se, but I think each relationship should be allowed to develop naturally, and it will work best if we don't share too much private stuff."

"You mean sex?" Heath asks with a slight frown, as if he's only just considered this.

"I mean anything we talk about that's private or anything we do that's intimate. That should be private to each couple and not something shared. I think that'll help quell any jealousy too."

"Speaking of sex," Axel butts in. "I'm not into group sex. Not now. Not ever. I won't share in the bedroom."

"What?!" I screech, my eyes almost bugging out of my head as panic roars to life inside me.

Skeet chuckles. "You haven't fantasized about having all of us at once?"

"No!" I splutter. My mind wouldn't ever go there. I'm an open-minded person, and I'm willing to give this poly relationship a try, but that's not something I believe I'll ever be comfortable with. All the tiny hairs on the back of my neck lift, and my stomach sours, but I push all invading thoughts from my mind, refocusing on the conversation. "I'm with Axel. That's not something I'm into or will ever be into."

"Great, so we're all in agreement," Heath says, emitting a relieved breath.

I peek at Skeet, glimpsing the fleeting disappointment flaring in his eyes before he disguises it, fixing a smile on his face as he turns to me. "We need complete honesty if this is to work, so I need to ask you this, Blaire, but don't be offended."

"Ask me." I think I know where he's going with this, but I'll let him pose the question.

"Have you had sex before, or are you a virgin?"

"I'm not a virgin, but I've only had sex with one boy. My ex-boyfriend Cam."

"How long were you two together?" Heath asks.

Both boys' knees are pressed against mine, and we're so close we're almost sitting on top of one another. I'd expect to feel crowded, and tense, but I don't. I feel … secure, protected, and I like it. I like it a lot. "A little over a year, but I'd known him most of my life." I wet my dry lips. "He was my brother's best friend."

"And you broke up because you moved here or …" Skeet lets the sentence trail off.

I shift uncomfortably on the couch, averting my eyes as I speak. "We broke up just after Ethan died. Cam dumped me," I admit.

"What a fucking asshole." Skeet runs a hand up and down my spine, and I'm every bit as tense as I was when I first stepped foot in the door of this house.

"His loss is our gain," Heath adds, trying to make me feel better.

"What about you guys?" I inquire, tipping my chin up and working hard to keep emotion from my tone. "What's your history with girls?"

"I've never had a girlfriend," Axel says. "But I already told you that. I've had my fair share of hookups, but that stops now."

"I haven't had a girlfriend since ninth grade," Skeet supplies.

"How come?"

"Didn't meet anyone I wanted to date," he replies, shrugging. "And I've indulged in hookups too, but none since you arrived in town."

"I had a long-term girlfriend." Heath confirms what Shaznay already told me. "She moved out of state, but things were on the outs anyway. Then I had the whole Cassie fiasco, and I've been single ever since."

115

"If we do this," Skeet interjects. "Then it's an exclusive arrangement. No dating or hooking up with anyone else."

"Agreed," Heath and Axel say as one before all three boys turn to me.

"Uh, agreed. I'm not interested in anyone else." I'll be lucky if I can handle these three. Adding more guys into the mix is not on my agenda. It's a miracle I'm even doing this, and I've no desire to push my boundaries any further.

Skeet pecks my lips briefly, grinning like he's just won the lottery. My cheeks flush, and I look over at Heath and Axel to see if they're bothered by his PDA, but both look unflustered. Which leads me to another question. "So, it's okay if I kiss and touch you around one another or … what?"

"I'm cool with that provided it doesn't become too intimate," Axel says, piercing me with a grave look. "I'm a naturally jealous person, and I don't want to see you getting it on with either of them. I'm likely to knock the shit out of someone that way."

Skeet smirks while Heath looks deep in thought. "What about in public," Heath asks a second later. "What are the rules then?"

Skeet loses the smirk fast. "Blaire, what are your thoughts?"

"I don't want anyone to know," I blurt, quickly rephrasing when I see the hurt look on Skeet's face. "It's not that I'm embarrassed, but a lot of people won't understand, and I don't like being the center of attention."

"It's none of their business, but people will talk the more we hang together," Axel agrees.

"What if I was Blaire's boyfriend in public?" Heath suggests. "That would deflect curiosity."

"It shouldn't be you," Skeet says. "Because Cassie will freak the fuck out, and we don't want to give her additional ammo to go after Blaire." He scrubs a hand over his chin. "And if it was me, it'd probably only invite speculation because of my parents."

"I'll do it," Axel readily supplies. "Blaire and I will be boyfriend and girlfriend in public." His laser-sharp focus pins me in place. "If that's okay with you?" His voice lowers a few decibels as he lets me make the decision.

I want to fling myself at him and hug him tightly. I don't act on my impulse straightaway, convention keeping me rooted to the couch, but it only takes a few seconds for me to toss convention aside. I jump onto his lap, circling my arms around his neck. "Yeah, that's more than okay with me." I smile at him, and he kisses me firmly on the lips.

"Except that Cassie already saw me kissing Blaire," Heath adds, and I tear my lips from Axel's mouth. "If you show up to school on Axel's arm, she's going to figure it out."

"Shit." Skeet's brows knit together. "You're right. And she already insinuated that. Looks like there's no choice. You and Blaire will have to be the official couple."

I glance at Ax, and he reluctantly nods. "That's the best way of keeping Cassie off the scent."

"My turn." Heath pats his knee, motioning me forward with his fingers.

I climb out of Axel's lap and into Heath's. He cups my face and kisses me deeply until I'm seeing stars.

"Anything else we need to agree on?" Axel asks, directing his question at Skeet.

I rest my head on Heath's shoulder, watching Skeet as he thinks about it. This has got to go down as one of the strangest conversations ever. All formal and business-like even though we're discussing something so intimate. But I like that Skeet corralled us into talking about it, forcing us to set some rules. Hopefully, it will help limit the arguments and jealousies. I'm curious, excited, and a little anxious about it, but pushing myself out of my comfort zone is good for me too.

"I think we're good. The main thing we've got to remember is to openly communicate. If anyone has a problem, there's no point letting it fester. None of us have tried this before, and it probably won't be smooth sailing, but if we talk about it, we can work through our issues one at a time."

"I like that," I pipe up. "And the last thing I want to do is cause any friction in your friendship."

"Then we're doing this." Heath grins like a Cheshire cat, holding out his clenched fist.

We all bump fists, chanting in unison. "We're doing this."

Like I said, strangest conversation of my life.

Chapter Sixteen

"And how do you feel now you've had twenty-four hours to let it all sink in?" Shaz asks as she drives me to my first shift the following evening. Axel is working, Skeet is rehearsing with his band, and Heath had a session with his football buddies at the gym, so none of them could give me a ride. Heath was willing to cancel his gym session, but I insisted he stick to his plans. My suggestion to take the bus was instantly shot down, and Shaz jumped in with an offer before we had our first argument.

I've just finished summarizing the previous night's conversation with the guys, and apart from Skeet's parents, who are in the know, she's the only other person privy to our new relationship.

"It's a little surreal," I truthfully admit, wiping my clammy palms down the front of my jeans. "And I'm worried about people finding out and judging me, but I'm also really happy." I smile across the console at her. "The guys are great, and they make me feel good about myself in a way I haven't felt in a long time."

She squeezes my hand momentarily. "The guys *are* great. They're all like brothers to me, and I'm happy to vouch for them. I still can't believe it though," she adds, pulling up in front of Jacinta's store and killing the engine. "I never thought I'd see this day. Heath's always been traditional in his views, and Axel's always been possessive. I suspected Skeet was into exploring it, but I never thought he'd get the guys to agree." She pulls me into a quick hug. "It just took a very special girl."

"Stop it. You'll make me blush," I joke, rubbing a hand across my chest, willing the butterflies to scatter.

"What would Ethan have thought?" she quietly asks.

I blow air out of my mouth. "It's funny you should ask me, because that's exactly what I was thinking about last night." I bite down on my lip. "I think, if he knew the guys, he'd be okay with it once the initial shock had worn off, but, if he was here, if he saw how it actually happened, I think he'd freak out until he learned to trust the guys."

"That's understandable, and I think Skeet would be the same if it was me even if he is more open to the idea because of our family. He'd still be wary until he knew the guys were good guys."

"I'd better head in," I say, clasping the door handle. "I don't want to be late on my first day. Wish me luck?"

"Luck," she singsongs, hugging me again. "But you won't need it. You're going to knock it out of the park."

"Thanks for the ride," I say as I climb out of the car.

"No probs. Any time. I can pick you up later if you like?"

I rest my hands on top of the car and lean in. "Thanks, but one of the guys will pick me up when my shift's over."

"You know," she says, tapping a slender finger off her chin. "I might reconsider my whole stance on poly relationships. The thought of having a bunch of guys at my beck and call really appeals to me."

I lift an amused brow. "They're not my slaves, Shaz."

Her eyes glisten mischievously. "Not yet, but they will be."

I bark out a laugh. "You're devious."

"Always." She grins, waving as I close the door, and she pulls out of the parking lot.

Jacinta greets me warmly, wasting no time as she starts showing me how to work the register and how to track sales. In between serving customers, she takes me through the racks, showcasing her beautiful stock, explaining each piece in detail. By the time nine rolls around, my brain is basically fried, but the time has flown, and I've enjoyed shadowing her. It's obvious she's a natural people person and a born seller, and I only hope I can live up to her exacting standards.

"How did it go?" Skeet asks, pushing off the back of his truck and striding toward me when I emerge outside after Jacinta confirmed I could go home.

"Great! I really enjoyed it, but there's a lot to take in."

"You'll nail it. It just takes time." Hauling me into his chest, he leans down to kiss me. I instantly get lost in his velvety-soft lips and the way his mouth glides against mine. When we break apart a few minutes later, I anxiously look around the empty parking lot. "I thought we weren't supposed to be doing that in public?"

"I already scouted the place out. No one is around, and if Jacinta noticed, she can be trusted to keep our secret."

"Okay." I try to relax, but I only feel less anxious once we're in Skeet's battered old truck, en route to my house.

"I'm sorry if I upset you," he says, glancing at me briefly while he drives. "I shouldn't be breaking rules already. I just find it hard to keep my hands and my lips off you."

My mouth lifts into a smile. "I can't get mad at you for that." I lean across the gap and kiss his cheek. "I just don't want people at school finding out and talking crap about me." I've had enough of that to last a lifetime. "My privacy is important to me."

"I get that, babe, and we won't let anyone talk crap about you. Trust me." He pecks my lips lightning fast. "We've got you covered."

A comforting warmth traces a path through my body at his reassuring words, and it's incredible to have a support system again. I've missed having friends. Having people I can count on.

"Your parents aren't home?" Skeet inquires, squinting at the dark house when he pulls up in front of my house.

"Nope. They had dinner at my aunt and uncle's house in Tensen City. I got a free pass thanks to my new job. You want to come in?"

"Hells yeah."

The instant I'm inside the house, Skeet grabs hold of me, pressing me up against the wall in the hall where he proceeds to kiss the shit out of me. I cling to him, running my fingers through his messy hair and tugging on the longish strands. When he deepens the kiss, I moan into his mouth.

"We better stop," he murmurs as his lips glide from my mouth to my neck. "Or I won't be able to control myself for much longer." He thrusts his crotch into mine, pressing his hard-on against me.

I grab hold of his ass, keeping his body tucked against mine. "Maybe I don't want you to control yourself," I whisper, nipping at his lower lip.

121

"It's been almost six months since I last had sex, and I'm horny all the time around you guys."

He crushes his mouth against mine, grinding against me while ravishing me with his lips and his tongue. I'm putty in his arms, and I never want to let go. "I'm glad to hear it, babe." He nuzzles against my neck. "Because I'm horny for you too, but there's no rush." He kisses the tip of my nose, staring deep into my eyes. "I like the anticipation." His eyes glint mischievously. "It'll make it even hotter when we eventually fuck."

I close my eyes, whimpering. "That sounds a lot like torture."

"Yeah, but the best kind." He traces my face with his fingers. "Have you any idea how gorgeous you are? You could be a model with that face."

I snort. "I think you might be biased, or maybe your eyes need checking."

He kisses me again. "There's nothing wrong with my eyesight, and I might be biased, but then half the guys in town are too. You're gorgeous, babe, and I'm not just talking about your pretty face. You're gorgeous in here too." He lays his hand on my chest, right over the place where my heart is thumping wildly for him. "And I happen to be crazy about you."

I throw my arms around his neck, hugging him close. "I'm crazy about you too, Skeet. You make me happy."

He pulls back a smidgeon, tilting my face up with one finger. "I'm already falling hard for you, Blaire."

"Me too, and I love how honest you are. How comfortable you are expressing your feelings. It's so refreshing." Most guys would rather walk over hot coals than talk about their feelings.

He shrugs, dropping his hands from my face and taking my hand. I let him lead me into the kitchen. "I guess I'm just confident in my own skin, and I've never seen the point of lying. All it does is tie you into knots."

His words attack me head-on, and I almost keel over from the imaginary gut punch.

"What's wrong?" A frown puckers his brow as he inspects my face.

"Nothing," I whisper, faking a yawn. "I'm just tired. It's been a long day."

"I should go. Let you get to bed." He reels me into his arms, holding me close to his chest while peppering light kisses on top of my head.

When he releases me, I walk him to the door. "Thanks for picking me up."

"No problem, and one of us will drive you and pick you up every time you're working."

"You don't need to do that, but I'm grateful."

"We like to take care of our girlfriend," he says, and the ache in my chest eases a little.

I stretch up on tiptoes and kiss him goodbye. "You already do. Night, Skeet."

He takes my hand, pressing a kiss to my knuckles. "Night, beautiful. See you tomorrow."

My heart is split in two as I walk upstairs to my room. The guys make me happy, bringing light into my life, but they still don't know the real me, and guilt is starting to eat away at me again. I know we're still getting to know one another, and I'm sure there's stuff about their pasts I don't know, that they're anxious for me to discover, but I'm betting it's not on the same scale.

I wonder if my happiness is short-lived. If they'll dump me like Cam did once they find out.

These fears, and visions of the things I'm not telling them, keep me awake half the night.

💜💜💜

"You're dead on your feet," Axel exclaims the following morning after we've run only a couple miles.

"Sorry. I probably should've skipped today. I didn't get much sleep last night, and my limbs ache."

"We can turn back."

"No." I shake my head, cricking my neck from side to side in an attempt to liven up. "Let's keep going. My body's already feeling the effects of not running for a few days."

Axel slows the pace, and we jog companionably side by side. When we reach the lake, he leads me to the edge of the water, and we sit down, with our knees bent, staring at the placid water. There's a distinct chill in the air, but it's a welcome balm to my sweat-slickened skin. "What keeps you awake at night?" he asks, not looking at me as he skims a stone over the flat surface of the water.

I shrug even though he can't see. "Just stuff. My brother mainly."

"You were close." It's more of a statement than a question.

"Ridiculously so. We did most everything together, and he was always there for me." Tears stab my eyes, and I look away as the first one breaks free. "I miss him so much sometimes it's hard to breathe. Not when he isn't here, sharing the same air as me."

"I know what it's like to have someone ripped away from you," he admits after what feels like an eternity of silence.

I glance at him and he turns toward me at the same time. "Is this about your mom?" I softly inquire, and he nods, staring absently off into space.

"I mean, she wasn't the greatest mom in the world, she had her issues, but she tried. And in the end, she came through for us."

I frown a little. "I thought she left you?"

"She did, but it wasn't by choice."

"I don't understand."

He sighs. "I know. And I'll tell you." He stands, extending his hand to help me up. "But not now. I have to get back to the house and shower before school, and if I dredge up all that shit, I'll want to go and punch something."

My eyes widen, but I don't push it, understanding, on a personal level, how difficult it is to open up about the things that slay us on the inside. Exposing pent-up thoughts and feelings is the first step toward healing, but the pain is excruciating, and it requires enormous courage to go there. And while it helps lessen the pain, it never truly eradicates it. At least, not in my experience.

I stretch up on tiptoes, planting a light kiss on his cheek. "It's okay. Once you know I'm here for you. Whenever you want to talk, I'll listen."

Chapter Seventeen

*J*acinta lets me handle a couple of customers by myself tonight, and I even manage to make a sale, so I'm pleased as punch as I skip out the door at ten past nine, my grin expanding when I find both Heath and Skeet waiting for me.

I climb in the empty passenger seat, and Heath leans over to give me a quick kiss. I drop my bag on the floor and twist around, eyeballing Skeet in the back. "Why are you sitting there?"

He glances around the dark parking lot before reaching forward and dropping a soft kiss on my lips. He pulls back before I can properly savor it, and I resist the urge to pout. "We thought we'd head to the diner. It's usually packed with seniors Friday night, and it's a good opportunity for you and Heath to highlight your relationship before you return to school Monday. You should be seen beside Heath because all eyes will be on us when we park."

I chew on the corner of my nail while I consider it. "Yeah. That'll probably make things easier. I'm game."

"Cool." Skeet winks at me, before slouching back in the seat. I buckle my seatbelt as Heath drives out of the parking lot. "Ax's just finished his shift. He'll meet us there," he confirms.

Axel is quiet when we arrive at the diner. Propped against the side of his Harley, he looks tired, like he hasn't slept much either.

I feel eyeballs on me the instant Heath parks, right in front of the diner. He stretches over the console to kiss me. "You sure you're up for this?"

"Yeah, I'm good." I disarm him with a glowing smile, and his shoulders visibly relax. He hops out, jogging around the front of the car to open my door. I slide my hand in his, pretending to ignore the gawking faces staring out the window at us, and we follow Axel and Skeet into the busy diner. Tiny goose bumps lift all over my arms as a pretty brunette waitress leads us to the last vacant booth at the back of the diner, and every pair of eyes in the place fixates on me. A bead of sweat glides down my spine, and my pulse skyrockets as nervous adrenaline floods my body.

"Relax, babe." Heath discreetly squeezes my hand, jerking his head up in greeting as we pass a couple of his football buddies. He lets me slide into the booth first before scooting in beside me. Axel and Skeet sit across from us, facing the diner. Air whooshes out of my mouth, and I attempt to relax, to not overreact and draw further attention.

"I'll be back in a few minutes to take your orders," the waitress says, handing out menus. Her mouth twists into a sneer as she thrusts a menu at me, but I school my lips into a neutral line, determined she won't see how rattled I already am. When she's gone, Skeet leans across the table. "Why are you nervous?"

My knee taps up and down as I pin eyes on him. "I just hate being the center of attention. Always have. Knowing everyone is talking about me makes me uncomfortable."

Heath lands a reassuring hand on my knee, quelling the anxious movement. "We'll be the focus for all of five seconds, and then they'll move on to someone else."

I nod, hoping he's right. When the waitress returns, Heath makes a show of pulling me into his side, wrapping his arm around my shoulder. She barely manages to contain her look of disgust, but she's on the clock, and she doesn't seem entirely stupid. She takes our orders and leaves. I tip my head up to Heath. "Let me guess, she's a member of Queen Cassie's fan club?"

"Got it in one."

"She's also tried to get in Heath's pants for years," Skeet adds. "Not that Cassie is aware of that fact."

"Maybe I should enlighten her," I suggest. "Give the bitch someone else to hate on."

"Speak of the devil," Axel murmurs, glaring at something over my shoulder.

"Good," Skeet says, also narrowing his eyes. "I'm glad Cassie's here. Let her see you two together and take the weekend to process it."

The waitress returns with our sodas and silverware, still glowering at me, and I'm done with pretending she's not being a prize bitch. "Is there a problem?" I drill her with a deadly look. "Because if you have an issue serving us, I can always ask the manager to assign another waitress to our table."

"There's no problem," she barks, slamming my soda down so hard that it sloshes over the rim onto the table.

"Then you won't mind bringing my girlfriend another soda." Heath takes the offending drink, extending it to her. "And cleaning up the mess you just made."

"Girlfriend?" she splutters.

"Girlfriend." His determined tone matches the expression on his face.

Her cheeks redden, and she takes the soda and disappears.

"You've got to be kidding me." Cassie materializes like a bad smell, standing over the table with her hands perched on her hips. "You're seriously making it official?"

"Not that it's any of your business," Heath says, "but, yes, Blaire and I are exclusively dating."

"And it doesn't alter your deal, so you can fuck off and annoy some poor, unsuspecting sap." Axel leans back against the booth as he delivers his cutting statement.

She flips him the bird. "Asshole," she spits before spinning on her heel and leaving us.

"I don't know how you could spend a solitary second in that bitch's presence let alone fuck her," Axel adds, taking a long pull from his soda.

"I was trashed," Heath growls. "And I'd rather not be reminded of it. Unless you want to trade stories and share some of your unmentionables with Blaire?"

"Dude. Don't." Skeet levels Heath with a cautionary look.

"Speaking of unmentionables," I say, claiming their attention. "Want to hear about the time I accidentally flashed my math teacher?"

My diversion works, and by the time our food arrives, all tension related to the poisonous Cassie has been long forgotten. We trade goofy stories from our childhood, keeping it deliberately lighthearted, and I forget the curious stares and nosy interest. I even manage to eat half my burger, which is the most food I've kept down all week.

"I need to pee," I say, nudging Heath in the ribs. "Let me out."

"I'll come with," he says, standing.

I push him back down. "Don't be ridiculous. I'm well capable of making it in and out of the restroom alive."

"Cassie's gone," Skeet confirms, glancing over our shoulders.

"And there's a difference between protection and suffocation," Axel chastises, earning the middle finger from Heath.

I'm still smiling as I enter the restroom, walking straight into an ambush. "I thought you'd left." I slant a confident look at Cassie, determined to keep my cool during this confrontation. The pouty waitress is by her side, looking at me like I'm dirt at the bottom of her shoe.

"You think you're so superior," Cassie says. "But you're trash. Dirty. Disposable." She puts her face right up in mine. "Disgusting."

"Heath doesn't agree, but think what you like. Your words don't hurt me."

"Only an idiot would think that stupid deal protects them." Her smug smile competes with the malicious glint in her eyes. "I know how to play the game, and you're no match for me."

Come on. *Could she be any more cliché?* "Are you threatening me?" Briefly, I wonder if she's the one behind the email, but I quickly dismiss it. There's no way she could know about my past.

"Watch your back, whore." She shoulder-checks me as she walks past, but it doesn't register over the blood thrumming in my ears and the screams bouncing around my brain. The word repeats over and over in my head, and deep-seated anger races to the surface. I grab hold of her elbow. "What did you call me?" I say through gritted teeth.

She smirks, and her eyes glimmer with delight. "Whore." She enunciates the word, her mouth making an exaggerated "O" sound, and I'm dragged kicking and screaming into the past. I squeeze my eyes shut as my entire body trembles. Cassie tries to wrench free of my hold, but I've a vise grip on her arm, and she's not getting away any time soon. "Let me go, whore, or I'll scream."

My head is yanked back so fast it's a wonder it didn't detach from my neck. The bitchy waitress has a firm hold of my hair, tugging sharply, as if she's determined to pull every strand of hair out of my head. She drags me away from Cassie, pushing open one of the stall doors and trying to force my head down. Rage consumes me, and I jab my elbow into her gut before my face hits the toilet bowl. She stumbles backward, losing her grip on me, and I straighten up. Before I've had a chance to think about my next move, she's lunging at me, dragging her nails down one side of my face.

Immediate pain slices across my cheek, and I lose it.

Pressing my palms flat to the wall on either side of the stall, I use my upper body strength to swing my legs around into her stomach, pushing her out of the way. She soars backward across the bathroom with her arms and legs flailing, emitting a loud shriek of frustration.

Out of the corner of my eye, I spy Cassie making a beeline for me with a look of fierce determination etched on her face. "Fucking whore!" she yells. It looks like she's determined to get involved in the action this time. She repeats the word "whore" over and over, like a mantra, as she advances, and a switch flips in my head.

A frustrated roar rips from my throat, and I race toward her like a wild animal. She backs up, her eyes widening in alarm, but I'm on top of her in a flash, forcing her up against the wall. My hands automatically encircle her neck, and I zone out, having lost all control. She frantically grabs at my wrists, trying to remove my chokehold, but I'm not in the moment.

I'm back in the past, and I can't see straight or think clearly.

Years of torment fuel the violent energy coursing through me, and I'm not in the present. My hands tighten around her neck, and Cassie makes a strangled sound, but it's not her face I'm seeing, and I can't stop.

Ethan's face swims in front of my eyes. *Stop, B. This isn't who you are.*

I snap out of it. My hands fall away from her neck, and I jerk back, horrified at my actions. Cassie drops to her knees, gasping, crying, and clutching at her throat. Blood is pounding in my ears and my heart is beating way too fast. Shame, and a host of other emotions, washes over me. "Oh my God. I'm so sorry." I move cautiously toward her. "Are you okay?"

She scoots over to the other side of the bathroom. "Stay away from me, you fucking psycho!" she screams. "Keep her away from me!" she yells at her friend.

I'd almost forgotten about the other girl, but as I turn around, she grabs me by the hair again, shoving me, face-first, into the nearest stall door. Blood gushes from my nose, but I hardly feel any pain because my body is on edge, juiced up and raring to go. I turn around, swaying on my feet, as my vision blurs in and out, and remaining upright becomes challenging.

"Stupid fucking whore." The waitress kicks me in the leg, and I stagger back into the stall, grasping hold of the doorframe to keep myself from falling. Pinning me with a malicious look, she kicks me in the stomach, and I lose my grip, crashing to the ground on my butt. My back slams into the toilet, and pain shoots up my spine, but it barely registers as anger roars to life inside me again. She lashes out when I'm defenseless and sprawled on the ground, kicking me again, in the face this time, before backing away, smirking.

My head spins, and there's a metallic taste in my mouth as I scramble to my feet, but the surge of adrenaline still working its way through my body overtakes the pain, and I charge out of the stall toward her like a madwoman.

She's crouching over Cassie, and they are both screaming for help. A red haze sweeps over me, and I jump on the waitress's back. We both fall to the floor at an awkward angle, wrestling for control. She digs her nails into my injured cheek, and I lose all sense of reason.

Roaring, I gain the upper hand, straddling her as I rain punches on her face.

Her features transform.

The monsters from my past laugh at me, and I pummel them harder, ignoring my throbbing knuckles and the pain lancing across my chest. I just keep lashing out.

"Holy fucking shit."

I'm ripped off the girl by strong hands, and I thrash about, resisting the motion. I'm not in the moment. I still can't see over the red haze and the nightmares of my past.

"Blaire. It's okay," Axel says, looming hazily in my line of sight. "We've got you." The person at my back—Skeet, I'm guessing—wraps his arm around my waist more tightly, holding me flush against his body.

"I'm calling the cops." Cassie's fingers hover over her cell. Heath is beside her, his back flattened against the locked door. Someone thumps on the door from outside, demanding to be let in.

"Take her." Skeet lets me go, handing me over to Axel while he bends over the girl whimpering on the floor.

"She's a fucking psycho!" Cassie shrieks, making a grab for Heath as he snatches her cell and holds it out of her reach.

"You're the psycho," he barks back. "I told you to leave her alone, but you ignored me! And I'm fucking done with you. I'm telling your parents about the crash and your coke habit."

"Tell them! They won't believe you. You have no proof. All it'll do is bring heat down on you."

"We'll get proof," Axel hisses, keeping me close to his chest. I'm shaking all over, and my limbs are jittery and infused with adrenaline that refuses to dissipate.

"I think she might need stitches," Skeet says, helping the waitress to her feet.

"You're going down for this," she says, cradling her injured cheek. There's a small cut under her eye that probably does need stitches. My head is a mess. I'm disgusted at myself, but I'm still raging.

"Whore," she adds, and I lunge at her, the word like an incendiary device.

Axel reacts fast, restraining me before I can reach her and forcing me back behind him. He clasps a firm hand on my hip, keeping me in place.

"Get Blaire out of here." Heath speaks directly to Axel before stalking to my side. He stares at me with apprehension in his eyes. "We'll fix this, baby, but you need to go. Ax will take care of you, and everything will be okay," he reassures me.

I nod, gulping over a million conflicting emotions. Then Axel tugs me toward the open window at the back of the bathroom, pushing it up fully. "You go first." He lifts me up, swinging my legs over the ledge, and carefully sets me down on the ground outside before joining me. He takes my hand and leads me around the building, back out onto the sidewalk. When we reach his bike, he flips me around, clasping my face in both his hands. "What the hell happened back there?"

I open my mouth, but nothing comes out. I don't know how to explain it. Not when I'm still all fired up. My gaze darts all over the place, and my hands shake. I can't force my body to calm down, and it's refusing to cooperate. I'm twisted into a million knots, and my mind is spinning in a million different directions.

"Blaire. Eyes on me." Axel grips my face tighter, forcing my gaze to meet his concerned one. "You need to let off steam?"

I nod. "I ... I feel a little crazy right now."

"It's the adrenaline. It needs an outlet."

"I'm such a fuckup." I swallow over the nasty taste in my mouth

"Stop that." Axel's tone is harsh. "We're all fuckups in our own ways."

I hold my arm up, my hand shaking uncontrollably. "What the hell is wrong with me?"

"You need to get this out of your system." He weighs something up in his mind before gripping my face firmly again. "You trust me, baby? You trust me to look after you right now?" I nod. "Okay. Then I know what you need." After cleaning up my nose and wiping streaks of blood off my face, he hands a helmet to me. "Put that on, and let's get out of here."

Chapter Eighteen

J don't ask where we're going, which is becoming a bit of a habit when it comes to Axel. I hold onto him tightly as he navigates the bike in the dark, hoping the chilly ride will eliminate this crazy insanity thrumming through my veins, but I'm still pumped up when we reach our destination.

Loud whoops and hollers emanate from the disheveled barn we've arrived at. We're in a field in the middle of nowhere, and lighting is virtually nonexistent. Thin slivers of light snake out from some gaps in the wall as we walk alongside the structure, but it's the only brightness for miles. Empty fields surround us on all sides as we walk over uneven, grassy terrain.

Axel slams to a halt just before we turn the corner, twisting me around in his arms. "You still trust me to know what's best for you now?"

"I do. I trust you."

He's staring at me, but it's too dark to read his expression. "I know what you're feeling. Our rage may originate from different sources, but I feel your pain pulsing through me, Blaire." He plants his hand on my stomach. "I understand how destructive it is to try and breathe through it. No one else gets it." He sighs, and his chest heaves. "I used to come here when I needed to release it. It's not pretty, and you could get hurt, but it'll help." He holds my face between his hands. "I won't let you get seriously hurt. I'll keep you safe. I promise."

I grab hold of his wrists. "I trust you."

"It's dangerous, and the others won't approve."

My heart jumps at his words, and butterflies scatter in my chest. I'm equal parts scared, exhilarated, and reckless at the same time. "I don't care.

This is about me. About needing release. It feels like I'm destructing from the inside out." A tiny cry escapes my mouth. "Make it stop, Axel. Please make it go away."

He fuses our mouths together in a searing-hot kiss, and we devour one another for a few minutes, clinging tightly to each other, before he pulls back, snatching my hand and hauling me around the corner. I freeze at the sight of the two men guarding the barn entrance. Both are older. Early thirties, if I had to guess. They have shaved heads, lip piercings, full tatted sleeves, and bulging biceps to rival Heath's. But it's the guns tucked into the bands of their jeans that set my nerves even more on edge. The sight of the guns brings me out in a cold sweat, and I jerk back, wondering what the hell type of place this is.

"Blaire?" Axel pulls me against his chest.

"We're not going to shoot, are we?" I ask, my voice quaking.

He shakes his head. "No. It's nothing like that." He pauses for a beat. "We don't have to go in. I can take you home right now. Or we can go in, and if you don't like it, we can leave." He tucks my hair behind my ears. "It's always your choice."

That's exactly what I need to hear to settle my nerves. "I want to go inside."

"Thorp." One of the burly bouncers acknowledges Axel with a slight nod of his head, stepping aside to let us enter.

The first thing that registers is the smell. Stale sweat mixed with the metallic scent of blood and smoky fumes assault me as I clasp Axel's hand, letting him lead me into the barn. The unruly shouting is the next thing that registers. All around me, questionable-looking men with tats, piercings, and dubious expressions jostle toward the top of the space, hollering and fist pumping the air. An aura of danger permeates the room as we make our way through the noisy, sweaty crowd.

Even though I keep my eyes trained on Axel's back, I'm conscious of leering looks and lingering gazes. Someone pinches my ass, and I shriek, clutching Axel's hand so tightly I'm probably restricting the blood flow. Suctioning me to his chest, he glares at the nearest guy, not at all perturbed that he's got at least forty pounds on him and he looks like he eats puppies for breakfast. "Don't fucking touch her."

"No harm, no foul, Fury." The scary douche holds up his hands in surrender.

"Stay in front of me," Axel commands, altering our positions as we continue our journey.

"Fury?" I shout to be heard over the noise.

"It's my stage name."

I'm about to ask another question when we break through to the top of the room, and my mouth slackens as my eyes scan the cage. It's kind of similar to ones I've seen in MMA except cruder. Ethan and Cam were big MMA fans, and I used to watch some of the fights with them. Three steps lead up to a medium-sized ring that is surrounded by metal bars. It's not enclosed on top, but the steel sides are tall enough not to be breached. The gray stone floor looks brutal, and there are no mats in sight. Two men dance around each other in the ring, both sporting facial injuries and bruising to their bodies.

"Thorp. Long time no see." A tall, wiry man with greasy slicked-back hair greets Axel like a long-lost son, slapping him on the back. He's wearing an ill-fitting black suit, and bits of dandruff stick to the collar and shoulders, making my stomach turn. "You here to fight?" he asks, turning an inquisitive eye on me.

Axel shakes his head. "You got any girls looking to fight?"

A slimy grin spreads over his face. "It is free for all Friday, and your luck's in. Got a regular looking to fight. I was about to send her home."

"Give me a sec." Axel gestures at me, and the man steps back a few spaces.

Axel surveys me closely, his eyes penetrating mine. "This is what I do when I need to release steam. I get in that ring, and I let the anger fuel me. If you want, you can fight tonight."

Anxiety combines with excitement in a strange concoction flowing through my veins. "I've never fought in a ring."

"But you have fought before." Again, it's not a question. It's a statement. The fact he can see me so clearly is alarming for a whole heap of reasons.

I nod. "And I'm trained in self-defense."

"I can give you some additional pointers, and if you fight without a fee, you can call a halt to it if it gets too much."

This is crazy. I should say no, but I'm already nodding. "I'm in."

Ax spends a couple minutes making arrangements with the sleazeball in the suit while I watch the action in the ring. "C'mon." He takes my hand, pushing around the back of the stage and leading me behind an enclosed area. "You're up next, so we don't have much time." The area is divided into a makeshift men's and women's changing rooms, and there's a small communal area where a bunch of people linger, drinking and talking. Ax opens an overhead cupboard, pulling out some items and handing them to me. "Get changed in there, and let me know when you're done."

I eye the tight shorts and skimpy bra top with derision. "Exactly what kind of fight is this?"

"It's a regular fight, Blaire, but they like to give the largely male audience something pretty to look at every once and a while."

I mutter under my breath as I walk into the changing room and pull on the offending outfit. "I feel naked," I tell him when I step back outside. "I usually wear more clothes to the beach."

"You look fucking hot," he says, his eyes shimmering with desire. I expect him to pull me to him, but he's all business, explaining how to assess my opponent's strengths and weaknesses and how to use a few simple techniques to incapacitate her. The girl I'm fighting is a regular, so I probably don't stand a hope in hell of winning, but I don't care. I'm not here for the win. I'm here to unleash my demons through my fists. Unfortunately, inflicting pain is my usual go-to-method, so I'm not overly surprised I've ended up here.

When we're called, I hold my head up high and step back out into the main area, shaking off Ax's hand as we walk to the side of the cage. "Remember what I told you," he whispers in my ear. "I saw you earlier. You can do this."

My opponent is announced into the ring first. Demolition Girl looks like she's ready to bulldoze me into the ground. She's way shorter than me, but she's built like a tank. A tank full of muscle. There isn't an ounce of fat anywhere on her body, but she is ripped in a way I've only seen with those female bodybuilders on TV. My slender frame works against me, but at least I'll have speed on my side.

"What's your name, sweetheart?" the burly guy in charge asks.

I wrack my brains for an appropriate stage name and blurt out the only name that comes to mind. "Katniss." I inwardly cringe when he makes my introduction, but there's no time to backtrack now. In a way, it's fitting. Katniss had to fight to survive, and while our circumstances may be different, that's exactly what I'm doing tonight.

The bell dings, the crowd hollers their approval, and the fight commences. Demolition Girl charges at me, and I only just manage to duck down in time. She reacts faster than I gave her credit for, grabbing me by the hair and yanking me upright. Her arm goes around my neck, but I lash out before she gets me in a chokehold and it's lights out. I'm guessing the usual elbow jab to the gut won't work, so I take the only action I can. Reaching behind me, I grab one of her boobs and squeeze it hard.

It works.

She yelps at the unexpected pain, letting go of me. The crowd is going wild, screaming all manner of disgusting suggestions at me.

Ax said the fights are dirty and to play the same game, so I am.

I smirk at Demolition Girl as she comes at me again. I wait till the last second, flip my wrist up, and smash my palm into her face, flattening her nose and pushing her back. She stumbles, and I lift my leg, planting my foot in her stomach and pushing hard. Her abs are like a frigging wall, and it doesn't have the required impact, only throwing her off for another few seconds.

When she comes at me this time, she looks like she's ready to throttle me. Her fist crashes into my jaw, and my head whips back as stinging pain rattles around my skull. She hits me again, and I stagger back, my vision turning blurry. Behind me, I can vaguely hear Ax shouting. The one thing he told me to avoid at all costs was hitting the ground. A fall on that hard floor could cause serious damage. No doubt, he's shouting instructions at me, but I zone him out, channeling all my pent-up emotions and using that to refocus.

We trade blows, swinging and punching, ducking and diving, dancing around one another. Sweat glistens on my skin, causing tendrils of damp, wispy stands of hair to come loose from my ponytail. My jaw throbs and my stomach hurts from the few punches she landed, but the pain doesn't shut me down; it spurs me on.

She tries to get me in another chokehold, but I do everything to avoid that. I know once her arm wraps around my neck I'm done for, and I'm not ready for this to end yet. I've still got far too much aggression inside me.

My back is against the steel bars before I realize what she's done. She's backed me into a corner, and I need to think fast. Her fist comes at me, and I grab hold of it, my biceps strained to bursting point as I work hard to contain her punch. Before she can figure it out, I slam my forehead into hers, instantly seeing stars. She lets loose a string of expletives before stumbling away, clutching her head and screaming at me. Blood trickles down my forehead from an earlier cut, and I swipe it away as I clutch onto the bars, trying to stop myself from passing out.

I watch as she climbs to her feet, recovering and coming at me again. I'm almost out of juice, and I either end it now or let her take me down. I feign movement to the left, and she angles her body in that direction, reaching for me. Swinging from the right, I deliver a sharp, swift jab to her neck right in the place where her carotid is. My self-defense instructor was ex-military, and he taught me how to hit in the precise point to weaken my opponent. You have to be careful, to strike with enough force to disable someone, but applying too much force could actually kill someone. We practiced for weeks, perfecting the move, but this is the first time I've used it in a real-life situation.

Demolition Girl staggers back, her eyes fluttering before they close, and she starts falling. I jump into action, catching her before she crashes into the ground.

I don't want any other death on my conscience.

I'm struggling to hold her, and my legs are trembling, but I manage to place her carefully on the ground.

An arm lifts around me from behind, and I'm put back on my feet. Then the beefy guy in control of the cage lifts my arm aloft screaming out my victory. The noise of the crowd is almost deafening.

At some point, I'd actually tuned out all the background noise, but now it blares so loud, as if one hundred trumpets are blasting directly into my eardrums. I wince, looking around for Ax, only my eyes lock on a clearly furious Heath. He's standing with Skeet at the front of the cage, and from the expression on both their faces, I know I'm in serious trouble.

138

Chapter Nineteen

"*A*re you out of your ever-loving mind?" Heath roars once we're outside, away from the main entrance and inquisitive ears. His fists clench and unclench at his side as he shoots daggers at Axel. "Why the fuck would you think it was a good idea to take Blaire here?!" He jabs his finger in my direction. "Look at the fucking state of her! How is this helping?" There was only enough time to change into my clothes, and I didn't even look in the mirror, so I've no idea how bad I look.

"It *has* helped," I interject, feeling like I need to defend Axel. "Please stop shouting at him. It was my choice. He didn't force me into anything." Skeet places a cautionary hand at my hip, keeping me in place.

Heath throws his hands up into the air. "Great. Now we're saddled with another screwup to fix."

My stomach lurches to my toes at his hurtful words. I don't blame him for coming to that conclusion, and it's not that he's wrong, but it's still painful to hear it articulated.

"Fuck you, asshole." Axel shoves Heath in the shoulders, and he stumbles back. "Don't spout crap about shit you know nothing about!"

"And you do?" Heath pushes Axel this time and he almost falls to the ground, righting himself at the last minute.

"You know I fucking do."

"Did you tell her?" he challenges. "Does Blaire know about the stealing and the drugs and juvie?"

Skeet releases me, planting himself in between them. "Quit this shit. There's nothing to gain from rehashing the past." He puts his face in Heath's. "I know you're pissed. I'm pissed too, but throwing that shit in his face isn't cool. We all know he's paid the price, and bringing it up in front of Blaire is a low blow."

He doesn't wait for Heath to reply before turning around to face Axel. "And bringing Blaire here was the fucking wrong move, dude. I know you think you were helping, but this isn't the way to solve anything. You know I'm right." Both guys glare at one another over Skeet's shoulders, and it's clear no one's backing down tonight.

This is all my fault, and I hate myself for it. I never wanted to cause issues between them, and I'm already doing it. I step up to the guys. "Be angry at me, not one another. This is all my fault."

"Assigning blame isn't helping anyone," Skeet says in a calm, controlled voice. "Fuckups happen. It's not the end of the world. We need to go home and sleep it off. We'll figure this out tomorrow."

"Fine." Heath snaps, rubbing a hand around the back of his neck.

"I'm out." Axel stalks off, pushing Skeet away when he reaches for him. His face is contorted in pain, and I glimpse a host of competing emotions. Heath's words have hurt him more than he'll ever admit.

"Fuck. Shit. Crap." Heath kicks the side of the barn, resting his head along the corrugated iron.

I watch Axel's retreating form, concern for him overriding concern for myself.

"Go." Skeet jerks his head to the side. "He can't be alone, and I know you get him. He needs you."

"I'm sorry. For everything tonight."

He walks to me, clasping the back of my head and pulling me to him. He presses a quick kiss to my forehead. "I know you are, sweetheart. Don't sweat it. We'll thrash it out tomorrow, and all will be good."

I'm not so sure I share his confidence, but I don't stop to debate it because Axel is almost at his bike. I race over to Heath, wanting to say something to him before I leave. "Don't." His gruff voice spits out the word before I've even said anything. "Just go."

Skeet sighs, shaking his head sadly. Then he points at Axel's retreating form, and I don't need to be told twice. With pain spearing me on all sides, I run after him, pushing my limbs to the limit in my quest to reach Axel in time.

He's straddling his Harley, getting ready to take off when I reach him. I throw myself on the back of the bike, grabbing hold of his waist. He freezes for a second before glancing over his shoulder at me. We stare at one another. No words are spoken, but none are needed. Silently, he removes the helmet from his head, putting it on mine. Then he positions my hands more securely around his waist, and we take off.

The edgy, angsty feeling is still buzzing under the surface of my skin. Yes, the fight expended most of this reckless energy, but I'm still wired, still pumped full of indecipherable need. It's been a long time since I've felt this out of control, and it scares me. Ethan was usually the one to talk me down, but he's not here anymore, and it slays me all over again.

Axel brings the bike to a stop at a curb close to our neighborhood. "Home or my place?" he asks.

"Your place." There's no hesitation. My parents probably haven't even noticed I didn't come home after work. Last I checked, I had no worried voicemails or texts. No one will notice I'm not there if I don't come home.

Axel's house is in complete darkness when we arrive, a little after midnight. His brother is obviously still at the bar. He flicks the light on in the hall, taking my hand and leading me up the stairs. A new layer of butterflies descends on my chest, and a throbbing ache takes up residence between my thighs.

Ax guides me into the compact bathroom, sitting me down on the closed toilet seat. I remove my jacket, tossing it on the side of the tub as I watch him removing several items from the cupboard over the faucet. Then he crouches down in front of me, attending to the injuries on my face first. I flinch as he dabs ointment on my skin. "How bad is it?"

"It could be worse."

That's not the most reassuring statement, but I don't really care. I study him as he diligently treats my wounds, noting how long and thick his black lashes are, how plump his full lips are, and how sharp the angular lines of his cheekbones are. Axel is beautiful, and I've an almost overriding need to lose myself in him. It's more than a simple desire. It's an intense craving I must sate, so I have no problem going there. "Can I stay with you tonight?"

He looks up, piercing me with those stunning silvery-blue peepers. Lust washes over me, and I drag my lower lip between my teeth, squeezing my legs together in an effort not to squirm. His eyes examine mine carefully, and I hold nothing back, maintaining the intense eye contact. "Are you sure?"

I nod slowly, never taking my eyes off his. He doesn't say anything else, but he doesn't need to. His eyes do all the talking for him. His gaze rakes over me slowly, like a gentle caress. He gulps, and his eyes darken as he lowers his hands from my face to my torn knuckles. Electricity crackles in the space between us, and I close my eyes, soaking up his essence, enjoying the anticipation while he cleans the shredded skin on my knuckles before applying a couple Band-Aids.

Without uttering a word, he scoops me up into his arms, carrying me into his bedroom.

He places me down carefully on the bed, and I lunge for him, grabbing him down on top of me before he can guess the movement. His lips collide with mine instantly, and his hands creep under my shirt, inching upward. He grabs one of my breasts, kneading it roughly, and it's exactly what I need to erase the last vestiges of this recklessness. I slide my hand down between our bodies, palming his erection through his jeans. He rocks into me, and I moan, throwing my head back to give him more access to my neck. His hot, wet mouth trails a path down my neck, along my collarbone, and in the crevice between my breasts. I rub his hard length through the denim, my movements growing more and more frantic until it feels like I'll self-combust.

I shove him off me, and he falls back onto the bed beside me. Jumping up, I rip my sweater and shirt up over my head, kick off my shoes, and shimmy my jeans down my legs until I'm hovering over him in just my underwear. With a braveness I didn't realize I possessed, I watch his every eye movement as I unpeel my bra and panties, standing buck ass naked in front of him.

A dark flash of desire glistens in his eyes, and the protruding bulge in his pants tells me he wants this too. I crawl up the bed, straddling his lap, completely naked. The denim rubs against my core, and I welcome the friction, moaning and licking my lips as I bend over him. "Fuck me. Please."

He yanks my head down to his. "You never have to beg. Never." He stares deep into my eyes. "I need to ask you again though because you've been through a lot tonight. Are you sure this is what you want?"

"Yes. I need you to fill me up, Axel. I need you to fill this empty void inside of me."

He melds his mouth to mine, kissing me with an aggressive passion I can relate to. Without warning, he pulls back a few minutes later, and I cry out at the loss of his touch. His lips curve into an amused grin. "Relax, baby. I know what you need, and I'll look after you. I promise." He brushes his mouth against mine, and his kiss is more tender this time, warming me in a different way.

I watch him undress with my eyes out on stalks. He takes his time, watching my every reaction, in the same way I watched his when I was stripping. I've seen his naked chest before, but it doesn't diminish the impact of his carved abs and chiseled torso. I lick my lips as I watch the trail of dark hair snaking into his jeans gradually revealed. Axel has those "V" indents on both hips, and they're almost as sharp as the angles of his jawline. He pushes his jeans down his legs, taking his boxers with them, and his cock springs free, standing tall and proud. He strokes himself slowly, from root to tip, over and over, while he kicks his jeans away.

I'm a puddle on his bed, wet warmth trickling down my legs. I've never been so turned on in my life.

He walks to the table by his bed, removing a few silver packets from the drawer. He tosses a few on top of the table, ripping one open with his teeth. Saliva pools in my mouth as he slowly rolls the condom on. He climbs onto the bed, nudging my legs apart with his knees. Lowering his head, he looks down at me, urging my legs farther apart until I'm fully exposed to him. "Axel." I whimper, writhing on the bed in desperate need.

"Shush, baby." He runs the tip of his finger up and down my slit before pushing it inside. "Is this what you need?"

"Yes. God, yes."

He adds another finger, and then another, and he starts pumping furiously inside me. I lean my head back, closing my eyes and letting myself get immersed in blissful sensation. When his mouth suctions on my clit, I almost buck off the bed, and the moans leaving my mouth would embarrass me if anyone else was in the house.

"Let go, baby. Fly for me." He pinches my clit, pumping his fingers inside me at a rapid pace, and I explode, shattering into a thousand tiny fragments.

This, this is what I need. Nothing else haunts me in this moment. No horrid thoughts plague my mind. There is only pure sensation. Pure joy. Pure pleasure.

I feel him at my entrance, and then he thrusts inside me in one fast movement. I buck my hips up, crying out his name as he thrusts into me hard and fast. I open my eyes, needing to see him, marveling at the ripples in his abs and the throbbing of the veins in his arms as he fucks me into oblivion.

He's not gentle, and a string of dirty words flies from his mouth as he thrusts harder and harder, sending me over the ledge again. Before I've had time to recover, he flips under me, pulling me on top and yanking me down on his dick. I scream, fisting my hands in the comforter as I roll my hips, bouncing up and down on him. Then he takes control, holding my hips in place as he thrusts up into me. I hold on for dear life as he fucks me furiously.

I get the sense Axel is exorcising some demons of his own.

Not that I'm in any way complaining.

He's rocking my world, and if it was possible to stay here with him and never leave, I'd do it. He roars out his release, just as I climax for the third time, thrusting into my body continuously until he's completely sated.

We collapse on the bed in a sweaty heap. My messy hair forms a coarse blanket over my face as I lie on my side with my back to his chest. He grabs my hip, pulling me flush against him. The only sound in the room is our joint panting. Brushing my hair aside, he runs his lips against my heated skin. "Did that feel good?" he asks in a gravelly tone of voice.

"Better than good," I say with a grin as I shove the remaining hair off my face and twist around to face him. I scrape my nails down his chest. "But I'm still a little restless."

His lips kick up at the corner, and he pulls my mouth to his, kissing me deeply. "I was hoping you'd say that," he whispers against my swollen lips. "Just give me a couple minutes, and we'll go again." He gets up, disposing of the condom and disappearing. He returns after a bit with a glass of water and two pain pills. Perched naked on the edge of the bed, he holds them out to me. "Take these now so you won't hurt as much in the morning."

"I want to hurt," I honestly admit.

"Oh, you'll hurt, baby." He grins. "But in the right way."

I pop the pills, my heart overflowing as I watch him watching me, the look on his face telling me he's going to fulfil his promise, and then some.

And as we explore each other's bodies, fucking until the early hours of the morning, I know, without a shadow of a doubt, that Axel Thorp is a man of his word.

Chapter Twenty

I wince at my reflection in the mirror the next morning. I didn't check my face before I snuck out of Axel's bed at four thirty a.m., and when I got home, I crawled under my covers straightaway. I apply more makeup to the scratches and bruising on my cheek and cover the gash on my forehead, stifling a yawn. I've only had three hours sleep. Max. But I'm not feeling tired.

I feel invigorated.

Last night was just … wow.

Cam always treated me with kid gloves when we were in bed. Afraid to experiment in case he pushed me out of my comfort zone. I respected him for that, but after last night, I realize what I've been missing out on. Axel is adventurous, and he proved it over and over again. I'm sore down below in a way I've never been sore before, but all it does is inflate my desire to return for more.

Axel made me feel alive last night.

Made me feel normal.

All negative thoughts were banished, and I could get addicted to the feeling. And him.

Downstairs, I wrap up warmly, writing a quick note for my parents who are both still asleep. Mom in her bedroom. Dad on the couch, again. Then I slip outside the house, tumbling head-first into Skeet's arms. "Oh my God." My voice is muffled against his jacket, and he chuckles.

"Morning, gorgeous." He pushes my hair back off my face, inspecting it. "Good job." He lightly traces my injured cheek. "I can hardly see it."

"It'll probably be more noticeable as it darkens, but I've done my best." I shrug, taking his hand as we walk to his truck. "Nothing much I can do about the swelling in my nose though."

"Ice it when you get home tonight and tomorrow, and it should be fine by Monday."

He cranks up the heater once we're both strapped in, reversing the truck out of the driveway.

"You okay today?" he asks, risking a quick glance at me as he drives down the road.

"Yes. I'm sorry for losing it last night. I shouldn't have let her get to me like that."

"You don't need to apologize. I was just worried about you. We all are."

"Well, I'm okay now, so you can stop stressing out." A muscle ticks in his jaw, but he doesn't probe any further. "So, what happened? Considering I wasn't arrested during the night, I'm guessing the cops weren't involved?"

"The cops won't be involved. It won't go any further, so you can relax."

"How did you get both girls to agree to that?"

"Kelsie, the girl who waited on our table, isn't as much of a pro as Cassie. Her coke habit is well known around school, and Heath acquired photographic evidence. Her parents would send her abroad to live with her aunt if they knew she was using again, so it's enough to guarantee her silence."

"Why would Cassie back down because of that?"

"Cassie wants Heath." He eyeballs me. "It's as simple as that. That's why she backed down."

I harrumph. "She all but told me that's just for show. She has no intention of laying off me."

"Heath made it very clear she wasn't to even look sideways at you. He won't hold back if she provokes you again. She understands this is her last warning."

He pulls up in front of the store. "Besides, I think you scared the shit out of her last night. I don't think she'll be risking it again."

I chew on the inside of my cheek, not wanting to admit this but needing to get it off my chest at the same time. I draw a brave breath as I face him, knotting my hands in my lap. "I could've choked her to death, Skeet. I had my hands around her neck, and if I hadn't come to my senses, I…"

"You stopped. That's all that matters." He unfurls my clenched hands, taking them in his callused ones. "Don't beat yourself up about it. Honestly, it's a wonder no one's strangled Cassie yet."

"Please don't make light of it," I whisper. "It's not something to joke about." Now that I've come down from my adrenaline rush and the high of last night, old doubts resurface, mixed with new ones.

Are the haters right? Is there some destructive gene inside me that was inside my brother? Is that why he snapped? Do I have the same violent streak? Or is the stress of the last few months finally finding an exit?

"Hey." He tips my chin up. "I'm just trying to make you feel better." He rubs soothing circles on the back of my hand. "I'm a good listener if you ever want to talk about it."

Tears prick my eyes and I hate how volatile my emotions are right now. "I want to tell you. All of you," I whisper. "But I just can't."

He pulls me over the console onto his lap. We shouldn't be doing this in public, but it's still early, and there's no one around. "It's okay, Blaire." He wraps his arms around me, enveloping me in a reassuring hug. "We're going nowhere. When you're ready to talk, we'll be waiting."

♥♥♥♥

"What the actual fuck?! What the hell happened to your face?" Jacinta asks the second I walk through the door.

I groan. "I didn't think it was that noticeable."

She examines my face, tilting my head from side to side. "It's not. Unless you're like me." I quirk a brow, but she offers no further explanation, rummaging in her purse and pulling out a small bag. "I've professional foundation and concealer in there, stuff they use on movie sets. It'll disguise it fully." She gives me a gentle nudge toward the back area. "Go, put it on. I can't have you scaring all my customers away."

I emerge a few minutes later feeling like I'm caked in mud, but it does the job, and I pass Jacinta's inspection. She insists I take it home with me, so I slip the makeup bag into my purse and get stuck into work.

This is my first Saturday shift, and the store is busy, so I don't notice the hours ticking by until it's almost time to close up. The bell chimes while I'm on my hands and knees behind the counter unloading new stock from a box. "I want a word with you," Jacinta bites out, striding out to greet the customer in a less than pleasant manner, which is so unlike her. While Axel was right—she definitely has a potty mouth—she is never anything but polite and professional with her clientele.

"What'd I do?" a familiar voice says, and I pop my head up over the counter. Axel has his arms folded, and he's in a serious face-off with Jacinta.

"Why does your girl have bruises on her face, and why is she walking like she's in pain?"

Shoot, have I been that obvious? I should've brought some pain pills with me to work.

"What the fuck are you accusing me of?" The venom in Axel's tone sends shivers down my spine, and not the nice kind.

"I don't want to think that of you, but I know what someone looks like after they've taken a beating."

I climb awkwardly to my feet, ignoring my protesting muscles. "Axel didn't hurt me," I say, rounding the counter. "It's not what you're thinking." I quickly explain, giving her as much info as she needs to know.

She shoves Axel's shoulders. "What the hell were you thinking bringing her there!? Are you out of your fucking mind?!"

"Save it. I already got the lecture from Heath and Skeet."

"Well, good." She plants her hands on her hips, her glare bouncing between Axel and me. "At least someone has sense. And you!" She prods her finger in the air in my direction. "Do you have a fucking death wish? Because that's the risk you take in that barn. You think any of those assholes give a shit if you get brain damage or pick up a spinal injury? I didn't realize I hired someone with shit for brains."

"That's enough," Axel growls. "It's none of your business."

"The hell it isn't. Blaire's my staff, and she turned up to work looking like she walked face-first into a wall. It's my responsibility when my staff isn't presentable or fit to work."

"It won't happen again," I rush to reassure her, because I can't lose this job. "I promise. And please don't blame Ax. It was all my idea."

"I'm not buying that for a second." Her foot taps off the floor as she regards Axel. "Do I need to call your brother?"

He purses his lips, looking like he just swallowed something sour. "Do what you like. I'm eighteen now, and he can't do jack shit to me."

"He can throw your punk ass out on the street!" she roars, and I flinch.

"Griff wouldn't do that, and you're overreacting."

"Blaire," she snaps, not looking at me. "Go, grab your things. You can clock out now."

I shuffle to the back room, collecting my jacket, purse, and the paycheck Jacinta handed me an hour ago before hurrying back out. Axel and Jacinta have their heads bent together, and they're talking in hushed tones, so I can't hear what's being said.

"I'm ready." I land beside Axel with a fake cheery smile on my face.

"Let's go." He places his hand on my lower back and leads me to the door.

"Ax. Wait." Jacinta walks toward us. I hover with my hand on the door handle while Axel turns back around. "I'm only saying this because I care. I know you're a good kid, but it's too damn easy to fall back into old habits."

"Like I said, you don't need to worry." Axel's entire body is rigidly still.

Jacinta raises her hand, cupping his cheek. "I'll always worry. Just like I'll always care. And I meant it. I'm here if you need to talk. Anytime."

"Thanks." His tone is sincere, and I'm glad they seem to have worked through their issues.

"Now go look after your girl. Take a warm bath and pop some pills for the pain," she says over his shoulder to me. "I'll see you next Thursday."

"What was all that about?" I ask when we're outside.

"She's worried I'm regressing."

"You fight a lot?"

"Not anymore. For a while, after mom was gone, I went a bit crazy. That's why J was upset." Looping his fingers in the waistband of my jeans, he tugs me toward him, piercing me with a penetrating stare. "Are you okay today?"

I know what he's asking. "Yeah." I smile at him, encircling my arms around his neck. "I've no regrets if that's what you mean."

A layer of stress seems to lift off his shoulders. "Was I too rough with you?"

I shake my head. "No. You were perfect."

151

He slips his hands under my jacket and shirt, and his fingers start caressing my bare skin. I sway in his arms, his touch bringing back a host of delicious memories.

"Perfect, huh?" His lips kick up into a smug smile.

"Cocky much?"

He laughs, a deep full-bellied laugh that does weird things to my insides. "I think you know the answer to that." A red flush creeps up my chest. "You okay to come to my place?" he asks, moving me over to his bike, the smug smile still planted on his mouth. My cheeks inflame as my mind totally goes there, and his smirk expands. He presses his lips to my ear and whispers, "As much as I'd be down for rounds four, five, and six, the guys are coming over. We thought we'd order pizza and watch a few movies."

I ignore the little pang of disappointment that races through me. "That sounds fun."

"Fair warning. Heath will rip us a new one. He doesn't let shit go easy, but it's best to just let him vent and get it out of his system."

"He has every right to be pissed at us, and once it clears the air, I don't care. He can scream and shout all he likes."

Skeet is already inside Axel's house when we arrive. "Hey, dude." He does some elaborate knuckle touch with Axel before swooping me up and swinging me around in his arms. "Hey, gorgeous. How was work?"

"Good. Busy."

He puts me down gently, like I'm precious cargo. "Shit, sorry. Are you sore?"

And, my mind totally goes there again, my cheeks heating alongside my thoughts. Skeet looks at me funny while Axel pins me with a predatory look that doesn't help. I clear my throat and my mind. "A little but I'm fine."

"Griff let you in?" Axel asks Skeet, pushing open the living room door.

Skeet nods. "He was just leaving for work when I arrived." We pile inside the homey living room, and I plop down on the couch, immediately kicking my shoes off.

"Where's Gilchrist?" Axel asks, sitting on the chair across from us and leaning down to untie his boots.

"He's not coming." Skeet flings his arm around my shoulder, crushing me into his side.

Axel stiffens, and a sinking feeling churns in the pit of my stomach. "He's still pissed?" Axel inquires.

Skeet sighs, dragging a hand through his hair. "Yeah, but that's not the full reason. His mom sprung some family dinner on him. They're going over to the McFarlands for the night, and he says his mom wasn't letting him duck out of it."

Axel harrumphs, and Skeet sighs again. "Dude, you know he hates you going to that place, and the fact you took Blaire has infuriated him, but he'll cool down." Skeet sits up straighter. "Provided you both agree not to go there again."

"I've no desire to return," I jump in, trying to rescue the conversation. "It was a one-time thing."

"I'm glad to hear it." He winds his hand through my hair, pulling my head toward his. "This face is far too pretty to mess up." Axel snorts as Skeet melds his mouth to mine, kissing me slowly and deeply. When we surface for air, Axel is perusing a takeout menu. We make our choices, and Axel places our order before pulling up the movies app on the TV.

"Come sit here." I pat the empty space the other side of me.

"I'm good here."

"Pretty please?" I pout my lips and send doe eyes at him. Skeet watches in amusement as Axel rises, crossing over to the couch.

"Don't say it." He pokes his finger at Skeet. "Not one word."

Skeet fake coughs, muttering "pussy whipped" under his breath. Axel glares at him, and I grab his face, smushing it up as I lean in and kiss him. The instant my tongue enters Ax's mouth, he forgets everything, submitting to a heated duel as our tongues battle one another. We're both flushed when we break apart, and I can't keep the grin off my face. I lean back, keeping both boys close beside me, resting my head on Skeet's shoulder, as I settle in to watch the movie.

"You're sneaky," Skeet whispers in my ear. "But I love it."

Chapter Twenty-One

I roll over in bed the next morning, and my body aches all over. I groan, reaching for the pain medication on my bedside table, popping a few pills and washing them down with water.

My hair is still damp after my shower when I mosey downstairs. My parents' bickering reaches my eardrums as I'm descending the stairs, and a heavy weight presses down on my chest.

"Morning," I say in a cheery tone as I enter the kitchen, hoping my presence might break up the argument. But no such luck. My parents don't even acknowledge me as they trade insults.

"I'm only suggesting the local diner," Mom hisses. "Not a Michelin-starred restaurant!"

"It doesn't matter, Mir!" Dad snaps back. "We don't have the money for that either."

"We need to start rebuilding our lives again, Archie. And I want us to go out for dinner today." She finally glances at me, offering me a small smile. "As a family."

"I can treat us," I suggest. "I got paid yesterday."

"That's just fucking great," Dad barks, glaring at Mom. "Now I'm forced to rely on my wife *and* my teenage daughter for handouts. I didn't sign up for this." He starts pacing the tiny kitchen. "I didn't spend countless years studying to end up like this!" The pained look etched across his face slices through me. He looks between Mom and me before hanging his head. "I'm sorry, but I can't do this. I'm going out." He walks with purpose toward the door without looking at either one of us.

"Please, Archie. Don't. Drinking isn't going to solve anything," Mom calls after him.

"It'll make me forget," Dad barks. "And I don't want to think about the shitshow that is my life now."

I watch, helpless, as he grabs his jacket and leaves. Mom is hunched over the kitchen table, sobbing. I cradle her from behind, holding her while she cries. My cell pings in my back pocket, but I ignore it. Rubbing Mom's back, I whisper false assurances that neither one of us believes. When she finally cries herself dry, she looks up at me with haunted eyes. "I think we're losing him. I don't know how to reach him. I don't know what to do!"

Neither do I. And I don't know how to console Mom either, so I'm grasping at straws when I make a suggestion. "Maybe we could look for jobs for him? Send his resume out and try to line up some interviews?"

"Oh, honey. I know you're trying to help, but that might only make things worse. He hates that he can't provide for us, and I'm not sure he has the confidence or the sobriety to attend any interviews right now."

"Well, what about trying to find him a therapist?"

"I don't think he'd go." Her shoulders sag, and her features are thick with sad resignation.

"What does Aunt Jill say?"

"I haven't really spoken to her about this." She scrubs her hands over her face. "We've asked too much of them already."

I crouch down in front of her, pulling her hands from her face. "Talk to your sister, Mom. You need to talk to someone about this, and you know she'll be sympathetic."

She nods, patting my hand. "Yeah, I'll do that." She stands, and I straighten up. She pulls me into her arms. "I'm so sorry, honey. I know this is tough on you, and I appreciate that you aren't causing us any hassle."

I stare at her like she's grown an extra head. "Mom, did you forget I got suspended from school?"

She flaps her hands in the air. "I've spoken to the principal. You were just trying to defend yourself. You didn't cause trouble on purpose."

I turn stiff in her arms, unwilling to accept her understanding, feeling guilty again. She doesn't know about Friday night because Jacinta's magic makeup and Axel's strong pain pills are enabling me to hide the truth from my parents. If she knew what I'd done, she'd be ashamed of me. She certainly wouldn't be thanking me.

"Honey, it's okay. This has been a difficult time for all of us. And you've kept your head down and studied hard this week. You found a job, do more than your fair share around the house, and you barely make a peep." She kisses the top of my head. "So, thank you, for trying to ease the burden." She smiles at me. "I love you, honey. Things might be tense right now, but we both love you so much. Never forget that."

I rest my head on her shoulder, hugging her like I might never get to hug her again. "Thanks, Mom," I whisper. "And I love you too."

After Mom's gone upstairs to call her sister, I fish my cell out of my back pocket and check my messages. I have one unread text from Axel, and I race to the door the second I read it. Grabbing my coat, I slip outside, and thankfully, Axel is still there, sitting on the top step waiting for me.

"Sorry. I only read your message now," I say, sitting down beside him. The stone step is freezing cold, and my butt doesn't thank me for it. I shiver uncontrollably, and Axel moves in closer, lending me some of his body heat.

"S'okay." He looks into my eyes. "Is everything all right?"

His look isn't judgmental, but it's informed. I sigh. "You heard my parents arguing?"

"I caught the tail end, and your dad almost knocked me over when he came charging out of the house." Heat floods my cheeks, and he shakes his head, strands of his jet-black hair tumbling over his forehead with the movement. "Don't be embarrassed."

"He's not usually like this." I pick at a loose thread on the end of my coat. "Things have been strained since Ethan died. Dad hasn't been able to find another job, and that's hard for him to deal with."

"My dad used to hit me," he bluntly says, staring straight ahead.

"I'm so sorry." Reaching out, I brush the loose strands back off his forehead.

He stares at me with that intense lens of his, before pulling me to my feet. "You mind if we go to the lake?"

"Of course not. I love it there."

We ride Axel's bike to the lake, walking side by side as we head to the water's edge. The weather is frigid today, and there aren't that many people about. We sit down in our usual spot, throwing stones into the water.

After a while, he starts opening up. "I spoke with Heath and smoothed things over. He's cool now."

"That's good. I'm glad." I angle my arm back, putting real power behind my throw. We both watch the stone skip over the water before plunging under the surface.

"I need to ask you something." He twists his head around to face me. "Does your dad hit you or your mom? Is that what's going on?"

I vehemently shake my head. "No, that's not it at all. He's never laid a finger on either one of us."

Air whooshes out of his mouth in grateful relief. "Thank fuck."

"I'm sorry if I gave you the wrong impression."

"It's probably just me jumping to conclusions." He skims another stone, and it far exceeds mine, disappearing out of sight before it's even dropped below the surface. "My dad was a bastard," he admits. "Used to hit my mom, and when she wasn't around, he'd hit us too."

A muscle pops in his jaw as he speaks. I want to reach out to him. To offer him comfort. But two things hold me back. One, I sense he wouldn't like that. And, two, we're in public. I can't be seen touching him when I'm now officially Heath's girlfriend. It's something I have to constantly remind myself of when I'm around Skeet and Axel because it's becoming second nature to touch them without thinking.

"Griff took the brunt of it," Axel continues explaining. "When Dad showed up drunk, he'd deliberately provoke him, deflecting attention from me. As he got older, he'd intervene when he was beating Mom." Pain slashes across his face, and I long to hug him, but I say nothing, keeping silent while he unburdens his soul. "The day before my fourteenth birthday, Dad was let go from his job, and he came home in a foul mood. Griff was at football practice, so Dad took his frustration out on me. I tried to fight him off, but he was a heavy fucker, and he had me pinned to the floor, hitting me repeatedly, alternating between a baseball bat and his fists. I could hardly see through all the blood, and I was losing consciousness when he slumped on top of me." He pauses, taking a shaky breath.

Screw this. I slip my hand in his and give him a comforting squeeze.

His face is contorted in pain as he looks at me. "Mom stabbed him in the back. He was bleeding all over me until she pulled him off. I stood in our kitchen watching as she stabbed him repeatedly, over and over again. I mean, we both knew he was dead, but I couldn't move, and she couldn't stop."

I squeeze his hand again, fighting tears.

"Griff called the cops when he got home, and I was taken to hospital for treatment. We both gave statements, and Mom told them about the abuse, but it wasn't enough." His eyes turn cold. "They sent her to prison for murder."

"What? How? It was self-defense!"

"The justice system in this country is a fucking joke. She'd never reported my father, and we were still kids. Griff was almost eighteen but even his word wasn't taken seriously. Dad was well liked in the community. Always the life and soul of the party. Always happy. No one knew what we'd endured behind closed doors. And no one believed us." He shakes his head. "People we thought were our friends turned on us. Others snubbed us like we'd brought shame to the town."

I can relate so well to his experience, and I wish I could tell him my story.

"The only ones who helped were Skeet's parents. Chandra and Michael took on Mom's case pro bono. They did their best to defend her, but criminal law isn't their area of expertise. They did everything to try and prevent her from going to jail, but it didn't work."

"That's awful, Ax. I'm so sorry."

He shrugs. "I lost both my parents that day. Griff became my legal guardian. He gave up his NFL dreams, forgoing college to stay home with me. I owe him everything, and I was a horrible little shit."

"In what way?"

He pulls me in close, cradling me against his chest. "I went off the rails. Fell in with a bad crowd. Spent a couple years high as a fucking kite. Was fighting all the time. I was a hot mess. Almost got expelled from school, and my GPA plummeted. Got sent to juvie for six months for stealing, and it's the only thing that saved me."

He lifts my head up, and I peer into his honest eyes. "I haven't touched drugs since, and I've tried to turn my life around. Got a job and I've been focusing on my studies. I want to repay Griff for all he's done for me. He wants me to go to college, and I owe it to him to try. I've applied for a scholarship to UF, and I'm hoping to join the guys there."

Heath previously mentioned he was going to the University of Florida, but I wasn't aware Skeet was going too and that Axel plans to join them.

At one time, attending university was my primary goal. But my parents were forced to tap into my college fund, and I haven't even completed any college applications, so I doubt I'll be going anywhere after I graduate high school in a few months.

I refocus on Axel. "You hadn't been back to the barn since juvie either. Am I right?" He nods, and I hang my head in shame. I dragged him back into that scene. "Hey, it's okay. I went there for you. Because I knew it'd help."

"And you'd no desire to fight?"

He bites down on his lip. "I'm not going to lie. I was itching for a fight, but I didn't give into it, and I'm not going back." His gaze drills into me. "I've too much to lose to risk it."

Silence engulfs us, and he continues holding me in his arms as I mull over everything he's told me. I'm guessing Axel doesn't tell that story a lot, and I want to return his faith. I want to tell him the truth about me. More than ever, I'm convinced he won't let me down. That none of them will.

"Ax," I whisper. He turns to me with a questioning expression. I swallow nervously over the wedge of emotion clogging my throat. "I lied. My brother didn't die from cancer."

Chapter Twenty-Two

Both our cell phones vibrate at the same time I blurt out my half-truth. Neither of us reaches for them. We stay locked in position, staring at one another. I'm trembling. Trying to force the rest of the words out of my mouth, but they refuse to come. I've always had trust issues. Wanting to be up front isn't the issue. Trusting others to accept the truth is the real problem.

"It's okay, Blaire." Axel looks deep into my eyes, as if he can see all the way through to my blackened soul.

"No, it's not. I want to tell you, but I'm scared." All my bravado has evaporated, and now, I'm petrified to tell him. *What if I'm wrong? What if they all think I'm a monster too? What if they turn on me and tell everyone our secret?* I promised my parents I wouldn't tell a soul and they'll be devastated if this gets out. I scramble to my feet, staggering back. "I'm sorry. I have to go."

I run off, and he follows, taking me by the arm and forcing me to stop. "Blaire. Stop."

I can't even look at him. My head's a mess. And guilt threatens to destroy me. *He* trusted *me*. He bared his soul, and I can't do the same. "I can't," I cry. "I want to, but I can't."

"It's okay." He grips my face between his palms. "You don't have to tell me until you're ready. Or ever."

"I really want to, Ax. I really do, but I'm so scared you'll all want nothing to do with me when you find out."

"Trust me, there's nothing you can say that'll change our minds."

Our cells vibrate again, and Ax lets out a frustrated sigh, pulling his out and checking the unread messages. "It's Skeet. Inviting us to his house for dinner."

I nod my head in agreement. "Let's go." Hanging with Shaz is just what I need right now. "I'll text my mom."

Axel doesn't mention anything else about my little outburst, and I force it from my mind. When we rock up to the Taylors' house, Heath is waiting outside for us. He shuffles awkwardly on his feet while Axel helps me off his bike. "Can we talk?" Heath asks, once I've removed the helmet from my head.

"Sure."

Axel strides off without a word, automatically giving us privacy.

"I'm sorry." We both speak at the same time, and then we both smile.

"I shouldn't have lost my temper like that," he explains, pinning me with an earnest look.

"And I shouldn't have acted so recklessly."

"Does that mean I'm forgiven?" His brows climb to his forehead.

I press up against him. "There's nothing to forgive."

His arms sweep around me, and he kisses me softly on the lips. "Did Axel tell you?" he inquires, and I nod. "Axel and Skeet are like my brothers. When something happens to one of them, it's my problem too. We lost Axel there for a while, and seeing him around that place again ..." Sadness ghosts over his handsome face as he trails off.

"I get it. And he's lucky he has such good friends." There's no doubt Heath and Skeet are at the top of the loyal-friendship pyramid.

"So, we're good?"

"We're good." I peck him on the lips briefly. Tucking me under his arm, he leads me into the house.

Dinner is a blast. Everyone is crowded around the dining table, passing dishes around, as conversation flows naturally. I'm seated in between Heath and Shaz, and there's never a dull moment.

After cleanup, we hit the basement. Skeet's dad Liam joins him in an impromptu session, and we lounge on the couch listening to them play a full set.

I ditch the guys for a while to hang with Shaz in her room, and we take turns painting our nails and shooting the shit.

When it's dark outside, Heath drives me home. He gives me a long, lingering kiss that steams up the windows of his SUV before walking me to the front door like the gentleman he is. The curtains twitch, and I scowl. "My mom would make a lousy spy."

Heath grins. "At least you're forewarned."

"True."

He takes my hands in his. "Are you still okay being a couple in school tomorrow?"

I stretch up on tiptoes and kiss him one final time. "Yes. Let's do this."

"Cool." His smile radiates happiness. "I'll drop by and pick you up first thing." He dots a quick kiss on my lips. "See you in the morning, Blaire."

I wave him off and then step inside. Predictably, Mom is waiting for me in the hallway. "Did you have fun with your friends?"

"I did. Thanks. Skeet's family is great."

She leans against the wall, a chaste smile playing on her lips. "So, do I have to drag it out of you?"

I might as well get this over and done with. "You saw me kissing Heath."

She bobs her head. "He seems like a nice boy."

"He is, and, yes, we're dating."

Tears prick her eyes, and a wave of concern washes over me. She steps forward, tucking my hair back behind my ears. "This move has been good for you. I'm glad. You deserve to be happy."

I'm not sure I do. "Thanks, Mom. I'm going to grab a shower, do some studying, and then get an early night." I kiss her on the cheek. "I'll see you in the morning."

"Okay. Night, honey."

I peek in the living room, but Dad is nowhere to be seen. I hope he hasn't been in the bar all day because that's one surefire way of guaranteeing my parents will be arguing tonight.

After I shower, blow dry my hair, and change into pajama pants and a long-sleeved top, I power up my laptop and log in to my school email. I need to double-check the time I'm to report to the principal's office in the morning.

All week, my nerves have been hanging by a thread each time I've logged on, expecting to see another nasty message. My breath escapes in a shuddering puff of air when I notice no new emails in my inbox. I recheck the time of my meeting and text Heath so he knows what time to pick me up. Then I get stuck into my books, quickly losing track of time.

My laptop pings a couple of hours later, when I've just decided to call it quits for the night, and I freeze. Bile floods my mouth, and butterflies scatter among my chest. I sit ramrod straight on the bed, as if frozen and mute, unable to force myself to move. After a couple minutes, I give myself a stern talking to, slowly getting up, and walking to my desk. With shaking hands, I open my laptop and stare at the new message in my inbox.

I wrap my arms around myself as I stare at the screen in horror. It's from the same person: truthseeker101. I'm tempted to delete it or move it over to the folder I set up for these messages without reading it, but that would be taking the coward's way out. If someone is targeting me, it's better to know what I'm up against. I open up the email.

You can run, but you can't hide. No matter where you go, I will find you. Does your new boyfriend know what a lying bitch you are? If you won't tell him the truth, I will.

I clasp my hand over my mouth and stare at the words in shock. I can't figure out how this person knows so much. And I don't know whether the threat is an empty one or not. My stomach tightens at the thought of Heath, or any of the guys, finding out the truth from a stranger. I'm in a daze as I log off my laptop, switch off my light, and crawl into bed.

My mind churns restlessly the whole night as I debate scenarios in my head.

By morning, I'm no clearer as to what I should do, and I have no choice but to push my concerns aside as I join Heath for the ride to school. I need to keep my wits about me today, and freaking out over these emails won't do anything to help.

People stare as Heath and I walk hand in hand through the hall toward my locker. I pull at my collar, my skin itching like bugs are crawling all over me. "Relax, Blaire," he whispers, squeezing my hand. "Just pretend they're all naked." He winks, and I burst out laughing.

"Eh, yeah, I don't think that'll help much," I mumble, as we pass a bunch of his football buddies, and now I'm imagining them without clothes on. My skin heats. Yeah, definitely not helpful. A few catcalls ring out, and Heath flips his teammates the bird, but he's smiling.

I manage to make it through the rest of the day unscathed. Even Cassie and her crew stay out of my face, although they glare at me any chance they get, but at least Cassie finally seems to have gotten the memo, and she's leaving me alone.

The rest of the week flies by. Between school, work, homework, helping Heath study, and hanging with the guys, I flop into bed exhausted most nights. And I'm grateful. Because I fall into such a deep sleep that it keeps the usual nightmares at bay.

Chapter Twenty-Three

 *H*eath collects me after work Friday, and we catch a movie at the local theater. I kinda feel bad that I can't go on normal dates with Axel and Skeet, but there's no way I'm ready to let the whole town know about our relationship. I need to build my courage before I can face that one.

We make out like demons in the back row, groping each other in a way that proves we're both hot for one another.

"Want to come back to my place for a while?" Heath asks as he bundles me up in his arms when we leave the theater.

"Won't your parents mind?" It's after eleven thirty already.

"They're at a party. Won't be home till late, and my younger brother and sister will be tucked up in bed by now."

"Okay then. I can stay for a little while." I send Mom a quick text in case she's wondering where I am. She knew about my date with Heath, but she's probably expecting me home soon.

This is my first time at Heath's house, and my jaw hits the floor as we pull up in front of ornate gates, fronting a massive, modern two-story property. It's all glass and wood, and it looks super stylish. "Wow, what did you say your dad did again?" I ask as Heath pulls into a wide garage, parking alongside a sleek, silver Aston Martin. Another new SUV is parked beside it, and a red sporty number completes the collection.

"He owns his own engineering company. They won a couple of massive contracts a few years back that set them on the map, and my parents bought this place after that. Before that, we lived five houses up from Skeet."

"That's impressive," I add, climbing out of the car.

Heath takes my hand, leading me into the house through a side door. "Dad's firm is the number one engineering company in the state now," he proudly declares.

"Are you expected to take over when you're older?"

He nods, leading me into the kitchen and making a beeline for the refrigerator. "You want something?" he asks with his head in the fridge.

"Water, thanks." He takes out a couple bottles of water and some strange red concoction. "What's that?" I ask, scrunching my nose up.

"One of my shakes. I didn't consume enough calories today."

"Ah. Of course." The guys were right. Heath is diligent.

He guides me to a large room at the side of the house, and we flop down beside one another on a long couch. He flicks on the TV, handing me my water. I watch, mesmerized as he knocks back the contents of his shake in three steady gulps before washing it down with water. The way his throat works is sexy as hell. Add his rippling muscles to the package and my libido is suddenly wide awake. He glances at me, grinning when he notices my expression. Pinning me with a heated look, he wiggles his fingers at me. "Come closer, baby."

I set my bottle down and crawl into his lap. His lips instantly seal to mine, and I kiss him back with the same fervor, wrapping my arms around his muscular arms and up over his shoulders to his neck. My fingers rub across the velvety-smooth hairs at his nape, and he groans into my mouth, deepening the kiss while rocking his hips into mine. I reposition myself so I'm straddling him, and he takes advantage, his hand creeping under my sweater and shirt, caressing the bare skin of my back.

"Heath," I whisper, against his lips, grabbing fistfuls of his hair.

"You feel so good," he whispers back as his hands start climbing. I thrust my crotch against him, and he pushes back, hardening against me and elevating my desire another couple of levels.

When his hand cups my breast through my bra, and he starts kneading my sensitive flesh, I cry out, rocking against him with more urgency.

"Heath? What on earth is going on here?" a deep masculine voice demands, and I jerk back with a shriek. My cheeks instantly flare up as I look at the well-dressed man and woman staring at us in horror.

Heath pales, lifting me off him and helping to straighten my clothing. I don't say a word, waiting for him to set the lead. "This is Blaire," he says. "She's new to town."

I smile awkwardly. "It's nice to meet you, Mr. and Mrs. Gilchrist."

"It's late," his mom snaps, and I balk at her tone and the derision on her face. "I think it's time your guest went home."

Heath nods curtly. "I'll drop Blaire home."

"I'd like a quick word please, son," his father says. "My wife will show you out, Blaire." He offers me a small smile that seems genuine. "Welcome to town."

"Thank you, sir."

I don't look at Heath as I follow his mother out of the room. She walks slightly ahead of me, not uttering a word. But her steely spine and the frigid air swirling around us is enough to tell me all I need to know.

And I get it.

They think Heath's with Cassie and I'm some slut on the side. I wish that didn't bother me so much. I knew what I was getting into when I agreed to this relationship, so I've no right to complain now.

The second we reach the garage, she spins around, facing me with a furious expression. "I don't know what your game is, young lady, but you need to stay away from my son. He's in a serious relationship." She looks me up and down. "And it's clear he's only after one thing with you."

Pain stabs me through the heart, and my stomach twists into knots at her insinuation. I want to retaliate, but I don't know how to respond without getting Heath into trouble, so I say nothing, staring at the ground and wishing it could swallow me alive.

"Here." She shoves her cell in my face, and another pain slices across my chest. "This is my son's girlfriend, his future wife. See how happy they are?" I stare at the photos of Cassie and Heath with a sick feeling in my stomach. The date stamp clearly indicates it was the dinner from last week. Not only does Heath have his arms draped all over Cassie, but he's kissing her too.

A myriad of emotions assaults me from all sides, and I'm momentarily tempted to tell her the truth. But that's only hurt talking, so I do what I do best, keep my lips sealed, trapping the truth inside.

"Mom!" Heath shouts from behind me. "What are you doing?"

She jerks her chin upright. "I'm just educating your little slut."

"Mother!" Shock splays across his face. "Blaire is not a slut, and please don't speak to her like that." He shakes his head in disgust. "If you must know, she's my—"

"Can you please take me home now." I deliberately cut him off. "I want to go home."

"Goodbye, Blaire." Mrs. Gilchrist's tone is like ice. "And in case I wasn't clear, you're not welcome in my home. Leave my son alone. He's already spoken for."

"Mom!" Heath looks disgusted. "I won't allow you to treat Blaire like that. No matter what you think you know, you're mistaken. You don't have all the facts."

She walks right up to her son, jabbing his chest with her finger. "I know this is my home, and I make the rules. That slut is not to step foot in my house again. And don't you dare speak to me like that. Don't test me, Heath. I'm warning you."

She holds my gaze for another few seconds before striding off, her stiletto heels making a clackety-clack sound on the granite floor.

"Blaire, I'm so sor—"

"Can we please leave. Now." I round the car, grabbing the passenger door handle and climbing inside.

"Blaire, please. Don't be like this," he says, sitting behind the wheel but facing me. "This is all my fault, and I'm so, so sorry. She had no right to speak to you like that, and I'm sorry she upset you."

I harrumph. While I didn't like being spoken down to like that, his bitch of a mom isn't the reason I'm struggling to keep my tears at bay. That's all on Heath.

"I shouldn't have brought you here," he continues, "but they're never home before two from these things. I honestly thought it was safe."

"Please drive," I say, talking to the window. I can't look at his face. In this moment, I don't trust a single word that comes out of his mouth.

"Baby, please."

Fire blazes in my eyes as I pin my angry gaze on him. "Don't call me baby. I don't want to hear any more of your lies. Just drive me home."

"I know you're mad, but—"

"You don't know how I feel, so stop pretending like you know me." I fish my cell out of my bag. "Either drive me home or I'm calling Axel to come get me."

A muscle ticks in his jaw. "That won't be necessary." The engine purrs to life. "I'll drive you home."

We don't speak again until we reach my house. We both sit there in the dark, fuming.

"I'll tell them the truth. I'll tell them you're my girlfriend," he says, breaking the silence.

"But am I?"

"What does that mean?"

"You know what it means," I hiss. "Don't play me for a fool."

"Look, I don't know exactly what my mom said, but it's not true. And I'm sorry for how she treated you. I'd like to say it's because of the misunderstanding, but it's not. Mom's a snob, and she has very set ideas for my future."

I grip my bag close to my chest, fighting angry tears. "I get it. I'm not good enough for her precious son, but that manipulative bitch is."

I move to get out, but he reaches over, pulling the door shut again. "Blaire, please don't leave like this. I'll fix this, I promise."

I turn the full extent of my rage on him. "How? You can't exactly un-kiss Cassie now, can you?"

He pales again. "What?"

"Don't even try to deny it. I saw the photos."

He wets his lips, and his chest heaves. Guilt splays across his face. "I know it looks bad, but I can explain."

I harrumph. "Ya think?" Sarcasm is thick in my tone.

"I didn't want to kiss her, I swear, but I was backed into a corner. Mom wanted some photos of us, and both sets of parents were teasing us to kiss. They would've smelled a rat if I didn't do it."

I shove his arm away. "Whatever, Heath." I get out of the car. "I don't know what sick and twisted game you're playing, but I want no part of it. I shouldn't have agreed to this, so I guess I'm partly to blame, but I'm out now." I slam the door shut and walk briskly toward my front door.

Heath races after me, grabbing my elbow. "What do you mean, you're out now?"

"I mean we're finished. I never should've gotten involved with you in the first place. All it's done is bring Cassie down on me. If she wants you that badly, she can have you." I wrest my arm free. "Just leave me the hell alone."

Chapter Twenty-Four

My mood hasn't improved by the following morning, but I'm not sorry I spoke my mind. I won't be played for a fool. I'm sickened at the thought of Heath kissing Cassie behind my back. Oh, how she must have gloated over that. And even though Heath defended me to his mom, her vitriol still hurts, prodding at festering wounds that never fully heal.

I was a fool to think this would work. I'm not equipped to deal with the drama. The plan was to come here and lay low. Not to invoke more unwanted attention. I let stupid fantasies fill my head instead of focusing on reality. There's no reality where me being in a relationship with three guys will ever work out. Public scrutiny and my past will always be the obstacle in my path. Cutting people out of my life is the only way to survive the fallout from Amber Springs. My hormones and my heart might have forgotten the memo, but my brain needs little reminding.

I'm not surprised to see Skeet waiting for me outside. I knew either him or Axel would show up this morning. "I'm taking my mom's car today, so I don't need a ride," I say before he can speak.

"Let me drive you. Please. We need to talk."

I sigh. "I know, but I can't do this now. I have to get to work."

"At least let me pick you up after your shift, and we can go somewhere to talk."

"I'm in a shitty mood, Skeet, and I just need some time."

"We don't want to lose you." His eyes plead with me, and all I want is to collapse into his arms and let him comfort me, but I can't.

"I'll talk to you later." I brush past him and climb into Mom's car, reversing out of the drive and leaving him standing, looking all forlorn, on the sidewalk.

I stay locked in my shell at work, focusing on my tasks and keeping myself busy so I don't think about the three guys who are a permanent fixture in my mind. Jacinta notices, asking me if I need to talk about anything, but I downplay it, plastering fake smiles on my face every time she inquires. My jaw actually hurts from all the fake smiling by the time my shift draws to a close.

For the first time, no one is waiting for me outside the store, and my stomach tightens in pain, which is stupid because it's what I told them I wanted. I'm such a hot mess right now. I told Heath we were done, and I told Skeet this morning I needed space, so I have no right to feel pissed at the fact no one showed up tonight.

The house is bathed in darkness, and deathly quiet, when I arrive home, much like my mood. I take a quick shower and change into my pajamas. Grabbing a tub of ice cream and a spoon, I sprawl along the couch with a blanket covering me, while I binge-watch *Vampire Diaries* for the millionth time. But even Damon and Stefan Salvatore can't rouse me from my rotten mood.

I give up trying, crawling into bed at ten, snatching my cell up every ten minutes to check for new messages that never arrive. Pain lodges in my throat, and tears linger at the back of my eyes. My heart is heavy as I glance at the picture on my bedside table. Ethan's beautiful smiling face mocks me from the photo, and the tears fall free, streaming down my face.

"Why, E?" I whisper, running my finger across the image of his face. "Why did you have to leave me? I don't think I'm strong enough to do this without you." A shuddering sob rings out in the empty room. "You were always my better half, and now I'm just sinking." I continue talking to the photo, while rubbing my hand across my chest, attempting to ease the piercing pain spearing me from the inside. "I don't know what to do, and I need you. I need you to tell me what to do. To tell me everything's going to be okay even if it's not." My tears transform to full-blown sobs. "Even if it's a lie, I need to hear it." I flip onto my back, clutching the photo frame to my chest, staring through blurry eyes at the ceiling. "Please, E. If you're there, please give me a sign. Please help me. I need you."

I'm well aware of how pitiful I am, staring into the dark, appealing to my brother's ghost to appear. It's how I spent every night the first couple months after he died. Begging him to show up. To haunt me. I'd take him any way I could get him. I've heard stories, watched movies, and read books where loved ones showed up after death, and I silently begged for it to be real. But maybe my previous cynicism worked against me. Because my brother's ghost never appeared, and I stopped clinging to falsehoods.

The fact I'm back in that space isn't a good sign. Nor is the fact I strip off my pajamas, redressing in one of Ethan's old shirts, crying harder when the faint masculine smell tickles my nostrils, my brother's scent still clinging to the fabric even though he's no longer here. I ball up into a fetal position, hugging the photo to my chest as I cry myself to sleep.

A subtle *tap-tap* rouses me from sleep very early the next morning. Confused, I sit up, looking around the semi-dark room. The noise sounds again, and I swing my legs out of bed, placing the photo on top of the comforter. My hands are stiff from holding it all night, and I curl and uncurl my fingers as I walk to the window, pulling the drapes aside.

Axel is perched, rather precariously, on the thickest branch of the old tree that rests alongside my bedroom window, gesturing for me to let him in. Shaking off my shock, I open the window and help him inside. He's dressed in his running gear, his hair hidden behind a snug hat.

"How the hell did you scale that tree?"

"It wasn't without challenge." He smirks, looking pleased with himself.

My eyes drift to his muscular legs, noting the multitude of scrapes and the small trickle of blood running down his left shin. "You're crazy."

He shrugs, smiling, like it's a compliment. "You didn't answer my text, and I didn't want to ring the bell so early in the morning."

"You could've just run alone."

He pins me with an earnest stare. "I like running with you." His eyes drop lower, raking up and down my bare legs. "And something tells me you need the physical exertion today." Axel mustn't have received the "give Blaire space" memo. Or he's choosing to ignore my directive, which is more his modus operandi. His eyes move up my body. "Nice shirt. I love *Reckless Scary Bastards.*"

"Ethan loved them too," I whisper, wrapping my arms around my body, feeling exposed and vulnerable.

"Hey." Carefully, he inches toward me. "I'll go if you really want to be alone."

"Don't go," I whisper, failing to make eye contact for fear of what I'll reveal.

He closes the gap between us, reeling me into his arms. Warmth seeps from his body to mine, chilling some of the newly frozen parts. "I'm not going anywhere," he promises, resting his chin on my head. We stay like that for a few minutes until a huge shiver rocks my body, and I'm trembling in his arms. "You cold?" he inquires, tipping my face up, and I nod.

"Could you … could *we* just lie in bed for a while?" I peek up at him, and all I see is empathy in his eyes. "Could you just hold me?"

Without uttering a word, he takes my hand, leading me back to the bed. He tucks me under the covers and moves to get in alongside me, faltering when he spots the photo tossed on top of the comforter. His eyes flit to mine, and I'm sure he sees the panic there.

What if he recognizes Ethan?

His picture was splashed everywhere for weeks after the shooting. But it's too late. Axel is staring at the photo of me and Ethan, our arms wrapped around each other. "Wow. You both look so alike." Kicking off his shoes, he climbs into bed, instantly opening his arm for me. I snuggle into his side, scarcely breathing. Axel clutches the photo frame in his free hand. "Why does he look familiar?" His brow puckers, and I damn near have a coronary.

Snatching the photo out of his hand, I place it facedown on my bedside table. "He just has one of those faces, and I'd rather not talk about him or the fact Heath's been kissing Cassie behind my back."

Axel's response is to draw me closer to him, wrapping his other arm around my body. The steady beat of his heart under my ear is soothing, and I'm almost lulled back to sleep. After a short while, he checks the time on his watch and clears his throat. "As much as I'd love to stay here with you, I'm sure your parents wouldn't be pleased to find me here." He tilts my face up to look at him. "How about a quick run, and then you can come back to my house, and I'll make you breakfast."

"Are you sure your brother won't mind?"

He shakes his head. "Griff won't surface till lunchtime. Saturday nights are always his busiest, and he rarely gets in before five. And even if he was up, he wouldn't mind." He pauses for a beat, biting sexily on his lip. "He knows about you, and he'd love to meet you."

"Yeah?"

He kisses my forehead. "Yeah."

I snuggle into Ax, holding him tighter for a couple minutes before I release him. "Okay. Let me get changed, and then we'll go."

Ten minutes later, we set off, running our usual route. We don't speak, and I love how in tune he is with me. An hour and a half later, we arrive at his house, both sweating profusely and in bad need of a shower.

"You go first," Axel says in a whisper on the landing, thrusting a fluffy white towel into my arms.

I channel my inner seductress, narrowing my eyes and licking my lips. "We could always shower together."

He pushes me into the wall, caging me between his arms while leveling a dark gaze on me. "Showering won't be all we're doing if I go in there with you," he warns, his voice rough and husky.

"Why do you think I suggested it?"

His lips descend on mine, and he kisses me deeply. I pant into his mouth, clutching at his waist, pulling him flush against me. The evidence of his arousal, prodding my stomach, coils my insides into delicious knots, and I'm already so wet for him. I whimper when he suddenly pulls back. "Are you sure, Blaire?" His eyes examine mine carefully. "I thought you needed space."

I was right. He *was* purposely ignoring my wishes, yet I can't find it in me to criticize him for it. Not when he seems to know what I need better than I know myself. "I do." I sigh. "I don't. I … I don't know."

"And that's exactly why we shouldn't." He kisses my cheek, moving to step away.

"No." I fist my hand in his shirt, pulling him back into me. "I need to feel … something real." My eyes convey every emotion racing through me. "Please, Ax. I just … I just need you."

He nods slowly, understanding washing over his features. Grabbing another towel from the cabinet, he leads me into the bathroom. Locking the door, he stalks toward me with fierce determination. He makes quick work of my sweaty clothing, peeling the layers off until I'm stark naked in front of him. I watch as he strips off his own clothes, adding them to the sodden pile on the floor. Then he turns on the shower, tests the water, and gets in, holding out his hand for me.

We take turns washing each other, still not speaking, but we don't need words. His hands linger on my breasts, and my breath hitches in my throat when he lowers the sponge, washing between my legs. Heat pools in my core, throbbing and pulsing as expectation rises. I close my eyes, moaning, as he washes and conditions my hair. Then I turn the tables, relishing the feel of his body under my hands as I wash every delectable inch of him.

His cock stands proud and erect, and I drop to my knees, without invitation, taking him deep into my mouth. He steadies himself with one hand against the tile wall, doing his best to stifle his moans as I work him over, licking him from tip to root before drawing his full length into my mouth and sucking him hard. After a couple minutes, he pulls me off, lifting me up and positioning me with my hands spread on the wall and my butt jutting up in the air. I suffer a bout of momentary panic, squeezing my eyes shut to ward off the images. His hands move to my hips, digging in hard as his length nudges my entrance. "You sure you want this?"

This is the most vulnerable I've been with him, but I still can't say no. "Please, and I'm on the pill," I add, considering we've no condom with us. My raspy plea is all he needs, and there's no further hesitation.

He ruts into me from behind, bucking in fast, furious thrusts while his mouth trails up my spine and over my neck. He plants hungry kisses along my neck and jawline, tugging on my earlobe, making me moan louder. "Shush, baby. I'd rather we didn't wake Griff."

His hand snakes around my front, and he plays with my clit, rubbing it softly, then firmly, matching the thrusts of his cock. Every time I'm close, he pulls back, leaving me whimpering and writhing underneath him. "Together, babe," he whispers before sucking on my neck, almost painfully. He picks up the pace, squeezing my hips as he rotates his pelvis, sliding deep.

"Axel," I moan, needing release as much as oxygen.

"Let go, baby." He pounds into me, harder and harder, flexing his hips the same time he pinches my clit. I explode, and he plants a hand over my mouth, containing my screams of pleasure. He comes deep inside me, gritting his teeth and restraining his own blissful roars.

He stills inside me, and we both try to get a grip on our breathing. I don't realize I'm crying until he turns me around, his face turning ashen. "Shit. Did I hurt you?"

"No! Not at all." I cup his horrified face, smoothing out the furrowed lines on his brow. "You make me feel alive, Axel. Sex with you makes me feel alive, and sex has never been like that for me. I'm just a little over-whelmed but not in bad way."

"Are you sure?" He doesn't look convinced.

I cup his face more firmly. "I'm sure. I love having sex with you. The fact I'm crying is all me, not you. I told you I was a hot mess, and I meant it."

"If it helps, sex with you is different for me too. I've never felt con-nected to anyone the way I feel connected to you." He kisses me softly on the lips. "And it's not just sex. I've told you things I don't tell anyone. Usually, it's hard for me to open up, but not with you." He caresses my cheek. "Never with you."

"And you don't mind that I'm a little cray-cray?"

He smirks, arching a brow. "You really want to play that game? Because I'm sure my cray-cray beats your cray-cray hands down."

A genuine smile graces my lips, and I'm opening my mouth to respond when someone knocks unexpectedly on the door, startling me. I shriek, grabbing Axel and using his body to shelter me from unwelcome visitors. "Relax," he whispers, extracting my hands from his waist. "The door is locked, and he can't come in." Axel switches off the shower and steps out, securing a towel around his waist. Grabbing the other towel, he hands it to me, and I wrap it gratefully around my body, hanging back while he goes to open the door. The towel hugs his body like a glove, showcasing his muscled back, slim hips, and shapely ass. Beads of water cling to his skin, and with his wet, slicked-back hair and muscular physique, he looks like he just stepped off the pages of *GQ*.

He eases the door open a bit, ensuring I'm protected from view. A hushed conversation ensues which I'm not privy to. Ax shakes his head before closing the door a couple minutes later. "C'mon. The coast is clear."

I take his outstretched hand, glancing nervously around me as we move from the bathroom to his bedroom. Axel rummages in his closet while I curse my lack of foresight. I should've brought a change of clothes, but clearly, my brain had disengaged. "Will these do?" He hands me a long-sleeved T-shirt and a pair of his boxers. "I'll put our stuff in the laundry while you get changed." Dropping his towel, he pulls on sweatpants and a tank while I try my best not to ogle him.

He looks over at me, still standing with the pile of clothes in my arms, and his gaze turns heated. He stalks toward me, and I suck in a breath. "Keep looking at me like that, and we won't make it down to breakfast," he growls, pulling me against him and crashing his mouth down against mine. I sway against him, drowning in his heavenly kisses. My lips are swollen when he finally pulls back. "Fuck, you make me so horny."

I beam at him, wondering what alternate universe I've wandered into. I still can't believe three of the hottest guys in town are into me as much as I'm into them.

Screw my dark thoughts from yesterday.

There's no way I can keep my distance from the guys. They're *mine*. And, as the saying goes, there's no pain without gain. It may be messy, it may get messier, but the best things in life usually are. And I believe our relationship is worth fighting for.

So, I'll just have to find a way to make it work.

Chapter Twenty-Five

The hum of quiet conversation filters out of the kitchen to greet me as I walk down the stairs and along the small hallway. Axel's brother must have people over. Glancing down at myself, I self-consciously smooth a hand over the front of Axel's clothes. Stepping into the kitchen dressed in his clothes will be a dead giveaway, but it's not like I've any choice. I can't cower in the bathroom until they leave, no matter how appealing that sounds.

My heart thrashes around my ribcage as I hold my head up high and step into the kitchen, instantly gasping when I see who it is. "What the hell's going on?" Suspicion combines with hurt in my tone.

"Don't get mad," Skeet says, moving quickly to my side. "We needed to stage an intervention, and we were afraid you wouldn't come if you knew we were all here."

Heath's gaze roams over my clothes, and a strange expression appears on his face. I whip my head around to the stove, staring at Axel with hurt in my eyes. He's in front of me in an instant, pulling me to him. "Don't even think it for a second," he whispers into my ear. "What happened upstairs was real and unplanned. All I agreed to do was get you here for breakfast so we could speak to you."

His words and the genuine expression on his face reassure me, and my shoulders relax. "Okay."

He closes his eyes briefly before kissing me softly on the lips. With a cheeky wink, he returns to the stove.

"I know you said you needed space," Skeet continues, linking his fingers in mine, "but we also agreed to openly communicate and not let things fester. Let's talk it through, and if you still need some time, then you have it."

I bob my head. "Okay, and I'm not mad." My head jerks involuntarily in Heath's direction, and my eyes narrow before I refocus on Skeet. "At you or Ax." I'm not letting Heath off that easily. I'm still hurt over his betrayal, even if I can understand he felt trapped into it.

Heath rounds the island unit, stopping in front of me. "I'm so sorry, Blaire. I fucked up, but I promise it won't happen again."

"We've only just gotten together, only just gone public with our relationship, and you're kissing her behind my back?"

"Blaire, please. It wasn't like that." He rubs a hand along the back of his neck.

"How would you feel if I was having cozy family dinners with my ex and my mom thrust a photo of me kissing him in your face?"

His eyes drop, and shame washes over his face. "I'd be hurt and disappointed in you, and I'd want to kick the shit out of your asshole ex."

"And that's exactly how I feel. She hates me, Heath, but I could be any girl. She'd hate any girl who has the potential to take you away from her, in her eyes. She's not going to stop, and if I can't trust you to be on my side, then why are we even dating?"

"You can trust me. I swear. I don't want her to ruin things between us, and you're the only one I care about. I don't care what my parents want anymore. I'm going to prove to you that I'm genuine." Determination glints in his eye as he moves toward me, gingerly taking my hand and planting a soft kiss on it. Before I have a chance to respond, he rushes on. "I'm going to come clean with my parents. Fess up about the fake relationship with Cassie and tell them you're my real girlfriend."

"You'd really do that for me?"

"Yes. And I'll do whatever else you want me to do to prove I'm serious about us. Just tell me what you want me to do and I'll do it."

"How do you think they'll react?" I inquire, peering up at him. He shrugs casually as if it's no biggie. "Don't do that," I protest, shaking my head. "Honesty. Remember?" I plant my hands on my hips and slant a pointed look at him.

He sighs, clawing a hand through his dirty blond hair, sending waves tumbling in every direction. "They'll be pissed that I've been lying."

"And," Skeet prompts, spearing him with a cautionary look.

"And they'll probably threaten to pull my college fund, and insist I join Dad's firm instead, but they won't mean it."

"No." My tone brokers no argument. "You can't tell them the truth if it risks your dreams. No way." I cannot have that on my conscience.

Axel sends a smug look over his shoulder. "Told you." Heath flips him the bird, and Skeet chuckles.

"What did I miss?" My gaze dances between them, waiting for someone to fill me in.

"Ax and I both predicted you'd respond like this, but Heath was insistent you'd want him to fess up."

"You think I'm that selfish?"

"What? No!" Heath gulps. "That's not it. I saw how hurt you were Friday night, and I know how important the truth is to you. Even before you said it just now, I could see it in your eyes."

His words penetrate bone deep, and it's like someone just stuck a dagger in my back. I work hard to contain my true emotions. "The truth *is* everything, but sometimes the truth has to be sacrificed for the greater good." I almost choke on the words, but if they notice, they don't comment. "I don't think you should tell your parents the truth. Not if it risks your future. I don't want that."

"Are you sure? I hate that I'm putting you in this position." Heath wears a strained look.

"I'm sure. I couldn't live with myself if you lost out on your football dreams because of me. I'm hurt and upset, but I'll get over it once you promise I have your loyalty."

Skeet lets go of my hand, kissing my cheek before walking to Axel's side, helping him plate up our food.

"I won't touch her again," Heath rushes to reassure me. "I promise. No matter what, I won't let you down again."

I exhale loudly. "Okay, I believe you."

His arms go around me instantaneously, and a shuddering breath of relief leaves his body. "Thank you, and I'm so sorry. I never want to hurt you. Ever."

All the tension has left the room, and we enjoy our breakfast, chatting and making plans for the coming week. It's like a bucket-load of stress has been lifted from my shoulders, and I know, without a shadow of doubt, that these guys are the glue holding me together right now. I'm not sure why they need me, but I know *I* need *them*. They are the first people I've truly connected with in years, and I was a fool to even consider walking away. I feel almost normal, almost human, when I'm with them, and I want to drown in those feelings until I believe it's real.

Heath is the first to leave. To go to another family engagement. A lunch gathering this time. Sans Cassie and the McFarlands—thank God. I walk him to his car, swathed in Ax's leather jacket. "So, we're good?" Heath asks, shoving his hands in the pockets of his jeans. "Shit, I seem to always be saying that to you."

"Let's try not to make it a habit," I suggest, stretching up to kiss him. He takes my chaste kiss and multiplies it a thousand-fold, worshiping my lips and exploring my mouth with his tongue. When we break apart, I'm panting and in need of an oxygen fix.

"Maybe we should fight more often," he teases, palming my face. "If it means we get to make up like that."

"Eh, no thanks. I've had enough arguing to last a lifetime." He frowns, but before he can quiz me, I push him toward his car. "You need to go, and I need to get back inside before the neighbors spot me dressed like this." I gesture to myself, and Heath opens and closes his mouth in quick succession, obviously thinking better of whatever he was about to say.

He calls out to me as I'm just about to return inside. I spin around. He's sitting in his SUV with the window lowered. "I'll pick you up at the usual time tomorrow morning, and I'll call you later tonight." Then he blows me a kiss and drives off. I'm smiling like a goober as I step back into the comforting warmth of the house.

"Where's Ax?" I inquire, plopping down on the couch beside Skeet.

"He went to check if your clothes are dry."

My cheeks turn pink, and he chuckles, sliding me over onto his lap. "It's okay, you know."

"It's all still a little weird," I admit.

"It's not as weird as I thought it'd be." He sneaks his hand under the back of my shirt. "And you shouldn't feel embarrassed. If Ax can give you what you need right now, then that's all that matters."

"It's not that, it's—"

"Babe." He shuts me up with a kiss. "You don't have to explain." He traces my face with his fingers. "You and Ax have an intense bond. It's different from what you and I share and what you have with Heath, and there's nothing wrong with that." He rubs his thumb along my lips. "You're good for him, you know. He's way more relaxed since you arrived. And"— his eyes widen and his lips kick up—"shock, horror, I've even spotted him"— he leans in, glancing furtively over his shoulder before pressing his mouth to my ear—"smiling and laughing." He whispers the words like it's some big secret, and I giggle. I'm rewarded with another quick kiss. "We've both noticed the changes in him, so whatever you're doing, keep doing it." He grins, smothering another chuckle as the stain on my cheeks darkens.

"He helps me unwind too," I sheepishly admit.

"And that's great." He runs his eyes over my clothes. "By the way, you look hot in his clothes." A cheeky glint appears in his eyes. "But you'd look even hotter in mine." I bark out a laugh, leaning in closer to him. "Or wearing nothing at all," he adds in a lower, huskier tone, grazing his nose along the column of my neck. His head whips back, and his eyes pop wide. "You seen this?" His voice contains a hefty dose of amusement.

"Seen what?" I jerk upright on his lap, and he groans, adjusting himself in his pants.

"Axel gave you a hickey."

My jaw slackens and I'm speechless for a split second. "Oh fuck."

Skeet chuckles again. "It's low enough to disguise it, but …"

I quirk a brow. "Finish that thought."

"But it seems lonely, all by itself." His fingertips dance across my neck on the other side. "I think you might need a matching one."

My lips curve into a smile. "You want to brand me too?"

"That sounds so wrong yet oh so right," he quips, nuzzling into my neck.

I tug the shirt aside, granting him more access. My body hums with excitement, and my voice oozes delight when I say, "Do it."

He grins at me. "Hells yeah, baby." He kisses me fiercely on the lips before gliding his mouth to my neck, right at the point where it meets my collarbone, and sucking hard. I close my eyes, moaning and shifting on his lap as he marks my ticklish skin.

"What the actual fuck?" Axel exclaims, and my eyes snap open.

Skeet's mouth doesn't leave my skin, but his body rumbles with silent laughter. "You gave me a hickey." I faux glare at Axel.

"And what?" His brows climb to his hairline. "He's giving you a matching one?"

"Exactly." Skeet lifts his head up, keeping his eyes locked on my neck, admiring his handiwork, as he responds to Axel.

"You two are so fucking weird." Axel shakes his head, fighting a smile.

"Bite me." Skeet flips up his middle finger, and Axel can't contain his smile this time. Skeet looks at him strangely. "You know, I thought for sure you'd be the jealous one, but you're handling this well."

"Unlike some we won't mention." Axel waggles his brows.

Skeet chuckles. "Gilchrist's always been so in control. I'm not sure he knows how to deal with all this."

"Did you see the look he gave me when Blaire came in wearing my clothes?" Axel smirks gleefully.

"Stop it!" I poke Skeet in the ribs and shoot a warning look at Axel. "Don't do that when Heath's not here to defend himself."

"Sure thing, sweetheart," Axel says with a wink, handing me my freshly laundered clothes. "Just prepare yourself. Heath's the most competitive of all of us, and you're not going to know what's hit you when he next comes at you." He tweaks my nose playfully. "Don't say we didn't warn you."

Chapter Twenty-Six

*H*eath is a man on a mission at school on Monday. Every second we're together, he's all over me like a rash—minus the itching and scratching, thankfully. I'm not usually one for PDAs in school, but there's no resisting Heath's magnetic allure. Whether he's pinning me to my locker and kissing the shit out of me, pulling his chair in so close during lunch that he's practically sitting in my lap, or finding ways to sneakily touch me during class, he ensures he has his hands on some part of my body every time we're together. While I sense there's some truth to the guys' musings that he's jealous, I also suspect it's his way of making things up to me and sticking one to Cassie at the same time. She still hasn't come near me, but she embeds imaginary daggers in my back whenever we're in the same vicinity.

By midweek, I've forgotten I was ever angry at Heath. I'm laughing as I'm trying to retrieve books from my locker—completely unsuccessfully—because Heath has his arms circled around me from behind and he's tickling the side of my neck with a slew of feather-light kisses.

"Could you sink any lower?" a grating voice says in proximity, and Heath immediately tenses.

Snatching my books, I close my locker and whirl around, smiling pleasantly at my arch-nemesis. "Could you be any more obvious?" I retort, deliberately running my hand up and down Heath's back.

Cassie deliberates her next words carefully. "Funny, joke's on you, *Arizona*," she taunts before flipping her hair over her shoulder and sauntering off.

"She is getting on my last nerve," Heath grits out, steering me toward our next class, but I've zoned out.

The way she pronounced Arizona has me wound up tight, like a ball of yarn. It isn't a secret that we moved here from Arizona. Mom and Dad felt it was best to be as honest as possible in order not to trip ourselves up, but they cautioned me to avoid going too deep or giving too many specifics away. So, all anyone knows is that I'm originally from Arizona. It's a big enough state not to draw too much attention.

But Cassie doesn't say anything without meaning.

She wanted me to know she knows something.

What exactly is the million-dollar question, and I barely sleep a wink that night wondering about it.

I'm unusually quiet the next morning, and the guys notice. Skeet pulls me away from Heath, pinning me with a concerned look. "Has something happened?"

I scrub a hand over the back of my neck. "Cassie makes me nervous, and I don't like feeling like I'm in the dark."

"You think she's up to something." His bright green eyes probe mine.

I nod slowly. "Yeah. I do."

I'm not sure what he sees in my expression, but he reaches out, discreetly hooking his pinkie around mine. It's as much as we can risk in the school hallway. "Whatever it is you're worried about, you aren't alone, Blaire. We're here for you."

On the spur of the moment, I tug Skeet back over to where Axel and Heath are talking. "Can we meet after school at your place, Ax?" I cut in, dropping my hold on Skeet's arm. "There are some things I need to tell you," I blurt before I lose my nerve. "Things about my past that you should know." I chew on the corner of one nail, my insides twisted into a million knots.

They exchange subtle looks. "I'm cool with that." Axel sends me a penetrating stare. "Are you sure you want to tell us?"

"No," I honestly admit. "But I don't want to *not* tell you either." I lower my voice. "It doesn't feel right keeping this from you even if my parents will be mad if they find out."

Heath tucks me under his arm. "We'll keep it between the four of us."

We are all summoned to the assembly hall for a meeting just before the last class of the day. Apparently, there's some important group session the entire school needs to attend. Seniors and juniors are attending the first session, so I walk with Heath and the guys, and we manage to find seats together near the front of the podium.

The noisy rumbling of chatter only dies down when the principal takes to the stage, commanding quiet. A bunch of other adults sit in a line of chairs behind her. The principal clears her throat, looking around the room. "As you are all aware, gun violence, and gun violence in schools, is a very real concern for every educational institute across our great nation."

Alarm bells start ringing in my head, and a line of sweat coasts down my spine. I rub my clammy hands down the front of my jeans, trying to hear over the thrumming of blood filling my ears.

I gulp, giving myself an inner pep talk in an attempt to control my burgeoning anxiety. I'm sure this is just routine. *If there was anything personal, the principal would have informed me, right?*

"Here at Kentsville High, we have always taken the security and safety of our students very seriously," she continues, and I try to focus on her words rather than giving in to the temptation to flee. "And we believe it's our duty, in conjunction with parental support"—she waves her arms in the direction of some of the people sitting behind her—"to educate our students appropriately as well as invoking necessary safety precautions."

She smiles at a tall, severe-looking man with sharp features and a pinched mouth, and he stands, coming alongside her on the podium. Heath visibly stiffens at my side.

"Thanks to the generosity of Lionel McFarland," she continues, "we are delighted to welcome a panel of experts here today to give a wide variety of presentations on mental health, social media vigilance, coping in the aftermath of tragedy, safety precautions we can all adopt, and the threat of gun violence in our society today." She places her hand on his arm. "Before the session begins, Mr. McFarland would like to make an introductory speech." She steps aside, giving him the floor.

"Thank you, Principal Ivers, for affording me the opportunity to say a few words." He looks out across the crowd, his eyes locking on his daughter's as she slips into the room, late, with her trail of minions skipping behind her. Mr. McFarland beams proudly as Cassie and her crew take up the row of seats right in front.

Suck-ups.

"As a businessman and a father, the escalation of gun violence in schools has alarmed me for some time, so I'm honored to be in a position to offer my support, and the support of my family, to Kentsville High in whatever way I can."

I'm squirming in my seat, and my shirt is now glued to my back. An ominous sense of foreboding washes over me, and the urge to run is riding me hard. But I don't know how to do that and not draw attention to myself, so I grip both sides of my chair hard and try to breathe. A challenge that is more difficult than it sounds.

"Are you okay?" Skeet whispers in my ear, his brow creased with worry lines. I don't know how to respond so I just stare at him, fighting panic and paranoia, and he grows more concerned.

"I asked for a few minutes," Mr. McFarland goes on, "because I wanted to show you something important." He looks to the crowd, zoning in on his daughter now, and I start shaking. I'm vaguely aware of Skeet whispering something to Heath behind my back. "And I'd like to thank my daughter Cassandra for the suggestion." He beams proudly before flicking a switch, dimming the lights in the hall.

Cassie turns around, searching the crowd eagerly. Even in the low light, I can spot the telltale gleam of success in her eyes when her gaze lands on me. My lower lip wobbles, and I glance frantically around.

I need to get out of here.

"Blaire." Heath's worried tone has me twisting around. "Blaire, what's wrong?" He looks over my shoulder as he wraps his arm around me. "Baby, you're shaking all over."

"I was going to tell you," I mumble, horrified as the screen starts to load. Bile travels up my throat, and I genuinely think I might puke. "Oh God, no." Tears leak out of my eyes unbidden as the full scene is unveiled.

It's a church or chapel of some sort. The large, ornate room is packed to maximum capacity, and the camera zooms in on the framed photos of the seven victims, surrounded by bunches of cream and gold flowers. Their faces have always tormented me, yet my eyes are adhered to the screen, and I'm unable to tear my gaze away.

"Today would have been Todd DeLaurentis's eighteenth birthday," Cassie's father continues explaining, "and his parents are hosting a memorial service to remember him and the other victims of last year's Amber Springs Academy shooting. The ceremony is being televised via live feed, and I felt it was fitting to begin today's session by remembering some of the latest victims of gun violence in our high schools."

My eyes climb up, meeting the horrified gaze of the principal. She shakes her head, starting to move in my direction.

"It's about to begin. Please be respectful and attentive," Cassie's father adds just as I jump up, my chair screeching with the movement. I push past Skeet's and Axel's anxious faces, past the inquisitive stares of other students, tripping over feet and almost tumbling in my rush to get out of the room. My throat swells to the point where I'm struggling to draw enough oxygen into my lungs. Hushed voices follow me as I stagger toward the exit, silent tears cascading down my cheeks as I claw at my throat, rasping for air.

Can't breathe. Need air.

I don't hear the footsteps following me.

Not as I crash into the doors and race out into the empty hallway.

Not as wracking sobs rip free of my throat and the choked sound of my anguish bounces off the walls.

Not as my blurry eyes finally focus on the multitude of pictures pasted to lockers up and down the hallway.

Pictures of my brother.

Pictures of me.

The word monsters slashed across the images in blood-red ink.

No, I don't hear the footsteps following me until they slow down.

Until they're joined by others as people leave classrooms to investigate.

In my panic to get away, I stumble over my own feet, falling to the ground at an awkward angle.

I manage to land on my butt, face up. Pushing off my hands, I sit up, in a perfect position to watch as Heath, Skeet, and Axel stare in horror at the images and insults tacked to the walls. The principal runs toward me. "Blaire. Wait!" she calls out, as crowds form a circle around me, and I shrink back, trembling and shaking.

Dark shadows flicker across my retinas, and the eerie sound of crying is the only noise in the hall.

"Monster!" Someone shouts, shattering the creepy silence, and it starts a cacophony of similar taunts. The crowd swarms around me, closing me in. Blood thrums in my ears, and my heart is beating a hundred miles an hour. Little beads of sweat form on my brow. I try to take deep breaths, to focus on calming down before I have a full-blown anxiety attack, but the shouting and loaded looks are too difficult to ignore, and my breath oozes out in panicked spurts as I start to lose my grip on reality. In the distance, I hear other shouts and the principal demanding people move back.

Someone kicks me, and I instinctively raise my hands in protection, wincing as pain registers in my ribs. My anxiety flares, and the pressure on my chest intensifies to the point where it feels like I'm dying.

I wish I was.

I wish it was all over.

The eternal pain and torment are something I can't withstand any longer.

I'm not strong enough to go through this again.

Another foot connects with my torso, and lancing pain spears me on all sides. I curl into a protective ball as more kicks land on my back. Others join in, and I zone out, going to that special place in my head that frees me from reality while I'm attacked from several corners.

Just before I lose complete consciousness, I pray to God to take me. I beg him to let me join Ethan.

Because if this is what my life's going to be like again, then I don't want to live.

Chapter Twenty-Seven

"Give the girl some space to breathe," an unfamiliar voice says as I slowly regain consciousness. My eyes flicker open, and dazzling white light almost blinds me. I press my eyes closed as a warm hand entwines with mine.

"Blaire?" Heath's voice is hesitant.

"You're in the nurse's office," Axel quietly confirms, his fingers fleetingly brushing against my cheek.

"It's okay," Skeet reassures me. "You can open your eyes. It's just us, the nurse, and Principal Ivers."

Drawing on hidden reserves of courage, I force my eyes open, blinking profusely as I adjust to the brightness. I attempt to sit up, groaning as aches and pains swamp my body.

"Nice and slowly, Ms. Adams." The nurse has salt and pepper hair and kind eyes. I don't bother correcting her as she helps me sit up. "How badly does it hurt?"

I'm sore but I don't ache as much as I did after the fight in the barn. "It's not too bad. I'll live." I offer her a weak smile.

"Did you see who assaulted you?" the principal asks, looming in my line of vision.

I shake my head, and she sighs deeply. She moves to my side, placing a gentle hand on my arm. "I'm so very sorry, Blaire. I had no idea Mr. McFarland had that planned, or I would've forewarned you."

"What about the photos?" Axel asks, his rage barely concealed. "Did you approve those too?"

"Axel." Heath's tone carries a caution.

"Of course not." The principal looks flustered. "And I will find out who's responsible, and they'll be dealt with accordingly."

I almost believe her. Except I've been here before. And no punishments were ever doled out. People have zero sympathy for me because of my brother. And I get it. I do. My suffering is nothing compared to the suffering of the families of the victims or the fact those boys and girls lost their lives in such a horrific manner. I love my brother, but I've never condoned his actions, and it makes me sick every time I think of it. Doesn't mean it sucks any less to be me.

"Can I go?" I beg her with my eyes.

The principal shakes her head. "Not until your parents get here. I've called them, but—"

"But neither of them picked up." My smile is tight. "If we're waiting for them, we'll be here half the night." I turn pleading eyes on her again. "I need to get out of here. Please."

"We'll escort Blaire home," Skeet offers. "We'll keep her safe."

She sighs again, looking at her watch as she considers it. "Okay, but wait here until I check that the school has been fully cleared and everyone went home."

I guess I must've blacked out for longer than I thought.

The tappity-tap of her retreating heels pierces through my skull, and I grab my head in my hands. The nurse hands me some pain pills and a small plastic cup of water. "I'd like to examine your injuries, if that's okay. I want to ensure there's nothing broken." I nod, still not properly looking up at the guys. She shoos them outside to wait, and a shuddering breath works it's wait through me. "There, that's better," she says, smiling softly at me. "There was way too much testosterone in the air for such a small room."

I can't even muster a smile at that. She gently helps me lift my sweater and shirt off, and I bite the inside of my mouth to keep from crying out. A dark expression crosses her features as she examines my back. A large purple bruise is already mushrooming on my stomach, and I spot similar markings on both sides of my body and one side of my ribs. She mutters quietly under her breath. "You're sure you didn't see who did this?" she asks.

"I'm sure." I'm *not* lying, but even if I'd seen, I wouldn't tell. Nothing good would come of that. "Why are you being nice to me?" I blurt, and she falters, peering strangely at me.

"Why wouldn't I be?"

"Don't you know who I am? Who I really am?"

"Ms. Ivers informed me. I know who you are, Ms. Simpson."

"Then why don't you hate me?" I eyeball her, genuinely curious.

"You're not responsible for the actions of your brother," she quietly states, and waterworks threaten.

It takes me a few moments to compose myself enough to speak. "That's not how people usually see it in my experience."

"Well, people are wrong." Her eyes turn glassy, and I hate the look of pity on her face.

"Can I go now?" I bite out.

"Of course, honey." She rummages in a cupboard, pulling out a few tubes and handing them to me. "Get someone to help you put that cream on twice a day. It'll help you heal. And get one of those boys to drop by the pharmacy and pick up more pain medication. You'll need it in the next few days." She pats my hand as I struggle to my feet. "You mind yourself, Blaire."

Her kindness almost undoes me. "Thank you," I whisper, fighting tears again. I can't remember the last time anyone showed me any compassion, and I'm not sure I'm equipped to handle the influx of related emotions.

The boys have furious expressions on their faces when I step out into the hallway. They are locked in some sort of battle of wills with the principal. They stop talking the minute they see me, but I'm too anxious to get the hell out of this place to care.

"You ready?" Heath asks, sliding his arm behind my back with care. I nod, still unable to look him in the eyes. I hate that they found out like that. Just as I'd plucked up the courage to fess up. I don't know how they can bear to stand by me after this, but I'm not going to look a gift horse in the mouth. I'm terrified of what lies in store outside the safety of the school building. Although I can fight, it's of little use if I'm hugely outnumbered. Or if I tune out, like I did earlier.

"I don't expect to see you in school until Monday," the principal confirms, "and, rest assured, I will be conducting an investigation to identify the guilty party or parties."

"And you know where to look first," Heath cryptically says, pinning the principal with a look that would probably earn him detention at any other time.

"I haven't forgotten, Mr. Gilchrist, but this is *my* school, and I will conduct this investigation in a professional manner, as I see fit."

"Thanks." Skeet shoots her an expansive smile. "We have full faith in your ability to unearth the culprits and administer the appropriate penalty."

Spot the guy who lives with two attorneys. This time, a small smile breaks free on my face, but I hide it before the guys notice.

"You can leave now." The principal's tone is curt, and she's clearly running out of patience.

We don't talk as we make our way outside. The boys match my slow pace without argument, surrounding me protectively as we step out into the parking lot. I'm aware I'm shaking again when Heath pulls me closer, pressing a soft kiss to the top of my head. Tears sting the back of my eyes at his gesture.

"Aren't twins supposed to share the same traits?" someone asks in a deliberately loud tone of voice from somewhere off to the left. I ignore the natural urge to look, to spew some retaliation, focusing on putting one foot in front of the other. *Just keep moving, Blaire.*

"It's a proven scientific fact," some other asshole agrees. Tension lingers in the space between me and the guys, but I forge on, determined to ignore the haters.

"Then we've all just been put on notice," the first voice says.

A shadow darkens the path in front of us, halting our progress. "You're a murderer just like your scum of a brother," he growls as I lift my chin, facing my accuser. Heath keeps a vise grip around my shoulders. I don't know this dude. He's average height with cropped hair, menacing eyes, muscles stacked upon muscles, and he's wearing a thunderous look that says he means business. He cracks his knuckles as he stares me down. "You shouldn't have come here, and you'll regret the day you did."

"Back off Jenkins before I make you," Axel snaps in a threatening tone.

Jenkins guffaws. "Your days as reigning champ are over, Thorp. I'm not scared of you."

"You should be." Axel steps up to him, and he's a good two heads taller. He looks down his nose at Jenkins. "If you so much as look at Blaire funny, you'll have us to deal with."

"Why the fuck would you defend that psycho bitch?" some girl asks, pushing her way to the front of the small crowd. "Is she the reason you tossed me to the curb?" She sneers at me, looking up and down my body in a derogatory manner. "You clearly need your eyes examined as well as your brain." She flicks her fingers at his forehead, and Skeet reaches across, taking her wrist and gently pushing her away.

"Fuck off, Shelly. He tossed you to the curb because you're a skank who can't keep her legs or her mouth closed. Blaire is worth a million of you."

"Screw you, Skeet." She flips him the bird before her eyes glint maliciously. Cocking her head to one side, she adds, "Oh, I already did."

"And I still have nightmares about it," Skeet coolly replies, moving closer to me.

"Shell." Jenkin's warning works and Shell slithers away like the poisonous viper she is.

"This is the only warning you'll get," Jenkins says, jabbing his finger in my face. I swat it away and steam practically billows from his ears. "Get the fuck out of our school and out of this town. Come back here, and we'll show you what we do to murderous sluts."

"She didn't murder anyone!" Heath's hands are balled into fists.

"She as good as did. What is it they say about twins? They're two peas in a pod? She knew what that fucking asshole brother of hers had planned, and she did nothing to stop it. That means she's as guilty as him." A small chorus of approval swirls around him. I'd retaliate, but it'd do no good. They believe what they want to believe. They've no interest in the truth.

Axel steps up to Jenkins, ready to pound him into the ground if the expression on his face is any indication.

"Let it go, Ax. Trust me, there's no point arguing." His body is rigid and primed to attack. I reach out, touching his elbow. "Please. I just want to get out of here." He takes a step back, reluctantly nodding.

"I meant what I said," Axel adds as we prepare to walk away. "Anyone messes with Blaire, they mess with us. Pass the word around."

"Fuck you, asshole." Jenkins bridges the distance between them. "You've just declared war, and you're already on the losing side. Don't say I didn't warn you either." He stalks off, his motley crew trailing after him, making rude hand gestures and shouting insults at me as they go.

Chapter Twenty-Eight

*I*t's deathly quiet in Heath's SUV. Axel and Skeet are following us separately. "I was going to tell you," I finally admit when I can't take the ominous silence any longer.

He looks sideways at me for a moment, and the expression on his face is strained. "I know."

Exhaling noisily, I look out the window, pulling my knees in tighter to my chest. My cell pings again, and I glance at it. I've hundreds of unread messages and texts. I don't need to open them to know what they say. Clearly, someone shared my cell number, and now half the school wants to tell me what they think of me and my brother. Except this latest text is one I can't ignore. It's from Shaz, inquiring if I'm okay. I tap out a quick reply.

ME: *Can you meet us at Axel's house asap. I'll explain everything.*

SHAZNAY: *I'm on my way.*

When we arrive at Axel's place, Skeet parks his truck at the curb while Axel pulls his bike up alongside Heath's SUV in the driveway. Skeet is opening my door before I've had a chance to. He lifts me out, keeping hold of me as he pulls me into a strong embrace. "You hanging in there?"

"Just about," I truthfully reply.

"We're not going to let anyone hurt you." Fierce determination shimmers in his eyes, but I know it's not as simple as that. He takes my hand and leads me into the house. Axel and Heath head into the kitchen while Skeet guides me into the living room, pulling me down onto his lap on the couch. I rest my head on his shoulder, trying to siphon his warmth and his reassurance to help calm myself down. I'm in a strange half-dazed, half-terrorized state. "It's okay, beautiful. It's only us here." He rubs his hands up and down my trembling arms. "Breathe, Blaire. Try to relax."

"How are you okay with this?" I ask, staring into his eyes. "Why don't you hate me?"

"The feelings I have for you are as far from hate as they can get." He swipes his thumb under my eye, collecting the dampness there. "You're not a bad person. We all know that."

Footsteps thump down the stairs and my back stiffens. An older guy with Axel's piercing gray-blue eyes enters the room, his eyes widening when he sees me. "Hey there." His smile is welcoming but inquisitive.

"Hi," I squeak, as Skeet tightens his hold on me.

"I'm Griff. Axel's brother. Nice to meet you."

"This is Blaire," Skeet quickly explains, and Griff's forehead puckers in confusion.

"Blaire?" He stares at Skeet. "But I thought she was dating my bro—"

"Griff," Axel cuts in, suddenly appearing in the doorway behind his older brother. "Can we do this later?"

Griff looks over his shoulder at his brother. "Sure." His pleasant smile is back when he turns around again. "Nice to meet you, Blaire. Maybe we'll get to talk next time." Then he walks out of the room, gesturing for Axel to follow him.

"I'm guessing Ax didn't tell him the part where I'm also dating you and Heath."

"I think he was working up to that," Skeet admits with a low chuckle. "Now he'll have no choice."

Heath steps into the room carrying a mug and a plate. He sets them down on the coffee table in front of me. "Hot sweet tea and a grilled cheese sandwich." He touches my cheek. "You should eat."

"I honestly don't think I can. My stomach's in knots."

The bell chimes, and Griff walks past the living room door with his jacket on. Sounds of muted conversation filter into the room, and then Shaz materializes in the doorway, followed by Axel carrying a tray with more drinks and sandwiches. Shaz hurries to my side, grabbing me off her brother's lap into a mammoth hug. "Are you okay? How badly are you hurt?"

"You heard about that?" I shouldn't be surprised this kind of news has traveled fast.

She winces. "There's a video doing the rounds."

"Of course, there is." I squeeze my eyes shut, willing my body to calm down. "I can't believe this is happening all over again."

Heath and Axel take the two chairs across from us, exchanging looks as they sit down.

"They did this kind of shit to you in Amber Springs?" Shaz asks, disbelief clouding her face.

I nod. "They needed someone to blame, and my brother was dead, so …" I shrug.

"Do you feel up to telling us about it?" Heath asks, pinning solemn eyes on me.

"I was going to tell you." My gaze bounces between all of them. "I swear. That's why I asked if we could meet tonight."

"We believe you." Skeet slings his arm around me, squeezing my shoulder in a show of support.

I draw a deep breath and start into it. "Things were bad in Amber Springs, and we'd no choice but to leave. My parents made the decision to change our surname to Adams, my mother's maiden name, to avoid recognition. They made me promise I wouldn't tell anyone about our real identities, but I felt so bad keeping it from all of you." I knot my hands in my lap, sitting up a little straighter. "After today, I know I made the right call deciding to tell you the truth. Doesn't mean I wasn't terrified."

"You thought we'd turn on you?" Axel asks, leaning his elbows on his knees.

"I hoped you wouldn't, but people I'd known for years disowned me, and my boyfriend dumped me the day of the shooting. Cam was someone I'd known practically my whole life. If he reacted like that—"

"Then you had good reason to fear we'd react the same way," Skeet says, completing my sentence.

"A little faith would've been nice," Heath says, and there's a slight edge to his voice.

Axel glares at him. "Your whole life has been nothing short of a picnic, so you don't understand how secrets eat away at you and how fucking scary it is to let people in. Don't you dare judge Blaire for protecting herself in the only way she knew how."

Heath slams his coffee down on the table. "Don't fucking patronize me. My life is not all rainbows and unicorns. I've my own shit to deal with, and I'm not unsympathetic." A muscle clenches in his jaw before he forcibly calms down. He looks over at me. "I can't even begin to understand what you must've gone through, and I don't want to upset you anymore than you already are, but it hurts that you'd doubt us."

"Ultimately, I didn't, because I'd still decided to tell you even if a part of me was terrified you'd walk away."

He nods, his eyes softening, and I muster my courage before continuing. "My brother, Ethan, was the best brother a girl could have, and he was my best friend. Above everyone else, he was always there for me." I smile sadly. Shaz squeezes my hand, and Skeet presses a kiss to my hair. "Mom used to say we were the same soul, split in two different bodies." I recall the memory with fondness. As kids, we used to think it was so cheesy, but as we matured, it made more sense to me. Gave even more meaning to the intense bond Ethan and I shared.

"We were virtually joined at the hip, and we did most everything together. As we grew older, it was often just the two of us at home because my parents both worked irregular shifts. Ethan was my whole world. He protected me and took care of me in so many ways."

A stabbing pain infiltrates my chest, and I have to pause to draw a fresh breath. I look at everyone, and they're all focused completely on me. "We had that weird phantom twin thing going on. I'd feel things when he'd feel them and vice versa." I smile, brushing a tear away. "It never freaked us out. We loved having that connection."

My smile fades as my mind meanders in the past. "Of course, it meant we rarely could keep any secrets from one another." I hang my head, remembering the parts of the story I want to tell but can't.

You can't ever tell anyone, B. No one can know.

I return to that horrible morning, and the images are so vivid in my head that it's as if I'm transported back to that time. "He locked me in my bedroom the morning of the shooting," I whisper, struggling to keep my tears at bay. "And I think he did something to Cam's truck to keep him away from school too." Shaz hands me a tissue, and I dab at my eyes as Skeet pulls me over into his lap again. "He was acting weird, and he'd cooked me pancakes and eggs and bacon for breakfast, which he never did on a school day. I asked him what was wrong, but he deflected." I sniffle, loudly blowing my nose. Shaz fishes in her purse, handing the whole tissue packet to me.

"It's my biggest regret. I sensed something was wrong, and I should've pushed him harder. Should've made him tell me what was on his mind."

"It probably wouldn't have made any difference," Skeet softly says. "If he was that determined to keep you out of it, nothing you said would've made him tell you."

I nod, sniffling as I twist on his lap to look at his face. "The logical part of my brain agrees with you, but it doesn't help offset the guilt."

"Do you know why he did it?"

This is the hard part. "Not really," I lie. "I mean, I've no idea why he woke up that morning and decided to steal my father's hunting rifle and shoot those four boys and three girls dead, but I've an inkling as to why he targeted them." I made a promise when we first moved here that I'd be as honest as I could be, and this is as far as I can go without breaking my promise to Ethan.

"They were all bullies and not very nice people." I swallow the bile building in my mouth. "They'd bullied me for a while, and I guess Ethan just snapped. Not that it makes it okay," I rush to reassure them. "My parents and I were, *are*, horrified over what he did. It doesn't matter that I didn't like any of them. It doesn't matter how they treated me. None of that gave Ethan the right to take the law into his own hands. They didn't deserve to die, and I still wake up every morning in a state of disbelief, because I can't reconcile that version of Ethan with the Ethan I knew and loved."

Truth.

The room is deathly quiet.

"Why were they bullying you?" Axel asks after a couple minutes. I refuse to look at him although I feel his intense radar attempting to drill a hole in my skull. I'm terrified if I face him that he'll see the full truth. He's the only one with the potential to discover the truth, and I can't risk it.

I shrug, trying to downplay it. "The usual stuff. The guys were mad I'd rejected their advances, and their girlfriends were jealous and took it out on me." It's not a million miles away from how it went down.

"When did you find out?" Shaz asks in a low tone.

Tears prick my eyes at the memory. "When the cops showed up at my house. They let me out of my bedroom and explained." It all comes flooding back, crashing into me like a tsunami, and I'm knocked off my feet, metaphorically speaking. Sobs wrack my body, and every part of me shakes uncontrollably as I collapse against Skeet. He holds me close, and then Shaznay's arms go around me too, from behind, and I hear her quiet cries. She sobs as I sob, and the only sound in the room is the haunting sound of our joint crying.

When I've composed myself enough to speak, I lift my head up and continue. "The police shot him dead because he turned around to face them with the rifle still in his hand, but the chamber was empty. I know my brother, and he had no quarrel with the cops. He was going to turn himself in, but he never got the chance."

"I'm so sorry, Blaire." Shaznay is full-on crying now, and Axel crosses over to us, lifting me out of Skeet's arms so he's freed up to comfort his sister. Axel sits back down in the chair with me on his lap.

"I feel so guilty for grieving," I admit as my tears dry up. "It feels like I have no right to mourn him because he is a … a … killer." I can't ever bring myself to use either of the *M-words* to describe my twin. Even on days when I hate him for what he did, I still can't call him that. I won't ever fully understand what prompted him to do that. I won't ever know whether he just finally snapped or whether he'd planned it all along.

His letter didn't mention that.

I continue. "Ethan killed those seven people in cold blood, and I don't feel like I've a right to mourn my loss or to moan about how my life has changed when those people aren't even here anymore. Their families are the ones who have the right to grieve and suffer. Not us."

"That's complete bullshit." Heath shakes his head. "He was still your brother. He was still your parents' son. His actions were deplorable, but that doesn't mean you don't miss him, and it doesn't erase the love you still clearly have for him."

"No one else understands that, and I don't blame them. Honestly, I don't. We couldn't even hold a funeral because of the public reaction. After the police released his body, he was cremated with just myself, my parents, and my aunt and uncle in attendance. And that hurt so bad." The tears start again, and this time, Axel holds me tight.

Over on the couch, Skeet holds Shaz in his arms, trying to soothe her. She's crying again too, and I hate that I've upset her like this, but it feels good to get all this stuff off my chest. "It doesn't seem right that we were born together but died apart. Or that we couldn't even give him a proper funeral. It's so wrong."

Axel rubs his hands up and down my arms, pressing soft kisses to my cheek as my words sink in.

"I've spent countless hours putting myself in their shoes, and I can't fault them for their thoughts on my brother or for their retaliation against my family. And it wasn't just the families of the victims impacted. There were other students in the school who saw it all go down. They're most likely traumatized for life. It's an impossible situation."

"What did they do to you?" Heath asks, his shoulders stiff and his face tense.

"Pretty much anything you can imagine. I couldn't go back to the Academy, the private school I attended, so I enrolled in the public school, stupidly thinking I wouldn't be as victimized there, but if anything, it was worse because Amber Springs High lacked the discipline and structure of the Academy, and the students basically got away with tormenting me on a continual basis."

I look down at the floor as I dredge up a host of unpleasant memories. It pours out of me like lava oozing from a volcano. "They spat at me, pushed me around, beat me up, stuffed dead animals and rotting food in my locker, stole my bag, destroyed all my books, plastered posters with horrible shit written on them all over school. They set fire to Ethan's SUV. I was forced to change my cell number constantly, and I had to shut down all my social media accounts because of the vile comments. People didn't hold back, telling me to kill myself because I deserved to die. I was afraid to leave my house because other sick bastards threatened to rape and kill me, and I didn't feel like they were idle threats. My mom pulled me out of Amber Springs High after a month, and I studied at home. I was a virtual recluse. Both my parents were fired from their jobs, and no one else would hire them. They couldn't sell our house. We were stuck there until my aunt and uncle offered us a way out."

"Jesus Christ." Heath drags a hand through his hair, shaking his head. "I can't believe you were subjected to all that."

"Why would they do that to you?" Shaz cries. "It wasn't your fault."

"Most of them believe the same thing Jenkins believes. That I knew what my twin was planning and didn't stop it. Especially in the Academy where they knew I'd been bullied by that group. People assumed I was happy they died, but that couldn't be further from the truth." I look them all in the eye, one by one. "I never wanted them dead, and I never wanted my brother to kill them. He lost his life over it, and that's not something I would've ever wished for."

I fight a new wave of tears. "I feel so lost without him, yet some days I hate him so much I wish he was still alive so I could scream at him and punch him and tell him what a stupid asshole he was." A choked sound rips from my throat. "He's destroyed so many lives, mine included, and I don't know how I can ever forgive him for that."

Chapter Twenty-Nine

"*I* still can't believe your boyfriend abandoned you like that," Heath says as we sit outside my house in his SUV. I'm trying to work up the courage to go into the house and confront my parents. The numerous texts and missed calls on my cell, and the car parked in the drive, confirm the news has reached them. While I'm not responsible for the revelation, I'm sure they'll blame me.

"You and me both. I thought I knew the type of person Cam is, but I guess I never knew him at all."

"We would never do that to you." Heath takes both my cold hands in his much warmer ones.

"I know that. I'm still in shock that you've all taken it so well."

"We *were* shocked, Blaire, and no matter what Axel said back at his house, we are all disappointed that you didn't confide in us, but I understand better now why you didn't. And ultimately, concern for your safety overrode anything else. I thought Axel was going to beat up half the school if they didn't step away from you when you were on the floor. He definitely threw a few punches when Ivers wasn't looking."

"Thank you so much for being here for me. I've felt so isolated and alone for so long. It's hard to trust anyone, but I know I can trust all of you and Shaznay, and you've no idea how much that means to me."

"We care about you. Unlike that fuckface you were dating in Amber Springs." His expression darkens. "Have you had any contact with him since?"

I shake my head. "Nope. Not a word. I did look him up on social media before we moved here, out of curiosity." My stomach tightens in pain. "He was already back on the dating scene and living his life like nothing had happened." Bitterness fuels the blood flowing in my veins. "I was so tempted to confront him. He didn't just let me down. He let Ethan down too."

"What a fucking asshole."

"Yeah. You won't hear me disagreeing."

He rubs a hand across the back of his neck, looking a little uncomfortable. "Have you ever thought of speaking to someone, Blaire? A professional?"

"You mean a shrink?" He nods. "I was meeting a therapist at first, but then money became tight, so I stopped going."

"Maybe you should consider returning to therapy," he tentatively suggests. "What you've had to endure would devastate anyone, and I can't begin to imagine how you coped with all that."

"I'll think about it," I say, as Mom opens the front door, gesturing at me to come inside. "Shit. Time to face the music."

"You want me to come with?"

"You're sweet, but no. I've got to do this alone."

"Call me after?" he inquires a minute later as he walks me up to the door. Mom has retreated inside but she left the door open in a clear sign. I nod, not resisting when he gently brings me into his embrace, kissing me with the same devotion and tenderness Skeet and Axel displayed when they were kissing me goodbye. "You're not alone anymore, Blaire. We're all in this together."

AXEL

Heath stomps through the front door, and a herd of elephants wouldn't be as loud.

"Is she okay?" Skeet asks from his seat at my kitchen table.

"As okay as anyone can be in the middle of this shitstorm." He drops his keys on the counter and plonks down in the seat across from us. "I picked up pain pills at the pharmacy and made her promise to take it easy," he adds. "But I'm worried about her parents' reaction. What if they make her leave town?"

Skeet and I exchange knowing looks. "We were just discussing that. No point worrying about it until we hear what they say."

"I know I was a little pissed at her initially," Heath continues, "but I can't stay mad at her. Not after what she told us."

"I want to kill every single motherfucker who ever hurt her," I grit out.

"We all do," Skeet agrees.

"This doesn't change anything for me," Heath quietly adds. "If anything, it makes me more determined to make this relationship work. The thoughts of losing her …"

"That's not happening," I growl, frustrated at the thought of anyone taking her away from us. Blaire has gotten under my skin like no girl ever has. And it's more than just this intense connection we share. I want to be there for her. To protect her and make sure she isn't the one paying for her brother's sins.

"Even imagining her not being around scares the shit out of me." Skeet looks earnestly at both of us. "I already love the bones of that girl." I wish I had such confidence when it comes to my feelings, but Skeet's always been way more comfortable expressing that shit than either Heath or I ever will be. "It's okay," he says, smirking. "I know you both love her too. You don't need to say it."

I flip him my middle finger, and he laughs, shoulder-checking me.

"We need to protect her from Jenkins and other assholes like him," Heath cuts in, trying to keep us on track.

"I got my dad on the case," Skeet supplies. "He's working on getting all that crap taken down from the net." Tons of shit has popped up on social media and on the school network since Blaire's real identity was revealed. Chris, one of Skeet's dads, is a graphic designer by trade but a bit of an overall tech genius, so he's working on removing all the content before Blaire sees it.

"What else are we planning?" Heath asks, looking between us with complete trust.

"One of us is with Blaire at all times. While we can't attend every class, we'll make sure one of us is there to escort her to and from each class. You continue to drive her to and from school, and Skeet will handle the work journeys. I'll go running with her and spend as much time as I can with her."

"We'll be like her shadow," Skeet confirms. "And we instantly shut down anyone who dares take this out on her."

"I'm also worried about her mental health." I stop for a second before I share this. We've agreed not to breach privacy, but this transcends that. "I'm not sure if either of you have noticed the scars on her thighs?" Neither guy even attempts to crack a sleazy joke. They just shake their heads. "I didn't comment, and she didn't volunteer any information, but I knew a couple girls in juvie who self-harmed, and I'm pretty sure that's what they are."

"Shit." Heath shakes his head.

"Do you think it's related to the shooting?" Skeet asks, always trying to get to the root of the issue.

"No. The scars were old. Definitely not recent."

"Well, that's good." Skeet frowns. "I think."

We're all quiet with our thoughts until Heath raises another question. "What about that bitch Cassie?"

Skeet and I trade looks again. "We all agree she's behind this. She wasn't exactly discreet, but we thought we'd let you decide how to handle her, because of the family connection."

"I thought of nothing else on the drive back. It's a tough one." Heath leans back in his chair, scrubbing a hand over his jaw. "This news won't help with Mom. She'll be more insistent I have nothing to do with Blaire, but I'm done playing pretend with Cassie. I'm quite likely to throttle her the next time she's around, so I'm going to come clean. My parents can go screw themselves if they don't like it."

"What about your place in UF?"

A sly grin spreads over his mouth. "You know I always like to have a Plan B." He produces a letter from his inside pocket, sliding it across the table. "I got a full ride, so my parents can yank my trust fund if they like. It won't stop me from following my dreams."

"Fucking-A, man." Skeet touches knuckles with Heath.

"That's great, especially since I got confirmation of my place and full ride this morning."

Skeet punches me in the arm. "Why the hell didn't you say something?"

"I wanted to tell Griff first although the news was overshadowed by the discovery that Blaire is also your girlfriend."

"I'd love to have been involved in that conversation."

"Trust me, you wouldn't," I murmur, recalling the heated words exchanged.

"Have either of you mentioned college to Blaire?" Skeet asks. We both shake our heads. "We need to discuss it with her. I want her with us."

"Me too," I admit without hesitation.

"I do too, and we definitely need to have a group convo, but can we refocus on the Cassie issue," Heath says, like the control freak he is. "We need to figure out payback. She isn't getting away with this."

Oh, Cassie is definitely not getting away with this. When we're through with her, she's going to wish she hadn't been born. "I agree, but we need to plan it carefully and leave it for a while. Lull her into a false sense of security, and then bury her."

We spend a few minutes exploring options, agreeing on a few ways we can retaliate. After I call for takeout and grab beers for me and Skeet and a water for Heath, I raise my concerns. "Did any of you think Blaire was deflecting when she spoke about the victims?"

"In what way?" Skeet asks, frowning.

"I think there's more to the story than she's telling us." Heath arches a brow. "Ethan clearly loved Blaire, and from what we've learned of him, he wasn't a bad guy. So, what prompts a guy who is a good student, a good son, a good brother, to take such drastic action?"

"What if he isn't that guy?" Heath replies. "What if Blaire *didn't* know the real Ethan? What if he was actually a psycho, and he just flipped that morning? It's not unheard of for loved ones to be in denial, both before and after. Most psychos stay hidden in plain sight and no one is any the wiser."

I shrug. "You could be right. Or maybe he was dealing with stuff she wasn't aware of, like depression or some other mental illness. We didn't know the guy, but Blaire doesn't strike me as the delusional type, and you heard her say some days she hates him. That doesn't sound like denial to me."

"I agree, and I get where you're going with this, Ax. It's more than bullying," Skeet says, sitting up straighter.

"What else could it be?" Heath asks.

I look them both in the eye. "That's what we need to find out."

Chapter Thirty

BLAIRE

My parents are arguing again. I think they might've been at it all night. I'm not sure because I stole one of Mom's sleeping pills, and between it and the pain medication, I was unconscious all night. Just how I wanted it.

My body hurts like a bitch as I dry myself after my shower and get dressed. I already texted Heath to come pick me up. I know Principal Ivers doesn't expect me at school today, but not showing my face will only make things worse. I don't plan on spending the next four days fretting over school on Monday. Best to tackle the bull by the horns.

I'm remarkably upbeat today which surprises me. In a pleasant way. And I know it's down to the guys and Shaznay. I'm wading into battle today, but I've other soldiers by my side. It makes a hell of a difference. And it beats staying home and listening to my parents' constant fighting.

"Are you sure this is a good idea?" Heath asks as soon as I climb into his car.

"No, but I'm still doing it."

His smile is proud. "Fair enough."

Axel and Skeet are waiting in the parking lot for us when we arrive at school. Skeet opens the passenger door, helping me out. "How are you feeling?" he asks, inspecting my face. Thank God, I still had that heavy-duty makeup Jacinta gave me. I never thought I'd need it again so soon, but it came in handy this morning, disguising the large bruise that materialized on my right cheek. Axel must've told Jacinta what happened, or she heard the gossip that's no doubt circulating around town, because she messaged me this morning telling me I didn't have to show up for my shift if I wasn't up for it. I replied telling her I'd see her at the usual time.

It would be easy to let this derail me. If I stop to think about it for too long, I feel myself falling, dropping, sinking into that black hole again, and I'm not going to be a victim here too. I'm going to fight back. To stand up for myself. As long as my reserves hold up.

"Babe." Skeet touches my cheek. "You okay?"

I offer him a small smile. "I'm okay. Just zoned out there for a bit."

"You have your pain pills with you?"

"Yep." I pat his arm. "I'm good. Thanks."

"I missed you on my run this morning," Axel says, leaning in to kiss my cheek, uncaring who might be watching. It's something a good friend would do anyway.

"Yeah, I think I might be out of action for a few days." Despite all my bravado, I can't risk more serious injury by running when I'm so bruised and battered.

"It's better to rest until you feel up to it." He shoots daggers over my head at someone while he talks. I'm conscious of the myriad of eyeballs glued to my form, but I'm trying to forget they exist, vanquishing them to an imaginary otherworldly realm.

Heath threads his fingers in mine, eyeing me carefully. "Let's do this."

I keep my head up and my eyes straight ahead as we walk toward the entrance. Crowds of students stand around, pointing and whispering. A few brave—some might call them stupid—souls shout out insults. Skeet and Axel are all over them in a flash, and the insults die out. "One of us will be with you at all times," Heath murmurs as we walk. "And you're not to go anywhere by yourself. If you need to go to the toilet, hold it till the bell goes, and then one of us will escort you."

It's on the tip of my tongue to tell him that's taking it a tad too far, but I stop myself. Because the truth is, it's not an overreaction. I've been jumped more times in the girls' bathroom than anyplace else. Some girls might think it's weak to rely on my boyfriends for protection, but I think it's the opposite. Only someone lacking a few brain cells would refuse every protection available. In Amber Springs, I had no choice but to go it alone. Here, I'm choosing to let my boyfriends help keep me safe, and that knowledge bolsters my confidence, assuring me I can ride this storm out.

I don't want to leave Kentsville, and I'm sure it's already on my parents' agenda, so it's in my interests to prove to them I can cope with this. That we are better off staying and facing the music than running again.

"Psycho bitch!" someone shouts, pushing me from behind.

Heath whirls around, keeping a tight hold of me as he prepares to tackle the culprit, but Axel has beaten him to it. He holds a scrawny-looking guy with glasses in a chokehold as he glares at him. The guy looks ready to pee his pants. "Want to say that again to Blaire's face, you fucking coward?" Ax spits.

"I'm sorry." He folds instantly, fear gripping his face. "I take it back."

Ax shoves him off. "Stay away from Blaire, or the next time, you'll get my fist in your face." The guy doesn't need to be told twice, racing away as if his life depends on it.

"Thank you," I whisper, my heart surging with unnamed emotion. Ax just nods, and we set off again.

Heath curses when we reach my locker. It's busted open, the contents destroyed. *Die Bitch* is spray painted on the botched door. "Ms. Simpson." Principal Ivers comes up behind us. "Can you come with me for a few minutes."

Heath walks with me while I wave a hasty goodbye to Axel and Skeet. The hallways are devoid of the usual chatter. Students move aside to let us pass, staring and whispering under their breath. Every stare is like a dagger thrown at my back, but I refuse to look at any of the bystanders.

"Get to class!" the principal snaps. "Anyone found loitering in the hall will be given detention." The place empties in seconds, and a tiny layer of stress peels off my shoulders. What a pity I couldn't hire the principal as my personal bodyguard. No one would dare approach me with her by my side.

In her office, she explains that she's held a meeting with all the teachers, informing them of the situation and advising them to report any instances of abuse or victimization. She also asks my permission to make an announcement during first period. I'm touched she thought to ask me, and any ill will I've been nurturing over yesterday's fiasco disappears. I'm also shocked to discover she was at my house last night, talking to my parents about how to handle the situation. It must've been while I was at Ax's, or perhaps I was asleep by that stage. Either way, I'm glad she's taking such a proactive response. It's the direct opposite of how Amber Springs High dealt with the situation, and it's good to know *some* adults are capable of acting like adults.

The hallways are empty as we hurry to class. Entering the room when everyone is already seated, and the class has commenced, isn't ideal, but Heath refuses to let go of my hand until I'm securely in my seat. The teacher doesn't even interfere when Heath forces the student at the desk behind me to move so he can sit with me. I keep my head down while the principal makes her statement over the communal speakers, advising all students of the punishment if they make any threats or physically harm me. Hushed whispers echo around the room, but no one approaches me directly, and I get through all my morning classes unscathed. I can deal with the venomous looks, the finger pointing, and the whispering once they physically leave me alone.

I have my first run in with Cassie during lunch in the cafeteria.

"I can't believe you," she fumes, hovering over our table and pointing her bony finger in Heath's direction.

"Fuck off, Cassie," Heath hisses. "No one wants you here."

"How can you still choose her now that you know?"

I refuse to look up at her, quietly picking at my fruit salad, but I just know she's got her hands on her hips and that her nostrils are flaring.

"I've always known," Heath lies coolly. "And it makes no difference because Blaire hasn't done anything wrong."

"Your little plan backfired," Axel adds with a wicked gleam in his eye. "And Heath has already told his parents everything."

"He wouldn't! You didn't?!" Her panicked tone lifts my spirits to no end.

"I did. My parents know it all. I expect my mom is probably telling your mom right this very second."

She shrieks. "You fucking idiot! This is all going to blow up in your face."

"Do I look like I care?" Heath glares at her before standing. He raises his voice, making sure everyone hears. "You're going to regret that stunt you pulled yesterday. You're a nasty, petty, vindictive, spoiled bitch, and I wouldn't touch you if you were the last woman on Earth. Now get the fuck out of my face, and don't ever come near me again." Under his breath, for her ears only, he adds, "And if you think you're going to get away with this, you're as stupid as you look. I warned you. You have this coming."

"Heath, please." She tugs on his arm, and I pluck her hand off.

"Get your hands off my boyfriend, and go crawl back into that pit you came out of."

"You think they can protect you?" she snarls in my ear. "Think again. You're going to get what you deserve, murdering whore." She pours her soda over my head, and I jump up, sticky brown liquid stinging my eyes, dripping down my face, and trickling under the collar of my shirt.

A teacher appears at our table with a stern expression on his face. "You need to come with me to the principal's office, Ms. McFarland."

"She provoked me!" she lies.

"Save it," the teacher barks. "You're in enough trouble as it is."

Word is buzzing in the halls by the end of the day. Cassie has been suspended along with her crew for graffitiing the lockers and for the stunt she pulled at lunch. I know it's only a temporary reprieve.

But I'll take the wins wherever I can get them.

"Did you really tell your parents?" I ask Heath later that night when we're at my house, studying. Jacinta insisted I finish my shift early which gave me some unexpected free time. We've a history test in the morning, and I thought Heath could use a last-minute go-over even if he is well prepared.

Only Mom is home. Dad is probably out drinking again. Mom let us study in my room, provided we keep the door open, so we're currently lying on my bed with books sprawled out around us.

"I told them about the fake relationship and what really happened with her car, the night she drove drunk and landed in a ditch." He lifts his head up. "I didn't tell them about her coke habit. Thought it was wise to hold something back to dangle over her head. I don't trust her not to pull more shit."

That's a smart move, and I don't trust her either. "How did it go down?"

"About as well as you'd expect," he says, returning his focus to his books.

I tap his back. "Please look at me." He raises his eyes to meet mine. "No more secrets," I say, ignoring the way my pulse spikes.

"My mom's a snob, Blaire."

"Meaning she still wants me nowhere near you and thinks Cassie did the community a favor by outing our true identities."

He tweaks my nose. "Still razor sharp." I roll my eyes. "Yeah, that about sums it up. My dad was actually sympathetic, and he told me he's glad I've ditched the bitch. He said he never wanted me saddled with someone like that."

"You sound surprised."

"I am. I always thought Dad bought into the notion of Cassie and me as much as Mom, but I'm beginning to see it was all Mom's idea."

"So, he won't withhold your trust fund?" I twist on my side, anxiety bubbling to the surface again.

"Oh, Mom's threatening it, but Dad told me he'd handle her. Besides, I secured a full ride, so I'm covered either way."

"You did?"

"Yep. Seems there isn't much they won't do for their next potential star player." He puffs out his chest, and a smile graces my lips.

"Wow. Someone's got a healthy ego."

He pecks my lips. "Sometimes you've just got to own that shit." We grin at one another. "What about you?"

"What about me?" I ask, wondering what he means.

"Have you thought about college?"

I flip over onto my stomach. "My parents had to dip into my college fund, and with everything going on, I haven't given it much thought. I don't even know where I'll be living after graduation, so it's hard to make any concrete plans."

Heath flips me over onto my back, hovering over me. "Come with us to UF."

"What?" I splutter.

A lopsided grin appears on his face. "We talked about it. We want you there with us."

"Why?"

"Why?" Incredulity creeps into his tone. "Because you're our girlfriend and we lo—we want you by our side."

I know what he was going to say, and my heart is ready to burst. But that doesn't mean I'm going to be the first to openly acknowledge my feelings either. "I care about you guys too," I whisper, "and I'd love nothing more than to go to UF with you, but I don't see how. I've probably missed the deadline, and unless I got a scholarship…"

"It's not too late to apply, but you have to make up your mind soon. The priority application deadline has passed, but you have until March first to apply on a space-available basis. I can talk to the coach, see if he can do anything to help."

"I don't know, Heath." Could I seriously consider this? The thought of going to college with all of them seems like a far-fetched dream that's way out of reach, but maybe I'm being pessimistic.

"Promise you'll think about it?"

"I promise." Leaning in, I distract him with a kiss, and soon, studying and future college plans are the furthest things from both our minds.

Chapter Thirty-One

$\mathcal{J}$acinta lets me leave the store a little earlier on Saturday so I can get ready with Shaznay at the Taylors' house. Skeet's band is playing at a local bar, and we're all going to support him. "This would look fab on you," Shaz suggests, holding up a black silky jumpsuit that is cut indecently low at the front and dips down at the back.

"Maybe, but I'm not showcasing my bruises for the whole town to see." I'm already a little antsy about the night, but at least I'll be protected with my guys, my best friend, and Skeet's parents who will all be there.

"Shit, sorry, forgot."

"It's fine." I pull the short green lace dress out of my bag. "Jacinta loaned me this to wear." The dress has a high, round neck and it's fully covered at the back. But the sleeves are sheer lace, and it stops a good couple inches above my knee, placing all the focus on my—bruise-free—legs.

"Oh, wow." She fingers the dress. "That will look stunning with your height and your coloring. The guys won't know what's hit them."

We're both dressed, sitting side by side in front of the mirror applying our makeup when she starts her subtle interrogation. "How are things at home? Please tell me your parents have given up on the idea of moving?"

"They have. For now. While it's tempting to run, we all agree it's probably pointless." I press my lips together until my lipstick dries. "In hindsight, it was foolish to think we could hide who we are, and we can't run every time someone finds out. It's exhausting. But it'll all depend on how things go. I know there are people at school waiting to pounce as soon as I'm unprotected, the minute they feel they can take action and get away with it."

"Then just make sure you're always with the guys. It's only for another few months anyway, and then you'll all be going off to college."

I fumble my eyeliner at her words. "Skeet talked to you about that?" I haven't even spoken to Skeet about it.

"He might've mentioned something. Shoot. Was I not supposed to say anything?" Her worried eyes meet mine.

"No, it's not that. It's just Heath only recently mentioned it to me, and I honestly don't see how it's going to be possible."

"Don't you want to go with them?"

"I want to be with them, but this is a big decision, and I don't want to rush into it either, but time is running out." I swivel on my seat facing her. "I always thought I'd be attending college with Ethan. It's just another bittersweet moment."

"God, Blaire, I hate everything you're going through. It's so unfair. I can't imagine losing Skeet. Especially like that. It'd kill me."

"It very nearly did," I admit. "My parents are the only reason I didn't seriously contemplate taking my own life."

She whacks me in the arm. "Don't you ever say or think that!" Tears pool in her eyes. "I hate that you're hurting, but suicide is never the answer. Think about what it'd do to my brother and me. And Axel and Heath, as well as your parents and your aunt and uncle."

I hug her. "Shaz, relax. I never seriously considered it, okay, but I was depressed."

I still am.

"Life was shitty, and I was missing my brother, but ending it all would mean he died in vain."

"What do you mean?" Her brow furrows.

I quell the panic waiting to rise to the surface. "Just that Ethan believed he was leaving me in a good place, and it'd be like making a mockery of that," I lie, relieved when she seems to buy it.

I want to tell her the rest of the story. I really do. But then I'd be going against Ethan's last wishes, and I can't do that even if I disagree, in part, with his thinking. Besides, it's too late now. The time for opening that can of worms has long since passed.

"Wow." Skeet whistles as I step into the kitchen, and a faint blush stains my cheeks. His entire family is here, and I hate being the center of attention. Not that they seem to mind. Skeet reels me into his arms, pressing a barely there kiss to my lips in front of all of them. His mom smiles while the rest of his family continues their conversation as if this PDA isn't happening in the vicinity. "Don't want to ruin your lip gloss," he whispers into my ear. "I'd love nothing more than to cancel tonight and lock you downstairs with me." His hand skims low on my back, and he presses me in closer. "Feel that?" he murmurs, planting a feather-soft kiss on my neck while discreetly pushing his erection against my stomach. "That's what you do to me. All the damn time."

"Oh my God," I whisper back. "You can't say that to me in front of your family!"

He chuckles. "They can't hear. Besides, my parents are all about the PDAs. They're probably mentally high-fiving me right now."

"Are you nervous?" I ask, deliberately switching to safer topics.

"A little." He tilts my chin up and his eyes shine with unnamed emotion. "I'm debuting a new song tonight, and that always gives me the jitters."

"I'm sure it's amazing. You know I love your original stuff."

He kisses the tip of my nose. "You're probably biased."

"No way." I shake my head. "If you sucked monkey balls, I'd tell you."

He barks out a laugh as his dad Liam plants a hand on his shoulder. "Ready, stud?"

"As I'll ever be." Skeet winks at me, entwining our hands and leading me outside.

❤❤❤❤

The venue is packed when we arrive, and there's limited standing room. Thankfully, Skeet's mom had already reserved an area at the front, just off to the side of the stage. Skeet gives me a sly kiss on the lips before disappearing backstage with his dad and the rest of the band. Ax and Heath are already seated, and Ax pats the empty stool beside him. I hop up, and Shaz claims the stool the other side of me.

"Everything okay?" he asks, pinning me with those gorgeous eyes.

"Yeah." I look around again. "I don't think anyone in here will pay much attention to me." The crowd is older, and I don't recognize anyone.

I highly doubt anyone from school will make an appearance, and that shaves a buttload of stress off my shoulders.

"Skeet's talent is wasted playing to these crowds," Ax admits, taking a sip of his soda. "I know he loves playing with his dad, but he's missing out on other opportunities."

"I've talked to him about it," Shaz says, sliding a Coke to me. "And you're right, he doesn't want to let Liam down."

"That's crazy," Heath interjects. "Because Liam is the most laid-back of your dads and the one most likely to be cool with Skeet following his own path."

"I know, but try telling Skeet that. He's so stubborn sometimes."

I take small sips of my soda as we wait for the gig to start. Twenty minutes later, the lights dim, and the owner of the bar announces the entertainment for the night. A loud cheer emanates from the room, accompanied by catcalls and hollers. I'm smiling as Skeet takes to the stage alongside Liam. Both are up front, guitars strapped around their torso, sporting big smiles as they wait for the other two guys to get settled.

They play a few covers to start, whipping the crowd into a frenzy. The dance floor is crammed, and the atmosphere is electric. It's funny to see all the oldies letting loose, and the four of us laugh as we watch some of the old school moves on the dance floor.

"We're going to slow it down for this number," Skeet says into the mic. "So, grab your woman and hold her tight."

"Man, he's such a fucking pussy," Axel exclaims, rolling his eyes.

"Want to dance?" Heath asks, leaning across the table toward me.

"Sure."

Gripping my hips, he lifts me down and leads me out onto the dance floor as Skeet continues talking to the crowd. Heath positions us right under the stage, directly in front of him. I give Skeet a thumbs-up, and he grins back at me. "Recently, a girl came into my life, and she's inspired me like no one ever has before. She doesn't know this, but I wrote this song for her. Hope you like it, B."

His use of Ethan's pet name is only upsetting for a nanosecond. I'm determined not to do anything to upset Skeet or throw him off his game, so I flash him a genuine smile.

How can I not smile when he's written a song for me?

When he starts singing, my smile is so wide it threatens to split my face in two. It's one of the songs he played for me in the basement except this time there are words to match the soulful music. Heath holds me close, and we sway to the music as Skeet pours his heart out in the song. He stares at me as he sings, and I can't look away. Our eyes remain locked on one another, and it's as if no one else is in the room. It might as well just be the two of us.

I feel Heath's smile as he bends down to my ear. "He wanted it to be a surprise, and he asked me to bring you up here so he could sing directly to you."

"I can't believe he wrote this for me. It's beautiful." My heart is full to bursting point. I don't know what I did to deserve these three guys, but I thank God every day for bringing them into my life. They are saving me in ways they can't even begin to imagine.

"And you look stunning, by the way," he adds, and I momentarily drag my eyes away from Skeet to smile at Heath. "Best-looking woman in this room by a mile."

I snort. "Considering most of them are old enough to be my mom, I'm not sure how to take that," I tease.

"Trust me, it's a compliment." He lifts my arm, pressing his mouth to my wrist and placing a delicate kiss there.

I rest my head on his shoulder, grinning like an idiot as one of my guys sways me gently in his arms and another one serenades me from the stage.

"Thank you," I mouth when the song ends, and Skeet takes a bow as rapturous applause breaks out around us.

"I love you" he discreetly mouths back, and happy tears prick my eyes.

I blow him a kiss before we return to our table. Axel lifts me onto my stool before placing a tray with fresh sodas on the table. "Our boy is quite the romantic," he murmurs, peering into my eyes with that intense lens of his. "And I still can't believe he kept it a secret. Skeet was dying to tell you."

"I'm glad he didn't. No one's ever done anything like that for me before."

"We'd do anything for you, Blaire. You know that, right?" He tucks a few stray strands of hair back off my face.

"I know, and I'm grateful."

His hand slips subtly up the outside of my thigh as he leans into me, whispering in my ear. "You look fucking hot tonight. All I can think about is peeling that dress off you later and worshiping every inch of your body."

My core pulses with deep longing at his words, but before I can reply, Shaz butts in. "I need to wash my ears out after that." She makes a gagging gesture.

"It wasn't meant for your ears." Ax waggles a brow. "And maybe you shouldn't eavesdrop if you don't like what you hear."

She flips him the bird, and her mom slants her a cautionary look. The oldies have mostly been sticking together, chatting and drinking and leaving us to hold our own conversation on this side of the table, so it's been easy to forget they're here.

"Maybe you need to tone it down a level or ten," she retorts with a flirty wink. "Unless you were aiming to turn your girlfriend on in front of everyone." Heath chuckles, listening attentively to our conversation but not joining in.

"I liked you better when you were four with those cute pigtails and a more limited vocab," Ax deadpans.

"Ouch." She grins, pulling me down off the stool. "It's just as well I know you love me like a sister, or I might take that to heart," she tells Ax, darting in to plant a chaste kiss on his cheek, before looping her arm in mine. "Bathroom break. C'mon."

Grabbing my purse, I waggle my fingers at the guys. "Back in a bit." Heath blows me a kiss, and Ax drills me a look that promises wicked deeds later. I shiver all over from the force of their attention, and I'm floating on a cloud as we walk away. I force Shaznay to walk through the crowd toward the restroom so I can wave at Skeet as we pass by.

"God, you're so nauseatingly in love with them. I can't decide if I'm jealous or just genuinely ill at the thought." She shivers, as if a chill just tiptoed down her spine.

"When it's your turn, you'll see." I shoulder-check her, grinning as we enter the bathroom.

I remove my cell when I'm in the stall to text Mom like I promised. My parents are wary of letting me outside now the news has been leaked.

I tap out a quick text telling her I'm fine. Before I put my cell back in my purse, a new text pops up with a link.

I know I shouldn't look.

I've become adept at ignoring stuff online, and I know better.

So, there's no excuse for my actions.

I click on the link, and all the blood drains from my face as the video uploads.

Chapter Thirty-Two

I watch with the volume turned off, my heart sinking with every frame. The first image is Heath and me kissing at the party. The next one is Axel and me cuddling intimately down by the lake. The third scene shows Skeet kissing me outside Jacinta's store.

My stomach lurches at the thought someone's been watching me and secretly taking footage of me and the guys. I shudder at the thought of what other stuff they might've captured on film.

A barrage of insults ends the video reveal. Words flash by on the screen. *Whore. Slut. Psycho.*

I shut it off after that, unable to watch any more.

"Blaire, you okay in there?" Shaz inquires, knocking on the door of my stall.

"Yeah." I shove my cell back in my purse, rubbing at the moisture under my eyes, inhaling and exhaling successively until I feel back in control. "Hey." I plant a false cheery smile on my face as I open the door and face my friend.

A small frown puckers her beautiful features. "You sure?"

"I'm peachy. Chill, Shaz." I brush past her, ignoring the twisting in my stomach and the blood pounding through my ears as I make my way to the sink. I shove my shaking hands underneath the water, keeping the fake smile plastered on my face.

"Shoot," I say, when we're back outside in the hallway. "I forgot I've got to call my mom." I shrug casually. "She'll freak out if she doesn't hear from me." I take a step back toward the restroom. "You go. I'll follow in a minute."

"I can wait." She makes to come with me.

"Shaz, seriously?" I send her an incredulous look. "I know the guys are overprotective as shit but not you too. Nothing's going to happen to me in here. I'll be back before you know it."

"I don't mind waiting."

"That's your brother and your dad out there, and their set will be over soon." I give her a gentle push. "Stop being an idiot and go!" I roll my eyes, smiling. "I'll see you in a bit."

"Okay." She still looks hesitant, and I wonder what instructions Skeet gave her in regards to me tonight.

I wave her off, and my smile crumples the instant I turn around and stride toward the bathroom. I waste no time once I'm in there. No one else is here, thankfully, so I lock the door and head straight toward the window. It glides up easily, and I climb outside, wrapping my arms around my body as the cooler evening air greets me. I'm shivering as I walk away from the venue, but it's not purely from the weather.

I can't believe we've been outed. If I had to hazard a guess, I'd say Cassie's behind this too.

She's never going to leave me alone.

She's going to torment me until she's driven me out of town.

I don't want to let her win, but I'm not sure I can take any more finger pointing and slurs. It's bad enough everyone thinks I'm a monster who enabled her brother to kill in cold blood, but now they'll be adding whore and slut to the repertoire of names they call me. They won't understand our relationship, and it'll only give them further ammunition to ramp up the bullying. The school can't protect me from this. And my parents will go ballistic when they see this.

They won't get it either.

My good mood has been erased, replaced with dark thoughts I thought I'd long since buried. I don't know how I ever believed happiness would be mine for keeps. There is no silver lining for someone like me. That's the reality I have to accept as my future.

And I can't drag the guys down with me. I *won't*. They have bright futures, and I won't be responsible for ruining them. I don't know how I'm going to stay away from them, but the only way to put the rumors to bed, to protect their reputation and safeguard their futures, is to break up with them.

I knew that as I watched the video play out, and I couldn't return to that bar and hide all this from them. Axel would see through me in a split second, and they'd talk me around. I don't want Skeet to look down from the stage and notice something isn't right. Nothing should take away from this night for him.

I pull my cell out of purse and call Mom to come get me. I keep walking in the direction of home, fearful of stopping in case the guys come after me. It won't take too long to realize I've run off and I need to put as much distance between us before that happens.

I'm halfway up the deserted road, freezing my butt off, with blisters forming on my aching feet, when the sound of approaching vehicles tickles my eardrums. I keep closer to the side of the road, not looking back.

"Oh my God, it's her!" some girl yells, and blood turns to ice in my veins. Keeping my eyes forward, I quicken my pace praying for Mom to hurry up. "Slut!" another girl shouts as the car draws up alongside me.

I refuse to look over at them, walking as fast as my legs will carry me while the car keeps pace with me. "What's wrong, sugar?" a male voice says. "Grown tired of your boy toys already?"

"If you're looking for some new fuck buddies, we're game," a different boy says.

"Do you fuck all three of them at once, whore?" one of the girls hollers.

Tears stab my eyes, but I keep walking, still refusing to look at them.

"Look at me, bitch," the guy roars, but I ignore him, pushing my legs as fast as they will go in these heels.

Suddenly the car revs up, speeding ahead, and relief courses through me. But it's short-lived.

The car swings around, coming to a halt in front of me. It's horizontally positioned across the road, blocking my path. The screeching of tires behind me raises my blood pressure to coronary-inducing levels. I glance over my shoulder, horrified to notice a second car blocking me in from the rear. Tall fences line the road on both sides, so I'm pretty much hemmed in. "Leave me alone," I hiss, hating that my voice trembles. They're all getting out of their cars now, moving toward me. With trembling fingers, I reach into my bag for my cell, but it's yanked out of my hands before I can call the guys for help. "My mom's on her way," I blurt even though I know it won't deter them.

"I'm quaking in my boots," Jenkins says, putting himself right up in my face.

Another guy presses against my back, way too close for comfort, and a single tear rolls down my face. "Is that where you learned to be a slut? From your mom?" he whispers in my ear while his hand slides up the back of my thigh.

"Don't touch me!" I shriek, trying to elbow my way out from between them, but Jenkins grabs my arm, digging his nails in.

"I told you what would happen if you stayed around here." He smirks. "The assholes aren't around to protect you now."

The guy's fingers move up under my dress, and a hysterical scream rips from my mouth. Jenkins clamps his hand over my mouth, stifling my cries. At the same time, he looks over my shoulder, narrowing his eyes at the other guy. "Enough."

"What the fuck, man?"

"Much as I'd like to teach the bitch a lesson, that kinda shit won't end well. I'm not doing time for banging a murdering slut."

"You wouldn't want to put your dick in her anyway. God knows what you'd catch," one of the girls says.

Jenkins turns to the two girls behind him, one I recognize as Shell, the girl from the parking lot the other day. "You got the stuff?" They nod. He turns back around to the asshole behind me. "Strip her."

"Gladly." I hear the smug tone in his voice.

"No!" Adrenaline courses through my veins, and self-preservation kicks in. I simultaneously stab my stiletto heel in Jenkin's shin while I hit that sensitive spot in his carotid. His eyes loll back in his head before his hold on me loosens, and he slumps to the ground, out of it. The guy behind me makes a grab for me, but I stab my heel in his foot while simultaneously elbowing him in the gut. It catches him off guard, giving me enough time to attempt an escape. Kicking off my shoes, I race forward, shoving both girls out of the way and running toward the back of their car. Up ahead, in the distance, I spot lights, and I'm silently praying it's Mom.

I slam into something solid, falling backward and landing hard on my back. Pain ricochets up my spine, and I cry out. "Fucking bitch." A different guy looms over me, lounging against the hood of the car. He crouches down, disgust lining his face even in the dark. He opens his mouth, and I scream as his spittle lands on my face. Then something cold and sticky lands on my forehead, and I look up in time to see the others crowding around me. They pelt me with eggs and pour sticky soda all over me. I scream as I thrash about on the ground. Ignoring the pain splintering me from all sides, I twist around, attempting to crawl away, but someone stomps down on my hand, and an agonizing scream tears from my lips. Someone else grabs hold of the hem of my dress. A loud ripping sound mixes with laughter as my dress is torn off me. Someone puts their boot on the middle of my back, pressing me face-first into the ground, holding me in place for the others.

I zone out. I've no other choice. I'm not getting out of here with my sanity intact. Images torment my mind, and I'm powerless to stop them or the shivering covering my entire body. Burying my head in my hands, I pray the car in the distance is Mom.

They start kicking me. Inflicting new wounds over the existing ones which haven't yet healed. I block my ears to their insults, and I beg God to take me.

I just want this to end.

Life is too hard.

And I'm not strong enough to survive this kind of torment again.

The roar of an engine startles everyone. "Now the fun starts," some asshole male says.

Car doors slam, and racing footsteps come close. "Get the fuck away from her," Axel roars. Sounds of scuffling reverberate around me, but I don't lift my head. I've gone beyond the point where I'm grateful help has arrived. I don't want them to see me like this. Lying facedown on the ground in only my undies, covered in a sticky eggy mess and a fresh layer of wounds, only some of them they can see.

"Blaire!" Heath shouts amid the sounds of wrestling, panic underscoring his tone.

The glare of headlights hits me from the other side and expletives litter the air. "Shit. Scatter!" I recognize Jenkins' voice.

"Run away all you want, but you're still dead, assholes," Skeet shouts after them.

I keep my face pressed to the asphalt, praying for this nightmare to end. Tires screech, and the smell of burning rubber lingers in the air as my assailants make a hasty escape. Racing footsteps approach. "Blaire, oh my God, Blaire. Honey, are you okay?"

Mom's voice is like a balm to my soul. She touches my arm and I lift my head up, forcing my eyes open. "Can you take me home?" I plead, shivering profusely.

"I've got you." Axel scoops me up into his arms from behind before I've had time to protest. I cling to him, burying my head in his chest so I don't have to see the look in any of their eyes.

"Do you know who did this?" Mom asks them in a clipped tone.

"Yes. We know them," Skeet confirms.

"Good. I want all their names. They're not getting away with this."

"No." My voice is croaky. I raise my head and eyeball Mom. "It'll only make things worse."

"But, honey."

"No, Mom. Please."

She looks over my head at the guys, and they share a look. Her features soften as she refocuses on me. "We'll talk about it in the morning. Let's just get you home."

Axel places me gently on the backseat of Mom's car, pulling the blanket off the floor and covering me. His clothes are destroyed with the same sticky eggy mixture coating my skin. His eyes blaze with anger. "They are not getting away with this," he grits out. "Fair enough if you don't want to report it. We'll deal with it our way."

Heath and Skeet nod from behind him.

"I don't want you to do anything," I say in a voice devoid of feeling. "It's not your problem."

Mom turns the key in the engine, looking anxiously at me through the mirror.

"The hell it isn't." I've never seen Heath in such a murderous rage. "You're our girl, and they hurt you. If you think we're going to stand by and do nothing, then you don't know us."

"Will you be okay?" Skeet asks, pushing Ax aside so he can lean in over me.

"I don't know if I'll ever be okay," I truthfully admit.

"Blaire, honey. We need to leave. I want to get you home so Daddy can check you out."

I twist my head to the side, meeting her concerned gaze. "One minute." I close my eyes for a second, knowing what I need to do but hating myself for it already. I pull myself upright, biting down hard on my cheek to stop from crying out as pain whips through my body. I look at all three guys, committing their faces to memory. "I can't do this anymore." I shake my head, fighting tears. "I thought I was strong enough to handle it, but I'm not. Not on top of all the other stuff."

"Blaire, no—"

"I'm breaking up with you." I cut across Skeet and force the words out. "It's better this way."

For all of you. They've protected me; now it's my turn to protect them. The only way I know how.

"You don't mean it." Heath's tone beseeches me.

"I do. We're finished. Please leave me alone." I turn back around to Mom. "You can go now."

"Blaire."

Axel's tone holds a gravity no one else can suffuse with one word. I know if I look at him, my resolve will waiver. "Close the door, Ax. On the car and our relationship." I say it without looking up at him.

"Say that to my face, Blaire." Of course, he'd be the one to challenge me.

Summoning whatever strength I have left, I lift my chin up and stare at him. "We're finished. Goodbye."

"Boys. Please." Mom interrupts. "I know you're upset, but you need to give my daughter space right now. Please respect her wishes."

"We're not going anywhere, beautiful." Skeet's fighting spirit is alive and well. "We love you too much to just walk away now. Take whatever time you need, and when you're ready, we'll be waiting."

I can't acknowledge his beautiful words because if I do I'll cry, so I turn the other way, letting tears silently roll down my face as they close the door and Mom drives us home.

Dad cries as he attends to my injuries, and I can no longer hold back my own tears. Mom is sobbing too, and it's such a mess. I'm making things worse for them. My selfish decision to date all three guys has only added to this nightmare. They don't ask me about them, but I know it's coming.

I lie in bed a couple hours later waiting for them to go asleep. I can still hear them arguing through the walls. Mom wants to move again. Dad wants to hunt down those who hurt me and exact his own vengeance. I twist onto my side, hugging Ethan's picture to my chest. Silent tears continue to pour down my cheeks, and the pain in my chest is so intense it's a wonder I can still breathe.

The urge to hurt myself is riding me hard. I'm only in one of Ethan's old shirts and I lift it up, exposing my thighs and digging my nails in, scratching over the old scars as familiar emotions run riot inside me.

I could cut.

The physical pain would make it easier to deal with the pain in my head, but it will only be a temporary release. What I need is to remove these feelings permanently.

I'm so weak. So useless. Despite all those self-defense classes Ethan made me take in tenth grade, I'm still unable to defend myself. I still folded like a deck of cards out on that road. I let them do that to me. I let them make me a victim again. I haven't moved on. I've regressed.

I can't save myself because I'm too much of a fucking coward.

Ethan couldn't save me. In the end, my problems killed him.

Skeet, Axel, and Heath can't save me. And I won't stand by and destroy their lives like I did with Ethan.

My parents can't save me. Even if they knew the truth, they still couldn't help. It's too late. I'm beyond help. I'm a noose around their neck. Without me, their lives would be so much easier.

My cell pings from my purse, and I pull it out to torture myself some more. But it's not another message from the guys. It's another message from truthseeker101. Now they have my cell number I'm sure the abuse will only increase.

I want to inflict pain. I need to feel pain.

So, I open it up and read through numbed eyes.

You deserve everything that's coming to you. Do us all a favor and kill yourself, you lying slut.

I'd laugh at the irony if I wasn't afraid of waking my parents. The house has finally fallen quiet, so I get up and tiptoe to the bathroom, removing the items I need from the cabinet, before carefully locking the door.

I just want it to stop.

The pain has sunk bone deep, soul deep, eradicating every trace of the person I used to be.

The darkness has spread. Eating me alive from the inside out.

And I can't face it anymore.

I need it to stop.

I don't want to feel.

I don't want to think.

I don't want to exist.

I want to cease trying to survive on this plane.

These thoughts repeat over and over in my head as I empty the box with Mom's sleeping pills and the second one with her anti-anxiety medication. I fill the glass by the sink to the brim and knock back the medication, one handful at a time, until there's none left. Then I lie down on the floor on my side, hugging myself while I wait for the darkness to claim me forever.

Time passes, and my eyelids grow heavy. My body feels weightless. My mind is deliciously hazy.

The last thing I see as my eyes flutter shut is an image I've craved these past few months. His ghostly form stands over me, instantly relaxing me.

"Ethan," I slur, reaching out a hand. "Don't leave me again."

Part Two

Chapter Thirty-Three

SKEET – NINETEEN MONTHS LATER

"Y‍ou coming to the frat party Friday night?" Heath asks, walking into the living room of the house we share off campus and throwing his duffel bag on the ground by my feet.

"Maybe. Maybe not." I'm deliberately noncommittal. The girls at those parties are like predatory wild animals looking to sink their claws into any male in the vicinity.

"Dude. Not this again." He looks over my shoulder at my laptop and sighs. "Seriously, Taylor. You're not going to find her if she doesn't want to be found."

"I don't know how you can be so dismissive," I snap, rubbing a tense spot between my brows. "Aren't you the least bit worried about her?"

"It's been over a year and a half, Skeet. If anything had happened to her, we would know about it. Some media outlet would've picked up the story."

"Not necessarily." I continue scanning the monitoring feeds I've set up to see if there is any recent news about Blaire. But, as usual, it's empty. Snapping the laptop shut, I lie on my back, sighing.

"She left us, Skeet. She broke things off, and then she upped and left town. I don't know why you and Axel are so fixated on finding her. She didn't want us. It's as simple as that." A muscle clenches in his jaw, and I know what's coming next. We've had this same argument over and over since Blaire vanished. "We all went out on a limb for her, and she left us behind without a second thought."

"You're an asshole," Ax says, appearing in the doorway.

"You say that every time we have this discussion."

"And I'll keep on saying it if you keep up the bullshit." He tosses a beer to me, and it lands in my lap. He hands Heath a bottle of water and drops onto the couch alongside him. "Blaire was in a bad place when we last saw her. *That's* why we worry." Ax pins Heath with a menacing glare.

I honestly thought Heath wasn't going to room with us again this year. A divide has formed in our friendship. Since we lost Blaire, Heath has distanced himself from us. He was worried about her when she first upped and left, but then his feelings changed. His concern transformed to anger. I can partly understand. His relationship with his mom is more fractured than ever. He stood up to her for Blaire, and then she left. He's latched onto his anger and continuously feeds it.

Heath was never a player, but he's put Ax and me to shame since we came to UF. Ax hasn't so much as looked sideways at any girl since Blaire. Which is practically saint-like for a guy who once fucked girls like they were a dying breed. I've been celibate too although I had one moment of weakness. One time where I let frustration get the better of me. I almost hooked up with this girl at a party, but it was a disaster because she wasn't Blaire.

Blaire got under my skin, and there's no digging her out.

Other girls hold no interest for me, so I generally abstain from parties, same as Ax. Heath, however, is a whole other ball game. He's turned into a stereotypical man-whore, hooking up almost as much as Ax did during his dark pre-Blaire days. Heath can protest all he wants, but we both know the score. He's pissed and lashing out. Trying to fuck the girl we all still love out of his system, but it's not working. He might say he doesn't care anymore, but we both know he's lying. That does nothing to ease the tension that lingers between us all the time though.

"It doesn't matter how much time passes, I'll always worry about her. Until I find her. Until I know she's okay. Know she's happy. That's all I want for her," I semi-lie.

Ax stares at me, and I know he sees through me. He knows the reasons why I trawl the net every night searching for her. I won't give up on the girl I know is my soul mate. I may have only been with her a short while, but when you know, you know. That girl touched me to my core. Same way she did Ax and Heath. They're just less vocal about it.

And if that makes me a pussy, I'll gladly wear that crown.

"How long are you going to keep this up? For the rest of your Goddamned life?" Heath throws a pillow across the room in frustration. "We're in our sophomore year of college. This should be the best time of our lives. There is beer, parties, and pussy galore on this campus, and all you two do is pine over a girl who kicked us to the curb without a backward glance. Why the fuck are you wasting your time with this bullshit?" He sits up, a muscle ticking furiously in his jaw. "Wake the fuck up. Both of you. Blaire's gone, and she's not coming back. Period." He stands, draining the last of his water. "If you don't get over yourselves, I'm out of here. I'm not wasting another year sitting around watching you two mope over a girl who doesn't want us."

"You don't know that," I retaliate.

"Then where is she, huh?" He throws his hands up in the air. "She knew we were planning to come to UF. It wouldn't be that hard for *her* to find *us*. If she still wanted us in her life, she'd find us. It's been nineteen months, and she hasn't made contact. Enough said."

"Fuck you, Gilchrist." Ax stands, putting his face in Heath's. "No one is forcing you to stay here. You want to move out, join your football buddies in their house, go right ahead. We're not stopping you."

I put my beer down and climb to my feet, pushing myself in between them. "No one's moving out, and we'll go to the damn frat party if it means so much to you."

Heath visibly calms down. "I'm doing this for you guys. You need to get under someone else to get over her."

That pisses me off, and I snort, glaring at him. "Is that how you convince yourself it's not a betrayal?"

"It's not a fucking betrayal!" he roars. "She. Broke. It. Off. With. Us!" He shoves me. "What the fuck is wrong with you? She did a number on your brain. One day, you're going to look back at this and fucking regret throwing away college over a girl who didn't even care enough to tell us a proper goodbye."

"Just because we're not whoring ourselves around campus doesn't mean we're throwing away our college experience," Ax bites back before I get the chance. "I'm top of all my classes, and I'm on target to achieve my goals. I'm going to qualify for the bar and get my mom the fuck out of jail. I'm going to earn enough money to pay Griff back for all his sacrifices. I'm going to have a life that is a million times better than the life I grew up with, so screw you, asshole." Ax shoves Heath aside before marching out of the room.

I shake my head. "You've got to stop pressing his buttons. The fact he's not casually hooking up with anyone isn't a bad thing. Have you forgotten what he was like when he was spiraling? He's in a pretty good place, man. Don't ruin that."

"He's not in a good place when it comes to her. Neither of you are."

"That's your opinion. It's not ours. We're not giving up on her."

He shakes his head. "It's pointless to keep hoping. She's gone, Skeet. She's gone." He clamps his hand on my shoulder before stalking to the door. "I'm leaving in an hour with or without you."

💜💜💜

Axel and I hover by the doorway, drinking warm beer from red cups while surveying the carnage in front of us. Drunken girls are draped all over Heath and his football buddies, ignorant to the fact they are just one of a number.

"I hate that douche McKenzie," Axel admits, glaring at the back of the douche's head.

"Same. I don't know how Gilchrist puts up with him."

"Probably for the same reason the rest of those idiots do. His five-second forty-yard dash."

"Hey, Ax." A petite blonde with perky tits lands in front of us, interrupting us mid-conversation. She swoons at Ax, and I feel like pulling her aside and filling her in. She's wasting her time. If Axel was ever going to hook up with any other girl, it wouldn't be with a blonde. It's too much of a reminder of the girl we loved and lost.

"Larissa." Ax is polite but barely.

"I haven't seen you here before," she says, batting her eyelashes and placing her hand on his arm.

"That's original." Ax removes her hand, staring her out of it, but she's a feisty little thing and not to be deterred.

"You're so funny." She playfully shoves his shoulder, and I smother a laugh. "It's one of the things I like most about you."

Oh boy.

"Was there something you wanted?" I can tell from the way his jaw works that he's grinding down on his teeth and losing whatever semblance of patience he possesses.

"You." She sways on her feet, clearly smashed, smiling up at him like he hung the stars in the sky.

"Not going to happen, sweetheart." Ax's smile is tight.

"Why not?" She pouts, and it's not a good look on her.

I take pity on Ax, jumping to the rescue. "Because he's got a girl back home and he's loyal." It's only half a lie.

"So, do us both a favor, and stop wasting your time." Ax doesn't hold back. Not now or the hundred other times I've watched him deflect advances. He has zero interest in anyone but Blaire, and I love that we're both on the same page.

"Huh." Her nostrils flare, and I can tell she's debating whether he's telling her the truth or not. "Well, I hope she's worth it." She flounces off, and Ax visibly relaxes.

"Is it just me or does every girl pale under Blaire's memory?"

"It's not just you. No one else comes even close."

He sips slowly on his beer, watching Larissa make a beeline for Heath. "Do you think he's right?" He tips his head at Heath, who now, predictably, has his arm curved around Larissa's waist. "That we're foolish to think we can get her back."

"I don't believe that. If we want to find her, we will."

"But you've been searching this whole time and found nothing." He sighs, sounding resigned. "I think we might have to face facts, man. We might never find her. Not if she's changed her name completely."

This is the first time I've heard Ax sound so defeatist, and I feel like taking back my thoughts from a few minutes ago. "I refuse to think like that," I spit out, anger fueling the blood flowing through my veins. "And I can't believe you're capitulating."

"I never said that." Now he looks mad. "You know how I feel about her. She's everything to me, and I want her back. I'm just thinking out loud."

I drain my cup and crumple it in my fist. "Well, keep those kind of thoughts to yourself. I don't want to hear it." I toss the crinkled cup to the ground. "I'm out of here." I walk away before I say or do something I regret. Ax doesn't stop me or come after me, but I knew he wouldn't.

I'm still fuming by the time I get back to our house, so I don't spot the form waiting in the shadows. I'm fumbling with the key, trying to get it to turn in the lock when a soft voice speaks from behind me.

"Hi, Skeet."

I go still, my fingers curled around the key, my heart careening out of control behind my ribcage. Every muscle in my body has locked up tight, my breath faltering, shock splayed across my face no doubt. I've almost convinced myself I imagined it when she speaks again, her voice clearer and more confident this time.

"I know you probably hate me, and that you don't owe me anything, but I need to speak to you. Can you please turn around?"

Her soft, lyrical voice does funny things to my insides, and I can't deny her.

I never could.

In slow motion, I turn around, blinking profusely at the girl standing in front of me. Her hair is different now. It's a golden almost-white blonde color, and it's shorter and layered, resting gently on her shoulders. Her beautiful blue eyes turn glassy as she watches my reaction with a nervous smile on her lips. I skim her from head to toe, needing to assure myself that she's really here and that she's not some ghostly apparition. She glows. Exuding life and vitality, and my heart surges as all manner of emotions run wild inside me.

"Blaire?" I choke out, still rooted to the spot. "Is it really you?"

"It's me. I'm really here." Her smile grows wider, and I snap out of it, bridging the gap between us and reeling her into my arms.

Chapter Thirty-Four

BLAIRE

S keet pulls me into an embrace, and it feels like I'm home. I wrap my arms around him, holding him tight. This isn't the kind of reception I was expecting, but I shouldn't be surprised. Skeet always had the biggest heart. He buries his head in my hair, inhaling deeply. "I can't believe you're here," he murmurs. "I've wished for this moment every day since you left."

His words reach deep places inside me, and I want to stay enclosed in his arms and never let go, but there is so much that needs to be said, and I can't forget what I came here for. Reluctantly, I ease out of his arms, putting some distance between us. "I'm so sorry, Skeet. For just abandoning you all like that."

"It doesn't matter." Tears prick his eyes, and I melt all over again. "All that matters is you're here now."

His hair is much longer, almost touching his shoulders, and he has it pulled back in a ponytail. Thick leather bands encircle his wrist, and the telltale signs of a tattoo creep up the side of his neck. His eyebrow is pierced, and he's sporting a semi-grungy style with a crumpled black shirt and loose-hanging jeans that hug his body in all the right places. Unlaced scuffed leather boots adorn his feet. He looks like a bona fide rocker rather than your typical college student, and it looks really good on him.

I force myself to stop drooling, shaking my head. "It does matter, and it's why I came here. I owe you all an explanation."

"*That's* why you came here? Just to explain?" His face drops a little, and I close the gap between us, taking his hands in mine. "I thought, I hoped …" He trails off, looking dejectedly at the ground.

247

"You thought what?" I ask in a gentle tone.

"That you might go to school here. It's silly, I …"

He trails off again as my smile expands. I came here expecting anger and rejection, and I wouldn't have blamed any of them for reacting like that. But Skeet … Skeet seems to be genuinely pleased that I'm here. "I do go to school here," I confirm, watching as his face lights up. "I'm a freshman. I had to take a year off last year, but as soon as it was possible, I enrolled here."

Skeet picks me up, swinging me around, and my laughter rings out in the silent night air. "Put me down, you idiot."

"Never." He places my feet on the ground but hauls me back into his arms. "I'm never letting you go."

"Skeet," I whisper, looking up at him. "Why aren't you mad?"

"I can't fathom being mad when I'm so fucking happy to see you. Have you any idea how long I've tried to find you? How happy it makes me to see you looking so well? We were worried about you, Blaire. So fucking worried." His euphoria dies, his expression turning more serious. "We were scared we'd never see you again, and the thought almost killed me."

"We?" I inquire the same time a deep voice says "Blaire" from behind.

"Look who I found." Skeet spins me around in his arms to face Axel.

Axel drinks me in from head to toe, his laser-sharp, slow gaze like a sensual undressing. Images of our time together flash before my eyes causing tingles to fly through my body in a way I haven't felt for a long time. "Hey," I whisper. "I'm back."

He stands rooted to the spot, just looking me up and down, without saying anything. As usual, his face is a wall, and I can't see behind it to figure out how he feels about me showing up on their doorstep after all this time.

"Are you okay?" he asks after what seems like eternity.

I nod. "I'm good. I'm in a much better place."

He drills me with an intense look, still not moving from his spot on the grass. "I'm happy to hear that. I was concerned."

"I'm sorry for worrying you." I glance back at Skeet, clutching his arms around my waist, noting how his muscles are hard and strong under my fingertips in a way they weren't before. "And I want to explain. I want to tell you everything. Things I couldn't tell you last time. I was hoping we could meet tomorrow evening?"

He nods, looking up at Skeet. "Sure. Why don't you come here? We don't room with anyone else, so we'll have privacy."

"That would be great. I'm in one of the residence halls where privacy is a luxury I only enjoy once in a blue moon."

Skeet brushes my hair aside, grazing his nose along the column of my neck. I shiver all over. His touch affects me every bit as much as it used to. Skeet was always the touchy-feely one, but I still can't believe he's like this with me. It seemed like too much to hope for, and now I regret wasting a month before approaching them. But I was scared they wouldn't hear me out and scared to face the reality that I'd lost them forever. Perhaps there's some way of salvaging our relationship. Even if it's only as friends.

"Skeet." Axel's tone holds considerable caution.

"Don't," Skeet retorts. "I fucking missed her, and from the way she's holding on to me, I can tell she missed me too."

"I did." I look up at him, smiling sadly, before refocusing on Ax. "I missed you all so much."

Ax stares at me, looking uncharacteristically unsure. Electricity crackles in the space between us. "Come. Here," he says in a gruff voice after a bit. Skeet releases me, pressing a kiss to my cheek before letting me go. I walk toward Ax with my heart hammering in my chest. I stop in front of him and look up. His hair is styled the way he's always worn it, and he still wears his trademark scruff. My fingers twitch with the craving to reach out and touch him, but I hold myself back.

I can't assume anything.

His gorgeous eyes suck me in until I'm drowning in his gaze. Reaching out, he laces his fingers lightly through my hair, and I stifle a blissful moan. "I missed you too," he whispers, before clamping his hand on the back of my head and drawing me into his chest. I circle my arms around his waist as he holds me close. His heart beats wildly under my ear, and I close my eyes, absorbing his touch and his smell, remembering how good it felt to be touched by him. He didn't realize it, but he healed parts of my fragmented heart, helping put me on a path to today.

"You've got to be fucking kidding me." Skeet's disgusted tone has me pulling away from Axel and glancing around. A lump the size of a football lodges in my throat as I follow Skeet's gaze.

Heath is staggering toward the house, his arm wrapped around a tiny blonde. She's struggling to keep him upright, almost buckling under his weight. Heath has always been the biggest of the guys, but either my memory didn't serve me well or he's added even more bulk to his muscular form. He exudes potent alpha maleness, and my hormones sit up and take notice, obviously ignoring the fact he is already spoken for.

My heart plummets to my toes, but I give myself a silent pep talk. Coming here was an important part of my recovery. I had to explain, and I wanted to ensure the guys were okay. That they were living their dreams and were happy. It was never about picking up where we'd left off. I couldn't dare to dream like that, so I have no right to feel jealous of the girl draped around Heath or heartbroken at the thought he is lost to me. I gave up the right to those feelings the night I broke up with them. The night I chose death over life.

I draw a few deep breaths as he nears. He still hasn't noticed me. He's too hammered to notice much of anything. "Hi, Heath," I say as the couple come up alongside Ax and me.

His head jerks up so fast it's a wonder he didn't give himself whiplash. He rocks back on his heels, almost taking a tumble, but Ax's reflexes are fast, and he grabs hold of his arm before he hits the ground. Heath blinks repeatedly, rubbing at his eyes. "What the hell?"

Skeet comes up on the other side of me, placing his hand on my lower back and moving me in closer to his side. "Blaire's back," he says, cautioning Heath with a ferocious expression.

Heath stares at me, and I watch his emotions metamorphose. There's disbelief at first and then a flash of relief before anger raises its head and his features contort. "You're too late," he slurs, grabbing hold of the girl and plastering her to his side. "I've moved on."

"That's not why I'm here," I coolly reply, ignoring the narrowed focus of the girl's gaze. "I owe you an apology and an explanation."

"I don't want to hear it, and there's nothing I have to say to you either." He yanks the girl forward, moving past us.

"Heath." Skeet calls out after him, but I shake my head.

"Drop it. He's smashed." I shrug, as if my heart isn't splintering. "Can you mention the meeting to him in the morning?"

"We'll tell him," Ax supplies. "But you shouldn't get your hopes up. He's changed."

"And it's not for the better," Skeet adds.

"What do you mean?"

"He's angry at the world," Ax says. "And I think you and I can both relate to that."

I bob my head. "Yeah, we can." I pause for a beat. "Is that my doing?"

Skeet takes my arm, tipping my chin up with his finger. "It's complicated, and it's not down to just one thing."

I spin around watching Heath stumble into the house with his girlfriend with a heavy heart. Turning back around to face the guys, I catch them exchanging looks. "It's late. I should go. I'll meet you back here tomorrow."

"I'll walk you to your dorm," Skeet offers, but I shake my head.

"You don't need to do that."

"I'm not letting you walk back to campus by yourself. It's not safe."

My lips kick up at his obvious protectiveness. "I'm not walking." I gesture at my car over my shoulder. "I'm driving."

He looks displeased, and that only makes me smile more. At least two of my guys are happy to see me. They both walk me to my car, and Skeet opens the door while I get in and start the engine. They stand there, staring at me, and there are so many unspoken words between us. "Give me your cell," I say, holding out my hand. Skeet grins, placing his cell in the palm of my hand. I punch in my digits and return it to him. "You have my number now, message me so I have yours. I'll text you when I'm back at my dorm."

"You won't disappear again, will you, Blaire?" he asks, his face awash with vulnerability. It's a look I know I put there.

"I'm not going anywhere, Skeet. I promise." My gaze dances between them. "I will be back here tomorrow, and I'll tell you everything."

"We believe you," Ax says pulling Skeet back from the car. "Drive safe." He closes my door and I pull away with both guys watching me until I'm out of sight.

Chapter Thirty-Five

"Hottie alert. Over by the pillar," Nina says, waggling her brows and subtly gesturing to her right as we exit our building en route to the coffee shop for lunch.

Don't tell me how I know.

I just do.

My smile is wide as I confirm my suspicions, spotting Skeet lounging against the wall with buds in his ears. He notices me instantly, grabbing his bag and jogging toward us.

"Oh my fucking God," Nina rasps, like she's finding it hard to breathe. "He's coming over here!" She smooths a hand down the front of her shirt. "Do I look okay?"

I've no time to let my roomie down gently before Skeet has scooped me into his arms, hugging the shit out of me. Over his shoulder, I spot Nina's mouth falling open.

"Hey, beautiful," he says, holding me tight.

"Hey, Skeet. What are you doing here?"

He holds me at arm's length, tugging the buds out of his ears. "I couldn't wait until tonight, and I wanted to make sure I hadn't been dreaming."

This guy. He slays me. In the best possible way.

I link my fingers through his and squeeze his hand. "I'm real. I'm here. And I'm not going to disappear again. I promise."

I look up at him as he looks down at me, and something indiscernible passes in the space between us. My heart swells with love as we stare at one another. I hoped to shed some of my lingering guilt by meeting the guys and explaining. But I didn't expect to feel this flurry of emotions.

To feel like I'm falling all over again.

But I am. I've only spent minutes in their company, but it's enough to resurrect all my old feelings. I remember how exciting it felt to be with them. How adored and safe they made me feel. How they never looked at me as if I was broken.

Our relationship didn't end because we lost those feelings we shared. It was torn apart by circumstance and my damaged mental health. The love growing in my heart for them never died, and now I'm back in their presence, it swirls inside me, reminding me of how amazing it feels to be falling in love.

"Ahem." Nina clears her throat. "Aren't you going to introduce me?"

"Of course." I drag my gaze away from Skeet. "Nina this is Skeet. He's my …" I'm struggling to spit the word ex out of my mouth, and true to form, Skeet rides to the rescue.

"Boyfriend," he blurts, and now it's my turn to go slack-jawed.

He looks at me anxiously. "Unless you already have—"

"No, no other boyfriend," I rush to reassure him.

Nina frowns, looking between us. "Why do I get the sense there's a lot more to this than meets the eye."

"Because there is. Do you mind if I ditch our lunch plans and fill you in later?"

She hugs me briefly. "I'd ditch you in a heartbeat for him too," she quips, winking at Skeet. "I'll see you later." She waves, sending me a suggestive look before she skips off, and I just know she's going to grill me later.

"She seems fun," Skeet says, towing me across the grass.

"Nina's cool if a little excitable at times, but she's a good friend." Or I think she will be. It's a long time since I had any real female friends, and I'm still adjusting to letting people back into my life. To trusting them with my innermost thoughts and taking a risk in order to move forward with my life.

"There's this cool little diner just off campus we could go to if you like? Food is good and it's devoid of the usual college crowd. You don't have class for two hours, right?"

"How'd you know that?"

He looks sheepish. "Don't get mad, but I might've sweet talked one of the admin staff in the registrar's office into looking up my girlfriend's schedule."

I roll my eyes, but I'm laughing at the same time. "Why doesn't that surprise me."

He grins. "What good is charisma if you don't take advantage of it from time to time?"

I shake my head this time. "Next time, please convince the administration to switch my class to midweek. Trust me to pick an elective that has a Saturday session. Kill me now."

He darts in, kissing my forehead. "I'll work on that. Leave it with me." He shoots me a saucy grin, leading me off campus.

"So, what are *you* studying?" I ask once we're seated at the diner and we've placed our order.

"Computer science." He drums his fingers idly off the tabletop.

"Really? I thought you'd pursue music," I admit as the waitress sets our drinks down.

"Nah. That's only a hobby."

"But you're so talented."

He shrugs. "I'm only as good as my muse, and when she deserted me, the well dried up."

I pause with my mouth pressed against my glass. "I'm sorry."

He leans across the table, taking my hand in his. "I was trying to be funny, but that obviously failed. I don't blame you for anything, Blaire. It wouldn't have made a difference. I enjoy music, and I enjoy being up on stage, but I've no burning desire to be a rock star. I play with a band locally, and I love it, but it's not what I want to do with my life."

"And computer science is?"

He shrugs again, letting go of my hand so we can sip our drinks. "I've always been good with computers, and it was, honestly, the only thing that appealed to me when I was enrolling. I like the course, and it's not that taxing."

"Maybe not for you!" I tease.

He scrubs a hand over his prickly jawline. "Why'd you choose sociology as your major?"

"I like how broad the spectrum is although I'm pretty hellbent on becoming a social worker. I want to help others. To give something back."

His expression turns more serious. "I think that's great, and you'll make a fantastic social worker."

We chat about more mundane things while we eat, and I'm loving how relaxed and normal everything is between us. He insists on paying and walking me to my class. "Have you dated anyone since us?" he inquires. I shake my head, and he stops walking, pulling me over to a nearby bench. "Why not?"

"I was focused on other things and …" I'm not sure I should say this, but I'm trying to be more open and honest, so I suck in a brave breath and continue. "And I was still hung up on you guys."

"Honestly?" That vulnerability is back on his face again.

"It's the truth. I didn't want to break up with any of you. I thought I was doing the right thing."

"I figured as much, but it was still a terrible shock when we discovered you'd left town. I was in a major funk for ages."

"If it helps, I thought about you all every day."

"It does." He links his fingers in mine. "I haven't been able to forget you either. Tried hooking up with a girl last year, and I was a hot mess. Ran out of the room, leaving her half-dressed, because every time I looked at her, all I could see was your face." Shock splashes across my face and he notices. "That surprises you?"

"Eh, yeah. You're a guy." I'm sure the fact guys his age are horny bastards is pretty much self-explanatory, so I don't elaborate. "I didn't expect any of you to be waiting for me. I mean, it's clear Heath isn't, and that's fine," I rush to add. "His girlfriend is pretty."

"She's not his girlfriend. Heath only engages in hookups."

My brow furrows. "That's not who he is."

"It's who he is now." He stands, pulling me with him. "C'mon. I don't want you to be late."

We walk hand in hand to the building, and he seems reluctant to let me leave once we arrive. "I'm terrified to let you out of my sight," he admits. "In case you vanish into thin air."

Boy, I've really done a number on him. And I hate myself for that. "What can I do to convince you I'm here to stay?"

A flirty look shimmers in his eyes as he pulls me to him. "Kiss me."

My eyes dart to his mouth of their own volition. "Skeet," I whisper, tracing the pad of my thumb across his lower lip. "I want that more than anything, but you need to hear what I have to say first."

"One little kiss won't hurt," he pleads, arching a brow and pinning me with puppy dog eyes.

"It won't be one little kiss if I press my lips to yours, and we both know it."

He shoots me a lopsided grin. "Can't help a guy for trying. Especially when he's missed his girlfriend so much."

Shock splays across my face. "I thought you just said that for Nina's benefit. But you're serious?"

"As a heart attack." He caresses my cheek. "Unless it's not what you want?"

"We can't just pick up where we left off," I splutter.

An amused grin graces his lips. "Why not?"

"Because … because …" I trail off, unable to articulate any legit reasons why we shouldn't get back together. I still have feelings for him. He clearly has feelings for me. *Is it wrong to rush back into this? Especially when I have stuff I still need to work out in relation to Ethan and the past?*

"Don't fight me on this because you'll only lose." Then he places his mouth against mine, and time stands still. Our surroundings disappear, and it's only the two of us, kissing and kissing like we've never kissed before. Skeet's lips glide across mine in worship, and he holds me close, like he never wants to let me go. Our separation no longer exists. It's as if we've never been apart. When we finally tear our lips from one another, we're both flushed and grinning like fools. "I love you, Blaire," he whispers, tucking my hair behind my ears. "I never stopped, and I never will. I can't speak for the others, but you're my girl unless you tell me you're not mine. Unless I'm mistaken, and you didn't feel that the same way I felt it."

"You're not wrong. I love you too, but there's still so much you don't know."

"And I'm sure I won't feel any differently after you tell me." He fixes the straps on my bag before pecking my lips softly. "Now go before you're late. I'll see you at the house in a few hours." He backs away, mouthing

"Love you, beautiful," and I basically soar into the building as if I'm floating on love's wings.

❤❤❤❤

Axel opens the door to me, a few hours later, ushering me inside the house. He's not giving anything away, just politely offering me a seat in their spacious living room before striding to the kitchen to fetch me a bottle of water. Skeet lands in the room while he's gone, dropping down onto the couch beside me and pulling me onto his lap. His arms go around my waist as his mouth descends on mine. I kiss him briefly before gently pushing him away. "We can't." Axel chooses that moment to walk back into the living room, halting when he sees our intimate embrace. I slide off Skeet's lap and smooth a hand down over my dress. Ax walks toward us, not saying anything, but he shoots a dark look at Skeet before sitting down.

"I'm not hiding anything," Skeet states, resting one leg casually over his knee. "Blaire is my girlfriend again."

"Skeet," I hiss. "This isn't the time or place." I can't let this meeting get derailed. I need to get this stuff off my chest.

Ax and Skeet drill deadly looks at one another. Then Ax sits back, sighing. "What is it you wanted to tell us, Blaire."

I look toward the door. "Where's Heath? Shouldn't we wait for him?"

"Heath isn't joining us," Skeet says. "I didn't tell you earlier because I thought Ax could bring him around."

"I tried, but he doesn't want to know," Ax confirms. "I'm sorry."

My stomach drops like a lead balloon, and pain pierces my heart. It doesn't feel right to be here without him, but I can't force him to listen. I can only hope that he'll come around in time.

"It's not your fault, and it's not his. I don't blame him." I wet my dry lips. "Okay, so I guess I'm doing this without him here." I sit up a little straighter, eyeballing both guys, one at a time. "I have lots of stuff to tell you. Things about that night, and why I went away, and where I've been all this time. But it's more than just that. There's stuff from my past I never told you. Stuff you need to hear."

The guys trade knowing looks before Ax focuses on me. "I always suspected you didn't tell us the full story."

"I couldn't because of a promise I made to my brother, but everything's changed now, and I want to right all my wrongs. It might not be possible, but I'm determined to try." I smile at them. "It was never about you. You guys were the best part of my life back then, and you made me feel normal. Like I wasn't broken. I didn't want to shatter that illusion. I wanted to bask in the pretense. To believe I could turn things around, but the ties linking me to the past were too binding, and I couldn't break free."

Skeet slips his fingers between mine. "It's okay, Blaire. You can tell us anything. No one is judging you here."

I nod, smiling softly. "Thank you for always being so gracious." I wet my lips again, ignoring the flurry of anxiety pressing down on my chest. "What I have to tell you isn't easy to say or listen to, but I'm asking if you can try and not interrupt in case I lose my nerve. You can ask me anything you want after."

Ax moves, kneeling in front of me. "Don't be scared. Let it out. You've got this."

"In order to explain, I need to go back to a night I'd tried very hard to wipe from my memory." I fight the trembling threatening to take hold of me. "It was the summer just before I started tenth grade. And a night that set everything in motion."

Chapter Thirty-Six

"A couple weeks before my fifteenth birthday, I snuck out with some friends to attend a party at Todd DeLaurentis's house." Both guys stiffen, instantly recognizing his name. I'm sure it won't take much for them to join the dots. "Ethan hated Todd because he was dating the girl he was crushing on. There's no way he would've let me attend, so I went without telling him." I pause for a second, dredging up reserves of courage. "It's the biggest regret of my life."

Skeet squeezes my hand, moving closer to me on the couch. Ax sits cross-legged at my feet, giving me his undivided attention.

"I'd never drank alcohol before or attended any of their parties. While Ethan and I went to the Academy, and we had our own small circle of friends—other kids who came from middle-class families—we were mostly outsiders. Our parents weren't stinking rich like the majority of kids, and they looked down their noses at us. Except for Cam. He'd been Ethan's friend since they were three, but he was the only rich kid who didn't treat us like dirt. I should've smelled a rat when Todd told my bestie to make sure I came along that night. But I was too stupid to think anything was suspicious."

"What did he do to you, Blaire?" Ax grits out, and his lack of patience isn't anything new.

"Matt Carey was fawning over me all night, and I was flattered by his attention. I didn't realize how fast he was filling up my cup or that he'd drugged my drink." I swallow the bile forming in my mouth. "I started to feel unwell, and he acted all sympathetic, taking me upstairs to one of the bedrooms to lie down."

SIOBHAN DAVIS

My chest heaves up and down. I've gone over this with my therapist and spoken in group sessions about that night while in the facility, but retelling it doesn't get any easier. "My vision was blurring in and out, and I couldn't stand upright without his help. I started to panic. I knew, deep down, something wasn't right, but he bundled me upstairs so fast I didn't have time to call out for help."

I knot my hands in my lap, pausing for a split second. "Most of the rest of what happened is a blur. I was unconscious when someone undressed me, but I woke up as the first spear of pain shot through me." Tears fill my eyes despite my desire to recount this without sobbing. I don't want them to see me how I used to be because I'm stronger now.

"Here, take a drink," Skeet says, uncapping my bottle of water and handing it to me. My hands shake, and he holds the bottle to my mouth, helping me take small sips.

"They sodomized me," I whisper. "All four of them taking turns. Todd, Matt, Finlay, and Lucas." I don't need to explain who they were. Their names have been splashed all over the media since the shooting.

"You were *fourteen*, and they did that to you?" Ax's nostrils flare.

I nod. "I don't remember a lot of it, but I get these flashbacks. Of them laughing. Taunting me and calling me names." My voice trickles out in a soft whisper. "I remember the pain." Skeet runs his hand up and down my spine in a soothing motion. "I don't know which is worse. That I can't remember everything and my imagination fills in the blanks or whether it would've been better to have been fully conscious during it. Maybe I could have fought them off. Or screamed for help." I shrug, shaking my head.

"They called Ethan to pick me up in the early hours of the morning. I don't remember him coming to get me. Cam came too. The next memory I have is waking up at home, in bed, with Ethan holding me in his arms. He was crying. I'd never seen him cry like that."

My body aches to feel my brother's arms around me now.

"I was hurting so bad, and I couldn't sit down properly for weeks. And they left marks all over my body. They didn't rape me vaginally. I was still, technically, a virgin, but they left scars on the outside and the inside that will never properly heal."

"Why weren't they put behind bars?" Skeet inquires.

262

"I refused to go the cops." I hang my head. "I couldn't remember what happened. I didn't know if I'd consented at first or not. The whole night was a blur."

"It doesn't matter. You were under age, and it was still rape." Skeet continues rubbing my back.

"That's what E said too. He begged me to go to the police. He pleaded with me to tell my parents, but I blackmailed him into staying quiet. I was embarrassed. I'd gotten drunk and flirted with Matt, and I convinced myself I was responsible. They were all from extremely wealthy families, and I knew they'd destroy me in court. Ethan and Cam tried talking me around, but I wouldn't budge. I wouldn't talk about it. I just wanted to pretend like it never happened. And I was partly successful. For the rest of the summer, I banished it to the back of my mind, but I was unraveling on the inside. I'd wake up screaming, drenched in sweat, as flashbacks haunted my dreams. I was sneaking out, going to parties, getting drunk, and kissing random guys. My friends gradually distanced themselves from me, and I only found out why when we returned to school."

Ax rubs my legs, heating my frozen skin while I continue. "I'm not sure if it was deliberate or how it happened, but the guys' girlfriends found out what had happened, and they made my life hell from that point on. They were under the illusion that it was consensual. That I'd somehow gotten their boyfriends drunk and convinced them to have an orgy. They blamed me for their actions, called me a whore to my face, and made sure everyone in school knew what I'd done."

"I can't believe Ethan let all this happen," Ax admits.

I pin my eyes on him. "He didn't. Him and Cam were jumping in to protect me on a daily basis. Ethan got suspended numerous times for fighting. He begged me to tell our parents, but I thought it was too late. I told him there was no point reporting it now. People wouldn't believe me. I was ostracized in school, and I withdrew into myself."

"I don't understand why he didn't just tell them," Skeet says. "If that happened to Shaz, I wouldn't care how mad she was at me. I'd still tell my parents."

"Ethan would never go behind my back. Maybe it's a twin thing, but he'd never betray me like that. Instead, he did everything he could to help me. He protected me from the bullies, and when he found me cutting, he forced me into therapy. He gave my parents part of the truth. Told them I was depressed and suffering from anxiety, which wasn't a lie, but I refused to tell them what was behind it."

"And what about those assholes who raped you?" Ax asks.

"They kept their distance although I always felt their eyes watching me. And they stood back and smirked when their girlfriends slut shamed me and beat me up. I lived in fear that they'd come back for another turn, but I think they realized they were lucky to have gotten away with it, and they weren't risking it a second time. I don't know."

I rest my head on Skeet's shoulder for a minute. "I begged my parents to let me move schools, but they wouldn't hear of it. The Academy was the best school for miles, and my grades were great. Focusing on schoolwork during the week was the only thing that distracted me from the pain and self-loathing. I threw myself into my schoolwork during the week and partied hard on the weekends, making sure to avoid places where any of those guys would be. Until Cam and I got together, and he helped me in ways Ethan couldn't."

I lift my head up. "I know you guys have a bad impression of my ex, and I'll never forgive him for dumping me like he did, but he isn't a bad guy. He helped me cut out the partying, and he made me happy. He helped me regain some of my self-confidence, and he kept me safe at school. The bullying died down once everyone saw our relationship was serious. Cam comes from money, and he was one of the popular kids in school, so people wouldn't cross him. And it helped Ethan too. He was happy to see me happy again, and he trusted his best friend to look after me. It finally seemed like things were turning a corner until Ethan went into school day one of our senior year and shot them all dead. The four guys who'd raped me and three of their girlfriends. Lucinda Jamison got a reprieve. She was the girl Ethan had wanted, but she'd been Todd's girl-friend the whole way through high school. She never participated in the bullying even though I never understood why."

I take the bottle from Skeet's hands and guzzle water. My throat is parched but my soul feels lighter.

"That's why you don't drink?" Skeet asks.

"Haven't touched a drop since that night."

We don't speak for a few minutes, all lost in our own thoughts, until Ax breaks the silence. "What happened that last night we were together sent you spiraling," he quietly says, instantly understanding.

I bob my head. "That night was one of the best and worst nights of my life." I cup Skeet's face. "You sang me that beautiful song and told me you loved me, and I was ready to burst I was so happy."

I look to Ax, cupping his face with my free hand. "You loved me with your body and made me feel desirable, like a normal woman. I never thought I'd feel so free when it came to sex, but you gave me that. And Heath stood up to his family for me. He put me first when I'd felt like I was scraping the bottom of the fish pond for so long, unworthy of love and devotion. I loved you guys, I really did, but I wasn't strong enough to deal with everyone pointing fingers at me again. I was struggling already in the aftermath of the revelation of my true identity. When that video was posted online, and our relationship was outed, I just shut down. All I could think was I was going to ruin your lives like I'd ruined Ethan's. I loved you enough to walk away. But it was Jenkins and his crew that truly sent me into a tailspin. When they attacked me, it brought everything back, and I just wanted it to end."

This is the real hard part. Because I know when I admit this they're going to feel like they failed me.

"I wasn't in my right state of mind, or I never would've done it." I gulp. "And when I got the email, it seemed inevitable. At least, that's what I convinced myself back then."

"What email?" Skeet questions, frowning.

I bite down on my lower lip. "I never told anyone, but I was getting threatening emails from someone who knew about my past. Someone who was telling me I should've died instead of Ethan."

Ax and Skeet go rigidly still.

My chest pumps up and down, my heart thumping wildly, and I crick my head from side to side, attempting to loosen my stiff shoulders. There's no easy way to do this, so I just rip the Band-Aid off. "I tried to kill myself that night, and I almost succeeded."

Chapter Thirty-Seven

"Jesus, Blaire." Tears roll unapologetically down Skeet's face. "I didn't know you felt like that."

"We never would've left your side if we knew you were thinking those thoughts," Ax ads in a solemn tone. "We thought we were doing the right thing by giving you space."

A portentous silence engulfs us as my statement hangs in the air.

"It was all too much. I was suffocating, and that was the only way I could see of escaping my inner prison. Ethan would've been so disappointed in me." The memory of that night flits through my mind. I remember seeing him. Reaching for him. Being happy we were going to be reunited. I don't know if it was a hallucination or if he was really there. I like to think he was. And that it means he's looking over me. I find comfort in that. And in the days immediately after I attempted suicide, it was that vision of him that kept me going.

"If you'd died Blaire …" Skeet shakes his head, his glassy eyes sad as pulls me into his arms. The couch dips as Axel sits down on my other side, hugging me from behind.

"I'm sorry we weren't there for you," Axel whispers, his warm breath lifting all the tiny hairs on the back of my neck.

We stay like that for a while. Just holding onto one another, not talking, but it's cathartic. I'm not sure there's much you can say when someone admits they tried to kill themselves.

I ease out of Skeet's arms a few minutes later, keeping hold of his hand while Ax slings his arm around my shoulder. We sit back on the couch, and I'm cocooned by two guys who mean the world to me. I blink back tears as I speak. "You guys helped me more than you ever knew, so please don't feel like you've let me down. You didn't." I look between them, hoping they can read the sincerity in my eyes.

"My mom found me slumped on the bathroom floor, unconscious. Dad performed CPR while Mom called an ambulance. They got to me just in time. My stomach was pumped, and I stabilized, but I wasn't in a good place. Not at all."

I swallow over the lump in my throat. "The next day, my parents packed up our stuff, and we flew to Florida, to my grandparents' estate. I'd never met them before. Dad was estranged from his parents since before Ethan and I were born. I don't know what went down, but I know it took a lot for him to swallow his pride and call them, asking for help."

I smile as my grandparents' faces swim before me. "They're so lovely. If they were holding any grudge toward Dad, they didn't show it in front of me. They paid for me to go into a psychiatric facility, and they're paying for me to come to school here."

I glance at the ceiling, struggling to formulate the right words to explain. "Trying to kill myself was hugely selfish, and it would've devastated my parents if I died too. I'm so grateful I didn't succeed but … in a strange way, it's saved all of us. Dad has a relationship with his parents again. They've loaned him the money to set up a doctor's office, and Mom's working with him. They're not arguing anymore, and after a lot of therapy, I've turned a corner. I've come to terms with my past, and I'm finally looking forward."

Skeet kisses me on the cheek. "I'm sorry you had to go through all that."

"What doesn't kill us makes us stronger, right?"

"Except it's easier said than done." Ax squeezes my shoulder.

"Yeah. It's one step at a time. And I'm still working through some stuff I need to do. Talking to you was part of it. I hated that I left without any explanation, and I've picked up the phone so many times to call you, but I wanted to tell you the truth face to face. And I wanted to be better before reappearing in your lives. I didn't want to come back with all this baggage."

"It wouldn't have mattered. We'd have welcomed you with open arms anyway." Skeet pecks my lips softly.

"I'm glad you're here and that you're okay." Ax presses a kiss to my cheek, and my heart soars.

I turn to face him, getting lost in those gray-blue eyes of his. "I don't expect anything, you know." My eyes probe his. "I didn't come back here expecting to pick up where we left off. I know a lot of time has passed. I owed you all the truth. I didn't dare hope for anything else."

"And like I told you," Skeet says, slipping his arm around my waist. "No measure of time apart will change the way I feel about you." There's a pregnant pause. "The way we *all* feel about you."

I wait for Ax to say something, but he's quiet, introspective looking. The longer the silence extends, the more my hope dwindles. Deep down, I was wishing they'd all react like Skeet, but I've got to be realistic. I dumped them and disappeared, and it's not something most guys would get over just like that. "It's okay," I tell Ax. "You shouldn't feel forced into anything, but I would like it if we could be friends."

Skeet mutters something under his breath, and Ax pins him with a "butt out" look. "I just need time to process," Ax proclaims. "But just so there's no confusion, there's no way I'm letting you walk away from me again. I'm glad you're here, Blaire."

I grace him with a smile. "I can live with that. Take whatever time you need. I'm just happy to be back with you guys. I'll take that however I can."

"So, what's the plan?" Skeet asks, brushing my hair aside and planting a delicate kiss on my exposed collarbone. A shiver skates up and down my spine, and delicious tendrils of pleasure whip all over my body.

"There's something else I need to do." My gaze bounces between them. "If we're going to be back in each other's lives, then it's only fair you should know. I've unresolved feelings about Ethan. About what he did. And I need to do something about it."

"I'm finding it hard to elicit sympathy for the victims now," Ax honestly admits.

"If others knew, I bet they'd feel the same," Skeet agrees.

I shake my head. "That's not what I'm talking about." I pin them with grave looks.

"Maybe it's time the truth came out about what they did to you," Skeet says.

"What good would it do now?" I ask, my brows climbing to my hairline. "No one would believe it. They'd think I was saying it to try and exonerate my brother. All it would do is throw a spotlight on my family again."

"I hate that I agree with you," Ax says. "But I think you're right. It's too late."

I grab my bag off the floor and pull out the crumpled letter, passing it to Skeet. "Ethan didn't want me to tell anyone either, and I tried really hard to abide by his last wishes, but it was the wrong call." I'm quiet as I watch first Skeet, and then Ax, read Ethan's last words to me. "I didn't tell my parents, didn't tell you, because it felt like I'd be betraying him if I spoke out." Ax hands me back the letter and I fold it carefully, tucking it back in my bag. "That only added to my guilt. My parents had no clue why Ethan had done that, and I lied to their faces over and over every time they asked me why."

I rest my head on Ax's shoulder. "I fessed up recently after a lot of soul searching. Telling them was awful. One of the most harrowing things I've had to do, but I'm not sorry they know. All these secrets were tearing my family apart, and it's good they're out in the open. But I still don't know what prompted Ethan to go to school that morning and kill them. I won't rest until I find out."

"Maybe it all just built up and he exploded. It must've killed him seeing those guys walk the halls at school knowing what they did to you. It's not that difficult to understand why he did what he did. If that was Shaz or Sage …"

"There's no justification for what Ethan did," I reply, eyeballing him. "None. Even though they hurt me, they didn't deserve to die. I might've thrown that sentiment out in anger when I was hurting, but I never wanted that. What I need to know is why Ethan did it. Why then? After more than two years? Something triggered him to do it *that day,* and I have to find out what."

"How are you going to do this?" Ax asks.

Steely determination crosses my face. "I know where I need to start. If anyone knew what was going through Ethan's head, it'd be Cam." I look between the guys. "I need to talk to my ex."

💙💙💙

A hammering on our front door wakes both me and Nina early the following morning.

"Hold your horses," Nina hollers, mobilizing faster than me. She crawls out of bed, exiting the bedroom and moseying through our small living area to the door. I sit up, straining my neck to see through the open bedroom door, watching her squint through the peep hole. "Oh my God." She glances over her shoulder at me, excitement splashing across her face before she returns to the peephole again. She emits a loud squeal. "Holy shit. It's the quarterback. The one everyone's talking about on campus."

I hop up, adrenaline forcing its way through my sluggish veins. "He's here for me."

Realization creeps across her pretty face. "Oh my God. He's the third boyfriend, isn't he?" Nina is already aware of who I am. I told her the second day because I'd rather she heard it from me before gossip spread on campus. She was incredibly understanding and grateful I'd confided in her. It was that moment that cemented the connection between us, and I knew she was someone I could trust to be on my side. I'd told her about the guys last night, but I'd deliberately kept Heath's name out of it. She was unbelievably excited at the fact I'd dated three best friends at the same time, and her lack of judgment only made me love her more.

"Yeah," I admit, opening the door and coming face to face with Heath. His features are twisted in pain, and from his pale skin to the bruising shadows under his eyes, it's clear he hasn't slept. I've no idea how he got up here, but the last thing I need is our RA discovering him and freaking out. I step aside. "Come in."

Nina is perched on the arm of the couch with her mouth hanging open as Heath steps into our space, soaking up all the air in the room. "Hi!" she screeches, unable to contain her excitement.

"Hey." His voice is coarse as he acknowledges her briefly before redirecting his attention to me. "Can we, uh, talk somewhere in private?"

"I'll go back to bed," Nina instantly offers, jumping up. "Take as long as you need." With one last appreciative glance in Heath's direction, she saunters back to the bedroom, closing the door behind her.

Tension builds in the room as we stand our ground, staring at one another. The space between us may as well be an ocean. I'm guessing the guys told him the news, but that doesn't explain why he's here. His actions, up to this point, have made it perfectly clear that he doesn't want anything to do with me.

"Blaire." His voice is strangled when he eventually speaks, and I'm shocked when a single tear leaks out of the corner of his eye. "I didn't know," he whispers. "I didn't know what you were going through. I …" He opens the window to his soul, and I'm witness to his inner torment. Pain has crept into every nook and cranny of his being, extinguishing the bright light that used to live inside him.

"Come here." I hold out my arms. If anyone needs a hug in this moment, it's the lost, lonely man standing in front of me. "It's okay."

"But it's not." More tears stream down his face, and my heart is breaking for him. Judging by the altering expressions fliting across his face, he's battling some inner war, so I ignore the urge to eliminate the space between us and bundle him into my arms. Instead, I wait him out. It doesn't take as long as I predicted.

Resolve smooths out the worried lines on his face as he locks gazes with me a few minutes later. Without any further indecision, he's crossing the floor, eating up the distance that separates us and snatching me into his arms, clinging to me for dear life.

Chapter Thirty-Eight

HEATH

She still smells the same. An intoxicating mix of vanilla and apple blossom. Like summer and innocence and all things good. But that scent is only skin deep. It masks the devastation underneath. I hold her against me more firmly as this unequivocal need to protect her resurfaces. It's an old sentiment, one I thought I'd left in the past. Losing Blaire was the catalyst for losing myself. And I've ambled through my life since.

"I'm sorry, Blaire," I whisper into her hair. "For everything you've been through, for not having more faith, and for failing you." I thought I was doing the right thing. Protecting her. Finally standing up to my mother. And, deep down, I believed I was helping Cassie. But I fucked up. And everyone's paid the price.

"Stop, Heath." She runs her hand up and down my spine, and it's unbelievably comforting. She leans back, tilting her head up so she's looking me directly in the face. "You didn't fail me. I'm responsible for my own actions. No one else."

"That's not the way I see it. We should've known something was wrong when you upped and left. Instead of helping Thorp and Taylor find you, I fucked my way around campus like I was king of the world." Shame slaps me in the face. All my mistakes regurgitate in my mind, reminding me of what an idiot I am.

"Heath." She grips both sides of my face. "You helped me a lot. All of you did, but I was depressed and carrying a lot of pain, and no one could've pulled me out of that. I needed professional help."

"The guys said you were in some place?"

She nods, pulling me over to the couch and pushing me down. "I was in a psychiatric facility for four months. They helped me work through all my feelings, and I see a therapist on a weekly basis now. Most likely, I'll continue seeing her indefinitely. But I'm cool with that. She's non-judgmental, and I feel safe telling her all the weird shit that goes through my brain."

She smiles, and her pretty blue eyes sparkle with so much life. Looking back, I don't know how any of us didn't see the true extent of her inner misery because it was obvious if we'd only known what to look for.

"I blamed you," I blurt. "For all the shit in my life since you left."

"I don't think any less of you for that," she says, rubbing soothing circles on the back of my hand. "But I'm worried about you. The guys haven't said much, but I can see how concerned they are."

I slouch on the couch, sighing. "I've been a giant asshole. It's a wonder they haven't kicked me out of the house." I turn my head so I'm looking into her beautiful face. The time apart has done nothing to diminish her beauty or the strength of my feelings for her.

"They love you. You're like brothers, and I know you were there for Ax when he was going through a rough time. They just want to do the same for you, and I do too if you'll let me."

"I'm not worthy of that devotion."

"I think I should be the judge of that." She twists around, pulling her legs up underneath her body. The movement causes her thin tank to rise over her belly, exposing smooth, tan skin. Lust stirs and my jeans start tightening in the crotch. One look at Blaire was always enough to make me hard as stone, so my current reaction is nothing new. I shift a little, discreetly adjusting my jeans so she doesn't notice the expanding bulge down south. "You don't have to tell me what's going on with you, but talking these things out works wonders. I speak from experience."

"You'll hate me." I rub a tense spot between my brows. I didn't come here to unburden myself. I'm not really sure why I did come here. After the guys filled me in, I just ran out of the house, and my feet somehow found their way here.

"I could never hate you. Never." She squeezes my hand.

I want to get this off my chest, and that's all the encouragement I need. "After you left with your mom that night, I went to see Cassie. I didn't need any evidence to prove she was behind the video leak. I was beyond enraged. I told her you'd been assaulted, and she laughed." A muscle clenches in my jaw. "She actually fucking laughed." I shake my head at the memory. "I knew she was a malicious bitch, but I still clung to the belief there was a part of her that was still good. That still resembled the girl I'd grown up with."

I touch Blaire's cheek, tracing my fingers over her soft, smooth skin. "I had one more card to play, if you remember." She nods. "I'd never told her parents about her coke habit, but that night I told them everything. Showed them all the photographic proof I had gathered, so there was no doubt I was telling the truth."

I hang my head, shame washing over me. "They were so grateful. They thought I'd her best interests at heart." I bark out a laugh. "They didn't realize it was my form of payback. My way of punishing her for what she'd done to you."

"What did her parents do?"

"They sent her to rehab."

"I know your motives might not have been pure, but you helped her. You did a good thing."

I shake my head slowly, pain spearing through my chest. "I didn't help her, Blaire." It's hard to force these words out of my mouth, but I need to release them. "She met this junkie asshole in rehab. Son of an oil baron with enough money to feed both their habits. The minute she was released, she took off with him. Her parents were devastated. They didn't know where she was or if she was safe. Five months later, they got a call saying she'd OD'd." I can scarcely talk over the wedge clogging my throat. "Cassie died Blaire, and that's all on me."

"Oh my God." She clamps a hand over her mouth, my statement hovering over us like a dark cloud. "That's awful, but it's not your fault. You didn't force her to take drugs. She made her own choices which led to her death."

"That's not the way my mother sees it." I grit my teeth. "Mom blames me. Her best friend is distraught at the loss of her daughter, and my mother pointed the finger at me. She said stuff she can never take back."

"Like what?"

"Like I'm a pervert and my obsession with you meant I turned my back on Cassie when she needed me most." I'll spare Blaire the truly gory details. Like how my mother called her every disgusting word under the sun. Like how she beat me with her fists until her knuckles turned purple. How she told me I was dead to her and I might as well have died with Cassie.

"She's wrong. That's not who you are." She pleads with her eyes, clasping both my hands in hers.

Her faith in me is misguided. "I am since I came here. I've treated girls like shit, screwing them and then discarding them like they're worthless, when really that's how I feel. I failed you. I failed Cassie. I failed my mother."

She scoots closer to me, forcing my eyes to lock on hers. "You are not worthless!" Her tone is laced with vindication. "Your mother has made you feel that way, but you are not worthless to me or the guys or the rest of your family or your football buddies." I look away, unable to stare into her earnest eyes.

She thinks she can save me.

I see it in her expression.

But I'm gone beyond the point of saving.

"Look at me," she demands, turning my face back around. "You are worth everything to me. And you have so much to offer the world. Don't let her hurtful words pull you down."

"My own mother hates me, Blaire. Have you any idea how that feels?"

"No, but I was invisible to my parents for a long while, and that hurt a lot. It felt like they cared more about Ethan than me, but I was mistaken. They were just grieving. Maybe your mom was too. You told me she wanted you to marry Cassie, and she was probably like a daughter to her in a lot of ways."

"It's been more than a year and a half, and she hasn't once picked up the phone to call me."

"Have you?" she quietly asks, and I shake my head. "Have you even spoken to anyone about this? A professional?" I shake my head again. "It would help, but you have to want to be helped."

I'm not sure that I do. Sure, I hate myself most days. Hate this asshole I've turned into but, I know if I follow this path I'm opening myself up to a whole new world of hurt, and I don't think I'm brave enough to do it.

"What if it's not enough?" I risk asking her. "What if my mother refuses to listen and I'm still dead to her. I'm not sure I could handle that."

"If she does, it's her loss, but you'll feel better for confronting your feelings and trying to put things right."

I shrug. "I don't know."

"Just think about it."

I deliberately switch the topic of conversation, sick of talking about myself. "I didn't come here to talk about me."

"Why did you come here?"

I shrug again. "I owed you an apology. I thought you didn't care. That it had all been a lie. That I'd thrown Cassie to the wolves for nothing. That I'd defended you to my mother when you hadn't loved me after all."

"It wasn't a lie," she whispers. "Everything I told you was true." She runs her fingers lightly through my hair. "I cared about you back then, and I still care about you even if you don't want anything to do with me. I just want you to be happy."

There's no doubting the truth when it's written all over her face. "I missed you so much," I tell her, staring deep into her eyes. "But then anger and hate took over, and it consumed me."

"I understand." She bobs her head.

"How can you? I'm everything you should despise." Self-loathing swathes me like a blanket.

"No, you're not. You've just lost your way, but you're still you." She places her hand on my chest, right over my heart, and it thumps wildly in response. "You're still the Heath I fell in love with."

I suck in a gasp. Her bravery astounds me. She's not afraid to be vulnerable in front of me. I wish I was a better man. A stronger one. To match her vulnerability and her bravery, but I'm not.

But I think I can be again. "If I go for therapy, would you … would you come with me?"

Her smile is as magnificent as the northern lights, and her entire face lights up. "Of course, I'll go with you. I'd do anything for you, Heath. Anything. All you have to do is ask."

Chapter Thirty-Nine

BLAIRE

The next week is kind of surreal. We settle back into a familiar pattern, yet it's not familiar at the same time. Skeet is as affectionate as ever, lavishing me with attention. Ax is holding himself back, and I can't gauge his feelings, but I don't pry, because I told him I'd give him space. Heath is around, yet he's not present. He hasn't brought up the subject of therapy again, and he isn't as talkative in my presence as he used to be, but I know he's dealing with a lot of stuff too, so I cut him some slack.

"I've been thinking," Skeet says Friday evening as we're all lounging around the guys' living room after a long week.

"Fuck. Should we be worried?" Ax teases.

Skeet throws a cushion at his head before flipping him the bird. "I'm trying to be serious here, asshat." He wraps his arms around my waist, and I lean back into him. We're stretched along the length of the couch with my back snuggled into his warm chest. "Before we talk to Cam, maybe we can do a little investigative work on our own."

I sit up straighter, twisting around so I'm looking him in the face. "One, who said anything about *all of us* talking to my ex, and two, what kind of investigative work?"

"Baby, if you think we're letting you fly to Rhode Island to confront that lame ass ex of yours alone, you don't know us very well." He arches a brow, challenging me to argue with him.

"But—"

"It's not up for debate," Ax adds. "And the flights are already booked. We reserved seats in the row beside you."

I booked a flight for one week from this Saturday. I'm planning on flying in and out of Rhode Island on the same day.

Cam is studying at Brown. It was always his lifelong dream. His father studied there and his father before him. It didn't take much effort to confirm that's where he is. And Skeet was able to locate his address in a matter of minutes. I've decided not to contact him in advance for fear he won't agree to see me. Surprising him in person is my best chance even if I'm nervous about seeing him after all this time.

It'll be good to have some moral support in case it doesn't go well. So, I'm not displeased they've done this behind my back, but it's fun to pretend I am. I cross my arms over my chest and scowl. "And you were going to tell me this when?"

"You sound like you want to be alone with him," Heath cuts in. "Do you have another agenda besides seeking the truth?"

I know this is coming from that angry, seething place lurking inside him and that he can't help it. Besides, it's a valid point.

"Don't be such a fucking asshole," Skeet chastises him, but I put my hand over his mouth, cautioning him with my eyes.

"Heath has a right to express himself, and I'm glad he brought it up, so I can lay that ghost to rest. I have no romantic or sexual interest in Cam. I only want the truth. And just so we're clear, the only men I'm interested in are in this room." I level a look at Heath. "Does that answer your question?"

His lips kick up at the corners, and it's amazing to see. "Sorry for being an ass."

"You're forgiven." I blow him a kiss, and I'm rewarded with a full-fledged smile this time, and it warms my insides. I'm confident I can thaw out his angry, frozen heart even if I'm only chipping away at it bit by bit. I palm Skeet's cheek. "Now, tell me your suggestion, baby."

Grabbing my head, he pulls my face to his, melding our mouths together in a long, slow, sensual kiss. I'm grinning against his mouth because I know what he's doing. Yes, Skeet is a huge believer in PDAs, and it's not unusual for him to kiss me in front of the others, but he's even more affectionate than I remember him being, and I think he's trying to show the guys what they're missing by touching me any chance he gets.

"You've made your point, Taylor." Ax's tone is glacial, and I think Skeet's strategy is working.

"Get your tongue out of Blaire's mouth, and tell us what you're thinking," Heath adds.

"Jealous?" he retorts when he finally pulls free of my mouth. My lips are swollen, and my mouth tastes minty, just like him. We're pressed against one another in all the right places, and the evidence of his arousal is digging into my lower stomach, elevating my own desire.

We haven't done anything except kiss this week, but I'm dying for more. It's been ages since I last slept with Ax, and my neglected body is crying out to be filled. I don't think I'll last much longer before I jump his bones.

"Skeet. Just spit it out." Ax is growing impatient.

Skeet ignores him, rubbing his lower lip while piercing me with a suggestive look that does funny things to my insides. It takes all my willpower not to glue my mouth to his and take what I want.

"Jesus Christ," Heath exclaims, jumping up. "Why don't you just fuck and be done with it." Then he storms out of the living room leaving a thunderous blowback in his wake.

"Was it something I said?" Skeet somewhat jokes, and I slap his chest. "Don't make fun of this."

"You haven't lived with his mood swings like we have," Ax interjects when I stand. "Don't go after him. Let him calm down, and he'll come back."

"Ax is right. Let him cool down." Skeet pulls me down onto his lap. "Did Ethan have a tablet or laptop?"

"He had an iPad. Why?"

"Do you still have it?"

I nod. "Yeah. It's in a box with his other things."

"Please say you have it here with you."

"I do." I tuck my hair behind my ears. "I like to look through his things sometimes. It helps me feel close to him again."

"Would you mind if I took a look at it?" He pushes strands of hair back out of his eyes.

"No, of course not. You think you might find something there?"

"It can't hurt to try, right? I was wondering if he was getting nasty emails like you, and maybe they said something which triggered him to do what he did." It's not a huge stretch because the email I got encouraged my suicide decision, but deciding to go out and shoot a bunch of kids dead is an entirely different matter. Still, it can't hurt for Skeet to look. Maybe we might find something.

"You're right. It can't hurt to look, but the police already checked his iPad and his iPhone, so I doubt you'll find anything."

"I'd still like to try." He runs his hands up and down my arms, and I sink back against him. "I'd also like to try and find out who was sending you those emails. Do you still have them?"

"I had saved them in my inbox, but it was my old Kentsville High email account, and I can't even remember the password."

"No problem. I'll hack into their servers and retrieve the info."

I arch a brow, tilting my head back to look at him. "I didn't know you could do stuff like that?"

"Chris has been teaching me hacks for years. There isn't much I can't do with a computer."

"Such modesty," Ax deadpans, and I giggle.

Skeet rises to his feet, taking me with him. "Why don't we swing by the residence hall before we head to the movies, and we can take a look."

"Sounds like a plan." I swipe my cardigan and book bag off the floor before fixing Ax with a hopeful look. "Do you want to come with?"

He rubs a hand across the back of his neck. "I've got crap to do, but you two have fun."

Disappointment crawls over me, but I plaster a fake smile on my face. "Okay, sure."

As I walk past Ax, he takes hold of my elbow, pulling me into his side. "It's not what you think. I have an assignment due on Monday, and I haven't written a word yet." His eyes bore into mine, and I sway on my feet. His warm breath ghosts over my face when he leans in closer. "I'd love nothing better than to snuggle up in a dark movie theater with you." He slides his arm around my lower back, holding me close. His scent swirls around me, hypnotizing me, and my core throbs with need. "How about a rain check?"

282

"Sure," I rasp in a breathless tone. His eyes flick to my lips as his pupils dilate, flashing dangerously. Electricity ripples in the air, and I fixate on his mouth, licking my lips in anticipation. His body locks up tight against mine, and I think we've both stopped breathing. My chest heaves up and down as I silently beg him to kiss me. I don't think I've ever wanted a kiss so much. I lift my eyes, meeting his desire-laden gaze, and a tiny whimper flies out of my mouth.

He brushes his lips against mine, but it's so fleeting I'm not sure I didn't imagine it. "Do you have any plans for Monday night?" he asks, resting his hands loosely on my hips.

"I've none now," I admit in a breathy tone, and his lips kick up.

"Then it's a date." His eyes linger on my lips again, and I hold my breath. *Kiss me. Please.*

Indecision is written all over his face, and when he lets me go, my euphoria floats away, replaced by rejection. "Enjoy the movie," he says with a soft smile. "Let me know if you find anything on the iPad."

"We will." Skeet swings his arm around my shoulders, steering me toward the door because I appear incapable of placing one foot in front of the other by myself. "Catch you later."

I let Skeet guide me out of the house in a daze. "Damn it," he says, and I break free of the Ax spell I'm under.

"What?"

"I was so sure he was going to kiss you."

"Me too."

"You sound disappointed."

"Would it upset you if I said I was?"

He crashes to a halt, pulling me against him. "Not in the slightest. The opposite in fact." I raise a brow, and he chuckles. "I want things to go back to the way they were. I know they both still love you and they're just being stubborn."

"Or cautious?" I suggest.

Skeet takes my hand, towing me toward his car. "Life is too short to waste even a single second being cautious. But hey, their loss is my gain." He winks before darting in and nipping at my earlobe. "And I'm going to enjoy my alone time with you before I have to share." He swats my butt, and I yelp. "Now get your cute ass in the Jeep, and let's get out of here."

The dorm is empty when we arrive, and I remember that Nina has study group this evening. Skeet takes the box of Ethan's things down from the top shelf of the closet, setting it on the bed. I locate the iPad and his iPhone, but both are powered down, so we plug them in to charge and set out for the theater.

I couldn't tell you what movie we just watched because Skeet and I spent virtually the entire time making out. "What was the name of that movie?" I ask as we make our way back to the Jeep.

Skeet throws back his head, laughing. "I couldn't tell you. I was too preoccupied with my hot date."

My core throbs, reminding me how damp my panties are. "If you wanted to dry hump me, we could've just stayed home," I tease as I climb into the car.

He pins me with a look so devilish it's as if he's stripped me completely bare. "If we'd stayed home, we wouldn't have been dry fucking, I can promise you that."

"I'd have had no problem with that."

His eyes smolder as he leans across the console, dragging my lower lip between his teeth. "Now she tells me," he growls.

"Fuck, Skeet." I pull the tie out of his hair, letting it fall loose around his shoulders, before burying my hands in the thick strands. "I need you. I want you."

He grips my head, plundering my mouth, and I drift off to some alternate realm. When I come back down to Earth, I giggle, high on love and happiness, and he shoots me an amorous grin. "Your place or mine?"

I mentally fist pump the air. "How about we grab Ethan's stuff and then go back to your place?" We'll have zero privacy at my place.

"I love how your mind works," he murmurs, nuzzling my neck before starting up the engine.

Chapter Forty

he house is quiet and dark when we return, and there's no sign of Ax or Heath. Skeet takes my hand, leading me up the stairs to his bedroom. He places Ethan's iPad and iPhone down on his desk before hauling me into his arms. "You sure about this?"

"Hundo P." I caress his cheek. "Make love to me, Skeet."

We undress one another slowly and meticulously until we're both in just our underwear. "Fuck, your body is a work of art," Skeet murmurs, pushing me flat on my back as he hovers over me, his eyes hungrily roaming the length of my body. "One I'm going to feast on all night." He winks before lowering his mouth to my ankle. He brushes his mouth against my heated skin, his lips trailing excruciatingly slowly up my leg. By the time he reaches the apex of my thighs, I'm a writhing, quivering mess on the bed.

"Skeet." A needy moan escapes my lips.

"What do you need, baby?" he murmurs, bypassing the place where I ache most for him and beginning a slow perusal of my other leg.

I bite back my screams of frustration. "For you to not be a tease." He chuckles against my skin, and my core pulses with need. "Skeet, please." I'm not above begging. Not if it'll give me what I need. "I can't wait. It's been ages since I had sex, and I need you inside me now."

"Shush, baby." He shoves my soaking wet panties aside, pushing one finger inside me. "I know how to take care of you. There's no rush. We've got all night." He strokes my inner walls with calm, deliberate movements, and I lift my hips, urging him to do more, go faster. He chuckles again. "So impatient."

"So would you be if you hadn't had sex since the Dark Ages."

He adds another finger inside me before stabbing me with a virile look. "I *haven't* had sex since the Dark Ages. Not since before I met you. This is as painful for me as it is for you." He straightens up, giving me full view of the tenting in his boxers. "I want you, baby. Badly, but the anticipation only heightens the enjoyment."

"Sadist," I hiss, and he smirks before adding a third finger inside me. I shriek, bucking my hips and moaning loudly.

"Fuck. You nearly made me come in my boxers. Those sounds you're making are seriously turning me on."

I prop up on my elbows as pressure starts building down below. "Obviously not enough, or your dick would be inside me already."

"Demanding, aren't you?" he says, removing his fingers as I cry out in frustration. He presses his full body down against mine, kissing me passionately. "I won't hold back any longer if that's what you want." I bob my head enthusiastically. His expression grows tender. "I love you, Blaire. Tell me you're mine. Tell me your body is mine."

"It's yours. I'm yours. Now and always."

He unclasps my bra and tosses it away. Then he hooks his thumbs in both sides of my panties, sliding them down my body. When I'm spread before him, completely bare and wanting, he stands, making a big deal out of removing his boxers, but I don't mind the show. Skeet was always lean and toned, but he's ripped now in all the best places. His abs look like they've been carved into his body, and he has those V-shaped indents at either hip, which I love. The muscles in his thighs flex and roll as he crawls back over me. "It feels like I've waited a lifetime to make love to you."

"I know." I take his hand, pressing a kiss to his wrist. "I love you, Skeet. There are so many things I love about you, but the way you love unconditionally and with your whole heart is my favorite thing." Tears glisten in my eyes as I hold nothing back. "My body, heart, and soul are yours for all eternity. I will never stop loving you."

His mouth collides with mine, and he devours my lips as his hand moves between my legs. He rubs my clit with his thumb as I moan into his mouth. I hate to admit he's right, but all this anticipation has only heightened my desire for him. I wrap my legs around his waist, digging my heels into his butt and trying to move him where I most need him. His hard length presses against me, and warmth floods my pussy.

His lips leave my mouth, sliding down my body. He stops at my chest, paying my breasts lavish attention. Meanwhile, his thumb rubs me, stops, and then rubs me again. I'm squirming on the bed, moaning and writhing like a woman possessed. When his mouth covers my pussy and his tongue delves into my channel, I detonate, and it's like a million fireworks exploding in my body all at once. I scream out his name, over and over, as I ride each heavenly wave.

I'm vaguely conscious of him rolling a condom on, and then he's inside me, thrusting gently, letting my body acclimate to his feel. "Jesus, Blaire." I brush my knotty hair out of my face to look at him. He's magnificent. Like a Greek god with his long flowing mane and his chiseled torso, thrusting into me with a look of sheer pleasure on his face. Taking my legs, he rests them on his shoulders, quickening his pace. "You feel amazing, and I don't think I'll last."

"Let go, baby." I stroke his abs before moving lower, running my fingers through his thick pubes. "I want you to feel the same high I just felt."

He rocks his hips into me more ferociously, never moving his gaze from mine as he toys with my clit. "I want you to come with me this time." His abs glisten with sweat as he grinds into me, going faster and faster, and I'm riding a new crescendo. My hands move to my tits, and I knead them, rolling my nipples as I reach another peak. We climax together, and Skeet roars out his release, pumping into me relentlessly, over and over, until we're both spent.

He gets up, disposing of the condom, before flopping down on the bed beside me. I cuddle into him, needing to feel his body against mine. We lie tangled in each other for a while, just holding one another without speaking, and it's everything. I bask in the afterglow of our lovemaking, bathing in the light of his love. No feeling is greater. "I love you, Skeet." I kiss his lips softly. "I love you so much."

"I love you too, beautiful, and that was incredible," he pants, grinning at me. "I've never experienced that, Blaire." He pulls me up over him, and I feel him hardening underneath me again. His hands slide up my belly, locating my sensitive breasts. His touch is feather-like as he strokes me there, alternating from one breast to another. His erection is rock solid under my ass, and I grin. "Ready to go again?" He laughs, a deep full-bellied sound that resonates throughout me. "By the way, I'm on the pill, and I'm clean, so you don't have to use a condom if you don't want to."

"Me too. Well, the clean part." He showcases a perfect set of teeth when he smiles, and I could stare at his gorgeous face all day long. "And I've never ridden bareback. I'm glad I saved that for you." He positions me over his cock, and I slowly lower down onto his hard length. We both groan as I seat myself fully. Then I flex my hips and start a slow rocking motion. "It's you and me, babe," he whispers, taking my hand and placing it over his heart. "Forever."

I don't know how long we made love for or how many times we did it, but we eventually fell asleep, wrapped in each other's arms.

I wake a while later, parched, and my mouth feels as dry as the Sahara Desert. I glance at the clock and it flashes five thirty-two a.m. Extricating myself from Skeet's arms, I plant a soft kiss on his head before crawling out of bed. I grab his T-shirt off the floor and shimmy it on, tiptoeing out of the room and downstairs.

The shadowy form lurking in the kitchen startles me, and I shriek. "It's only me," Ax says from where he's leaning back against the counter.

"You scared the shit out of me." I flatten my hand over my beating heart, urging it to calm down.

"Sorry." He smirks before his features soften. "Couldn't sleep?"

I pad toward the refrigerator, trying to ignore the fact he's bare chested and only in a pair of low-hanging sweats. "I'm thirsty." I open the door and lean in.

He comes up behind me. "I'm betting all that sex worked up a thirst."

"Shit," I mumble, snatching a bottle of water. "I didn't mean for anyone else to hear us."

"I doubt even earplugs would've worked." I hear the grin behind his words.

I close the door, attempting to maneuver around him. His body heat crashes into me, causing a new wave of desire to shoot through my veins. *Seriously, Blaire?*

"It's why I'm up," he whispers against my neck, thrusting his hips into me, leaving me in no doubt he meant the double entendre. "I was so turned on I couldn't sleep." My nipples stand to attention, poking through the thin material of Skeet's shirt. "I debated whether to inter-rupt. To ask if I could join in, which is something I never thought I'd consider, but I was seriously tempted because that's how badly I want you." He places a kiss in that sensitive spot just under my ear, and I shiver all over. "But I know that's something you'll never be comfortable with, so I restrained myself."

I turn around, and he's so close to me it'd take nothing to kiss him. I could just press my lips to his and pull his amazing body against mine. I could slip my hands under the band of his pants and stroke his thick erection, and—

"Blaire?" He steps back from me, and I want to cry out. "I'm sorry. I shouldn't have come the heavy. I—"

"No." I move back up in his space, placing one finger against his lips. "You didn't. I was just imagining all the things I want to do to you, and I spaced out." His shoulders instantly relax. "But you're not wrong about the group thing. I don't know if I'll ever be comfortable with that." Neither of us need to elaborate on the reasons why.

He nods. "That's completely understandable, and we wouldn't want to ever make you uncomfortable."

A saucy grin spreads across my mouth. "Well," I purr, tracing my hands over his impeccable pecs. "I am kind of uncomfortable now." I push my pelvis into his, gyrating against his hard-on. "I have an itch that I need you to scratch."

"You're not sore?" he asks, his eyes flaring darkly.

"Nope," I lie, pinching his nipple. I remember how he always liked that. His eyes darken to the point of almost black. "I want you to fuck me. Right here. Right now."

"How could I ever say no?" Keeping his eyes on mine, he slowly lifts the shirt up my body, exposing me fully. The shirt is discarded on the floor along with his sweatpants. "For the record, I really wanted to kiss you earlier, but I knew if I did, I wouldn't be able to stop at just that, and I didn't want to ruin your date with Skeet."

He tenderly cups one of my breasts. "You should never doubt how much I want you." He presses his body up against mine, holding me against him. "How much I need you." He hugs me fiercely. "You changed me, Blaire, and there is no other living being on this planet I feel as connected to as you." His erection presses into my belly, stirring my lust to new heights.

"I love how intense our bond is," I whisper, running the tips of my fingers over his stubbly jawline. "And I would wait until the ends of time if you needed that."

"I don't need any more time, Blaire. I just need you." He presses his hot mouth to mine, and we kiss leisurely, reacquainting ourselves with one another without any urgency. The feeling of his naked flesh flush against mine, the sensation of his lips gliding across my mouth, and the synchronized beating of our hearts reminds me of how much I've missed this, missed him. My hands start an exploration, roaming over the contours of his back and lingering on his delectable ass, and very quickly, our touches and kisses turn frantic. His erection stands up tall and proud, and I lick my lips, dropping to my knees and sucking him off just how he likes it.

"Blaire," he growls after a few minutes. "I need to fuck you." He helps me to my feet and then lifts me up, placing me on the counter. I shriek as my butt hits the cold, hard marble. Spreading my legs apart, he positions himself at my entrance. With huge tenderness, he drops his mouth to mine, kissing me softly and passionately.

It feels so incredible to be kissing Ax like this again. He has a way of devouring me that is intense and tender all at the same time. Winding his hands into my hair, he tugs me closer to him. "I need you to know something," he whispers, biting gently on my ear lobe.

"What?" I rasp, squirming on the counter.

"I've wanted you as my girlfriend from the moment you reappeared, but I didn't want to rush anything."

"This doesn't feel like rushing."

"I know. It's the way things are meant to be." He nips at my earlobe. "You're mine, Blaire. And that's never changing. Ever."

I grasp his face in my hands. "You're mine, too. I want you so badly. And Skeet is more than fine with it. He wants things to revert to the way it was."

"I'm not sure …"

I kiss him to shut him up. I don't want anything or anyone to ruin this moment. Heath is an anomaly we don't need to discuss right now. "I know." I examine his face. "I love you to the ends of the earth, Axel Thorp, but only if you stop talking and fuck me like you promised."

He grips my hips roughly, stretching my legs out even farther as he rubs his cock along my entrance. The loudest moan escapes my lips. "I never renege on my promises," he says, edging slowly inside me. "And I've been counting down the days until my cock was buried inside your pussy again." I clench around him, my body liquefying with his words.

"You feel so incredibly good, Ax." I hold onto his shoulders, staring into his eyes, and he starts pounding into me. "Never stop fucking me like this. It's exactly what I need to feel whole." Ax never treated me like I was fragile or damaged, and his rough form of love helped heal some of my scars.

He remains true to his word, fucking me mercilessly until I'm coming around his pulsing cock, and then he's spilling his warm cum inside me, and everything feels right with the world again.

Chapter Forty-One

Ax picks me up Monday night from my dorm, and my jaw drops as we step outside the building and I spot his Harley. "You brought your bike with you?"

"Heath and Skeet shipped it as a surprise." Taking hold of my hips, he pulls me into his body. "You up for a ride?" He wiggles his brows, and a suggestive smirk appears on his face.

"I'm always up for a ride," I tease back, stretching up to peck his lips.

"Blaire." He whispers my name across my mouth, wrapping his arms firmly around my back. I lay my head on his shoulder, content to just hold him. He kisses the top of my head. "It's so good you're back, baby. I've missed this."

I squeeze him tighter, and my heart skips to a new rhythm. "Me too, Ax."

We set off a few minutes later, and I can't keep the smile off my face as I cling to Axel's back. It brings a whole host of happy times to the forefront of my mind. A light breeze swirls around my neck, raising my hair, and a deep sense of contentment settles into my bones.

In no time at all, Ax is pulling into the entrance of a nature park. He parks the bike and helps me off, removing my helmet and fixing my wayward hair. "This is my new favorite place to run. It's not quite the same as the lake back home, but it's close to campus, there's a little creek and a clear path to jog, and it's usually not that busy."

"I already love it," I exclaim, inhaling the minty, pine-fresh scent.

"Want to take a walk with me?" He holds out his hand, and I lace my fingers in his. We smile at one another as we start walking. "Do you still run?"

I nod. "Yeah. At least a couple times a week at the indoor track in the recreation center."

"I come here early most mornings, so if you ever—"

"I'm in," I say, cutting across him. "Running alone hasn't held the same appeal since we ran together. I've felt lonely without you jogging by my side," I truthfully admit.

He raises our conjoined hands to his mouth, placing a kiss across my knuckles. "Same here, and I never thought I'd say that, but you changed something in me, Blaire."

"You changed something in me too. You all did."

We keep walking, chatting and catching up as we go, and an hour passes as if it's minutes. When we reach a small area with a few picnic tables, Ax insists we take a break. He pulls two bottles of water out of his backpack and hands one to me.

"So, pre-law?" I ask as I unscrew the cap on my bottle. "How's that going?"

"It's good. I'm really enjoying it."

I slowly sip my water as I contemplate how best to broach this subject. "Did your decision to study law have anything to do with your mom?"

He nods, drinking deeply from his bottle. I watch his throat work, and it's amazing how much that simple action turns me on. Everything about Ax exudes raw sex and masculinity, and he might as well just reel me in now. "I visited her in prison last year for the first time ever," he quietly admits, tossing the empty bottle into his bag.

"How did that go?"

"It was hard." He stares at me with glistening eyes. "She's aged in that place, and it's so wrong. She doesn't belong there, and I'm determined to get her out. That was the initial motivation behind wanting to be a lawyer, but I also want to prevent other injustices from happening. To prevent others from going through what my mom, Griff, and me have endured. What you endured."

I move over beside him, sliding my arm around his back. "You're going to be an exceptional lawyer, and you're going to free your mom. I just know it."

He kisses me softly. "Thank you, and I'm not giving up until I do. I want her back home where she belongs."

"Have you been back to see her since?" I look up at him.

"A couple times. It's difficult because of the location, but I'm making more of an effort, and I write to her. She likes that."

I smile. "I'm really glad you're reconnecting with your mom, and she's so lucky she has you fighting in her corner."

"I told her about you." He twists around, holding my face in his hands. "And I know she'd love to meet you."

"I'd love to meet her too. I'll go with you next time you plan to visit."

"You'd do that for me?" He brushes his thumb along my cheek.

I lean my face into his palm. "Ax, I'd do anything for you. For all of you."

He pulls me into his chest, cradling me close. "As we would for you." He rubs his hands up and down my back before breaking our embrace and standing. "As much as I'd love to stay out here all night, it's getting dark, and I need to feed you." He extends his hand, and I let him help me up. "I know this fab little Italian place not far from here. You want to grab something to eat?"

I circle my arm around his waist, and we walk off wrapped around one another. "Sounds great. Lead the way."

Ax wasn't kidding. This place is a little gem of a find. It's tucked away on a side road a few miles north of the park and only about fifteen miles from campus. The restaurant is small with cozy tables lined up on both sides of the room. Homemade cloths and little vases of fresh flowers cover the tables. The lighting is dim, and opera music is on low in the background. There are only two other couples in the place, so the service is fast. Ax scoots his chair in closer to mine as the waitress places steaming bowls of delicious-smelling pasta in front of us. We thank her as she refills our glasses before discreetly disappearing.

"Wow. The food is to die for here," I say after a few mouthfuls.

"I know. Skeet and I have come here so often I think they think we're gay." He winks.

"Tonight helps address the balance," I joke. "Thank you for sharing this with me," I add in a more solemn tone.

"We didn't get much opportunity to go out on dates last time, and I'm determined to make it up to you. I want us to agree to a weekly date night, just the two of us."

"I have no objection to that."

He puts his knife and fork down and peers deep into my eyes. "I worried about you so much, Blaire. I mean, we all did, but I got it." His eyes delve into mine. "I understand the darkness and the rage, and it terrified me that you were dealing with that alone."

A shuddering breath leaves my lips. "I'm sorry I did that to you. I'm sorry you worried for so long, but I wasn't alone. The facility I was in really helped me face up to everything. I had to meet with my therapist every day, and I had weekly group sessions. It helped to know I wasn't the only one dealing with heavy shit. Most everyone in there was dealing with serious issues, and it helped talking about it. Before I went in, I never would've thought I could sit in a room full of strangers and tell them about what happened to me at that party, but I did it, and I talked about how it made me feel and gradually I learned to let go of that darkness."

I pause to gather my thoughts for a sec, taking a drink from my water to wet my dry lips. Ax doesn't interrupt or question. He just patiently waits for me to continue. "I used to think I was powerless. That I was weak. That I'd handed over everything to my abusers that night. But I was wrong. I alone have the power to change my life. No one else can do it for me. What happened in my past only defines me if I let it."

I jerk my chin up. "I'm not going to be a victim for the rest of my life. I've taken back control. I'm going to find out what happened to cause Ethan to snap, and then I'm closing the lid on that part of my past. I'm going to graduate college with an honors degree and work with other victims to help them move on with their lives. I have more focus and more determination than I've had in years."

I stop again, smiling at him. "The things that happen to us help shape the kind of people we become. I'm not going to let one night ruin the rest of my life. I've risen above it, just like you have. We are taking something horrid and turning it into something positive, something life-changing. And there is no space for darkness in any of that."

He swivels around on his chair, taking both my hands in his. "I have never been prouder of you or loved you any more than I do in this moment."

Tears prick my eyes, but they're the happy kind. "Sometimes we have to reach rock bottom to learn how to climb to the top."

♥♥♥♥

"Are you nervous?" Skeet asks as we sit in the taxi en route to Cam's off-campus residence.

"Yeah. I've no idea how he's going to react. He could slam the door shut in my face or welcome me with open arms." I nestle into the crook of his arm, letting him soothe the frayed edges of my nerves.

"He'll find my fist in his face if he even breathes wrong on you," Ax growls, flexing his knuckles.

"He'll have to deal with all three of us if he doesn't treat you right," Heath agrees.

"It's bound to be a shock. We haven't spoken since that day. Maybe I should've forewarned him. Do you think I should call him now?"

"Nah." Skeet massages my hand with his thumb. "Let's just arrive and take it from there."

"Wow, nice crib," Ax whistles twenty minutes later as we stand on the sidewalk outside the impressive brownstone Cam calls home.

"Makes our place look like a shed," Heath adds.

"His family is loaded," I explain. "Cam's never been short of cash." Butterflies run riot inside my chest, and I wipe my sweaty palms down the front of my dress as I move toward the steps leading to his home.

It's a weird one—trying to decide what to wear when you're visiting your ex with your current boyfriends present. I don't want Cam to think I dressed up for him, but it's important to me that he sees I'm doing good. I don't want to look like a hot mess, so I dressed in a plain, fitted knee-length black dress and ballet flats. I'm wearing a lightweight pink jacket, and I have an umbrella in my purse in case it rains although it's partly sunny today and the sky is almost cloudless, so I think we're in luck.

I wet my dry lips, trying to ignore the pounding of blood in my ears as I press my finger to the bell. I run my hand anxiously through my hair before Skeet takes my hand in his, squeezing. "Relax, babe. We've got your back."

Ax places his hand on my lower spine in a show of support, and on the other side of him, Heath straightens his shoulders, wearing an "I mean business" expression on his face.

"I know. I want to uncover the truth, but I'm frightened of what he might tell me too," I honestly admit.

"Whatever it is, we'll face it together," Ax confirms just as the door opens.

A tall good-looking guy with neat sandy-blond hair stares at us. "Can I help you?"

"I'm looking for Cam," I say. "Is he here?"

"Yeah. He's here. What's your name?"

"Blaire."

His eyes pop wide as soon as I mention my name. "Give me a minute, I'll be right back." He doesn't ask us to step inside, but he doesn't shut the door in our faces either, closing it while he races off.

"Interesting reaction," Heath says.

"Cam's told him about you," Ax deduces.

"I wonder what version of the story he's heard," Skeet muses.

"The truth." I jerk my head up, recognizing Cam's voice instantly. He's leaning against the doorframe with a shocked yet resigned expression on his face. No one moves or says a word as we stare at one another.

In some ways, he hasn't changed at all. He's still wearing his hair in the same way—cropped close at the sides and slightly longer on top. And he's still dressed like the offspring of wealthy parents. His white designer polo is tucked neatly into crisply pressed pants, and signature loafers adorn his feet.

But in other ways he's different.

His face has filled out, and there's a thin layer of stubble on his cheeks and chin that was never there before. He looks more bulked up than I remember, too, his shoulders broader and more muscular. His polo is unbuttoned at the top, and the edge of a tattoo peeks out. That's new as well.

Cam was still a boy when I had last seen him. Now he's most definitely all man.

"Blaire." He takes a step toward me, and Ax flinches at my side. Cam shoots him a quick glance before refocusing on me. "It's … you look good. Happy." His eyes penetrate mine as if he can see inside me. "I'm glad to see you looking so well."

"No thanks to you," Heath snaps, and I shoot him a cautionary glance. I warned all of them before coming here that they were to leave the talking to me.

Cam's Adam's apple jumps in his throat. "I've no way of defending that." He eyeballs Heath. "I wasn't there for Blaire when she needed me and it's the second-biggest regret of my life."

"What's the first?" I blurt, already suspecting his reply.

"Not stopping Ethan."

I swallow over the lump in my throat.

"You knew he was going to do that, and you let him?" Ax's tone is laced with disbelief.

"It's more complicated than that." Cam steps to one side. "Look, come in, and let's discuss this inside. I don't need you to explain why you've just appeared on my doorstep. I've been expecting you. Expecting to have this conversation for years. I'm just surprised it took you this long."

"Well, maybe if—"

"Don't." I place my hand on Ax's arm. "You promised." I don't want Cam to know I attempted suicide. I don't want anyone else crippled with guilt and regrets. Wallowing in past mistakes helps no one.

Cam sends me an inquisitive gaze, and I know him well enough to guess where his mind is gone. He's noticed Skeet holding my hand. Me touching Ax. And Heath jumping to my defense. He's trying to work out which one of them is my boyfriend. But I didn't come here to discuss my love life.

I slip my hand out of Skeet's and step into the hallway. All three guys follow me, and then Cam closes the door. He leads us up one flight of stairs into a large, wide, open room with a huge bay window that offers a great view over the small but beautifully landscaped yard outside.

"Can I get you anything to drink or eat?" he asks.

"No thank you," I reply. "We ate at the airport."

"How's UF?" he asks, while gesturing for us to take seats. Heath drops into a recliner chair while Ax and Skeet sit either side of me on the couch. Cam sinks into the couch opposite, looking stiff and uncomfortable.

"How did you know I was at UF?"

He sits forward, resting his elbows on his knees. "I've tried to keep an eye on you although you disappeared for a while, and I …" Pain contorts his face as all the blood drains from mine.

He knows. He knows I attempted suicide.

"I don't want to talk about that. I came here to talk about Ethan. That's all." Skeet slings his arm around my shoulders, holding me tight.

Cam follows the movement of his arm before clearing his throat. "I'm really sorry, Blaire. I was so upset when I heard. I almost went to you then, but I knew my presence would probably only make things worse. And I've almost booked a flight to Florida so many times, but I didn't know if you'd want to see me. If you'd want to hear after all this time."

"Of course, I'd want to hear!" I snap. "He was my brother!" Tears prick my eyes. "He was the other half of my heart and soul, and I miss him every single day. I have so many questions, and I need to know. I can't fully move on with my life until I do."

"I'll tell you, Blaire, I promise. I'll tell you what I know, but you have to understand I did what I did because I thought I was protecting you." Heath harrumphs, and Cam shoots him a warning look. "I never wanted to break up with you. I wanted to be there for you, but one look at your face and I would've spilled everything. I didn't want to hurt you all over again. Not when you were in so much pain."

"You didn't even have the decency to break up with me to my face."

He clasps his hands out in front of him, looking tortured. "I couldn't face you, Blaire. You'd have been able to see the lies written all over my face."

"Did you know?" I whisper. "Did you know he was going in there that morning to shoot them?"

He shakes his head. "Not at first. I mean, I was worried about him, but I thought everything he'd said the night before was just anger speaking. I never believed he was serious, or I would've stopped him. I swear."

I nod, because I've always felt that if Cam knew he would've talked him out of it. "But you knew once we spoke that morning. That's why you ended our call so abruptly."

"I had a bad feeling when my truck wouldn't start. It was basically brand-new, and there was no reason for it to break down. It'd been fine driving home from the gym the night before. But then Ethan had shown up, and it didn't take much to join the dots. I hoped I was wrong, but when I called you and you told me he'd gone to school already and that he was acting weird, I knew. I couldn't believe it, but I knew he was planning on doing it." Cam casts a wary glance at the three guys.

"They know everything," I confirm. "And you can speak freely in front of them."

Cam gets up, heading to a mahogany cabinet. He pulls out a bottle of whiskey. "I need a drink for this." He glances over his shoulder. "Any of you want one?"

My nerves are stretched tight, and every part of me is on edge. I might look composed on the outside, but my insides are twisted into knots. I know Cam's about to deliver a bombshell. I feel it in my bones. Maybe a whiskey would help, but I'm not about to break my sobriety now. "Actually, could I have a water?" I ask.

"Of course." He bends down, opening a door fronting a mini refrigerator.

My guys all decline drinks, so Cam walks back over with his whiskey and my bottle of water. His fingers brush against mine when he hands me the drink, and I feel nothing. No tingle. No flare of recognition. No hint of desire. Whatever we were to each other also died that day. We both take sips of our drinks, and tension filters in the air as I wait for him to continue.

Cam sits back on the couch, swirling the amber liquid in his glass and sighing. "I never wanted to tell you this, Blaire. I thought I was doing the right thing. Ethan wrote me a letter, and he told me not to tell you, but I'd already figured that out for myself."

"I got a letter too," I admit. "Two days later. He must've mailed it on his way to school that morning. I kept it hidden. Didn't tell anyone about it until recently." I lean into Skeet's side, and he presses a kiss to my temple, helping to settle me. "He told me not to tell my parents what'd happened to me, and I thought I was protecting him by keeping quiet, but I was wrong too."

"It's easy to look back and see things that weren't so clear in the moment," Cam says, looking sad. He takes another swig of his whiskey before continuing. "Ethan showed up at my house that night in a terrible state, Blaire. Someone had sent him an email."

My eyes dart to Skeet's, and Ax and Heath sit bolt upright.

"What?" Panic flares in Cam's eyes as he fixes me with a questioning look.

"I was getting threatening emails for a while after we moved away from Amber Springs."

His hand shakes and the glass drops, liquid splashing the front of his pants and dripping over the carpeted floor. Ax reacts instantly, leaning forward and grabbing the empty glass. He walks to the cupboard. Silently, he refills Cam's drink while Cam's horrified expression grows more terrifying by the second. "They sent you the video too?"

Every bone in my body locks up, and I stop breathing for a second. "What video?" My voice cracks.

He slumps in the couch, relief washing over his features, accepting the glass from Ax with an appreciative nod. He knocks it back in one go, and my guys trade worrisome expressions. "Thank fuck. I don't ever want you to see that."

"Cam, please. Tell me. Why was Ethan so upset?"

"Someone anonymously sent him a video of *that night*."

The way he enunciates the words leaves me in no doubt of the night he's referring to. Nausea swims up my throat, and I clutch onto Ax with my free hand. "What?" Tears flood my eyes even though I promised myself I was going to do this without crying.

"He watched it before he knew what it was. He … he …" Cam squeezes his eyes closed, and when he reopens them, tears fall free. "He showed it to me," he whispers, "and it's haunted me ever since." He sets his empty glass down on the couch beside him, burying his head in his hands.

I've a fairly good idea what was on that video, but I need to hear him say it. "What exactly was on that video, Cam?"

Slowly, he lifts his head, uncaring that he's full-on crying now. "Someone was taping what happened in that room, Blaire. And someone sent that tape to your brother the night before the shooting. We saw what they did to you, Blaire. We saw them raping you."

Chapter Forty-Two

I throw up all over the floor. Shock races through my veins, and my body convulses uncontrollably. My surroundings fade away. I'm vaguely aware of voices and movement, but I'm not present. A dense pressure presses down on my chest, making breathing difficult. I'm lifted and I close my eyes, focusing on the jarring motion as I'm carried someplace else.

"Blaire, babe. Breathe, beautiful. I need you to breathe." Fingers stroke my face as I'm carefully placed down on the ground. Something cold is draped over my face, and the unexpected sting snaps me out of it. I gasp, grappling for air, bending my knees and hugging them to my chest.

"Baby." Skeet's anxious face fills my vision. "I need you to inhale and exhale, nice and slow, big, deep breaths." He joins me, and gradually, the panic subsides. A warm cloth brushes over my lower legs and feet, and I look over Skeet's shoulder.

"I'm just cleaning you up," Ax explains, his eyes flooded with compassion. "And Heath is washing your shoes." I look up, and Heath is bent over the sink, his arms working overtime as he scrubs.

"I'm sorry," I mumble, pressing my face into Skeet's chest, ingesting his scent and letting it ground me.

"Are you okay, Blaire?" Cam's concerned voice comes from behind, and I look over my shoulder. He's leaning against the doorframe of the bathroom with a troubled expression on his face.

"I'm okay." I eyeball Skeet. "Help me up?" He helps me to my feet, wrapping his arms around me from behind. Heath quietly hands my clean shoes to Ax, and he slips them on my feet. "Thanks." I smile at both guys before refocusing on Cam. "I don't know what I expected you to tell me today, but that never crossed my mind. I have no recollection of anyone taping things." Not that it's inconceivable. My memory of that night has always been sketchy.

"Can we go back to the living room and I'll finish explaining?" he asks, and I nod.

When we return, the pukey mess is gone, but there's a damp patch on the carpet where I was sitting. "I'm sorry about your carpet."

"It's only a carpet. Forget about it." Cam gestures for me to sit back down. "Are you sure you're up for hearing the rest?"

"Yes. I didn't come all this way to walk away with half-answers."

"Who sent the email?" Skeet asks. "And do you know which email account it was sent to."

"I don't know, and yes. I can write it down for you."

"I'm a CS major, and I've been going through Ethan's old iPad and iPhone to see if I could find anything. So far, I've come up empty-handed, but that has a lot to do with the fact the police wiped his hard drive clean."

"They did?" Cam frowns. "That seems strange, but I don't know how investigations work. I suppose Ethan could've destroyed it, but I don't understand why he would. That was proof of what they did to Blaire, and because she was under fifteen at the time of the assault, there is no statute of limitations. They could still be brought to trial. I tried to tell him he could use it to get those bastards locked up and clear Blaire's name, but he kept saying it was too late and mumbling stuff I didn't understand."

"Like what?" Ax asks.

"Something about it'd hurt her, and he couldn't choose."

I frown. "What does that mean?"

He shrugs. "I've no idea, and he wouldn't explain when I asked. He just kept saying it was too late and he had to take matters into his own hands." He scrubs a hand over his jaw. "That's when he told me he was going to take your dad's hunting rifle and shoot them. Honestly, he sounded crazy, and I didn't believe him. He was upset. I was upset and full of rage too. We spoke about how they deserved to die, but I thought we were just venting. If I believed he was serious, I would never have let him leave my house that night."

Silence engulfs us, and I try to digest everything Cam's shared.

"After I got off the phone with you the following morning, I sent him a hundred messages telling him not to do it," Cam continues, staring absently off into space. "Then I tried dialing the school, but he must've cut the phone lines, and I couldn't get through. I thought of running to school but knew I wouldn't make it in time. Then I remembered my aunt was friendly with one of the secretaries in the school office. By the time I got her cell number, I was too late. When she answered my call, she was screaming and crying, and gunshots were ringing out in the background. I knew I was too late."

"And you didn't tell the police about the video?" Skeet asks.

Cam shakes his head. "Ethan asked me not to, so I told them I knew he was upset and angry but not why. It's not like it would've made any difference then. Everyone was mourning those assholes, and any attempt at real justice for Blaire was lost. Releasing that tape would just have hurt her more."

He looks at me with pleading eyes. "I couldn't stay with you and keep that hidden. That's why I had no choice but to let you go. And it killed me because I've always loved you, Blaire. Always. And I hate that I let you down."

"We've all made so many mistakes. But we don't get a do-over. We just have to try and learn from them and move on with our lives."

"I carry the guilt with me all the time," Cam admits. "For failing you and Ethan. And I miss that stupid fucker so much. He was my best friend, and I feel his loss every single day."

"Me too." I smile at him through watery eyes. "And I've hated him for leaving me, but I can't be mad at him anymore. Not now."

"He loved you, B. I've never seen a brother so devoted to his sister. What happened to you killed a part of him, and he had it thrown in his face every day when he saw those degenerates around school. He hated himself for not being there to protect you." His face contorts in pain. "I did too, but Ethan felt the pain as if it had happened to him. I'm not sure he wouldn't have snapped anyway. The video just propelled him toward something that may have happened anyway."

"I can't say that I blame the guy," Skeet admits. "I didn't know him. Wish I'd gotten the chance, but if anyone hurt my sisters like that, I don't think I could hold back either."

"I hate that Ethan has come out like the villain in all this," Cam adds. "But there isn't anything we can do about that."

"I know. I've thought about it nonstop since Ethan died, but the truth can't come out now. It's not right to tarnish their memories because their families have suffered enough. They don't need to know their sons were monsters or that their girlfriends were horrible bullies who tormented me for years. I couldn't live with myself if I inflicted that pain on them. It needs to stay in the past."

Cam gives Skeet Ethan's email address. "Do you think the same person that sent Ethan the email is the one who sent Blaire the threatening emails?" he asks, shoving his hands in his pockets.

"I don't know, but I'm going to find out." Skeet's brow creases like it always does when he's lost in thought. I lean into Ax's side, and he slides his hand around my waist. "Is there anyone you can think of who might've sent them?" Skeet asks while Cam stares at Ax's arm.

"It could be any number of people. Emotions ran high in the aftermath of the shooting, and I know people unfairly blamed Blaire."

"While you just sat back and let them." Heath glowers at my ex, letting him know exactly what he thinks of him.

"I was weak and a coward. I don't need you to point that out." Cam pierces me with a look. "I will always regret leaving you to face that alone. I'm so sorry, B. I'd do anything to take it back."

"It's okay. I forgive you."

"I don't deserve that, but thank you."

Skeet smiles at me proudly, linking his fingers through my left hand.

"Okay, I've got to ask," Cam says, his gaze bouncing between us. "Which one of them are you dating, because I'm confused."

"I'm dating Skeet," I say, looking up at my long-haired boyfriend. "And Ax too." I grin as I snuggle into his arm.

"And me as well," Heath says, startling me, but I don't correct him.

"What?" Cam's mouth is practically hanging to the floor.

I beam at him. "I'm in a relationship with all three of them, and they make me incredibly happy."

He's momentarily lost for words until he composes himself. "That's, um. Fuck." He claws his hands through his hair. "I don't know what to say to that." Shock, and a hint of concern, is splayed across his face.

"Say you're happy I'm happy and it's great I've got three amazing guys in my corner."

"I *am* happy you're happy. That's all I've ever wanted for you."

"I hope you're happy too?"

He shrugs. "I'm getting there."

He walks us to the door, opening it slowly before turning to the guys. "I'd like a minute alone with Blaire."

"Then ask Blaire," Ax coolly replies. "We don't speak for her."

Cam looks like he wants to ram his fist in Ax's face.

"It's okay." I wriggle out of Ax's embrace. "Can you guys wait for me outside?"

"Sure thing, babe." Skeet pecks me on the lips, and I feel his eyes on Cam the whole time.

"I'd like to say it's been a pleasure," Heath grits out. "But I'd only be lying." He shoves past Cam out the door. Heath's like a big, grouchy bear these days, and I can't help smiling even though it's not something I should condone or encourage.

"Take your time." Ax kisses my cheek before him and Skeet leave together.

"You're really happy?" Cam asks, leaning against the wall and crossing his ankles.

"I am now."

"After what happened, I never would've seen you dating three guys at once."

"Me neither," I truthfully admit. "But it works. They're really good to me, and they've helped me heal."

"Well, then I'm glad." His features soften as he looks at me. "You look beautiful, by the way." Tentatively, he reaches out, caressing my cheek for one fleeting moment. "You've always been beautiful, but you've really grown into your skin. They're lucky guys."

"I'm the lucky one. For a time there, I never thought I'd be able to recover."

"I know what you mean. It might've looked like I was coping on the outside, but I wasn't. I didn't get a free pass either."

"I know, Cam, and it's okay. I meant what I said. I forgive you. Now, it's time to get on with our lives."

He pushes off the wall. "Can I hug you? Please? I just need to hold you in my arms one last time."

I should probably tell him no, but I need this closure as much as he seems to. I step into his embrace, and it's soft and tender. Like a hug from a brother or a close family member. In a lot of ways, that's what Cam is to me. He was my brother's best friend, and like an adopted member of our family, way before he was my boyfriend—and for much longer. "I nearly died when I saw what they did to you, Blaire," he whispers. "You're so incredibly strong and brave." He presses a kiss to the top of my head. "You're my hero."

I ease out of his arms then, smiling up at him. "Have a good life, Cam, and be happy. I know Ethan would want that for you."

I don't wait to hear his reply, stepping out of his house and closing the door to my past. The biggest smile graces my lips as I skip down the steps to where my future is waiting.

Chapter Forty-Three

"Can we talk about what you said back in Rhode Island?" I ask from the doorway of Heath's bedroom. We only got home at two a.m., and we've been sleeping since. Skeet and Ax have gone to work out leaving Heath and me alone in the house. I sense it was a strategic move, and it's not one I'm going to waste.

"Okay." His tone carries a hint of wariness.

I perch on the corner of his bed as he runs a hand through his dark-blond hair. "Did you tell Cam you were my boyfriend for his benefit or you meant it?"

"Direct. Wow."

I shrug unapologetically. "I'm not holding things back anymore. This is how I roll now. Open, honest communication. Starting with you telling me what's going through that obstinate head of yours."

A devilish glint appears in his eye. "Right now, my *obstinate* brain wants to kiss the shit out of you."

The biggest grin spreads across my mouth. "I shouldn't condone this, because we do need to talk, but kissing the shit out of me beats conversing any day." I crawl into his lap, snaking my arms around his neck before he changes his mind. "Show me how it's done, stud."

A rumbling sound tumbles from his mouth before he grabs my head forcefully, melding our lips together. I close my eyes, sighing contentedly into his mouth.

Heath kisses me like he thought he'd never get to do it again. Every time I try to draw a breath, he pulls me back to his lush mouth, nibbling my lips and holding my face firmly in his large palms. I lose track of how much time passes, just reveling in kissing him again and how everything feels perfect now that I'm back on track with all my guys.

When he finally releases me, I'm seeing stars. "Hot damn," I pant. "You weren't lying."

He pecks my lips softly, honoring me with the first genuine smile since I reappeared in their lives. Another layer of stress flitters away. "I'm sorry for acting like a giant bag of dicks." His gaze is adoring as he peers deep into my eyes. "I love you, Blaire, and I'm all yours if you still want me."

"You mean it?" My voice exudes excitement and a tinge of disbelief.

"I do." He hugs me close, squeezing me as if he's afraid to ever let me go.

I rest my head on his shoulder, grinning like a lovesick fool. "I want you, Heath. There will never be a time where I don't." I lift my head and cup one side of his face. "I love you too much to ever lose you again."

"I don't know what I've done to earn your forgiveness and a second chance, but I promise I won't let you down."

"What about all the other girls?"

He places his hand over mine. "None of those girls meant anything to me, Blaire. I told you I was a prick to them. A prick. Period. It was meaningless sex. That's all. No one ever came close to you."

"I want to believe you."

He grips my shoulders with both hands, moving closer to me. My hands drop into my lap. "I don't blame you for having doubts, but you know the real me, and the real me is not the person I've been on this campus. I'm done with random hookups. I love you. Only you. And I will commit to you one hundred percent. You never have to doubt my loyalty. I will never betray you. Never."

"Okay."

Air whooshes out of his mouth in grateful relief. "Thank you. And just so we're clear, I always used condoms, and I'm completely clean. I get tested every few months."

"That's good to know." I'm grinning like a goober as I grab my cell from the back pocket of my jeans, tapping out a quick text.

He frowns. "Whatcha doin', babe?"

"Texting the good news to Ax and Skeet. This is going to make them so happy."

He groans. "Skeet is going to be unbearable. This is all his dreams come true."

I playfully shove his shoulders and they don't budge. Like, at all. He's an unmovable mountain of a man, and my pants turn damp at the thought of scaling him.

"Hmm." Heath inspects my face carefully. "Mind telling me what's going through *your* mind right now?"

"It's too X-rated to share," I tease. "Unless you're ready to go from zero to sixty?"

His eyes blaze with heat, and he grips my hips, pushing his crotch up into me. "I've been sporting a constant boner since you returned." I grind down against him, and we both groan. "You make me so damn hard."

I move my hand to the waistband of his jeans. "I can fix that for you."

He curls his fingers around my wrist, stalling me. "You don't have to do that, and I thought you wanted to talk."

"Talking's overrated." I smirk, popping the top button on his jeans. "Besides, I think we've said all that needs to be said for now." I lick my lips in a deliberately provocative manner. "Let me make you feel good."

"Only if you let me reciprocate." He cups the apex of my thighs through my jeans.

A shudder works its way through me, and I grind down on his hand. "Hell yeah."

I get rid of my jeans while Heath does the same. Sexual tension is heavy in the air, and our eyes never waver from one another as we undress. I hook my fingers in the side of my panties, ready to remove them, when he stops me. "Let me." My body tingles in anticipation, and I nod.

He slowly drags my panties down my legs, and I step out of them, kicking them aside. Then he kneels before me, pushing my legs wide. Before I've had time to process his intention, his hot mouth is on me, his tongue running up and down my slit, turning my insides into Jell-O. I take hold of his shoulders, gripping tight as he devours me. His tongue moves inside me, and a primitive moan slips out of my lips as my release starts building. He slides one finger into me as his mouth moves to my clit, and he sucks hard. He pumps his finger in and out, his mouth moving over my clit at the same pace, and I detonate a couple of minutes later, barely able to maintain an upright position as my body spasms with liquid pleasure. He milks every drop of my arousal before pulling his mouth away and standing, gripping my hips and keeping me steady.

"Heath," I rasp before crushing my mouth to his. I kiss him passionately, greedily, while I stroke his erection through his boxers. He's hard as steel, and my pussy clenches with the need to feel him inside me. "Fuck me. Please."

"Blaire." His pained expression matches his tone. "I want to. More than anything, but are you really sure about this? We've only just gotten back together and—"

I put my hand over his mouth, quieting his protests. "I know what I want and it's you. All of you. We might technically have only just reunited, but it's not like we don't know one another, and it's not like we're kids anymore." I remove my hand, brushing my lips against his in a feather-soft touch. "I want to feel as close to you as possible, and I think you need this as much as me."

"I do." He hugs me to his chest. "I need you so badly, Blaire. The only time I feel good about myself is when I'm with you."

"Then make love to me, Heath." I run my fingers through his hair. "Or fuck me. Whatever floats your boat."

He laughs, lifting me up. I wrap my legs around his waist as he carries me to the bed. "I want to love you, all over, like you deserve."

I hold my arms up as he strips me of my shirt and bra, and then I watch, licking my lips as he removes his shirt and shoves his boxers down his legs. His cock is magnificent, wide and thick like every other part of his anatomy. I'm not sure what emotion he sees on my face, but he rounds the bed, sitting down beside me and taking my hand. "I'll take care of you. I promise. I'll make sure it doesn't hurt. I'll make this good for you."

I lean up and kiss him slowly, and he crawls over me, careful not to press down all the way. Heat rolls off his body in waves, crashing into me and warming me all over. His mouth moves from my lips, blazing a trail down my neck, over my collarbone, and lower. He plucks at my nipples with his teeth, and my back arches off the bed. He soothes the sharp sting by rolling his tongue around my sensitive flesh while kneading my tits and pressing his hard-on against my pussy. I rock my hips up into him, needing him inside me now.

I don't have to articulate the need. Heath seems to understand. He lifts his head up, piercing me with a lust-drenched look as he rolls on a condom and lines his cock up at my entrance.

"I've got you, baby," he says, slowly inching into me. I spread my legs wider, sucking in a breath as I feel him slide inside me. A wanton moan escapes my lips as he pushes in farther, filling me like I've never been filled before.

"Heath!"

He leans down, kissing me with more restraint than I expected. "It's incredible to be like this with you. I never thought I'd get to experience this." He's still slowly pushing inside, patiently waiting for my body to adjust to his wide girth.

"I wanted this back in Kentsville, but I wasn't brave enough to ask for it," I admit, staring into his beautiful blue eyes.

"You've changed," he says, pushing that last bit in. He holds himself still while I absorb the sensation of him inside me. I feel him everywhere, and the tip of his cock is angled perfectly, shoving me into a heavenly realm.

"We've all changed," I moan, flexing my hips and wrapping my legs around his waist. "Move, baby. I need you to move."

He starts thrusting, slowly and precisely, and his tender care brings tears to my eyes. "I won't break, Heath. Go faster." He picks up the pace and black spots mar my vision. Holy fuck. He's pressing all the right parts of me, and I'm already close to the edge. I dig my feet into his solid ass cheeks, urging him to go even faster, and he bucks his hips up, grabbing onto the headboard with one hand as he starts fucking me hard and fast. I scream the place down as my climax thunders through me. Sweat dots my brow as I clench around him. The headboard bangs against the wall, over and over, and then he roars out his own release, shuddering inside me in powerful waves that seem to last forever.

He collapses on the bed beside me, and a fit of giggles attacks me from nowhere. Soon, he's joining me and we're both crying tears of laughter. "I guess it's good I have a massive ego," he says a few minutes later, wiping tears from his eyes. "Or I might get offended that you started laughing right after we had sex for the first time."

I prop up on one elbow, tracing swirling motions on his chest with the tip of my finger. "It's only because I'm deliriously happy. You're all back in my life. I'm crazy about each one of you and so unbelievably happy right now. I never thought I could ever have that."

Tears of joy prick my eyes, and he pulls me down for a lingering kiss. "You deserve all that and more, and we are going to ensure you are loved and adored every day for the rest of your life."

"I love the sound of that," I say, resting my head on his chest. His heart thumps steadily under my ear as he circles his arm around my waist, drawing me in closer.

"How are you feeling about everything you heard yesterday?"

"I'm not sure. I'm still processing. The thought that someone was taping the whole time makes me feel ill." A shiver runs up my spine. "I don't even want to think about who they might've shown it to or what they did with it. I didn't think anything else about that night could disgust me anymore, but I was wrong."

"I want to kill those bastards all over again. I'm glad they're rotting in the ground. I know how you feel, but I'm glad your brother killed them. They were animals, and they fucking deserved to die."

I don't agree with him, even if I'm sickened all over again, but I don't argue the point. I don't want to fight after we've made such huge moves forward in our relationship.

"I'm going to talk it through with my therapist. She'll help me unravel my feelings. Until then, I'm compartmentalizing."

"About that." Heath's heart rate kicks up underneath my ear. "I did some online research, and I found a guy I think I'd like to talk to. Will you still come with?"

I lift my head up. "Try keeping me away. Make the appointment, and I'll come with you." Of course, I won't be able to go in with him, but I'll be there for moral support.

We make love again, more lazily this time, and then we spend the rest of the day in bed, watching movies, chatting about everything and anything, and eating takeout pizza. Skeet and Ax keep their distance, giving us much-needed privacy, and I respect them so much for that. When nighttime falls, we make love again before drifting to sleep soon after.

Sometime later, another warm body wraps around me on my other side. "Go back to sleep," Ax whispers in my ear, placing his hand over my naked belly. I'm only semi-conscious, so I fall back into a deep sleep with a huge smile on my face.

When I wake the next morning, I'm so hot it's as if I slept in the fiery pits of Hell. Tendrils of sweat have plastered strands of my hair to my forehead, and I feel icky all over. I try to stretch out my legs and meet resistance. "What the hell?" I murmur, just about managing to crane my neck. Heath and Ax are both still curled around me, on either side, and they are like furnaces. My gaze locks on Skeet, lying underneath the covers at the end of the bed, winking at me with a cheeky glint in his eye. I blink excessively, thinking I must be imagining it or dreaming. But nope. Skeet's trademark chuckle wafts to my ears, and his hand moves up my thigh.

I manage to wriggle out of Ax's and Heath's embraces and crawl under the covers, shimmying down the bed until I've landed on top of Skeet with our faces lined up. "What are you guys doing?" I whisper, not wanting to wake the two sleeping beauties at the top of the bed.

"I hope it's okay, but after Saturday, both Ax and I just wanted to stay close to you too. To make sure you were all right."

My heart swells with love. "Of course, that's okay. I have no issue with sleeping in the same bed as all of you. It's just the group sex thing I don't think I can handle."

"There was also something else," he says, looking uncertain.

"What?" I press a kiss to his chest, not wanting to inflict my morning breath on his mouth.

"I don't want to say it like this. Can we head downstairs, and I'll tell you over breakfast?"

I nod, and he helps me crawl out of the bed without waking the others. We are like two thieves in the night, stealing away from a house we've just pilfered. I grab my undies off the floor and hurriedly pull them on. Skeet is only in his boxers. He stops at the door, turning me around, and I have to smother my laughter. Ax and Heath have moved closer on the bed, and they have their arms wrapped around one another. Clearly, they think they're hugging me. "This is too good. I can't not capture this tender, loving moment," Skeet whispers, struggling to contain his mirth. "Stay there for a second and don't wake them."

It only takes a second for me to follow him to his bedroom. "I don't think you should," I say, stopping at the doorway to his room. "I know it's harmless, but after everything we've learned about—"

"You're right." He stalks toward me. "I wasn't thinking clearly. No incriminating photos." He pecks my lips briefly. "But that doesn't mean I'm not going to milk this for-everr." His eyes shimmer mischievously.

The serious expression slips off my face, replaced by a wide smile. "Oh my God, I know. That was hilarious but also extremely cute."

He's still smirking when he hands me one of his shirts. I slip it on, still grinning at the visual playing on a loop in my mind. Pulling on sweats, he pads out of the room in his bare feet with his naked chest on proud display, looking unbelievably H.O.T. So hot it takes all my willpower not to jump his bones. Reluctantly, I leave him to fix breakfast while I take a necessary trip to the bathroom, taking a pee, combing my wayward hair, and brushing my teeth.

The first thing I do when I arrive in the kitchen is kiss him long and hard. We have our arms wrapped around one another as we kiss, and it's both sweet and sexy in an innocent yet not-so-innocent way.

"I could get used to this," he murmurs, sliding his lips to my ear while continuing to hold me close. I love how velvety-soft he feels under my touch, especially the light smattering of hair covering his chest.

"We're all together again," I happily admit. "And everything feels right with the world."

"Except for one thing." I frown, and he kisses me softly. "Move in with us."

My eyes widen. "What?" I splutter before adding. "I can't."

"Why the hell not?"

"What about what other people would think? I mean, I don't care." And I don't. I've had enough time to think about it. I'm stronger now, and if I'm in a relationship with all three of my guys, then I'm not going to hide that fact. If people have issues with it, that's their own problem. Except there's one big obstacle. "But Heath has his football career to think about. I'd hate for our relationship to impact him."

"Hmm." Skeet rubs his prickly jawline. "That's a valid point and something we need to discuss. Let's just ask the guys later, and we can talk it through then."

"Sure. Now spill." I slip out of his arms and hop up on the stool, gratefully accepting the steaming mug of coffee he hands to me.

He sits down across from me, blowing on his own hot cup of coffee. "I can't find any trace of that video on Ethan's equipment. I think it's fair to assume the police found the recording and permanently wiped it."

"I've come to the same conclusion," I agree. "And it only reinforces what I think. They knew, as well as we do, that there was no point sharing that video."

"They had no right to bury it, Blaire. I grew up with lawyers, and hiding or destroying evidence is a crime."

"It doesn't matter now. And maybe it's for the best. I'm not sure I ever want to see that tape."

He nods, holding my hand across the table. "You're probably right. But that wasn't really what I had to tell you." He pauses for a minute. "I was able to trace the emails you received. I know who sent you those threatening messages."

I stop breathing for a split second, and an anxious feeling invades my chest. He pauses again, and the anticipation is killing me. "Skeet."

"I think this might change things. Call it a sixth sense, but I think there's even more to the story."

"Who is it, Skeet? Who hates me so much they told me to kill myself?"

"It was your brother's crush. The girl he couldn't have. The only one not killed that day."

I instantly know who he means, and I feel like smacking myself in the forehead for not realizing sooner.

"It was Todd DeLaurentis's girlfriend, Lucinda Jamison," he confirms.

Chapter Forty-Four

"*I* need to confront her," I immediately say.

"No. *We* need to confront her," Skeet says, waggling his finger between us. "We're a team now. All four of us."

I nod. "Which university is she attending?"

"None." Skeet props his elbows on the counter. "She never left Amber Springs."

Ice replaces the blood flowing through my veins at the thought of returning there, but this isn't the kind of conversation you have over the phone. I want to look her in the eye and find out why she hates me so much she wanted me to die. "That is extremely weird. Everyone, and I mean *everyone*, from the Academy goes on to university, most out of state. It makes no sense that she's still there."

Skeet shrugs. "Maybe the loss of her boyfriend sent her spiraling."

I purse my lips as I consider his assumption. I shake my head. "No, I think you're right. There is more we don't know. Her emails were not about Todd." My eyes pop wide. "They were about Ethan and how I should have died not him."

"You think Ethan wasn't the only one harboring a crush?"

I rub a tense spot between my brows. "I don't know what to think, and there's no point trying to second-guess it. We'll just have to wait until we hear what she has to say."

Heath and Ax join us a half hour later, arguing as they step foot in the kitchen. Skeet delights in teasing them about their cozy cuddling in the bed, and Heath looks fit to rip Skeet's tongue out of his mouth to stop him from talking while Ax is just taking it in his stride.

319

We all decide to skip classes, taking the day to just enjoy being together, back as a unit again. After lounging around in our pajamas watching back to back sci-fi movies, we get dressed and head out to a local diner for dinner. Skeet and I fill them in on the Lucinda connection as we walk. Neither of us had brought it up at the house because we didn't want to ruin our lazy Monday. We have a plan agreed by the time we're seated in an end booth in the diner. We're going to fly to Arizona next weekend to confront Lucinda.

"Done." Heath repockets his cell, resting his hands on the Formica tabletop.

"What's done?" I ask, taking a slurp of my soda as I look over at him. Ax and I are seated together with Skeet and Heath across from us.

"I just booked our flights and hired a car. I figure it's best we drive ourselves in case you want to make a quick exit after you speak to the bitch."

"You have to stop doing that." I shake my head at him.

"Doing what?" he looks genuinely confused.

"Paying for everything."

He sighs. "Don't even start with that. I have more money than I know what to do with."

"Let him pay if he wants to," Skeet says. "It's only money."

"Spoken like a guy who's never known what it's like to go without," Ax cuts in.

Skeet puts his drink down, leaning across the table. "You're right. I've been extremely fortunate, and I'm never flippant about that. And I know things were tough for you. I don't mean to dismiss it, but it's all the more reason why we shouldn't expend any energy arguing over money now."

"Once we have enough to look after ourselves, it doesn't matter whose pocket it's coming out of," Heath supplies.

I don't agree, and I'm definitely more on Ax's wavelength when it comes to this topic, but I don't want to get dragged into this conversation now. Not when we've other more important stuff to discuss. "Can we talk about our relationship," I cut in bluntly.

"What about it?" Heath asks.

"How do we want to do this in public?"

"Last time, you weren't so keen on people being all up in our business," Ax says, sliding his arm around my shoulder. "If we're going for one boyfriend in public again, then I'm calling dibs this time."

Skeet rolls his eyes. "Much to learn, you still have."

Ax flips him the bird. "You do *not* want to get into a *Star Wars* war of words with me, my young apprentice."

"Guys. Can we focus. Please."

"Sorry, babe." Ax kisses my cheek, pulling me closer. "What do you want to do?"

"I don't want to hide this time. I'm not ashamed of what we have, and if other people have issues with that, then I don't care." I glance over at Heath. "But I'm thinking it might not be a good setup for you. If you think it'll jeopardize your position on the team or your future NFL career, then we can do the whole one boyfriend thing again."

"Or we can do a two-boyfriend thing," Skeet says, pointing between himself and Ax. "And just leave Gilchrist out of the equation."

The waitress arrives then, placing our food down. She doesn't even attempt to disguise her blatant ogling of Heath. "I've been to all your games," she tells him, batting her eyelashes as she starts up a conversation.

"That's great." Heath gives her a tight smile.

"You're easily the best player on the team."

Skeet is grinning as he gets ready to tuck into his burger.

"That's kind of you to say," Heath says, giving her the briefest of attention, but she's not to be deterred.

"I'd love to hang out with you sometime." She grabs a napkin and scribbles her digits down. "Call me anytime." She thrusts the napkin in his face. Wow. Talk about pushy. My claws are threatening to come out.

"This happens all the time," Ax whispers in my ear. "You better get used to it."

Heath glares at Ax, and either Ax spoke louder than I thought or Heath has supersonic hearing. Heath pushes the napkin away. "Thanks, but I don't think my girlfriend would like that."

Her face drops. "You have a girlfriend? Since when?" Now she looks annoyed, as if she has some claim to him.

"Since now." Heath slides his hand across the table, circling his fingers around my wrist. Ax still has his arm around my shoulder, and I'm pressed up close to him. "This is my girlfriend, Blaire."

"Hey." I give her the biggest smile, and yes, I'm smugly gloating.

She frowns, her gaze darting from Heath's hand to Ax's arm. Her shoulders stiffen, and her eyes narrow. "Can I get you anything else?" she snaps in a prissy tone, finally remembering she's got a job to do.

"No," I jump in before any of the guys can respond. "I've got everything I need right here." I give her my best sugary smile while I'm mentally flipping her the bird.

She storms off without another word, and Skeet cracks up laughing. "I guess that's agreed now."

♥♥♥♥

The rest of the week crawls by in excruciatingly slow fashion. It's always the way when you're anticipating something. Whether it's something you're really looking forward to or something you're dreading like I am. However, by the time Saturday morning rolls around, I'm more than ready to do this. This feels like the last piece of the puzzle, and I just want to get it over and done with.

"By the way," I say, when we're on the interstate heading in the direction of Amber Springs. "My mom has invited you all to join us at my grandparents' house for Thanksgiving unless you were planning on going home for the break?"

"A. We're going wherever you're going," Skeet replies. "And B. You told your parents about us?"

I beam at them, proud of myself for taking the bull by the horns. "I did. I told them I'm dating all three of you and that I'm happy."

"I'm betting your dad loved that," Heath says from the driver's seat.

"He was too shocked to say much, but it's my life, and I'll live it the way I want to. Mom wasn't that surprised by the news. She said she guessed I'd been dating all of you by the nature of our conversation that last time we were all together in Kentsville."

She did overhear Heath calling me *their girl,* and she heard me breaking up with them, but she'd never mentioned it to me, and I'd forgotten all about it. I'm sure she'll have plenty of questions for me when I next visit. While my parents gave me their blessing to come to college and live on my own, it took a long time for them to stop fretting over me like I was a toddler again. I put them through hell, and they worry, so I understand if they have misgivings over our unconventional relationship.

Most people do.

Although some reactions are unexpected.

Heath spoke to his coach this week, and he surprised him, admitting he was glad he had a girlfriend and was no longer whoring himself around campus. It seems he's been gaining a bit of a rep, and that's not something the NFL likes to see in potential recruits. Although sharing a girlfriend with his two best friends isn't ideal either, it's preferable to his current rep, so it's working out better than we thought. He hasn't told his parents yet, but repairing his relationship with them in the first place is more important. He attended his first therapy session, and I think it went better than he was expecting, so he's scheduled a few more. I'm really hoping it helps him as much as it's helped me.

"I'm proud of you." Ax pulls me to him for a kiss.

"It feels good to finally be in control of my life," I admit.

Skeet leans through the front console, smiling at me. "My parents say hi by the way, and Shaz is beyond excited to catch up with you when she visits."

"I've been meaning to ask you for her number, but I want to apologize to her face to face. I abandoned her too."

"I've explained a little. I didn't tell her everything because I didn't know how much you wanted her to know, but she doesn't blame you, and she's ecstatic you're back with us. She was planning on visiting during Thanksgiving, but I can tell her to reschedule."

"No, don't." I shake my head. "She can come too. It's not like my grandparents' place isn't big enough. They have plenty of spare bedrooms."

"I'm going to message her right now. She'll be delighted."

"Tell her I can't wait to see her."

"Already on it."

I spend the rest of the journey attempting to listen to music, but it doesn't mute my brain. My knee jerks up and down until Ax plants his hand on my thigh stalling the motion. He finds different ways to touch me as we eat up the miles, but even his touch doesn't distract me.

My nerves get the better of me when we pass by the sign for Amber Springs. My heart is racing faster than a Formula One car during a Grand Prix, and sweat lines the back of my hands. I gulp back the bile traveling up my throat, and I'm sure I look as pale as a ghost. I genuinely think I could puke.

"It's going to be okay," Ax whispers, hugging me close.

"We're not going to let anything happen to you while you're here," Heath reassures me.

"Don't be mad," Skeet says, turning around to look at me. "But she knows we're coming."

"She what?" I shout. "How?"

"I called her," he admits.

"Why would you do that?" I shriek. "Now she's had time to prepare her answers."

"She wants to tell you the truth," he quietly confirms. "And I got the sense she's hugely remorseful over those emails."

"You should've told me." I fold my arms over my chest, a muscle tensing in my jaw. "We're a team, and we agreed no more secrets."

Skeet and Ax share a look. "You've been on edge all week. We worried this would make it worse," Skeet says. "I'm sorry if I overstepped, but this girl has threatened you, and none of us were comfortable coming here blind. We needed to know what we were likely walking in to."

I fiddle with a loose thread on the end of my shirt. "I know it was coming from a good place, but you can't hold stuff back from me again. I'm not the same fragile girl you remember. I'm stronger now."

"You were never fragile, Blaire," Ax murmurs. "You've always been one of the strongest people I know."

"You're our girl," Heath says, eyeing me through the mirror. "And we won't apologize for doing whatever we feel is necessary to protect you."

I blow air out of my mouth. "I don't want to fight with you about this, but this conversation is not over. It's just parked."

"Yes, ma'am." Skeet salutes me, and I stick my tongue out at him. He laughs before blowing me a kiss. "Love you."

"Love you too. Even if you are a giant pain in my ass sometimes."

"We're here," Heath proclaims a second later, and I look up, startled to see the elaborate gates to the Jamison family home.

"She wanted us to meet her *here?*" I can't keep the hysteria from my tone. The Jamisons are really close with the DeLaurentises, and I can't imagine Lucinda's parents will be happy to see me. "I don't know about this." I rub the back of my neck, nausea swimming up my throat. I think I'm about to make good on the whole puking thing.

"I disagreed at first too," Skeet supplies, "but she said this was the most private location, and she didn't want an audience for what she had to share."

"Relax, babe." Ax massages my shoulders. "If it gets uncomfortable, we'll leave."

The electric gates open, granting us access, and Heath maneuvers the rental up a long driveway edged with towering trees. He brings the car to a standstill behind a massive water feature just off to the side of the front entrance. The house is old school, and it's been in Lucinda's family for generations. Ethan attended a couple parties here back in the day, but I avoided parties like the plague after what happened that summer.

Ivy crawls the walls of the large two-story house giving it a creepy, haunted-house feel. Gravel crunches underfoot as we make our way to the front door. Skeet has his hand raised to knock when it swings open.

I swallow the lump in my throat, wiping my clammy hands down the front of my jeans, wishing I'd made more of an effort with my appearance. Screw that, my inner voice chants, I'm not here to impress Lucinda or her mother. Mrs. Jamison stares at me for a long moment, and the guys tense at my back, ready to go into battle if needed.

"Blaire. Look at you. All grown up and beautiful." She smiles at me before stepping aside. "Excuse my manners. Please come in."

I glance over my shoulder at the guys, perplexed. This is *not* the reception I was expecting. Skeet slips his hand in mine, walking into the house alongside me. "Mrs. Jamison." I nod politely as we stand awkwardly in a dimly lit hallway with a sweeping staircase behind us.

"Lucinda is expecting you. Follow me." She eyes the guys a little circumspectly but says nothing. Her heels tap off the stone floor as she leads us over to the west side of the house. She stops before a set of frosted-glass double doors, turning to face me. "Lucinda is just inside." She clasps her hands in front of her. "I know why you're here, and I know what my daughter has to tell you. I owe you an apology. I didn't know, or I never would've supported the DeLaurentis family after the tragedy." She pats my arm. "I can't begin to imagine how difficult things must've been for you and your family, and you have my deepest sympathy."

I almost keel over in shock, and I'm guessing it shows on my face.

"I don't condone what your brother did," she continues, "but I have more of an understanding now. I'm also appalled at how Lucinda treated you, and you should know she's suffered for it, in more ways than one. I have no right to ask anything of you, but I'm asking if you could go easy on her. She wants to do the right thing, and I'm proud of her for that, but she's ill, Blaire. She's lost the will to live, and I'm terrified I'm going to lose her. If you can find it in your heart to forgive her, I know that would mean so much to her."

I'm not sure how to respond, so I take a few minutes to gather my thoughts. "Thank you for your kind words, and, I've got to admit, I'm completely taken aback. This isn't what I was expecting. The last time I was in Amber Springs, we were virtually run out of town. Coming back here has been difficult, but I'm determined to try and uncover exactly why Ethan did what he did, and your daughter knows something. I'm sorry to hear she's unwell, and I promise I'll try my best not to upset her, but I can't guarantee anything beyond that."

"I understand, but if she's upset, I will have to ask you to leave."

"Fair enough."

She steps around us. "Go in whenever you're ready." Her heels make the same clackety-clack noise as she walks away.

"Well, that was weird as fuck," Heath says.

"I have no idea what's going on," I admit, my hand moving to the door handle. "But it's time I found out."

Chapter Forty-Five

I open the double doors and walk into a long sunroom, lavishly furnished with wicker furniture, plush couches, a multitude of soft overhead lights, and plants dotted around the room. Small vases filled with colorful flowers rest on top of the three tables in the room, and the scent of jasmine and honeysuckle wafts through the air.

Lucinda is seated at the far end of the room, looking out the window at the magnificent grounds surrounding the property. A lilac blanket is draped over her shoulders, hanging off her thin frame and trailing the tile floor. My ballet flats barely make a sound as I head in her direction, followed by noisier male footsteps. I'm about halfway to her when she wheels around in her chair. I work hard to smother my gasp of surprise and mask the shock splaying across my face.

Her beautiful face is gaunt, and bruising dark shadows paint the skin under her eyes. Her once lustrous, long dark hair is cropped close to her head in a pixie cut. But it's the sight of her in a wheelchair that startles me the most.

I stop in front of her, and we stare at one another. I've thought of a million ways this meeting could go down, and now I'm standing here, looking down at her, the only words that come out of my mouth are "What happened?"

Her eyes dart over my shoulder to the guys who have come to a stop just behind me. "Which one of you is Skeet?" she asks in a quiet voice.

"Me." Skeet steps up beside me, placing his hand on my lower back.

She casts an appreciative glance over him before checking the other two guys out. I arch a brow at her. Like, seriously?

"Sorry. I don't get much in the way of eye candy these days." She shoots me an apologetic smile before eyeballing Skeet. "Thank you for bringing Blaire here. Like I said on the phone, I've wanted to talk to her for some time." She wets her lips. "But what I have to say is difficult enough without having a larger audience. I'm not asking you to leave the room. I can tell none of you would agree to that." She points toward the other end of the long room. "Would you mind sitting there so Blaire and I can talk in private."

Skeet looks to me to make the call. I nod. "It's fine." He leans in and kisses me softly, and then all three of them walk away.

"Take a seat, Blaire," she says. I sit down on a two-seater couch across from her. "Would you like a water?" She gestures toward the large stash of bottled waters on the table.

"No thank you. I'd just like to get straight to the point." She pours herself a glass of sparkling water while I talk. "Who was Ethan to you?"

She screws the cap back on the bottle while I wait for her reply. When she tips her face up to mine, her eyes are shining with unshed tears. "He was my everything," she whispers, and a single tear drips down her face.

The more I reflected on it this week, the surer I was that something must've happened between them, but her statement is still shocking. "He was my everything too."

She nods. "I know. He talked about you all the time. He *worried* about you all the time. I think that's when my jealousy toward you started." Her amber-hued eyes glisten with honesty.

"What exactly was the nature of your relationship with my brother?"

"Ethan was the love of my life, Blaire." Her eyes well up again. "And if things had been different, we would've been a couple. Instead, we were forced to conduct our relationship in secret."

I lean forward a little. "Let me get this straight. Are you saying you and Ethan were together behind your boyfriend's back?"

She nods. "Technically, yes, but it's more complicated than that."

"Then uncomplicate it," I snap. I'm blown away by her revelation. That's if she's telling the truth. Ethan never said a word to me about any relationship with her, and I'm pretty certain Cam wasn't aware either. If he was, he would've said last week. Her next statement completely throws me.

"I despised Todd DeLaurentis, and I'm not sorry he's dead." Her eyes blaze with a variety of emotions. "My parents forced me into dating him when I was fourteen. I'd never liked the creep, but our parents were best friends, and they loved the idea of us as a couple. I thought I'd date him for a few weeks and then tell my parents it wasn't working, and they'd get it out of their system."

The similarity to Heath and Cassie's situation strikes me as ironic. *Is that how all rich parents operate? Forcing their offspring on one another to forge links between their families?*

"I know you dated him for years, so what happened?"

She clenches the glass between her fingers so hard I'm surprised it doesn't break apart. She gulps and a look of pure anguish appears on her face. "They did it to me too, Blaire," she whispers.

A cold sweat crawls over my skin. I know what she means, but I still ask the question. "Did what?"

"Gang raped me. The same four." She drinks from her water while I digest that news. She rubs the back of her neck, her bony chest heaving up and down. "From what Ethan told me, it was about five months before they attacked you."

"Ethan told you about me?"

She nods. "Not at first, but after a while, when we'd grown closer and I explained why I could never leave Todd for him, he shared your story with me. I never told anyone, Blaire. I keep your secret the same way I kept mine, until recently."

I don't know whether to feel hurt, betrayed, sickened, or some other emotion because I'm still reeling at the news Ethan was having a relationship with Todd's girlfriend behind his back.

"If you were Todd's girlfriend, why did he do that to you?"

A bitter look contorts her face. "He told his friends he needed to 'break me in.'" She makes little air quotes with her fingers.

"Oh my God. I'm so sorry." I came here hating Lucinda for what she did to me, but I can't hold on to that hatred in light of what's she's just told me. Maybe I'm too soft, because she said some horrible things to me in those emails, but I'm sensing her ordeal at the hands of those boys was worse than mine.

"He called my mom after they finished ruining me. Arranged for me to sleep over with his sister. We were friends, and we often had sleepovers, so Mom never questioned it. I don't know what he did to Emilia to get her to swap rooms with him, but he slept in the bed beside me. I was still drugged and not fully conscious of the fact he stripped me, posed me in provocative poses, and took pictures. The next morning, when I woke, he was sitting by the side of the bed with this malevolent grin on his face."

She shivers all over. "He told me I would be his girlfriend and then his wife and I was his to do with as he pleased. He said, if I didn't cooperate, he'd send the pictures to the media and the board of directors of my dad's company and destroy us." She looks absently out the window. "I know now I should've told my parents, but I was hurt and scared. He was only a little bit older than me, but he was as manipulative as a boy years older. I always thought Todd had an evil streak, but my imagination didn't do him justice. I became a plaything for him and his friends."

I place my hand over my mouth, horrified at the thought of facing what I'd faced over and over again. Silent tears roll down my face.

"Ethan found me once after a party. I was sobbing. Finlay and Todd had just finished with me, and it was the worst attack yet. I wanted to die. I truly wanted to end it all. That's when Ethan found me. I wouldn't tell him what was wrong, but we became friends after that night, and it gradually developed into love."

At least now I understand why Lucinda never joined in the bullying. She didn't do anything to stop it, but I could tell she was always uncomfortable. I thought Ethan had spared her the day of the shooting because of it. But he spared her because he was in love with her.

"He begged me to leave Todd," Lucinda continues, "and I eventually told him why I couldn't. It was about three weeks before the shooting. It was only then that he told me about you. He wanted us to team up. He said if both of us came forward with the same story then we'd be believed. We had a massive argument over it. I told him I couldn't do it. I couldn't ruin my dad's company, and at this stage, after three years of abuse at their hands, I thought no one would believe me." She pauses to drink more water. "I should've listened to him."

No wonder Ethan snapped. He was carrying so much on his shoulders.

"The night before Ethan died, he showed up here drunk, throwing stones at my bedroom window. I was furious with him. Terrified my parents would see him and put two and two together. He was pleading with me to go with him and you to the cops. I was mad at him, and I told him it was over and if he didn't leave I'd tell my parents he was stalking me."

She hangs her head and tears drip onto her hand. "He was rambling, not very coherent. He just kept saying I'm torn in two. I love you and I love her, and it isn't right." The look of agony on her face is unlike anything I've seen before. "I sent him away that night believing I didn't love him anymore, and I've hated myself ever since. I should've called you or Cam, but he'd promised me he wouldn't tell anyone about us, and I knew how honorable Ethan was. I knew if either of you had suspected anything you would've approached me. So, I didn't call anyone." She sobs quietly for a few moments.

I sigh, hugging myself, finding this so hard to hear.

"The following morning, he sent me a text begging me not to go to school. He didn't say why, but it became obvious when I got there." I knew she'd been there, and the media had speculated a lot as to why she was spared when Matt's, Finlay's, and Lucas's girlfriends were all killed. "Ethan looked me straight in the eye, and there was a crazy intense quality to his gaze that scared me. He said he was sorry, that he loved me, but there was no other way. That they must be stopped before they caused any more pain. Then he shot Todd, and I saw no hint of remorse. He was like a machine. Devoid of emotion." She gulps. "I just stood there watching him taking them out one by one, and I felt nothing either, Blaire. *Nothing*."

A strangled sob rips from her mouth. "He was turning to me when the police burst into the room. I saw it all go down. I screamed at him to drop the gun, but they shot him before he had a chance. *Then* I felt everything. Time seemed to stop, and I fell to the ground, crawling toward him."

She breaks down, sobbing uncontrollably, and I don't hesitate anymore. I sink to my knees in front of her and take her hands in mine. "I saw the light go out of his eyes, Blaire. He was looking straight at me and he mouthed 'tell Blaire I love her.'"

I start crying then, and I can't stop. Warm arms slide around me from behind, holding me tight as raw pain lances me on all sides. I hug Ax's arm as I release the last of my tears a few minutes later. He presses a kiss to my hair and one to my cheek, and I cling to him, feeling completely overwhelmed.

"You love her?" Lucinda asks him.

"More than life itself," Ax confidently replies.

"Then don't ever push her away. Don't ever let anyone tell you your love is wrong."

I feel him nodding as I wipe under my eyes. "I'm okay now. You can return to the others."

"You sure, babe?" He cups my face gently, and I nod, sniffling. He presses his mouth to mine in a sweet kiss before settling me back onto the couch. Then he pours me a glass of water, wraps my hand around it, and walks off.

"I came here today full of hatred toward you," I honestly admit. "But I was wrong. You were as much a victim as I was. I know how badly I was hurting, and I can't even begin to compare my suffering to yours. I don't care why you sent me those emails. It doesn't matter anymore."

"You're so like Ethan. He was always the better person. Always so kindhearted."

"He was the best brother ever. I cherish the years I had with him and hate that his life was cut short because of me."

"Because of both of us, Blaire. He wanted to do right by both of us, but that wasn't possible without someone getting hurt. If I'd told him that last night that I'd go to the cops with you, then he'd still be here." She pauses briefly. "It's haunted me," she whispers. "Every day I think about how that conversation could have gone, should have gone, knowing if I'd said the right things then Ethan would still be alive." She looks down at her lap. "I wasn't listening. I didn't see him, and I lost him because of it."

Her eyes are flooded with tears when she looks up at me again. "I went into a very bad place after Ethan died. My parents thought I was grieving for Todd, but I hope that bastard is burning in hell. I was mourning Ethan, and no one even knew we loved each other. No one knew how amazing he was and how he was the only person holding me together." She takes another sip from her drink, and I follow suit.

"It was easier to blame you," she continues, "but that was wrong, and I'm so sorry, more than you can imagine. In my head, I twisted it all up so that it was your fault. If you'd gone to the police after they raped you, they would've arrested the guys, and my torment would've ended. Ethan and I would've been free to be together, and he wouldn't have had to kill them. That's how I justified it in my head."

"I was scared to report it. Scared of their money and their connections."

"You were right to be scared, and they would've gotten off somehow. It wouldn't have made a difference. I know that now. But Ethan was right. If we'd teamed up, they wouldn't have been able to beat the charges. We could've sent them away."

"I wish Ethan had told me. Maybe he might've been able to convince me but probably not. Those guys ruled by fear, and I felt beaten down."

"Me too. I could never properly explain it to Ethan, but you understand because they hurt you too."

Silence engulfs us as we both process everything. It's an awful lot to take in. I feel a burden lift at the same time as a new weight presses down on my chest.

"I wanted to lash out, and you were the easiest choice," she adds. "It wasn't that difficult to find out where you went. I knew a guy in school who knew a guy who was amazing with computers. He found the post Cassandra McFarland put up on social media about you. You were going under a different name, but she had posted a photo of you. I reached out to her after that, and she supplied me with your school email addy in exchange for the truth about who you were."

Fucking hell.

Lucinda has the decency to look thoroughly ashamed. "I hated myself for it. Especially when I found out you'd tried to kill yourself." Tears run down her cheeks again. "I said it to you, but I meant it for me. There is no excuse that justifies my behavior, but I was hurting, and I wanted you to hurt too, which is crazy, because, of course, you were already hurting."

She wheels up close to me, facing me with an earnest expression. "I'm so sorry, Blaire. What I did to you is unforgivable. Ethan would be so ashamed of me. I'm ashamed of myself. When I found out that you'd almost died, I jumped off the roof of our house. I didn't want to be me anymore. I just wanted it to end. But I survived, and now, I'll serve out my punishment in this chair."

I open my mouth to speak, but she raises her palm. "Don't. It's what I deserve. I know now this is all on me. I blamed you, but the fault lies with me. I was the reason Ethan was holding back because he respected my wishes. He accepted my fears for my family and our reputation, and that stopped him from doing the right thing by you."

"There's something you don't know." I tell her about the recording sent to Ethan the night before the shooting. She's shocked speechless. "Skeet tried to find it, but it looks like the police wiped all evidence of it from existence. But that's what was the catalyst for Ethan's actions. That's what drove him to do it, and I refuse to blame myself for his actions any longer, and you need to stop blaming yourself too. We both could've done things differently but so could Ethan." I draw a long breath. "It's not anyone's fault. It just happened, and nothing we can do or say will ever change that fact."

I take her hands in mine again. "I forgive you, Lucinda. And all I ask is that you forgive yourself. Ethan died so we could have a better life. We both owe it to him to try."

The sound of running footsteps forces me to whip my head around. Heath lands on top of us the exact same moment Mrs. Jamison races into the room.

"Blaire. You've got to see this." Heath holds out his cell to me. It's paused on a CNN headline.

NEW EVIDENCE COMES TO LIGHT IN THE AMBER SPRINGS MASSACRE.

"It's on the TV," Mrs. Jamison says. "You both need to see this. Come on."

Chapter Forty-Six

*M*rs. Jamison leads us into an expensively decorated living room where a massive wall-mounted screen screams the headlines. She increases the volume, and we all stand around, watching. I lean back against Heath, and he wraps his arms around my waist. On screen, the reporter relays the news.

"In a shocking development, new video footage handed over to the FBI has, allegedly, provided motive behind the Amber Springs massacre and casts significant doubt over the heretofore unblemished reputation of the victims."

A photo pops up on the side of the screen, and Lucinda gasps.

"Denton Montgomery, a pre-med student at Harvard and a cousin of Todd DeLaurentis, handed the video evidence in to local FBI agents in the Massachusetts office early yesterday morning. According to our sources, he has since been detained, pending prosecution. We'll bring you further updates as the case develops."

The channel switches to a different story, and Mrs. Jamison switches the TV off.

"You know him?" I ask Lucinda.

She nods. "Todd hated him. Said he was weak, a fool, but I liked him. He was only around during the summers, so I didn't know him well, but he was always kind to me, and he was never involved in any of the assaults." My eyes dart to Mrs. Jamison. "It's okay," Lucinda says. "I told my parents everything last year." The guys share curious looks, and I know they are dying to discover what transpired between Lucinda and me in the sunroom, but they're too polite to ask in front of her mother.

"I need to get home." I pull my cell out of my jeans pocket, scanning tons of missed calls. I'd deliberately muted it while we were here. "My parents have been trying to contact me."

335

"I'll see you out," Mrs. Jamison agrees.

I kneel so I'm eye level with Lucinda. "Thank you for telling me, and it gives me comfort to know my brother had love in his life."

"Thank you for being so gracious; although I'm not surprised because Ethan was an incredible human being too."

"You take care of yourself. And remember what I said."

"You too," she agrees, clutching my hand.

We walk in silence to the front door. "Thank you for coming here today. I know my daughter needed to tell you that." Mrs. Jamison offers me her hand, and I shake it.

"I wish her well."

I proceed to fill my guys in on the ride back to the airport. The mood is solemn, and I'm not sure what awaits me back in Florida. I called my parents, and they are picking us up from Jacksonville International.

"Do you think it's the same video Ethan was sent?" Heath asks in a low voice when we're settled in our first-class seats awaiting takeoff.

"Probably but I guess we'll find out soon enough." Mom mentioned they were with the FBI, so I expect they'll have some answers when we land.

"Stuff's blowing up online," Skeet says, his fingers flying over the keypad of his phone. "I think you can expect the news will be all over campus too." He switches off his cell as the plane starts moving, threading his fingers through mine.

"I knew it would come out eventually. Maybe it's better it's now. We can deal with the backlash and then move on."

He kisses my cheek, and his eyes shine with love. "You never cease to amaze me. Most people would fall apart with everything you've learned recently, but you keep battling. I'm proud of you."

I kiss him softly on the lips. "The old me would've fallen apart, but I have better coping mechanisms now, and I'm not going to be a prisoner of my past. All I'm guilty of is bad judgment in not reporting the rape, but I haven't done anything wrong, and I'm not going to let anyone treat me like I have."

💜💜💜

A welcoming committee is waiting at the gate after we disembark the plane. Mom and Dad are standing with a tall, imposing-looking man in a charcoal-gray suit. Mom rushes toward me, enveloping me in her arms. "Are you okay, honey?"

"I'm fine, Mom."

"Good. Everything's going to be fine." She loops her arm through mine, turning her attention to the guys. "It's nice to see you all again."

"It's good to see you too, Mrs. Simpson," Heath says, as Skeet smiles at her.

"Is he FBI?" Ax asks, jerking his head at the guy in the suit.

She nods. "We've been talking with them and they'd like Blaire to come back to the field office in Jacksonville."

"Why exactly?" I ask.

She clears her throat. "They have some questions to ask you, but Denton Montgomery has also asked to see you. If you feel up to it," she tacks on the end.

I look over at my guys, and just having them here gives me the courage to see this through. "I want to talk to him. I need to know."

The trip to the field office is conducted mostly in silence, and I'm lost in thought the entire ride, wondering what Todd's cousin is going to tell me.

The FBI supervisory agent in charge is very nice, and he goes out of his way to make me feel comfortable once we are seated in the interview room. A female agent joins him as they ask me questions about the events at the party the summer before I turned fifteen. As I'm here voluntarily, Skeet insisted on coming into the room with me, and I'm glad he's here. Just holding his hand gives me the strength to relay those awful events again.

"Mr. Montgomery has confirmed he was the person who recorded the assault on you that night. Your statement corroborates the video evidence, not that we were in any doubt of the heinous nature of this crime. It's clear from the video that you were drugged, and it was not consensual," the supervisory agent explains in a gentle tone.

I force my anxiety aside, trying to avoid thinking about how many people have seen me like that.

"What happens now?" Skeet asks.

"While Mr. Montgomery didn't participate in the rape, he still stood by and let it happen. What's more, he had access to that recording, and he held onto it for all these years instead of coming forward sooner. While we appreciate he voluntarily handed it, and himself, in, he will be charged as an accessory to statutory rape."

"Why now?" I ask. "What prompted him to hand the evidence over now?"

"From what our colleagues have told us, it's tormented him for years. He attended a two-year memorial service the family organized recently, and he was sickened by the way people were talking about Todd like he was a saint. He said that was the tipping point for him. He knew the truth had to come out, and he finally plucked up the courage to do what he should've done years ago," the SAC confirms.

"I don't want the video made public," I blurt.

"Of course not. We would never release anything of such a sensitive nature into the public domain, and as Mr. Montgomery has already confessed, there is no need for a trial." He reaches across the table, patting my hand. "That tape won't ever see the light of day."

"What about those bastards who raped Blaire?" Skeet grits out. "Will the public record be set straight?"

"That's already out of our control," the female agent confirms.

"What do you mean?" I ask, glancing between them.

"Mr. Montgomery sent an open letter of apology to you via the *New York Times*. While he was respectful, he also makes it clear what they did to you and how ashamed he is that he did nothing to stop it." She pulls a newspaper cutting out of a manila folder and slides it across the table to me. "You can have this copy."

"And are any of the police officers involved in investigating the shooting being charged for burying evidence?" Skeet asks, eyeballing the SAC.

"The police didn't bury any evidence," he coolly confirms. "We've spoken to the officers involved in the case and the technician who conducted a forensic analysis of Ethan Simpson's iPhone and iPad. Both devices had been wiped clean and the archived files permanently deleted. We were unable to retrieve anything that could help. The police weren't aware of this recording. If they had found it, they'd have been duty bound to admit it as evidence."

Skeet look skeptical, but it makes sense to me now. "Ethan was still protecting me. He knew the police would take his things, so he got rid of the evidence because he didn't want anyone to see that recording. It's why he told me not to tell anyone what they had done to me." A lump wedges in my throat. "He knew everyone would think he was a monster, but he didn't care because he was sparing me from that."

No one knows how to respond, if there even is any response to that, and the room descends into silence for a couple minutes. When there's a knock on the door, the female agent gets up, popping outside for a second. I stare at the newspaper article in my hand before folding it up and placing it in my purse. I'd rather read it in private and after I've met Todd's cousin. I don't want to walk into that room influenced by anything I've read. He may not have raped me, but he did nothing to stop it, and I can't forgive him for that.

The female agent confirms Denton Montgomery has arrived. He was escorted here, from Boston, by members of the Chelsea FBI field office.

She brings me to the meeting room where he lies in wait for me. He's asked to see me alone and I prefer that too. I'm afraid if I bring any of the guys, or my parents, in with me, that one of them will end up on a murder charge.

"We'll be watching from the observation room," the female agent tells me, as my parents and the guys shuffle into the hidden room. "We don't believe he poses any threat to you, but we've still handcuffed him to the table. If anything happens, I'll be there straightaway."

"Thanks, and I'm okay." I glance at the guys as I head into the room before I lose my nerve.

The guy sitting at the table looks like any normal college student. He's wearing dark jeans, and a white Henley under an open checkered shirt. He looks up at me as I close the door and sit down, and it's a little like looking at a ghost. His resemblance to his cousin Todd is quite remarkable.

"Thanks for agreeing to meet me. I wasn't sure you would." His Adam's apple bobs in his throat.

I clasp my hands on my lap and school my features into a neutral line. "I've been searching for answers for years. You hold the remaining puzzle pieces in your hands. That's the only reason I'm here."

He nods. "I want to tell you how sorry I am, but sorry isn't a strong enough apology."

I'm not here to make him feel good about himself. "You can start by telling me how you came to be in that room and what part you played."

He gulps. "My parents used to ship me to Aunt Gabrielle's for two weeks every summer. I hated it and spent the weeks leading up to it in a state of pure fear. Todd was a horrible bully, and he made my life hell. It got worse as I got older." A muscle pops in his jaw. "Those jerks he hung around with were like Todd's clones, and they did anything he asked of them, without question. I'd seen them almost cross a line with girls before, but that night was the first time I realized they were monsters, predators of the worst kind."

Unshed tears glisten in his eyes, but I keep a neutral expression on my face.

"They dragged me into the room and locked it. I was frozen on the spot as I watched them do that to you. I wanted to stop it. To scream for help. But I couldn't do anything. The door was locked, and I knew they'd never let me leave, so I did the only thing I could think of. I slipped my cell out of my pocket and recorded it."

My chest heaves, and blood thrums through my veins, but I force myself to keep steady. To hear him out.

"They didn't notice. They were too high and too ..." He trails off, pursing his lips. "Anyway, the point is, they didn't know I was recording them. When they were finished, they tried to make me ..." He looks away, shame washing over his features, and he doesn't need to say it. "When I refused, they beat me up."

If he expects any sympathy from me, he's mistaken. "Why didn't you come forward? If you had evidence and you hated him, why didn't you do something about it?"

"Because he found out what I'd done before I could pluck up the courage to do the right thing, and he put me in the hospital when I refused to tell him where I was keeping the recording."

"And what did he blackmail you with after that to buy your silence?" I ask, guessing that's how it went down.

"He told me he'd tell my parents I was gay." His cheeks turn fire-engine red. "Before I'd been pulled into the room with you, he'd set me up with this guy, and we'd done stuff. Then another guy had joined us, and it turned into a threesome."

His entire face is flaming. "Turns out it was a setup. The guys were prostitutes Todd had paid to seduce me. When they came to get paid, they belittled me while Todd and his friends killed themselves laughing. As if that wasn't humiliating enough, I found out days later that Todd had filmed the whole thing. He said if I released the video of you that he'd release the video of me."

Neither of us says anything for a few beats. "I know you're not supposed to speak ill of the dead, but Todd DeLaurentis was one sick, evil bastard," I supply.

He bobs his head, and a look of abject sorrow splays across his face. "I wish I'd been brave enough to call his bluff, but I'd watched Todd get away with shit his whole life. His parents thought he walked on water, and I honestly believed he'd get away with it. But it tormented me. All the time. And I thought of you often. Then I heard they were doing it to other girls, and the guilt almost killed me. I stopped visiting his house the summer after tenth grade, and I tried to put it out of my mind, but it haunted me, until one night, when I reached breaking point."

He pauses for a breath. "I sent it to your brother the night before the shooting. I thought if I sent it to him, he could make the decision I was too weak to make." He leans in closer, his belly pressing into the edge of the table. "I would never have sent it to him if I thought he'd do that! I thought he'd go to the cops and the nightmare would end." Tears glisten in his eyes. "Their blood is on my hands too."

He doesn't know how conflicted and tormented Ethan was. "No, it isn't." I don't owe Denton anything, but too many mistakes have been made, and too many people are suffering because of that night.

It ends now.

"You might have helped set it in motion, but you didn't shoot them. That was my brother's choice. Not yours. And you're going to pay penance for the part you played that night. That's enough suffering. You need to forgive yourself and put it in the past. I know I'm going to." I stand. I've said my piece and there's nothing left to know.

I understand it all now.

For years, I drifted, like a lost soul at sea, craving rescue before I drowned in a pool of secrets, lies, and the unknown. The truth seemed like this vacuous, illusionary thing that was out of reach. It came with too much hurt and pain and I'd resigned myself to the fact the truth would have to remain buried.

But, eventually, the truth always finds a way to break free.

Releasing everyone from their suffering.

Epilogue

BLAIRE - THREE YEARS LATER

"What the hell are they doing in there?" I clamp my hands over my eardrums to protect them from the loud banging noises coming from the living room. Every so often, Heath curses and the hammering ceases only to start up again a few seconds later.

"It's a surprise." Ax is as informative as ever as he lifts another box off the ground and plonks it on the bed.

"I can't believe we're all finally here." I flop down on the bed, sneaking a moment to take it all in.

The bed bounces as Ax jumps down beside me. "I know. It's a little surreal." In a superfast movement Flash Gordon would be proud of, he has me lifted and settled on top of him.

My knees fall on either side of his hips as I straddle him with an amused grin on my face. I lean down slowly, my chest skimming against his body as I line up our mouths. I press a sultry kiss to his lips, and he automatically hardens underneath me. "You want to christen the bedroom first, baby?"

He grabs my shoulders, flipping me over onto my back again. Then he stretches the length of his rocking body over me, thrusting his pelvis against mine. "I look forward to christening every room in our new house, but I don't think the guys would be too pleased if I started right now and ruined the surprise."

"We can be quick." I slide my hand down the gap between our bodies, palming his erection through his jeans.

"You're killing me here, baby." He lowers his face to my neck, and his tongue darts out, running a line along my collarbone.

I shiver all over, still as turned on by him as I was at the very start. The same is true of Heath and Skeet. I'm incredibly attracted to all my guys and so very much in love with them.

Our love was truly put to the test after Denton told the world what'd happened to me and the real reason Ethan showed up to school with a gun that day. Intense national and international debate was sparked, dividing families, friends, and communities. Some came out in support of Ethan, claiming they'd do the same if anyone hurt their loved one, and that sparked angry outbursts and more heated debate on questions of morality, ethics, gun laws, and gun violence. Others denounced his actions, saying there was no justification for taking the law into his own hands even if they understood him a little better. Others sided with the victims and their families, refusing to believe the stories circulating about them.

Lucinda gave an interview to Oprah Winfrey, sharing her years of abuse at the hands of the victims, and a record number of people tuned in to watch. Slowly, other girls came forward with similar stories of abuse.

My parents and I issued a joint statement at the start, shedding light on the Ethan we knew, but we kept it short and respectful and avoided getting drawn into any moral or ethical questions as well as avoiding direct discussion of the victims or what had been done to me. Since then, we have maintained a blanket silence despite intense media scrutiny.

I became a mini-celebrity on campus overnight, and my relationship with the guys was thrust into the spotlight. Not everyone approved, and we had a few tough months, but we weathered the storm together. We never faltered. Not once. And the bond we formed back in those days lay the foundations of the relationship we have today.

The last couple years have been amazing, and I can honestly say my college years have been some of the best years of my life. I worked extra hard to gain additional credits so I could graduate with the guys this past summer.

Heath was drafted by the Patriots, and he moved to Boston a few weeks ago. We had stayed behind, needing to wrap things up back in

Florida and organize shipping of our stuff. We also attended Griff and Jacinta's wedding, and Ax looked completely gorgeous in his tuxedo, sending my hormones into a tailspin.

It was great to catch up with Jacinta after all this time, and I'm so happy she and Ax's brother finally realized they couldn't live without one another and made it official. Their adorable one-year-old son Charlie was the cutest pageboy ever.

But we're finally here. All together. In the house Heath bought for us to live in. And now the next chapter of our lives is set to begin.

Thanks to a high LSAT score, Ax was accepted into Harvard Law. His classes commence soon. He's also due to start interning part-time in a prestigious law firm downtown. They've already agreed to take a look at his mother's case, and he's hopeful he can lodge an appeal to have her sentence overturned.

Skeet is in the process of setting himself up as a freelance technical consultant, and we're transforming the spare bedroom into his office. I'm starting my new role in a victim support center in two weeks, and I'm exploring studying psychology part-time.

Everything has fallen into place for us, and I've finally laid the demons of my past to rest.

"We're ready," Skeet exclaims, popping his head through the door, instantly frowning.

While I've been having an intense conversation in my own head, Ax has been trailing a path of kisses up and down my body. I playfully shove him off me, jumping up and smoothing the wrinkles out of my clothes. "He's insatiable." I roll my eyes, fighting a smirk. "I told him it was a bad idea, but—" I shriek as Ax slaps me on the butt. Hard.

"Naughty, Blaire," he whispers in my ear. "Very, very naughty. And you know what I do to girls who misbehave."

My core pulses, my body humming in anticipation. I press a quick kiss to his cheek. "You can punish me later," I whisper, already on a countdown. I skip over to Skeet and fling my arms around his neck. "Love you, babe."

He melts against me, kissing me tenderly on the lips. "Love you too, beautiful. More and more each day."

"Are you coming or what?" Heath calls out from the living room.

345

"Is it just me, or is he even more impatient since he became this big hotshot NFL commodity?" Ax asks, copping a cheeky feel of my ass as he brushes past me and Skeet.

"I heard that!" Heath roars, followed by a deliberately loud "asshole."

"Now, now, boys," I tease, dragging Skeet after Ax. "Play nice. This is our first day all together in our new home, and we need to make happy memories. Not spend it tossing insults at one another." I fix a stern gaze on Ax and Heath. "Yes, I'm talking to you two." I jab my finger in the air.

"Fuck, I love when you get all feisty," Heath says, crossing the room and yanking me out of Skeet's protesting arms. He crashes his mouth to mine, dipping me down low until my hair is trailing the ground and I'm giggling into his mouth.

"Stop trying to distract me," I mumble in between kisses. "I want to see my surprise." Heath straightens me up, holding me close to his chest, and I sense the silent conversation going on around me.

"You can turn around now," Skeet says, and Heath wraps his arms around me, turning me in his embrace until I'm facing the fireplace and the massive picture taking center stage above it.

A sob tears from my mouth, but it's a happy one. "How in the world …" I trail off, speechless for once in my life. I walk toward the familiar picture, reaching up and trailing my fingers across the image of Ethan and me. It's a copy of the framed photo I have by my bedside, and it's one of my happiest memories. We have our arms wrapped around one another, and we're both laughing into the camera, an expression of sheer joy on both our faces. I place a hand on my chest, overcome with emotion.

"Are you okay, babe?" Skeet approaches with a slightly uneasy look on his face.

I smile through my tears, yanking him to me. "You did this?"

"We all did, beautiful. Your mom gave me the photo. Ax ordered it online, and then Heath collected it from the printers."

"And I almost ruined my football career before it's even begun helping this idiot hang it," Heath adds, coming up alongside me.

"You know you're more of a pussy than any girl I've ever known," Ax half-jokes, appearing with a tray containing four glasses of champagne.

I broke my sobriety when I turned twenty-one. I'll never be a big drinker, and I refuse to drink alcohol unless the guys are with me, but I like to indulge in the odd glass from time to time.

"Maybe, but you still love me." Heath pouts, blowing Ax a kiss, and Skeet opens his mouth to speak, but he doesn't get a chance.

"Don't you fucking dare!" they both shout at the same time, and I laugh. Skeet has never let them forget the cuddling in the bed incident, and I swear he'll still be teasing them about it when they're old and gray.

Ax sets the tray down on the table as Heath dims the lights and turns on the sound system with the small remote in his hand.

This place is the height of modern sophistication. The lighting, sound system, alarm, heating, and blinds are all remote-control operated, and the guys were like big kids on Christmas morning when we first got here, testing out everything, at least a half-dozen times, to make sure it worked.

Skeet's distinctive voice reverberates around the room as the song starts playing, and I arch a brow. "Is this something new?" I ask, not recognizing the words or the music.

"It is," he says, looking uncharacteristically nervous as he stands beside Heath and Axel. "We wrote it together. For you."

I open my mouth to speak, but I'm rendered speechless for the second time in minutes when all three of them drop to their knees in sync. Butterflies scatter in my chest. "What ... what are you doing?"

"The day you came into our lives, you turned everything upside down," Heath says, his eyes shining with more emotion than I've ever seen. "You made the impossible possible, and it didn't take long for me to fall crazy, head over heels in love with you. You mean the whole world to me, Blaire, and I will never love anyone as much as I love you."

Oh. My. Gawd. I press a hand to my mouth as the magnitude of the moment hits me.

"I was drawn to your light *and* your dark, and I've never shared such an intense connection with anyone before." Ax is choked up, and I can tell he's speaking from his heart. "You bring out the best in me, and you make me want to be a better man because I want to give you everything I can possibly offer. The love I feel for you is unsurpassed and infinite, and I will love you always and forever."

Happy tears cascade down my face as I turn to Skeet. The song continues playing in the background, and I'm overwhelmed and overjoyed.

"I fell in love with you the moment I saw you that night in the park. It was as if my entire future flashed in front of my eyes, and it was you. I've always known you were the other half of my heart, and this day couldn't come fast enough for me. I have loved you every day since we met, and I will continue to love you until my dying breath."

Together, they rise and approach me. "We love you more than life itself," Heath says, caressing my cheek.

"We cannot ever imagine our lives without you in it," Ax adds, running his hand around my waist.

"You complete us, Blaire," Skeet says, producing a box and popping the lid. "Marry us, baby."

I'm grinning like a maniac through my tears, and my gaze bounces between them. "I had lost my way until you three came bulldozing into my life. You saved me. In all the ways in which a girl can be saved. And you never gave up on me, even when I'd given up on myself. These last three years have been incredible, and nothing would make me happier than to spend the rest of my life with all of you."

I hold out my hand, and Skeet slides the glistening diamond on my engagement finger. "Yes, I'll marry you. A million times yes. Nothing would make me happier."

I kiss and hug each one of them separately, and the amount of love in this room is enough to fuel a small planet.

We drink copious glasses of champagne as we make plans for our future. We're not in any rush to the altar, so the wedding won't be happening anytime soon. We agree Heath and I should be the ones to get legally married, as he has a public image to uphold, and it makes the most sense.

It doesn't make any difference. We will all be married equally in our own hearts and minds, and our private commitment ceremony is the only ceremony that actually counts. That's where the four of us will cement our bond and our union as equal life partners in front of our families.

I rest my head on Heath's shoulder while Skeet holds my hand and Ax rubs my feet. I'm so unbelievably happy, and I commit this moment to my memory bank as my eyes drift toward the picture of Ethan and me.

I imagine my brother is here. Looking down on the celebration and smiling. Because he was always happy when I was happy. But more than that. He can finally rest in peace because I'm living my life the way he always dreamed for me.

"I love you, E," I whisper in my head. "Thank you for taking care of me. Thank you for loving me. Thank you for giving me this life. Now it's time to let me go. Until we meet again."

I don't realize I'm crying until the room goes quiet.

"Baby. Is everything okay?" Skeet eyeballs me with a face full of concern. I kiss him softly before doing the same to Heath and Ax.

"I'm perfect. Everything is perfect."

And as I curl up with my three guys in bed later that night, I vow to cherish this beautiful life I've been given, and to never take it for granted.

My happiness has been hard won, but I survived Amber Springs and came out the other side. A little broken. A lot stronger. And at peace now that I know I've done the best I can by my brother.

No day will pass where he isn't in my thoughts and in my heart.

And I will live each day to the fullest because he sacrificed everything for me.

The only love as pure is the love I share with the three amazing men who are my world.

And I intend to spend the rest of my life making sure they know it.

The End

Subscribe to my **romance newsletter** to claim a free
copy of *Finding Kyler*. Paste this link into your browser:
http://smarturl.it/KennedyBoysList

If you need to talk to someone regarding sexual assault, please call the National Sexual Assault Hotline in the U.S. at 800-656-4673

If you need to talk to someone regarding suicide, please contact the American Foundation for Suicide Prevention in the U.S. at 1-888-333-AFSP (2377) or via email: info@afsp.org

If you need support/counseling in dealing with the effects of a disaster or tragedy, please call The Disaster Distress Helpline in the U.S. at 1-800-985-5990 or text TalkWithUs to 66746.

Everytown provides opportunities in person and online for survivors of gun violence to connect with each other, honor the lives of their loved ones, create long-lasting bonds, share their stories, and become leaders in campaigns to support common sense gun laws. You can visit their website here: https://everytown.org/survivors/

Survivors Empowered is a national organization created By Survivors, For Survivors, Empowering Survivors. They provide support and referrals for services to survivors of violence and connect you to a support network of other survivors in your area. You can visit their website here: https://www.survivorsempowered.org/

If you live outside the United States, please contact your local support services.

Acknowledgments

If you have read some of my other books, you will know that I tend to write about topics that are sensitive or controversial, none more so than the subject matter in this book. I write the kind of books that I enjoy reading—books that are entertaining and dramatic, romances that are swoon-worthy, stories that are emotional and angsty, characters and topics that are sometimes dark, but they are always REAL. If you want a light, fluffy romance that is pure escapism from real life, then you will have to look elsewhere!

I always feel a certain pressure when I'm writing my books because I want to ensure I'm presenting the subject matter in an appropriate manner. While my books are meant to be entertaining, I also hope they are thought-provoking, because those are the kinds of books I love to read and are the ones that stick with me for a long time after.

While I don't live in America, I am still very much impacted by the culture of gun violence and the escalation of gun violence in schools in the U.S. When I watch the news and hear of another mass shooting, my heart aches for the victims, their families and friends, their communities, and those who were witnesses—the survivors who will have to live with those traumatizing moments over and over throughout the rest of their lives. It's impossible not to feel empathy for those involved. But I also feel for the family of the shooter. Every time, I wonder what their lives are like afterward and how they are treated by a community reeling from the devastation inflicted by one of their loved ones.

The idea for this book grew out of those feelings, and I have focused on that aspect of the story because I wanted to explore the impact on the shooter's family, namely Blaire. That does not mean I have no sympathy

353

for the victims or their families because I do. And just because there was motive in Ethan's case, it does not justify his actions. I want to be specific in stating that I, in no way, condone his actions or wish to imply that there is a justifiable reason for taking the law into your own hands. There is no justifiable reason for gun violence in my opinion.

I have put a trigger warning in place because the last thing I want to do is unintentionally upset anyone who has been traumatized by gun violence or lost someone due to gun violence. Nor do I wish to spark any political debate. I'm merely writing a piece of fiction which explores another side to the story, and my hope is that it is thought-provoking and allows people to consider the impact on the family of the shooter. I hope you understand where I'm coming from and that it has given you pause for thought.

As always, it takes a mini-army to birth a new book. In no particular order, I would like to thank my editor, Kelly Hartigan, Robin Harper of Wicked By Design, my assistant Lola Verroen, my critique partner on this project, Jennifer Gibson, members of my beta reading team (Karla, Deirdre, Sinead, Dana, Danielle, Jennifer, Donna.), Book Candy Studios, Tamara Cribley of The Deliberate Page, Sara Eirew for the beautiful photo of Chen Haskin, Siobhan's Squad on FB, my ARC team, Bobby Kim for his expert marketing advice, all my author friends the world over, and everyone who has helped in some way with this release.

Massive thanks to all my READERS who continue to enable me to write full time. Thank you for taking a chance on one of my books, and thank you for your messages of support, love, and encouragement. I read and respond to all emails and messages personally and you have no idea how much they bolster me on tough days, so thank you!

Thanks to my family and friends for their ongoing support, especially my husband Trev and sons, Cian and Callum.

Feel free to email me anytime—siobhan@siobhandavis.com—but please bear with me if it takes a little while to get back to you.

The Lost Savior

(ALINTHIA #1)

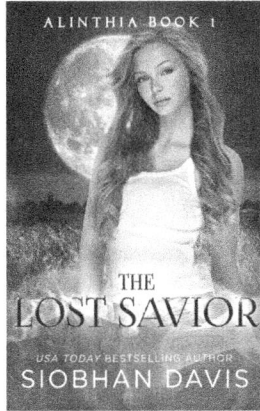

Tori King is a normal senior in high school. Head over heels in love with her childhood sweetheart, she is busy making plans for college when a chance encounter with an alien bounty hunter turns her world upside down. Now, she's experiencing terrifying changes and developing supernatural abilities that leave her questioning her entire existence.

Then the arrival of four hot new guys at school has everyone talking—especially when they become fixated on Tori, following her wherever she goes. She can't shake them off, and as they grow closer, she finds herself drawn to all four of them in ways she cannot explain.

When they finally reveal their true identity, and why they're here for *her*, she discovers everything she thought she knew about herself is a lie.

Because there is nothing normal about Tori King.

And she's about to discover exactly how underrated normal is.

Available in e-book, paperback, and audiobook format.

**Emotional, Angsty, Friends-to-Lovers,
Second-Chance Romance – Standalone**

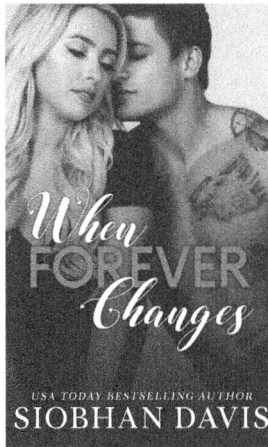

GABBY

Looking back, I should have seen the signs. Perhaps I did, but I subconsciously chose to ignore them.

From the time I was ten, when I first met Dylan, I knew he was my forever guy. Back then, I couldn't put words to what I was feeling, but, as the years progressed, I came to recognize it for what it was—soul-deep love. The kind only very few people ever get to experience.

Dylan was more than just my best friend, my childhood sweetheart, my lover. He was my soul mate. We were carved from the same whole—destined to be together forever.

Until he changed.

And I believed I was no longer good enough.

Until he shattered me so completely, it felt like I ceased to exist.

And I'd never experienced such heart-crushing pain.

Until he leveled me a second time, and I truly wanted to die.

But I had to stay strong because I wasn't alone in this cruel twist of fate.

I look to the sky, pleading with the stars, begging someone to tell me what I should do because I don't know how to deal with this. I don't know how to cope when my forever has changed, and I can't help wondering if I had seen the signs earlier, if I'd pushed him, would it have been enough to save us?

Or had fate already decided to alter our forever?

Available now in e-book and paperback.

About The Author

USA Today bestselling author **Siobhan Davis** writes emotionally intense young adult and new adult fiction with swoon-worthy romance, complex characters, and tons of unexpected plot twists and turns that will have you flipping the pages beyond bedtime! She is the author of the international bestselling *True Calling*, *Saven*, and *Kennedy Boys* series.

Siobhan's family will tell you she's a little bit obsessive when it comes to reading and writing, and they aren't wrong. She can rarely be found without her trusty Kindle, a paperback book, or her laptop somewhere close at hand.

Prior to becoming a full-time writer, Siobhan forged a successful corporate career in human resource management.

She resides in the Garden County of Ireland with her husband and two sons.

You can connect with Siobhan in the following ways:
Author Website: www.siobhandavis.com
Author Blog: My YA NA Book Obsession
Facebook: AuthorSiobhanDavis
Twitter: @siobhandavis
Google+: SiobhanDavisAuthor
Email: siobhan@siobhandavis.com

Books by Siobhan Davis

TRUE CALLING SERIES
Young Adult Science Fiction/Dystopian Romance

True Calling
Lovestruck
Beyond Reach
Light of a Thousand Stars
Destiny Rising
Short Story Collection
True Calling Series Collection

SAVEN SERIES
Young Adult Science Fiction/Paranormal Romance

Saven Deception
Logan
Saven Disclosure
Saven Denial
Saven Defiance
Axton
Saven Deliverance
`Saven: The Complete Series

KENNEDY BOYS SERIES
Upper Young Adult/New Adult Contemporary Romance

Finding Kyler
Losing Kyler
Keeping Kyler
The Irish Getaway
Loving Kalvin

Saving Brad
Seducing Kaden
*Forgiving Keven^*
*Releasing Keanu^*
Adoring Keaton*
Reforming Kent*

STANDALONES
New Adult Contemporary Romance

Inseparable
Incognito
When Forever Changes
*Only Ever You^*

Reverse Harem Contemporary Romance

Surviving Amber Springs

ALINTHIA SERIES
Upper YA/NA Paranormal Romance/Reverse Harem

The Lost Savior
The Secret Heir
The Warrior Princess
*The Chosen One^*

^Releasing 2019
*Coming 2020.

Visit www.siobhandavis.com for all future release dates. Please note release dates are subject to change based on reader demand and the author's schedule. Subscribing to the author's newsletter or following her on Facebook is the best way to stay updated with planned new releases.

Made in the USA
Monee, IL
21 April 2022

95164484R00215